PERFECT
ADDICTION

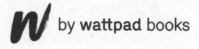 by wattpad books

PERFECT ADDICTION

The PERFECT *Series*

CLAUDIA TAN

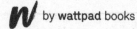 by **wattpad** books

An imprint of Wattpad WEBTOON Book Group

Copyright © 2022 Claudia Tan
All rights reserved.

Published in Canada by Wattpad WEBTOON Book Group,
a division of Wattpad Corp.

36 Wellington Street E., Suite 200, Toronto, ON M5E 1C7 Canada

www.wattpad.com

First W by Wattpad Books edition: July 2022
ISBN 978-1-99025-922-7 (Trade Paper original)
ISBN 978-1-99025-923-4 (eBook edition)

Library and Archives Canada Cataloguing in Publication
information is available upon request.

Printed and bound in Canada

1 3 5 7 9 10 8 6 4 2

Cover design by Mumtaz Mustafa
Images © Hill Creek Pictures
Author Photo by Louise Chan

To my readers—
You know I'm "lucky" to have each and every single one of y
Thank you for growing up with me and these characters.

ONE

Hit.

I was back in the living room of my apartment. It was pitch black; the only thing pelting light into the place was a small crack in the doorway to my sister's room. I shrugged off my coat and threw my keys into the ceramic bowl I knew was sitting somewhere on the shoe cabinet beside the door, the clink of keys and coins rattling softly in the dark.

Hit.

"Beth?" I called out, but my voice was drowned out by the sound of thunder crashing through the sky. "Beth, you busy?"

Hit.

Ever since my sister and I moved into this apartment, we had fallen into a solid routine. I'd come home from my evening shift at the gym and Beth would be in her room, buzzing with caffeine from her third latte of the day as she writes up her latest assignment. Sometimes, if my boyfriend, Jax, gets off *from training early, I'd find him perched on my bed, freshly showered and waiting for me with open arms.*

That was the way it was supposed to be.

Hit.

I hadn't anticipated getting off work early today, but one of my students had been a no-show and Julian told me I could leave. So I did. Truthfully, I was grateful for class being cancelled since I was more than ready to have an early kickoff to the weekend. I wondered if Beth was up for it too. We could order takeout and put on Gilmore Girls like we always do.

Hit.

I approached my sister's door, fist reaching up, ready to knock.

A soft moan drifts through the crack of the doorway, coupled with bed creaking noises.

My hand dropped to my side, suddenly feeling embarrassed. Beth never told me she was having a guy over tonight. She never has anyone over, really, so this was new for me. I wished she'd text me first so I could give her some privacy; she knew I'd be more than happy to give it to her. I'd usually shoot her something quick when Jax is over and we desperately need some alone time. I decided to let it slide for now. Maybe she'd tell me all about her mystery man later.

I began to inch away from the door.

But then . . . I heard it.

"Oh, Jax," Beth moans.

Shock paralyzed my body, forcing me to stumble back until my back collided against the wall.

HIT.

The squeaking immediately came to a halt. There were

sounds of frantic shuffling and clothes being pulled on, and then the door being flung wide open.

Jax was out first. Followed by Beth. Both looking shocked as hell.

Both looking guilty as hell.

I could feel the floor beneath me folding onto itself into one huge, black sinkhole.

HIT. HIT. HIT.

Jax's breathing was heavy and unsettled as he looked at me. I could feel my heart being cleaved wide open when his gaze locked with mine.

"Princess," he said softly and reached a hand out toward me. I recoiled from him, shaking my head. "Princess, wait—"

"How long?" I hurled out the first question that I could string together in my mind. I was surprised I was able to form words at all.

Jax's mouth hung open, no words falling out. Beth flinched at my sharpness, and in that moment, I felt bad for her, the shame unfurling across her face making me falter. But then my field of vision expanded and I saw the full, raw picture in front of me—Jax in nothing but a flimsy blanket to cover himself. Beth wearing a shirt that I recognize not to be hers.

Jax's shirt.

"HOW LONG?" I yell out, my voice nearly breaking.

"A couple months," Beth croaks out.

My heart absorbed the words upon impact.

I can't fucking believe it.

My boyfriend and my sister.

Fucking. Under the same roof.

For months.

While he was still fucking me.

Disgust slammed into my body with the force of a tidal wave.

HIT. HIT. HIT. HIT.

I needed to get the fuck out of here as soon as possible before I completely lost it.

I spun around and headed straight to the door.

My sister started sobbing hysterically, pleading with me not to leave. Jax tried to downplay the situation. A slew of excuses fell out of his mouth like he was reciting lines from every terrible movie cheating scene ever—"We were just messing around . . . It just happened out of nowhere . . . I swear we never meant to hurt you." God, how dense could he possibly be? Of course they meant to hurt me. If they didn't mean to hurt me, they wouldn't have fucking done it in the first place!

I couldn't breathe. I couldn't BREATHE. The pain in my chest kept expanding and expanding as they continued to hurl their stupid, half-assed explanations for infidelity at me until I finally had enough of it and the melting pot of emotions brewing inside me erupted.

"JUST STOP IT!" I screamed as I twisted back to them, wishing they could just shut the fuck up and leave me alone. But my pleas went unheard. The more they tried to reason with me, the more suffocated I felt; the more my lungs struggled to catch air.

"JUST STOP!"

I started to feel dizzy. Overwhelmed. My eyes blinked rapidly as I tried to gain some sense of control but the world around me slowed and warped and swiveled and everything became more unsettled, more constricting . . .

"JUST STOP JUST STOP JUST STOP."

HIT. HIT. HIT. HIT. HIT. HIT.

"JUST STOP JUST STOP JUST STOP JUST STOP."

HIT. HIT. HIT. HIT. HIT. HIT.

"JUST STOP!" I rasp to myself as the punching bag swings back so hard that it collides with my body, causing me to lose my footing and stumble to the ground.

I unravel the boxing wraps from my hands and fling them across the mat as hard as I can, frustration leaking out of me in tears and sweat as I try to get my breathing back under control. My head is spinning so hard my brain feels like it's about to fall out. If I don't get enough oxygen into my system right now, I might just pass out.

Calm down, Sienna. Deep breaths, I schooled myself. *In, out, in, out, in, out. . .*

My fingers dig into my blond hair but it's all tangled and in disarray, with strands sticking to my sweat-slicked face. When I drag my hands out of my hair, they feel weird and sore. I stretch them out in front of me, palms facing down. There's no mistaking the pools of red on my knuckles.

Looks like the no-gloves idea really panned out for you, didn't it? I think to myself, mentally slapping myself for being this stupid. I knew that it was a rookie move. I *knew* it, and like a fool, I did it anyway because I'd hoped the physical pain could override the emotional pain.

But my theory was bullshit. I feel both. Raw and definite.

Hot tears stream down my face as I snatch a bandage roll from my gym bag and wrap it around my knuckles. They'll probably hurt for a while, which means I might need a few days off from the gym to give them some time to heal.

I came to the gym after I mustered up the courage to return to the apartment a second time, with the sole purpose of clearing all my things from my room and getting the hell out of there as fast as I could. Jax wasn't there this time, and Beth did little to fight for me to stay, instead silently retreating into her room while I stuffed my clothes and whatever else I could into my bag and left. It was better that way. She probably knew that if she tried confronting me again things would get real ugly. My fists were aching to hit something, and while I knew that Jax could take it, there was no way in hell Beth could.

And I've showed them enough of my vulnerability for one night.

So instead, I'm here with the punching bag as my, well . . . punching bag. The Universal Fighter's Gym has always been a safe haven for me, the place where I feel the most at home when the world feels like it's caving in. I've been working as a mixed martial arts trainer since last summer, and I have every intention of turning that into a full-time gig once I've graduated from college.

As much as I'm on good terms with the boss who runs the place—Julian—he'll kill me if he finds me using the gym as my sleeping quarters. And jeopardizing my career over this is simply not worth it.

I still need a place to stay. There's no way I'm going back to the apartment.

My sister and my boyfriend are officially dead to me.

Staying with friends is out of the question too. When I called to tell Dakota and Trevor, my friends since high school, what had happened, I was shocked to hear that they were already aware of Beth and Jax's affair but hadn't had the heart to say anything to me because they "didn't want me to get hurt." As if that makes the least bit of sense.

So that just leaves family.

But family hasn't felt like a family in a long time. I haven't talked to my dad in weeks now. And last I heard, my mom was dancing with strangers in the heart of Rio.

I let the tears dry on my face for a little while longer before picking myself off the mats. I yank my bag over my shoulder and shut off the lights to the gym, then head out. I'm immediately greeted with the rain. It pelts lightly at my body at first, but soon soaks my clothes as it continues to pour. The winter chill has already begun to attack my wet skin, and while I usually don't mind the cold, I loathe it when it's combined with rain.

I wipe the rain off my face with the back of my arm, but I think I'm wiping away angry tears instead. I'm not sure.

Maybe I'm raining tears.

I don't think I've felt like I've ever hit rock bottom until now.

I have no home. No friends. No family. No boyfriend and no sister.

Bitter resentment crawls into my heart when I think about the both of them. How could they? I didn't think either had it in them to do something so malicious. Especially my sister.

Sweet, kind, soft-spoken Beth. She and I are so different that sometimes our friends would forget that we were related. Beth is artistic, shy but incredibly well-mannered— to the point where my dad truly believes that she's his biggest achievement to date. As much as I aspired to be like her, I just couldn't bring myself to stay away from trouble, getting sucked into the violent world of MMA and choosing to make a career out of it too. But that didn't mean that Beth and I didn't get along. We pushed each other's buttons, as sisters do, but when it came down to it, we had each other's backs. More so after our parents' divorce.

When she graduated from high school last summer, I thought it would be great to find a place together in the city. It was a certainly a convenient solution: we both got some breathing space from my dad, and since Beth was also attending Boston University—it being her first year and my third—it was much better than staying in the dorms or bunking with roommates that I barely knew.

Who knew it was also convenient for her to sleep with my boyfriend?

My body shudders with betrayal.

And Jax. Goddammit, *Jax*.

I was so certain that my relationship with him was the kind that was written in the stars. I met him around the time my parents announced their divorce, and he helped me through some of the darkest moments of my life. Boys have always been a struggle for me, but with Jax, falling for him was as graceful and effortless as witnessing a knockout punch in a ring. Even back then, he had a dangerous edge to him that was too tempting to stay away from. I liked it. And I liked that he understood the tempest roaring inside of me and helped me embrace who I really am.

I am nothing without him. Just an empty shell of who I used to be.

A car races past me on the road, sending a pool of water in my direction. A heavy breath falls out of me.

Seriously, I can't catch a fucking break tonight.

I run to the nearest bus stop and pull out my phone to search for some possible places to stay for the night. There's a budget hotel a few streets over. I'm too stubborn to call for a cab when the distance is so close, so I sprint as fast as my legs can carry me.

The hotel lobby is sinisterly dark when I step through the doors. Water pools beneath my feet and drenches the faded Persian carpet beneath me. I look up to see the receptionist staring with annoyance at the sight of my wet clothes. I'm not sure I care about inconveniencing her; I'm entirely focused on drying up in a decently sized room and sleeping off what happened today.

I rest my wet arm on the counter.

"I need a room tonight."

She gives me another glance over, then lets out a sigh before grabbing a key from one of the drawers and chucking it at me.

"Second floor. Room 104," she says flatly. "Enjoy your stay."

Dragging myself up the stairs is a challenge when I'm ten pounds heavier from the water clinging to every inch of my body. When I finally reach my room, the first thing that hits me is the stench of bleach. It smells sterile in here. Like a murder took place and forensics has just scrubbed the place clean. But the sight of a comfy bed and a clean bathroom is enough for me to momentarily forget about the unpleasant scent.

I peel off my clothes and hop into the shower. It's difficult to even clean myself properly because of the exhaustion of carrying around such heavy heartache. Instead, I settle for a light rinse, toweling myself off afterward and getting ready for bed.

I pull the blanket over me, wrap it around myself tightly, and try to shut off my mind.

I can't sleep.

The nightmare of finding Jax and Beth together keeps replaying in my mind. Every time I close my eyes, there he is—hands gliding over her skin, his mouth peppering kisses down her throat, his hips grinding against hers in a passionate, frenzied way that causes a loud, breathy moan to escalate from deep within her throat. God, I feel sick to my stomach again. Maybe if I threw it all up in the toilet the memory would get flushed away along with my sick.

How did I get blindsided by all of this? There must have been signs that I simply dismissed as paranoia. Instances when Jax and Beth got a little too close, were a little too affectionate. Maybe acting shady or too defensive when I would notice something and speak up about it. I sift through the memories, scrambling to dissect everything that either of them said to me for the past few months, but come up short, with not many red flags sticking out.

Perhaps they'd hid it from me well. Or I was just terrible at picking up the signs. But then again, even if there *had* been signs, I doubt I would have suspected that something like this would happen. Because how could I? I trusted Jax and Beth with my life.

And now, I feel like such a fucking fool.

Exhaustion soon gives way to a new kind of anger, slowly chipping away at my patience and resolve.

Do Jax and Beth think they can just drive an axe into my heart and not suffer any consequences? There's no fucking way I'll just let them go unscathed. I've been burned so many times in the past, but this feels different. It's a wild, untamed *nuclear* kind of anger. The sheer magnitude of their deception is too big for me to let slide.

This time, it's way too personal.

I flip over on the bed and clench my jaw so tightly that my teeth grind.

I'm not going to give either of them the satisfaction of breaking me. Because I can't break. It's simply not in my nature.

I may have fallen to the ground face-first but I can trust that I will pick myself up again. I'm not weak. I'm not.

I'm a *fighter*.

I'm going to make Jax and Beth pay for what they did.

And this time, they'll be sorry they ever fucked with me.

TWO

The budget hotel is an easy one-mile walk to central campus. The miserable weather from last night has retreated and, in its wake, a refreshing sunny day has settled in, the sneaky cool winter breeze tangling my hair. I think I miss the rain now. There's a certain soothing quality to it after having your heart violently smashed to pieces.

My classes start in an hour and while I usually look forward to them, this time they fill me with dread. The last thing I want to do right now is endure four hours of back-to-back lectures, but I drag myself to class anyway in hopes that it will distract from the shitshow that happened last night.

When I've found a place to sit in the amphitheater, I use the screen on my phone to check my reflection. I'm appalled by how terrible I look. My skin is sickly pale. My hazel eyes are glassy with the lack of sleep, with huge dark circles dragging my face down. It probably would have been a good idea to slap on some concealer around my eyes, but waking up sporting a raging headache had immediately dissolved any desire to doll myself up. So I guess the end result is partially my fault.

I drop my phone back in my bag, determined not to dwell on my appearance any longer. Instead, I poke my head back up, scanning the growing sea of students filing into their seats, and notice my favorite person right now giving me a thorough wave as he enters the hall.

I haven't known Brent long, but since meeting him on my first day last term, he's grown to be the best thing that's ever happened to this physics class. We like to share each other's notes—or, to be more specific, he shares his notes with *me*—and exchange cheesy pickup lines to get through the day. I'm not sure how this contributes to a degree in human physiology, but at least it makes the lectures easier to stomach.

"Are you my textbook? Because seeing you is the absolute *highlight* of my day right now," I say, almost like a sigh of relief, as he slides into the seat next to me.

"You better hope I am," Brent says, letting loose a dramatic sigh as he drops his bag in the available space on the floor beside him and jerks the bag's front zipper open. "Though I'm not functioning well today."

"What? Why?"

"Because I believe you've stolen a *pizza* my heart." He grins as he whips back to me, revealing a container with the lid peeled off and a couple slices of pepperoni pizza tucked inside. "I managed to cop several slices from the food sale today. I know you're always busy with work and stuff, but you up for some lunch later?"

"That's nice of you to offer but I'll take a rain check," I say, not wanting to elaborate further. But it's not enough to quell his curiosity. His eyes bulge in surprise when he takes a good look at my face.

"What the hell happened to you?" His eyebrows rush together. "You look like you got stomped on by Godzilla."

"Thanks." I try to swallow down the all-too-candid observation. "I found out that my boyfriend has been sleeping with my sister, so there's that," I say, albeit a little bit too harshly. "And then I lost my apartment because she's staying there and I can't really look at her face without wanting to bash it in."

"Holy shit." His mouth hangs open in shock as he processes the news. "That sucks. I'm so sorry."

"It's okay. I'll deal," I say, even though I doubt I believe what I'm saying.

"What are you going to do now?"

I bite my lip in contemplation. "I was planning to check if there are any available places to rent on campus after class but . . . I don't know. Term's just started, so I doubt there's anything."

He frowns, the thick-rimmed glasses resting on the bridge of his nose falling slightly. "Well . . . if you're looking for places off campus, I know someone who's renting out a room in Allston for, like, 500?"

"Seriously?" I ask. There's no way a room in Allston would cost that little. "Sounds like a scam to me."

"It's not," Brent assures me. "It's just . . . not about the money for him."

Interesting. Well, it wouldn't hurt to take a look, I guess.

"Fine. Let me check it out. Where do I find him?"

He peels off a Post-it note and scribbles down a name and an address. Then he slaps the note on my keyboard.

"His name's Kayden," he tells me. "But be careful, all right? He can be . . . intense."

Intense? Doesn't sound very promising.

"You're not sending me to a serial killer's house, are you?" I lift the Post-it to my face and trace the words on it with my eyes.

Kayden Williams? Rings a few bells. Julian might have mentioned him before. I'll have to ask him about it later.

"You'll be fine," Brent says, though a little hesitantly. "I think."

I wait for him to deny that Kayden's a serial killer but the words don't come. It amplifies my wariness.

"All right . . ." My voice trails off. "Any tips to get on his good side?"

Brent pauses for a second to think.

"Don't be yourself," he offers helpfully.

I snort. "Okay. Got it."

I hope I do get it. I'm not sure if I can survive another night being homeless.

***

Done with my classes for the day, I peel the note from my laptop and punch the address into my phone. Google Maps tells me that it's a twenty-five minute walk to Kayden's apartment. Not bad, though it could be worse. Mine and Beth's apartment was an agonizing forty minute walk to anywhere remotely close to the city, so we usually either took the T or just car pooled with Jax.

My jaw clenches hard as the thought of them slices through my mind. I had woken up to a barrage of missed calls and texts in the morning; most of them are from Beth asking if she could meet up with me to explain everything, and that she misses me and wants me to come home. After skimming through some of them, I decide to block her number, not wanting to get emotional about seeing her name light up my phone again. I want to hate her right now, not feel guilty for abandoning her and ignoring her messages. There are also several messages from my dad asking me to call him, and I'm hoping he's not going to try to convince me to make amends with Beth.

I check my call history again. At least Jax hadn't bothered with the call spamming. He probably thinks I'll be the one who caves in first and calls. Jax holds his ego too close to beg for me to come back. His detached nature was one of the things I used to admire about him, simply because there was nothing that could faze him. He was confident—often to the point of brazen arrogance—but it sure made him invincible to everyone around him.

Not this time.

I know there aren't a lot of things that Jax cares about—in fact, I used to be the only thing that he ever cared about, apart from fighting. Jax lives and breathes MMA. We used to train together at UFG, and all those sessions with him was what inspired me to take up training as a professional career.

If I really wanted to get back at him, I could go head to head with him in the cage. I'd maybe even win a round. But he's still got a hundred pounds on me and the fight wouldn't be fair with our physiological differences. It won't prove much other than the fact that I can barely hold my own in a fight against him.

It's going to be tough figuring out how to hit him where it'll hurt the most. I just need time to plan my next move.

Staring up at the exposed red brick exterior of the apartment complex, I soak the feeling of comfort and ease up eagerly as I slip through the gates and into the elevator. I hope Kayden's home. Brent didn't tell me what time he finishes his classes, so if he's not around I guess I'll have to wait until he returns.

I hear loud clicking of what sounds like heels against the concrete echo from the floor below me, and I peer over the ledge to see who it is. A mess of strawberry-blond hair bounces into my view as a woman leaves her apartment with her phone squashed between her ear and her shoulder.

"Are you guys coming home for dinner tonight? Simon's cooking lamb ragù and he wants to know how many portions to cook. And I'm asking now so Daniel doesn't get a chance to complain that we didn't cook some for him," she asks whoever's on the other end, loudly enough for everyone in the apartment building to hear.

She pauses for a moment, tips her head back to feign a loud laugh—a sultry and beautiful sound that fits her sharp, striking face—and continues with her chatter. After a while, I notice her end her call and walk to the elevator.

"Hi, excuse me, um," I say, quickly intercepting her at the stairs beside the elevator before she disappears from view. Her head tilts up upon hearing me. "I was wondering if you can help me? I'm looking for apartment 4-B but it's not between 4-A and 4-C."

She nods in understanding, climbing up the stairs to meet me at my level. "Yeah, that's cause it's behind there." She points to the little corner to the far left of me, blocked by a half wall.

"Oh right. Thanks," I murmur before stepping in the direction she gestured to.

"Hey, wait." Her voice stops me in my tracks. I whirl around and see her catching up to me, her Louboutins barely able to keep up with her legs. "Sorry. I didn't catch your name."

"Sienna."

She beams at me and sticks her hand out confidently. "I'm Cara. Nice to meet you. We don't get a lot of new people around here."

"Yeah. I'm actually checking out a space here," I tell her. "I heard this guy was renting out a room so . . ."

"Right." Her eyes flicker briefly toward the 4-B unit and a frown marks her lips. "Well, be careful. The guy who lives there . . . he's not so friendly. Tried offering him cookies once when he moved in. Took them and slammed the door in my face. My boyfriend, Simon, finds him superweird." When she registers the doubt on my face, her facial expression perks up into a reassuring smile in compensation. "But I'm sure you'll have better luck, though."

I like her optimism. It's been a while since I've encountered someone who has the same kind of radiant energy as hers. And she's undeniably gorgeous. Bright, gleaming face with angular cheekbones, a pair of plump lips, and a long, slender body to match. I would kill for her metabolism, to be able to keep a figure like that.

"Okay, then!" She clasps her hands together, as if she can't stand the small moment of silence. "Hope to see you around more. Might even introduce you to my roommate, Alex, if we ever bump into each other again. I think you'd like her a lot."

"Sure," I say awkwardly.

"Bye, Sienna." Her eyes crinkle with joy as she waves good-bye, her fingers wriggling like a posh socialite's.

I walk in the direction she pointed and face the door in front of me. I haven't even knocked on Kayden's door yet and he already makes me nervous.

Mustering up the courage, I tap my fist against the door. I hear shuffling inside the apartment and footsteps growing closer before the door flies open and a tall, dark-haired man steps out.

I'm immediately startled by how good looking he is. His form is magnificent: broad shoulders, huge arms, and a lean, ripped body with swirls of tattoos peeking out from the edges of his black shirt. My gaze then gets pulled up to his strong collarbone, hard jawline, and angled cheekbones, and finally lands on his eyes. They're a deep shade of grey—intense and quiet and magnetic. I've seen those eyes before. I'm not well acquainted with them, but I have a feeling I've felt them watching me, stealing glances, though it's hard to remember where.

Kayden's thick eyebrows rise in mild annoyance as he waits for me to say something.

I clear my throat and straighten myself up.

"Hi." I plaster on the widest smile I can muster. Smiling feels so weird after how dead I've been feeling inside since last evening. "I'm Sienna. Brent said that you were renting out a room. Is that right?"

He looks at me warily. "Yes."

"You mind if I take a look around?" I'm already moving forward but Kayden blocks the doorway with a strong arm.

"No."

"What?" I say, confused. Did I miss something from him between the first and second question I asked? "I don't understand. Is the room already rented?"

"No."

"Okay. Then, can I come in?"

Kayden pauses for a while. Glowering. Then, the dreaded word arrives again.

"No."

The skin between my brows crease with confusion.

What the hell is going on?

"Is *no* just, like, your favorite word or is there another reason why I can't rent a room from you?" I ask, annoyance flaring up my skin.

Kayden shakes his head. "None that you need to know about. Just find somewhere else to live."

He starts to close the door but my quick reflexes propel me to wedge my foot between it and the door frame.

"Wait, please," I say desperately. "Maybe I caught you at a bad time, but . . . " I swallow hard, my voice lowering in embarrassment. "I'm in a really tough spot here."

I expect at least some form of hesitation, but to my surprise, the decisiveness remains.

"Not my problem," Kayden snaps. His eyes scroll up and down the length of my body and he swallows hard, Adam's apple bobbing in his throat as he does. "I don't want any complications."

"Complications?" I take a step back, pausing to let his words sink in for a bit. Then my eyebrows relax when I figure out what he means. "Oh. I mean, I get that I'm hot, but trust me, you're not my type either."

"That's not what I mean," he says sharply.

"Of course that's what you mean," I shoot back with indignation. "Unless you're afraid of girl cooties?"

I can't believe those words just left my mouth. But it's the only reason I can think of that would warrant his shitty behavior toward me.

"No. Of course not." A dark look hardens Kayden's features. "I just think you're trouble. Trouble that I don't need," he says, like it's a stated fact.

"Seriously?" I arch a brow, my annoyance deepening.

What a weird thing to say to someone he doesn't even know. Maybe he recognizes me from somewhere before. From campus, maybe, or UFG. Or he's just a judgmental prick. Either way, it's clear he's not changing his mind about his assumption either. I don't think anything would convince him otherwise.

Do I even want to? His rudeness toward me is so off-putting that it feels like too much of an effort to attempt swaying him again. There's only so many times I can beg before it'll seem too pathetic.

And I'm not going to stoop *that* low.

"You know what? Fine," I say in finality, tugging on the

strap of my bag. "Have it your way, jerk. I'm sure there are plenty of other places I can live in."

The muscles in Kayden's face ease, and he looks almost relieved at me conceding.

"Good-bye, Sienna." He sighs, his hand clutching the door. "Don't come back. Ever."

And he proceeds to slam the door in my face.

THREE

I slump to the floor outside Kayden's apartment, bumping my head against the wall in defeat.

Well, that went well.

I don't think I've ever met anyone who treated me this shitty upon first meeting before. It was like he was repulsed by me. Or maybe he just took one look at me and assumed the absolute worst of me. Whichever the case, I'm not in the mood to stick around to find out.

Swallowing my pride, I collect myself and head out. I guess another night at a crappy hotel it is.

Finding another place to stay will take me weeks. Even then there's no guarantee. Maybe I can hold out until spring break, when there will be more availability, but I doubt I'll be able to endure even a couple more days of my paycheck getting eaten up by the cost of living in budget hotels. Brent might be willing to let me crash at his place for a while, but I'm not sure how I feel about asking for help from someone I'm not that well acquainted with yet.

I'll just have to keep myself busy on rental apps and hounding college officers. It'll be all right. I'm sure it will be.

***

It's not.

It's been three days and I've had zero leads. My nights since my encounter with Kayden have been spent eating out of noodle cups and scrolling endlessly on the college website, filling out applications for every listed accommodation offered. So far most of them have not gotten back to me, and when they do, it's usually doomed with the email opener "We regret to inform you . . . " Other off-campus places I've checked out are either too far away from the city or way out of my budget.

Deciding that a small break is in order to take my mind off this, I decide to pay a visit to UFG. When I arrive, the gym is unexpectedly sparse for a Saturday evening. Apart from the two guys sparring in the cage and the trainer who has just started their metabolic conditioning class, yelling at his three students to speed up their push-up burpees, the space feels somewhat empty.

My attention lingers on the class being held because it's the only thing that seems riveting to watch. I don't usually run big classes here, instead preferring one-on-one training because I like to give my full attention to whomever I'm training. Most of the people who come for my training sessions are beginners—usually guys who went down the YouTube rabbit hole watching UFC fights and decide that it's easy enough to get into the competitive sport. But while the sport is fun to watch, there are very few people with an appetite for getting punched in the face. And once they do, they usually don't stick around very long.

And unlike other kinds of sports, you don't have anyone to rely on but yourself. The fight falls completely on your shoulders, which usually comes with its own psychological and physical barriers that can be difficult to overcome. When I first started with Jax, it was incredibly overwhelming. The endless hours of conditioning, strength work, and martial arts training packed into a crazy six days a week schedule completely shattered my body for the first month until I finally built up my tolerance. The only reason I didn't give up was because I craved the emotional release I got from those sessions. I sought it like a miracle stimulant drug, dissolving all the pent-up anger of the week from my body once I got my boost of adrenaline and power.

I adored every minute of training with Jax. I could watch him in that cage for hours and never get tired of it. He's merciless when he fights, like a king cobra with its imposing size and deadly bite, looming over his prey, only to strike a viciously fatal blow that knocks them out for good. I love the way he moves so fluidly around the cage, bred with boldness and strength as he keeps pushing himself—both mentally and physically—until he's toeing the precipice of his limits yet still remaining fearlessly on top.

I particularly looked forward to him kissing the hell out of me afterward, claiming me wildly with his mouth, hands, and body. For a moment, it felt like I was the only prize that he ever needed.

Goddammit, Sienna. I mentally slap myself for letting

my thoughts catapult to Jax again. *He's not worth it. He cheated on you. He's not worth loving anymore.*

Banishing thoughts of him from my head, I set my gym bag down, then aim for Julian's office. He's a burly, middle-aged man with a shaved head and ink running down the sides of his arms. When I walk in, I find him perched behind his desk, his huge hands cupping a pink doughnut with sprinkles on it. I like that he just eats whatever the hell he wants. Since leaving the UFC several years back and opening this gym, he keeps up with a training regimen from time to time but can't be bothered with the strict diet.

He's still one of the best MMA fighters I know. Legendary, in fact. Everyone who fights in the area knows who he is: UFC Middleweight Champion for five consecutive years. He was known for having a dynamic fighting style and was skilled at exploiting the gaps in his opponent's game. A truly unique fighter. But to the shock of many, he decided to leave the UFC before he could make it to a double hat trick win. Said he wanted to quit while he was still ahead and leave a legacy that wasn't tarnished by the slow decline of age and sustained injuries. It was a move that invited a lot of controversy, and most people give him shit for it, but I respect his decision. It's the reason why Universal Fighter's Gym exists today, so I'm grateful.

Julian licks his icing-coated fingers and gives me a curt nod when I pop my head into his office.

"Hey." He acknowledges me, raising a perplexed brow as he straightens in his seat. "What are you doing here? I told you your evening class with Parker got postponed. Said he injured his leg hiking a few days ago."

"Yeah, I know. But I just can't seem to stay away from my favorite trainer," I say cheekily, and he makes a big show of rolling his eyes and scoffing his irritation. He hates that I still call him that even though he doesn't do training sessions anymore, preferring to focus on gym operations instead. My head whirls around to see the nearly empty gym. "Where is everyone?"

Julian looks disappointed when I remark about the turnout.

"You know where." He shrugs, his attention falling back to his half-eaten doughnut. "Watching the fight."

My lips pucker into a frown. Usually around this time of the year, Breaking Point, a rival MMA gym, holds the biggest underground fighting event in Boston. It's a no-holds-barred tournament where the stakes are high and one wrong move can quite possibly cripple you for life. This isn't just regular MMA shit. It's MMA on *crack*, where all the standard rules are thrown out of the window.

There's a strict no gloves and padding rule to maximize the carnage in the cage. The refs don't care about safety, and the fighters aren't insured, which makes watching someone snap a leg or break a rib much more difficult to watch. Every time I go to one of those matches it feels like being in a butcher's shop, the smell of sweat and blood and savagery making my stomach churn with discomfort.

The underground is illegal and circulates a lot of money, but they have a tight relationship with the Boston Police Department, so the force usually turns a blind eye to the gym's affairs.

Julian has a love-hate relationship with Breaking

Point. While he doesn't mind watching the occasional fight there, he has a strict no illegal shit rule when it comes to training fighters at his own gym. At UFG, he only breeds fighters he knows are clean—from both steroids and the underground—and those he's hopeful will be able to go pro someday. UFG has a stellar reputation because of this, but unfortunately, a stellar reputation doesn't always equate with profitability, driving some of the most promising fighters who are looking to dabble with the dark side from UFG to Breaking Point.

I only put up with the underground because Jax loved to fight there. He had been trained by Julian and was supposed to go pro before ultimately deciding he was too good for any of the big promotions and settling for fighting in underground circuits instead. He's so skilled at it that he's expected to win the championship title at Breaking Point for the third time without even breaking a sweat.

"Point's holding a fight tonight?" I ask.

Julian gives lazy nod. "The usual. Knockout rounds for the titles are starting in two weeks, so everyone wants to dip their toes in before jumping into the deep end."

Two weeks? That's sooner than I thought.

"Who's fighting tonight?" I can't stop myself from inquiring.

"Some Murphy guy, I think. And that other dude who's been turning heads since last year—Kayden Williams."

"No way." I breathe. "Kayden's an underground fighter?"

"Yeah. You remember him, right?" When I shake my head no, his eyebrows rise in confusion. "Come on. Jax went up against him during the finals last season. It was a pretty brutal and long fight. Lasted about twenty minutes, and it took Jax putting Kayden into a rear naked choke to get him to concede."

As soon as he mentions that, the memories rush back to me. I recall trying to soothe Jax's nerves right before he went into the cage against Kayden. It was weeks of intense training and preparation leading up to the big fight but he still felt on edge. It was a big deal because Jax rarely ever gets nervous. He can usually predict the outcome of a fight even before it starts, so the fact that Kayden shook him up means that this guy is a real threat.

"He's one hell of a fighter, though," Julian explains. "Apparently, just started getting into all this shit last season. You rarely ever get to see a rookie make it that far in the finals."

"That's quite impressive," I admit, despite my initial distaste for the guy.

I guess I should have put two and two together when I met Kayden earlier. It makes sense, since he's extremely athletic looking, his body strong-packed with lean, tough muscle but not bulky or overly defined in a way that a gym enthusiast's or a bodybuilder's would be.

There is also a certain kind of rigidness to him, an unyielding sense of determination in his eyes, which makes me wonder what happened during their last fight. Jax tends to leave all of his opponents in much worse shape than they were before they entered the cage, so I'm sure there's a lot of animosity there.

"Why are you so interested in Kayden, anyway?" Julian asks, the side of his lips tilting into a sneaky side-smirk.

"Unless you're looking for a side dude? I'm not sure about his sexual history, but hell, you've dated Jax. And I assume that these fighters are incredibly freaky and unhinged in bed."

"First off, I will not confirm nor deny anything," I tell him with a hint of a knowing smile. "Second of all, I'm not interested in him. Not in that way, anyway. I went over to check out his apartment a few days ago and he was incredibly rude to me."

"Maybe the world hasn't been kind to him," Julian suggests.

"The world hasn't been kind to me, either, and I'm such a ball of sunshine."

"Sure, you are," he says flatly, and I pretend to be unfazed by his sarcasm. "Anyway, I have a feeling this season's gonna get competitive if Kayden is in the roster." He pauses for a while before adding, "Jax will probably be joining, too, you know."

"I know. He's been training for the past few months. Or that's what he told me he was doing anyway. Maybe half of those were excuses so he could sneak off to fuck my sister."

Julian merely blinks back at me, unsure of whether to laugh to diffuse the tension or offer some sympathy. I think I'd rather him do the former. I'm aware that the entire situation is shitty, and I'd rather be snickered at than be pitied.

My thoughts drift back to Kayden. I wonder how he felt after his fight against Jax. It must have been a hard loss to swallow. I understand the feeling of being so close to having everything you ever wanted, only to have it ripped away from you at the last second. Surely he's looking forward to a rematch this year.

A plan begins to take shape in my mind, and I get so excited I start to jump up and down on the balls of my feet. "Oh my God. Oh my *God*."

Julian gives me a weird stare. "What?"

"Are you going?"

"Nah, I'm done trying to keep up with that shit. It's exhausting." He releases a sigh. But his eyebrows lift when he notices the knowing smile on my face. "You're thinking of going."

"Of course I am."

"To see Jax?"

"To see *Kayden*."

His dark eyebrows knit in confusion. "I thought you weren't interested in seeing him again?"

"Well, I've got a new plan now." I tug on the strap of my gym bag and blow him a kiss with my other hand. "See ya."

"But you just got here—" Julian protests.

"I'm a genius." I raise both middle fingers and kiss them before lifting them to the air. "A fucking genius!"

I know exactly how to get my revenge on Jax.

FOUR

To get into one of Breaking Point's fights takes a certain kind of commitment. Despite being all buddy-buddy with the police force, they still try to keep it very low key, so the only way you can be a spectator is through a recommendation from someone already affiliated with the underground. And the person who recommends you must swear in good faith that you won't bring any unwanted attention. A permanent ban from the premises and a brutal beatdown awaits both you and your friend if you snitch.

Beth and I were recommended to be spectators about three years ago by my now ex-friend Dakota, whose brother used to fight in the underground. He doesn't anymore because he was shit at it and got severely beaten within fifteen seconds of the fight.

It so happened to be the exact same night I first saw Jax fight in the cage. The second I watched him emerge from the shadows, clad in his signature black robe, every muscle in my body locked up. I fell so hard for him then, with his dark, unrelenting eyes and thick, loud confidence as he danced around his opponent like he'd just found the easiest prey to feast on and was going to relish ripping him apart.

Looking back at the moment, I can't help but feel a black stain forming over the memory, along with the many others I made with Jax. Did Jax know early on he intended to cheat on me with Beth? Or was it Beth who planted the seed of doubt in him? Who came on to who first? Whose willpower was the first to break?

I guess it shouldn't matter, as both of them are equally damned in my eyes. But still, I can't push away all these questions floating in my head. It's difficult not to feel this way when I feel so massively duped.

Staring up at the neon red Breaking Point sign this time around is enough to turn all my feelings about Jax into cold determination. I thought about going back to Kayden's apartment since I know his address, but I figured since he kicked me out the other day, I might just piss him off by going there again. If I attend his fight tonight and try to find him afterward, at least we'll be on neutral ground.

The underground is his playground, just as it is mine.

I can feel the vibrant energy thrumming from within the gym as I head toward the front doors. There are two lines to get in: one for first timers and the other for seasoned spectators. Thankfully, the latter is much shorter, so I get through within minutes. The bouncer checks my ID along with the small bag I brought with me, rummaging through my things before grunting with approval and stepping aside to let me in.

I haven't been here since Jax won his title last year, but I know that Breaking Point runs one-off underground matches every other weekend. Most of the time, Jax is here. And when he's fighting, he earns bank. All good fighters here do. Apart from entry fees, they also get a cut on any bets placed. If you're entering for the season, the farther you move up in the tournament, the more dough you rake in.

And if you're a reputable fighter who has fought in the underground for several years, fans may even bet on you based on blind faith. Which is why fighters usually engage and connect with their fans whenever they can during these events.

Jax has a ton of fans. He has a natural charisma, so it's no surprise he has a lot of loyalists under his spell. The income from the fights will provide him with enough financial security for the next decade.

The pungent stench of smoke and sweat hits me when I push through the doors to the basement. Rowdy patrons collide with one another, screaming final calls to place bets. A small group of people flock toward the betting table, waving their money, hungry to cash in on their favorite fighters.

It's a struggle to push through the mammoth crowd. Perched in the center, in all of its glory, is a raised octagonal cage, and it's the only thing that the overhead lights are directed at. It looks like it was quickly put together and easy to disassemble if the cops were to raid the place.

I glance at the time on my phone. Five minutes until the fight begins. *Good.*

The quicker Kayden's match is over, the sooner I can talk to him.

I call the bookie over and chuck one of the two remaining fifty-dollar bills I have left at him to bet on Kayden. I have a feeling I'll double my money. I want to prove myself right in case he's as good as I think he is.

Someone accidentally pushes against me, and I stumble back slightly.

"Sorry." The guy's voice is cut off when his eyes flare in recognition.

"Brent?" I shout, immediately recognizing the thick-rimmed glasses and shaggy brown hair. I didn't think he was the type to come to these kinds of events. He always felt like a board-game-night-with-friends kind of person to me. "What the hell are you doing here?"

"What the hell are *you* doing here?" He echoes the question back to me.

"I'm here for Kayden," we say in unison. When the joint statement clangs in the air, Brent and I both make a weird face.

He expression turns quizzical. "Wait, why would you be looking for him here? Didn't you find him at his apartment the other day?"

"I did. But he kicked me out," I mutter.

I expect Brent's face to fall, but the expression remains nonchalant. "I'm sorry. You're not the only one he's done this to so far."

I want to press him further about Kayden's cold behavior, but as I open my mouth, the sharp bleating of a horn pierces my ears. Brent and I turn our heads toward the cage as a thunderous roar vibrates from the crowd.

"Welcome to the Vortex, fuckers!" The announcer

screams like the megaphone isn't already helping him amplify his voice to the entire city. "THE ONLY RULE THAT EXISTS HERE IS THAT THERE ARE *NO* RULES! SO LET'S. GET. REAL. TONIIIIIIGGGHTT!"

More screams from the crowd.

"You come here a lot?" Brent asks, his face tilting toward me. "I probably should have put two and two together with you being into MMA and all," he tells me.

"Yeah, but this is a whole different ballgame, so I get why you didn't," I reply, looking at him with mild skepticism. "But I'm surprised to see you here, though. This doesn't really feel like your scene."

I peer down at his attire—a blue button-up shirt and black slacks. He looks like he's about to walk up to the front of the class and deliver a presentation about quantum mechanics.

"It isn't." He shakes his head. "But Kayden's my brother. I come to every fight he's been in."

"Wait a minute." Confusion ripples across my face. "Kayden's your *brother*? Why didn't you tell me that?"

Brent merely shrugs. "It's easier to say he's a friend than having to explain the alternative."

I scoot closer to him, curiosity getting the better of me when I recall Kayden's facial features filled with sharp lines and comparing them with Brent's chubby cheeks and round button nose. I also note the different colored eyes, with Brent's seaweed green a wild contrast to Kayden's grey ones. "You guys look nothing alike."

"Yeah, we get that a lot. We're brothers, but not by blood. My parents adopted Kayden four years ago, when he was seventeen," he explains to me.

"Oh." Is all I can say to that. "But if that's the case, why don't you live with him?"

"Kayden doesn't go to BU. I wanted the college experience so I applied to be in the dorms," he murmurs, sifting his fingers through his hair. "I still go over a lot just to check up on him and make sure he's okay."

Brent's comments about Kayden puzzle me even more. "Why wouldn't he be okay?"

Before he can shoot back a reply, our conversation gets cut off by the announcer again.

"All right! Let's get on with the fight, shall we?" The man screams again, and cheers reverberate through the crowd. "On your left, we have fresh meat—Murphy 'Menace' Davisssssss!"

When Murphy emerges from the shadows, a slew of *boo*s and insults get hurtled his way from the crowd. It's a response that I'm familiar with, as it's their fucked-up way of humbling newcomers. As much as the underground welcomes fighters from any kind of background, it feels more like an elite club than anything else. If newbies don't leave a strong impression in the community, they usually don't last very long.

Which is why Kayden is all that more intriguing to me. He's one of the newer fighters to enter the underground, yet still causes quite a stir.

"And ooover to your left, we have one of our crowd favorites, the relentless, powerful, penultimate gatekeeper of *death*: Kayden 'The Killer' Williamssss!"

I watch as Kayden, draped in a dark-red satin robe, materializes from the shadows in the corner opposite from

Murphy. Usually MMA fighters don't wear robes—only professional boxers do—but the underground has a flair for the dramatic. And boy, does the robe fit Kayden well. He looks like a phantom king, ready to take his place up on the throne.

I've never heard a more energetic, deafening roar from the crowd as I do upon his entrance. He's serious, his gaze hard as steel as he lifts his fist up to acknowledge the cheers, and then does a little jog around the perimeter of the cage, knocking people's fists and waving to others. All of the girls within a mile radius of me jump excitedly, screaming all sorts of nasty, sex-fueled one-liners at him.

When Kayden finally climbs into the cage, he shrugs off his robe, chucks it to the side, and walks to the center of the cage. His opponent does the same. They touch fists briefly before moving in the opposite direction and easing into their stances.

There's two types of guys in any fight: the one who comes out guns blazing with all that he's got and the one who calmly waits for his opponent to attack first, picking up his strengths and weaknesses along the way.

Unfortunately for Murphy, he appears to be the former.

Because the second the referee yells "Fight!" he is immediately pouncing on Kayden. He swings a right hook at Kayden's head but Kayden anticipates it easily, locking his arms tight over his ears. Murphy is relentless, though, choosing to go on the offensive, his fists darting at Kayden, but Kayden expertly manages to evade blow after blow. Murphy, frustrated that he has little effect on him, swipes his right leg over to trip him. It catches Kayden's foot slightly but he sidesteps him at the last moment, undeterred. In retaliation, Kayden strikes with an effective jab-cross uppercut combo, catching Murphy off guard.

It looks like Kayden's strategy is to get Murphy to gas out so when the time arrives, he can knock him out easily. I'm impressed. Most fighters don't understand that fighting is just as much about pacing as it is about skill.

Kayden controls his distance well, hanging back only to block Murphy's attacks or to score a couple of hits of his own. *Strong, precise movements.* I nod approvingly. *A definite sharpshooter.* However, I can tell Kayden is getting a bit antsy, his footwork already faltering, which gives Murphy the brief opening he needs to tackle Kayden by lifting him and flipping him over in a massive takedown, sending them both crashing to the floor.

From beside me, I hear Brent suck in a nervous breath.

Red flares in Kayden's eyes. Murphy has him pinned against the floor, but Kayden pulls himself into a better position and rams his knee straight into Murphy's ribs. Murphy immediately doubles over and Kayden seizes the opportunity to mount him and crash his elbow straight into Murphy's nose. But before Murphy can recover, Kayden's fists explode, knocking into him over and over.

Murphy grits his teeth to keep from crying out in pain as he sloppily blocks Kayden's blows. He's looking nauseated, drowning in his own blood. A more experienced fighter would be able to reverse the position by getting a grip on his opponent's body and entangling his legs, but because Murphy has spent so much of his energy keeping up with Kayden at the beginning of the fight, he's got little to no strength left. Kayden now has his arm pressed hard against Murphy's neck, his legs caging his opponent as he bashes his fists against the guy's bloodied face.

At one final blow from Kayden, Murphy taps his hand against the floor weakly.

"Annnnnd the winner is the one and only . . . Kayden 'The Killer' Williamssss!"

The crowd detonates into blaring cheers. From around me, cash changes hands. Some people writhe in frustration as they cough up their money, and others wave their winnings in the air smugly.

The host starts announcing the next fight. I swivel back towards the cage and notice that Kayden's no longer in it, which means he's gone backstage to cool down. That's my cue.

"Hey, I'm gonna set off," I tell Brent. "Gonna go find your brother."

My response earns a frown from him. "Is this about the apartment thing? If it didn't work out, there's no use asking him again."

I shake my head. "This isn't about the apartment anymore. Or at least, it's less about that now. I just need to talk to him. He'll want to listen to me."

"You're stubborn, you know that?"

"Some would say it's persistence."

He gives me a quiet stare before sighing.

"Fine. He's probably in the back corridor, far left."

I send him a grateful smile. "Thanks."

"Good luck, Sienna."

I'm not going to need it. I know Kayden will want to hear what I have to say.

I follow Brent's instruction and pivot to my left when I find myself in the hallway. A couple of fighters lurk around the area, and I'm acutely aware of them watching me with predatory eyes. It takes a lot of willpower to hold myself back from decking each of their faces. Any other day I'd be glad to, but I'm on a mission tonight, and I won't let myself get distracted.

When I reach the end of the hallway, I find Kayden leaning against the door of his room, icing himself down. I hate to admit it, but he looks really attractive like this, with his ripped body covered in a thick layer of sweat and his hair all messy and disheveled. However, the thought soon crumbles when a familiar scowl returns to his face, making his displeasure known.

"You really can't take no for an answer, can you?" Kayden huffs. "I told you to stay away."

"Technically, you told me to never come back to your apartment again," I say chirpily. "So I thought maybe you'll be a bit nicer to me if I came to one of your fights instead."

"And why do you think that would make any difference?" He lowers the pack of ice and tilts his head to the side. Despite his annoyance, there's no mistaking the curious gleam in his eyes.

"You knew who I was. When I came to your apartment. Didn't you? You knew I was with Jax."

His gaze falls to the floor briefly. "I was trying to be nice."

"That was you trying to be nice?" I say, baffled.

He ignores me, loosing an impatient breath.

"Sienna, what do you want?"

"What if I told you that I want the same thing you do?" I say, stepping forward.

FIVE

I hold my breath as I wait for Kayden's response. Seconds feel like hours when his lips part to respond to me.

"No, thanks," he says.

And then he has the audacity to turn on his heel and trudge the opposite way from where I came from.

What. The. Fuck?

"Seriously?" I say as I trail after him, my bag hitting the side of my hip with every frantic movement. "You're not even going to hear what I have to say?"

"I don't have to because I don't need your help," Kayden says gruffly as he moves along the hallway in long, purposeful strides to get away from me. "I'm sure you're good at what you do. But I work better on my own."

"Maybe that's your problem. And maybe that's why you lost last season," I explain to him as I jog beside him and talk in the same breath. "Come on, Kayden. You know beating Jax is no easy feat. He's had the underground in his clutch for two years now. A different strategy this season can help you go far. Might even help you win that championship that you so clearly want but refuse to admit that you do."

That gets his attention. Kayden stops in his tracks, a muscle pulsing in his jaw. He looks at me, waiting.

"Can we just talk about it?" I say, desperation cutting into my tone. "Five minutes."

He sucks in a breath as he considers what I've just said. I can practically see his mind whirling.

"Fine," he snaps. "Five minutes."

He spins around and closes his hand over the doorknob adjacent to him. As he gives it a twist, the door gives way, and he ushers me into a large room. The place is barren except for several collapsed cardboard boxes in one corner, a tiered shelf, and some leftover cleaning supplies. I set my bag down in a corner, wanting to give him my full attention. Kayden shuts the door behind him and leans a strong arm against the shelf, jerking his head at me in invitation to say something.

"Look," I start, building up strength within my chest. "I know I don't look like the solution to your Jax problem, but I *am*. I spent three years of my life with him. He taught me how to fight in that cage. I watched him as he fought with every opponent he's ever had, in and out of the underground. I know how he trains, how he works, how he thinks. He taught me everything that I know, and now, I'm right here in front of you. A copycat of your enemy."

Kayden continues to study me intensely. "And you're willing to just share all that knowledge with me?"

"I will do more than that. I will *train* you for the entire season. You'll stand a much better chance winning the rest of your matches with me by your side, especially the one against Jax," I say, my shoulders rounded back and my head tipped high. "Can you do that on your own?"

"Well, I got myself this far, so perhaps I should."

"Fine. You go do that. If you wanna lose," I point out dryly.

Kayden hums with annoyance. He does a slow pace around the room, thinking about how to respond. Then, his gaze returns back to me.

"Why me? You could have gone to any of the other fighters here. They've each had their run-in with Jax, too, and have a vendetta against him."

"You're better than any of them here. Not the best yet but I think you've got potential."

"Potential?" he says incredulously. "I don't know if you saw me out there but I owned Murphy in that cage."

"Yeah, you did. I also know that if you fight exactly like how you did just now against Jax, you'll lose. Big time," I state candidly, and irritation flickers in Kayden's grey eyes. I circle around him, sizing him up like how I usually would to an opponent in a cage. "You're smart and you know when to go in for the kill. You also know how to pace yourself well to outwork your opponent. But it's not enough. Jax has *twenty* pounds on you, so he'll wear you out easily. You need to work on your gas tank and focus on refining your fight IQ and agility. I can help you with that."

Kayden opens his mouth to protest but I don't give him a chance, instead resuming my cross-examination of him.

"If you've got no clear strategy, you will lose," I tell him.

"And it's not like you gave it your best out there either. That newbie had you on the ground rather easily, and a runner-up like you should have anticipated that. With me as your trainer, I'll make sure that never happens again."

Kayden scrunches up his face in deep thought. I hug myself, my fingers drumming over my biceps in anticipation of what kind of answer he'll give me.

Eventually, he breaks the silence.

"Fine. Say I'm considering your offer. What do you want in exchange?"

"I want a place to stay."

"What happened to your old place?"

I pull my gaze away. "I can't stay there anymore. Because my sister stays there."

"And you can't stand her because . . . ?"

"She and Jax were fucking like bunnies behind my back."

It's weird to admit what they had done to me to a complete stranger. But I'm not ashamed of what happened. I know better than to blame myself for being cheated on.

Understanding dawns in his eyes. "So all of this makes sense now. You're here to get even."

I nod tersely. "That championship is a big deal to Jax. And I want him to know exactly how it feels like to lose what you love the most." I swallow hard, feeling the emotion catch on some of my words. Straightening myself again, I clear my throat, not wanting him to hear me falter again. "And it's time you broke his winning streak, don't you think?"

His eyes are ablaze with fiery retribution. "Damn right, I will. That championship is *mine*."

The resentment dripping in his tone is enough to make

me wonder if Kayden's problem with Jax runs deeper than just him wanting to get even. I decide to hold off from asking him about it because I'd rather not get him fired up, and then backtrack on his decision to agree to the deal.

"So?" I prod him. "What do you say?"

There's still hesitation in his expression as a frown runs along his lips. "I'm just wondering if I can trust you," he says, eyeing me carefully. "If this is some elaborate ploy by you and Jax to take an opponent down . . ."

As much as his paranoia infuriates me, I can understand why he would be suspicious. Jax isn't exactly the friendliest guy in or out of the cage; antagonism is the only language he speaks when it comes to the sport. And my persistence about making this deal happen doesn't help ease the suspicion either.

"It's not." I shake my head vehemently. "I know he can be insane, but trust me, as much as he knows you're a guy to watch out for, Jax doesn't care about you enough to come up with a scheme like this. You can count on his massive ego for that."

Kayden gives me another long, contemplative look. Eventually, his eyes flutter shut and he lets out a long, defeated sigh.

"Fine," he grumbles, stepping toward me. "You'll train me to beat Jax and I'll let you stay with me. If you try any funny business—if I catch you relaying any kind of information to Jax, the deal is over, you got me?"

"Deal."

I stick my hand out and Kayden begrudgingly shakes it.

"Grab your things, Lucky. You're moving in with me tonight," he announces stiffly.

***

While Kayden packs up his things, I head back to the main room to collect my earnings and then swing by the hotel I've been staying at to grab the rest of my belongings. It's only a short walk away from Breaking Point, and by the time I return to the gym, Kayden has yet to appear. I spot Brent by the entrance and join him, and we chat about our upcoming assignment while we wait. Just as I'm beginning to suspect that Kayden has chickened out of our deal and made a run for it, he finally appears from the back alley looking slightly less disheveled than before, now sporting a plain navy-blue shirt, a fresh pair of gym shorts, and a damp towel slung around his neck.

His eyes light up when they connect with Brent's, and he draws Brent in for a brotherly hug.

"Hey," Kayden says. "Thanks for coming out."

"Of course. You know I wasn't gonna miss it." Brent gives him a squeeze on his arm before releasing him. "It was a good fight."

"Funny. I thought the same, but apparently it wasn't up to Sienna's standards," Kayden mutters, giving me the side-eye.

"Good luck with this one. You're gonna need it." Brent lets out a chuckle. *Excuse me? What the hell is that supposed to mean?* In response, Kayden grunts in agreement, as if he is already anticipating the responsibility. Brent turns back to me and gives me a wave. "I'll see you on Monday."

I nod back at him. "See you."

Kayden signals for me to follow him. "Come on, Lucky. Let's go."

My body twitches with annoyance. There it is again. *Lucky*. Every instinct compels me to tell him to knock it off, that I'm not some golden retriever he can just order around. But I don't want to piss him off right now. I have him in an ideal mood, and I don't want to ruin it.

I crane my neck to glance around the neighborhood. There's a stretch of parked cars that runs for about a mile, and the thought of having to walk that far fills me with dread. It's already been a long day and I want nothing more than to sink into a bed right now and shut off from the world.

"Where's your car?" I ask.

He pats on the hood of the insanely beat-up truck beside him. "Right here."

Huh. I would have thought that with all the money that he rakes in after every fight he could certainly afford a better car than this.

Kayden helps me haul my bags into the back of the truck, and then goes around to pull the front-seat door open for me. *What a gentleman*, I think to myself. I'm taken aback by his kindness since he's been nothing but cold and defensive toward me, but I slide into the seat anyway, grateful to learn that at least he has some decency.

This man is so perplexing. One second he's throwing me out of his apartment and the next, he's given me a pet name *and* opens doors for me. I don't mind the chivalry. But I'm not sure if I'm okay with the pet name yet.

As we drive, only the sound of the radio fills the car.

Kayden doesn't say another word to me, instead keeping his focus on the road and clenching the wheel tightly. I fidget with my phone in my lap in discomfort, unsure how to feel about any of this. Kayden and I aren't exactly friends, so I don't know how to be comfortable around him. He clearly wants little to do with me. But I guess I shouldn't let it bother me because it's not like I'm looking for a meaningful friendship with him anyway.

This is just a deal and it has an expiration date.

When we finally reach the apartment, I grab my things from the back, and he helps me carry them up the block. We still don't talk while he fiddles with the lock and pushes the door open to let me enter.

I'm surprised by what I see. The place, for the most part, feels vacant. The white walls are bare, with no paintings or framed photos. There's a sofa and a small television that sits on some stacked cardboard boxes and small antique dining table in the other corner, but other than that, the place is devoid of any furniture, color, or personality.

My gaze travels to the kitchen where takeout boxes litter the top of the kitchen counter. I cringe when I see the huge pile of dirty dishes in the sink, and I don't even want to know what creatures are crawling over those plates.

"Seriously? Don't you ever clean up?" I make an uncomfortable face.

"I got no time." He shoves his hands into his pockets. "I train almost every day."

"And that's all you do? Train?"

I squint my eyes at him. Brent did mention he was the same age as us, so you'd think he'd at least be in college.

When he senses what I'm implying, he says, "There's not much else to do. I dropped out of college."

"Why?" I feel compelled to ask.

Kayden looks away, clearly wanting to avoid the topic. "I don't see how it's any of your business."

"Fine." I sigh instead, gripping the sash of my bag hard. "Don't tell me. Just show me to my room."

He leads me down a small hallway. "That's the bathroom." He points to the right. "And that's my room. It's off limits so no going in there, okay?"

"Fine," I mutter, then my eyes travel to the room beside his. "And this is mine, I assume?"

"Yeah." He pushes open the door.

The room is big enough for me. Like the rest of the apartment, the walls are white. Brown curtains drape across the window and a decent-sized bed sits neatly in the middle of the room, along with a small closet shoved in the corner.

"Sorry, I didn't have time to decorate." He stands by the doorway, hands shoved into his pockets as he shrugs. "I wasn't expecting anyone to rent this place out so soon."

"Yeah, well, I can see why," I murmur, dropping my bag on the bed. I feel like I'm living in a murder house.

Kayden's eyes bore into mine. "It's just a place, Sienna. It's not my home."

"You should make it your home, then." I sit on the bed and stare up at him.

"I don't deserve to make this place my home," he mumbles, his throat clenching with hurt.

The words tumble out of my mouth before I have a

chance of stuffing them back in. "Did something happen to you, Kayden?" I say out of worry.

His eyes grow huge, like he's on alert. Another scowl shoots up his face, dissolving any softness that was there before.

"*Don't*. Don't ask me questions like that again."

He grips the door hard before closing it. Then he hesitates, muttering ever so softly, "Good night, Lucky."

And then I'm left on my own.

SIX

After unpacking most of my stuff, I head to bed a little after midnight but I don't fall sleep until an hour later. My mind keeps being invaded by thoughts of Kayden. What an enigma he is. I've been watching fights in the underground for years and most of these fighters are typically easy to read. Their motivations are usually simple and obvious in the way that they carry themselves—there's always a few local guy with grudges, blue-collar workers looking to blow off some stream, or ex-UFC fighters looking to reclaim their glory days. But with Kayden, he doesn't feel like he belongs to any of those.

I've only seen little bursts of emotions from him, but most of the time he's careful with me. Careful to keep his distance. And it's clear he knows how to do it well.

So I'm not surprised that Kayden doesn't trust me. And I can't really blame him either; I do seem like someone who's up to no good. But I don't know how to get it in his head that it's not because I'm planning a double cross.

I just really want to fuck my ex up.

When my alarm sounds at seven thirty, my body is on autopilot as I slide out of bed and shuffle into the bathroom. I've got a couple of training sessions booked starting at noon, and I always make an early start to the day to get some cardio in.

After slipping into a black sports bra, a pair of gym shorts, and a windbreaker so I won't freeze my ass off in this early February air, I head out of my room to grab my trainers. I notice Kayden's door is slightly ajar, and when I take a quick peek inside, the room is empty.

The rest of the apartment is eerily silent. I scour the place for any kind of note explaining where he ran off to but come up short. And then I realize Kayden probably isn't the kind of guy who would tell his new roommate about his whereabouts. I scribble a note for him anyway on the off chance that he suddenly swells up with yearning to know where I'm going today. I'm sure he doesn't care, but I like to think I grow on people over time.

Gone out for a jog. Let's talk when I come back.
– Sienna

When I head out, the roads are empty and quiet, which is ideal. I usually prefer doing my cardio away from UFG because I'm not a fan of treadmills or weaving through a mass of people and equipment every time I do laps around the gym.

I start out slow for the first few yards, and then increase speed when I feel like I've found a good pace. Adrenaline starts to spike in my body, propelling me forward with every step I take. I pick up even more speed a couple of minutes later when I spot a familiar inked body in front of me. Kayden's wearing a navy-blue hoodie and joggers, and he doesn't appear to notice me come up from behind him. As I inch closer, I notice he has a pair of wireless earbuds too.

"Hey!" I call loudly, and Kayden whips his head back, pulling out one of his earbuds. "You didn't leave a note before you went out."

"I didn't agree to do notes," he replies sharply, looking me up and down. "Nor did I agree to be stalked."

"What?" My eyebrows dip low in confusion. "I haven't been stalking you."

Kayden cocks his head sideways, eyes narrowed like he's waiting for me to rethink my answer. I purse my lips into a frown when I ruminate on the past couple of days.

Okay, *maybe* he has a point. I do seem sketchy as hell, with me first going to his apartment, then ambushing him yesterday at Breaking Point, and now this.

"I didn't follow you out here today, okay?" I point out. "I'm here to keep in shape, just like you."

"They have cardio equipment at UFG."

"Yeah, but I like the fresh air," I say. "And the sight of hot guys running." I jerk my head at a dark-haired man running in the opposite direction. Despite the white long-sleeved shirt that covers most of his body, his muscular frame alone is enough to draw my attention longer than it should. As we cross paths, I'm unable to stop myself from turning back to sneak a peek of his perky, rounded butt, cupped by those black tights. "Wow. Look at him go. He's *gorgeous*."

Kayden rolls his eyes, feigning annoyance at my brazenness, He remains quiet as he squeezes his earbud back into his ear and continues his jog.

There's more silence as we go for another mile, zipping through the endless rows of shops and restaurants then finally reaching Marsh Chapel, which is predictably sparse with students today. I'm half tempted to make an escape through there so I don't have to endure the tension between us as we jog, but on the other hand, the fighter in me pushes me to keep going and see if I can find some way to dissolve the awkwardness. I need to find some kind of common ground with this guy since I'm not only going to be his trainer, but his roommate as well.

"So I guess you don't like to talk much?" I ask lamely. I'm determined to find a way in, even if the observation was obvious.

Kayden presses pause on the playlist shuffling on his phone and glares at me. "I don't like talking when I'm jogging," he replies with a controlled huff. "So do you mind? I need to focus."

"Ah . . . and it looks like you can't focus around me," I say, humor injected in my tone. "Because I'm distracting you."

"Exactly," Kayden confirms. But then horror settles onto his face as he fully processes the meaning of my words. He stops abruptly in his tracks. "No. That is *not* what I mean—"

"That's all right." I flip my ponytail off my shoulder, gleaming with confidence. "I know I'm hot."

An earnest sigh escapes him as he eases into a walking pace. I follow suit. "Haven't you heard that modesty is the best policy?"

"*Honesty* is the best policy. And yeah, I'm being honest. I think I'm fairly attractive."

Kayden looks away hastily. But that doesn't stop me catching the slight flush creeping up his cheeks. "I haven't noticed."

"Come on. Of course you have." I goad him. "You just don't want to admit it because you don't like me very much."

Kayden gives me the side-eye. "It's not that I don't like you, Lucky. It's that I'm not sure whether I should."

He picks up his pace again and I break into a determined run alongside him. There's no way I'm backing down from him this easily.

"Well, let me tell you that you're missing out," I say as I attempt to catch my breath. "Brent told me that I'm his all-time favorite person in his class to hang out with."

"Funny," he says dryly. "Because Brent told *me* that you're bat-shit crazy. And that I should also watch out for you."

"That bastard." I faux shudder with betrayal.

Kayden cracks a faint smile, like he'd rather not reveal it. This is the first time I've seen him do that, and I hate to admit that I genuinely love the sight of it. It makes me want to steal every chance I can to make him smile again.

Ten minutes later, we come to a halt in front of the entrance to Fenway Park. Kayden rests his hands on top of his thighs as he catches his breath. Even with the sweat gleaming on his brow and coating the sides of his face, he still looks decent. Gorgeous, even. The morning light catches the dewiness on his face and highlights his rugged features even more. Like the dip of his cupid's bow. The tip of his slender nose. And that insanely cut jawline. He can probably cut through boxing wraps with that jaw.

But of course, the moment is undercut by the wariness that soon lines his eyes—the same expression he's worn since he met me.

Now that we've stopped, I take the opportunity to address the pink elephant in the room.

"Look, I'm not trying to double cross you, okay?" I assert. "I know you think you can't trust me. And to be honest, you're making it hard for me to trust you too. But I'm willing to set all that aside and focus on what we need to do to get you in top shape to beat Jax. I *need* that win. It's the only way I can make sure he pays for what he's done to me," I say, mouth tightening. "He can't just fuck up my life and get away with it. I'm not going to let him."

Kayden studies me carefully, his grey eyes pinning me down. Assessing if what I'm saying is true. His head dips for a second as he blows out a steady breath and pulls himself back up into a standing position.

"I believe you," he declares begrudgingly. I'm surprised that he would cave; I assumed he was ready to put up a fight about it. "I won't ask about Jax again. Not unless you want me to."

"Awesome," I say, clasping my hands. "I thought we could have a more extensive talk about our training schedule after this." I slide my phone from the hidden pocket in my pants and steal a quick glimpse at the time. "I have some time before my first training class. You wanna call it? I can go for another mile, but it's best if we stop here."

"Fine. Let's stop. Where do you want to go?"

"Caffeinated makes the best coffee in the city. It's only a couple of minutes walk from here," I explain, then immediately remember I left my wallet at the apartment. "Shit. I don't have any money on me, though."

"That's fine. Coffee's on me." Kayden beckons me to follow him across the street.

We walk together in silence for a while before the familiar coffee shop comes into view. I like to come here after class to fuel up before I have to clock in at the gym. Kayden is the first through the door, holding it open for me. "What do you want to order?" He asks.

"I'll have a dirty matcha latte, please."

"What's a dirty matcha latte?"

"It's when two people who really love each other do it over a cup of coffee."

"You're hilarious, you know that?" His gaze slides to mine, annoyance lighting his eyes.

"Relax. It's just matcha with espresso in it." I wrinkle my nose at him. "You believed me for a second there, didn't you?"

"Did not."

"Liar." I singsong, and Kayden merely grunts, turning his back on me and dragging himself toward the cashier. "You better not be having any sugar in yours!" I add, and he waves me off with a dismissive hand. Wondering if he would seriously disregard my first dietary advice to him as his trainer, I stay by the sidelines, eavesdropping as he recites his order to the barista. A satisfied grin pops on my face when I hear him say *no sugar*.

I scour the place for an empty seat, and wait a few

minutes for a couple to vacate their spot before I swoop in to grab their table. Kayden appears shortly after with two steaming cups. He hands me mine and slides into the seat opposite me.

"So, knockouts are in two weeks," he points out, his hands wrapping around his cup as he stares at the lid. "There's usually a week of buffer time before the semifinals and three before the finals, so that means we gotta be ready by then. I'm all ears for whatever kind of plan you have for me for the next six weeks. And I know you have college and MMA classes, so I'm wondering how we're going to find the time to do this."

"Six weeks is tight for prep, but I think with what I have planned we should be able to make do. I'm ahead in all my classes, so don't worry about me," I explain as I take a generous sip of my latte, the caffeine already doing a decent job of kick starting my senses after that morning jog. "What I wanna know is what your current schedule is looking like?"

"I train at Breaking Point. Every day. Twice a day."

"That's too much." I shake my head in disapproval. "Let's do six days a week. Twice a day with two half days of rest. You need adequate rest or you're going to overwork yourself and risk getting injured."

Kayden's grip on his cup tightens. He makes a sound of protest. "Six days a week is too little."

"If you're training with me, you need to stick to that schedule. I'm not going to have you killing yourself for this fight. We don't want to take your street name too seriously." I lean back against my seat, crossing one leg over the other to make myself comfortable. "I'll be with you most of the time, if not, at least one of the two sessions of the day, and you'll carry out the remaining sessions on your own with the regimen I've created. I think you're cool and all, but codependency is unfortunately not my thing."

"What about diet?" Kayden inquires. "You gonna plan that as well?"

"You eat and drink clean. No sugar, no alcohol. I want you doing preworkout meals to have you primed for training. Carbs are a mainstay. Lots of protein. And apart from that, I have no other qualms. I just need you to stick to your current size," I inform him. "Jax might be bigger but that comes with weaknesses. We're not trying to be like him."

"That's fine." He nods in understanding. "What are the days we won't be training?"

"Let's do half days on Friday and Saturday, and Sunday a full day off. We'll still be doing our daily runs those days to keep up with cardio, but no high-intensity training."

"What am I going to do during the times we're not training?"

"You take a break. We both do." I say it like it's so obvious. "I want a social life. Don't you?"

"I have a social life," Kayden growls.

"Oh yeah? Name one friend," I shoot back, adding quickly, "And before you say Brent, your stepbrother does not count."

"Okay, fine. But give me credit where it's due. Stepbrother counts at least half a point." Kayden tries to argue with me.

"I didn't know we were even counting points," I say, mouth inching into a half smile. "I guess you could count me. But like you said earlier, you still don't know whether you should like me or not. And if you want me to count as your friend, the liking needs to be there."

Kayden stays silent for a while, assessing my words. He rubs a hand over his chin and shrugs. "I guess you're not that bad."

"You *guess*?" I echo, baffled.

"You do infuriate me, so I'm not entirely sure what that makes you," he says, tapping a finger against his jaw lightly.

"I'm going to settle for begrudging roommates and co-workers for now. Don't you agree?" I declare.

"I'm fine with that," he confirms, slumping against the chair, hands knotted behind his head. "I'll try my best to tolerate you."

"I'm sure after today it won't be such a difficult task."

"If you keep up with your sarcasm, it will be."

"Well, you're not the easiest person to be around either." My expression is fierce when I snap back at him.

"I'm sorry, but I can't help with that," Kayden tells me grimly. "Looks like we're stuck with each other until we each get what we want."

I can already sense the disjointedness between us as he allows his words to ring in the air. A sinking feeling spreads across my stomach and I frown, knowing all too well that it's not going to be easy—getting what we both want.

SEVEN

After our short-lived tolerance for each other this morning, Kayden has returned to being his usual cranky self, avoiding any kind of conversation with me. I finally decide that it's useless to be so affected by his indifference since I barely know the guy, so I let him do his own thing. A part of me suspects that he's suffered a great deal in his life, as it feels like he carries a heap of sadness around with him that drags my mood down as well.

I don't want to pry because it's clearly not my business. As long as it doesn't affect the deal that we have, I'll just learn to live with it.

And unsurprisingly, when I get up the next day, Kayden has already left the apartment. I check to see if he's left a note for me since I placed a paperweight on the spot where I left him my note yesterday, but there's nothing there.

I assume that he's gone off to Breaking Point, since

before we went to bed, I had laid out an extensive six-week schedule that involved a grueling session in the gym around this time. I should be checking up on him later this evening after I finish with my classes for the day.

I lock up the apartment and head downstairs. When the elevator doors swing open on the ground floor, I spot Cara waiting by the entrance, her laptop wedged between her arm and hip as she taps away on her smartphone. She has on a cute pink, long-sleeved dress underneath her black trench coat and knee-high leather boots that make her already spidery legs appear even longer. When she senses a presence walking toward her, her head swivels in my direction, and a warm smile spreads across her mouth.

"Hey, Sienna!" She beams at me. "I'm headed to central campus. You walking there too?"

"Yep."

"Awesome. Come join us." She waves me over excitedly. "I'm just waiting for Alex to show up."

Cara's best friend. I wonder if she lives in this apartment block, too, and just as I'm about to ask, my curiosity is confirmed when Alex bursts out of the elevator, her long, dark hair in disarray and her fingers fumbling with the top few buttons of her pink silk blouse.

"Sorry I'm late," she mumbles as she stumbles over towards our direction. "Overslept."

"Sure you did," Cara mutters softly, enough for me to hear. "The insanely thin walls of our apartment would argue otherwise."

"Huh? What did you say?" Alex asks.

"Oh nothing. This is Sienna, by the way," Cara muses as

she introduces me to Alex. "Met her the other day when she was looking at apartment 4-B."

"No way." Alex's mouth gapes open. "You moved in with the weird, hot guy?"

"Yeah, I did," I say as the three of us cross the road. At least I'm not the only one who thinks Kayden is a dangerously gorgeous mystery. "Is he like infamous in this apartment building or something?"

She leaps onto the sidewalk, her hair whipping in the wind like that of a model taking an candid shot. "I don't know about the whole building, but to us, yeah. We try to be friendly with our neighbors, and most of them are usually nice and welcoming back," Cara explains as she pulls her laptop to the front, now cradling it in her arms. She frowns when she adds, "Well, except Kayden."

Alex falls into step beside her, letting out a groan. "For months Cara made it her mission to get him to open up a bit more. Countless party, dinner, and hangout invites rendered meaningless. He won't even open the door for Cara anymore. Takes one look through the peephole and scrambles."

"I'm pretty sure he's actively avoiding me at all costs. He never comes out of his place the same time I leave ours," her best friend adds miserably.

"If it means that much to you, I'll talk to him for you," I offer, and she immediately perks up. "I highly doubt he'll listen to me, but I can give it a try."

"Kayden's being difficult with you, too, huh?" she says, her interest piqued. "It's a shame. He's *so* yummy looking. Every time the guys see him they get weird about it because Kayden's physique makes them feel really insecure. Alex's boyfriend, Daniel, always puffs out his chest and talks in a deep voice when they're stuck in the elevator together. It's hilarious."

"Wait a minute." I stop in my tracks abruptly, holding a hand outward as the gears in my head stop winding and click into place. "Daniel as in Daniel *Kerrington*? Of Daniel Kerrington and Alex *Woods*?" I snap my head toward Alex, my jaw dropping when she nods quietly in confirmation. "Holy shit, the two of you are like celebrities."

Toward the end of last year, it was nearly impossible to *not* hear about Daniel and Alex on the news. Daniel Kerrington is the son of Harry Kerrington who runs Kerrington Enterprises, one of the biggest developers in all of Boston. His family is practically swimming in wealth. It was announced sometime last fall that Daniel was engaged to Alex, and it seemed almost too good to be true given that it was never reported that they were even dating in the first place. Of course, it was later revealed—by Daniel himself on the *Charlize Matson Show*, a notorious Bostonian talk show—that the engagement was an elaborate ruse engineered by Harry to clean up Daniel's playboy reputation in exchange for pulling Alex's parents' company, Woods and Co., out of bankruptcy.

I guess despite the rocky start to Alex and Daniel's relationship, it worked out well for both of them since they're still together even after the truth was exposed.

"Well, I'm not a celebrity." Alex shakes her head, crimson staining her cheeks. "But Daniel's basically a Kardashian. He's just famous for being rich and good looking."

Cara loops a friendly arm through mine and tugs me

closer as we continue walking. "What's going on with you, Sienna? Anyone you've been eyeing? Or are you looking to nab your new roomie to yourself?"

"Yeah. No way." I almost scoff at the absurdity. Kayden and I barely even get along, and every time I open my mouth he looks like he wants to put a drill through his ears. "I'm taking a long hiatus in the love department," I proclaim.

"Wait, why?" She scrunches her face in confusion.

And then I tell them what happened. When I'm finished, we've touched down on the main campus, which is already teeming with students getting to their classes. It's almost noon, so there are more of them than usual. We bump into a few students as they stride past us, but Cara and Alex have shut themselves off from their surroundings, still trying to process the news.

"I can't believe it. What a couple of backstabbing assholes," Cara gasps, her mouth falling open in horror. "And your sister. What kind of sister would do that?"

Honestly, I've been asking myself that question. And so far, I've come up empty handed.

"What are you going to do about it?" Alex injects.

"I figured making both their lives a living hell would be a good start," I say dryly.

"I'm with you on that." Cara nods at me and gives my shoulder an encouraging squeeze.

I turn my head to face her, sending her an appreciative smile. But as soon as I do, I catch sight of the very last person I want to see right now.

Shit. On. A. Brick.

Every muscle in my body locks up.

"What?" Cara whirls around in the direction I'm looking and her body tenses. "You're kidding me. *That's* her?"

I nod wordlessly.

Beth is sitting on the bench a couple of feet away from us, her fingers tapping nervously against the textbook resting in her lap. When she notices me, she wedges the book between her arm and her body and immediately launches to her feet.

"Crap. She sees you," Alex says worriedly as Beth moves toward me with careful purpose. Clearly she's been waiting to catch me today. She knows I always take this path to get to my exercise physiology class. Alex continues to tug on my shirt a little too hard, whispering, "Crap! She's walking straight toward you!"

"Alex, shut up. We can see that." Cara jerks Alex away from me and toward her instead. "You need backup, Sienna?"

I shake my head, my eyes still zeroed in on Beth. "No. I've got it."

"Good." Cara breathes a sigh of relief. "'Cuz the both of us suck at being in a fight."

"Go." I give them a tight nod. "I'll catch up with you girls some other time."

Sensing that that's going to be the end of our conversation, Cara and Alex retreat. I can't tell if they're still watching by the sidelines, and to be honest, I don't really care. All I care about right now is figuring out what I want to say to Beth.

Do I even *want* to say anything to her? If I really wanted to, I could leave her hanging here and haul my ass to class so I don't have to bother with any more of her excuses.

But before I can even make a concrete decision, she's already right in my face.

"Sienna." She exhales, her wide eyes pleading with me before she can even get the apology out. "Can we please talk?"

"No," I say flatly. "You lost the chance to do that when you fucked my boyfriend."

"Please," she begs. In all the time we were growing up, I've never seen her this distraught before. Momentarily, I feel sympathy for her, for what appears to have been an agonizing few days for her, just as they've been for me. She looks like she's lost a good amount of sleep, if the crater-sized dark circles rimming her eyes are any indication. But the sympathy fizzles out once I remind myself that her actions are the reason we're in this terrible situation in the first place. Beth's voice is shaky when she adds, "I don't know what else to do. You haven't been replying to my messages. I tried calling you but you wouldn't pick up. Even Dad's getting worried."

I let out a dry laugh at the mention of him.

"You tattled to Dad about this? What are we? *Five*?"

"That's not what I intended," she replies nervously. "I just thought that maybe he could help me get through to you."

"Has it ever occurred to you that maybe the reason why you can't get through to me is because I don't want to talk to you?" I seethe through my teeth, my cheeks burning from the adrenaline rush.

My frustration is loud enough that it attracts a few onlookers. Beth's eyes scan their faces, acutely aware of their gazes burning into her. She hugs herself tightly, head tilted low in embarrassment, and her false modesty makes me want to make a scene in front of all these people just so they can hear how ridiculous she's being right now.

"I'm sorry," she says. "I really didn't mean for you to find out this way."

"Yeah. So you're not sorry that you did it. You're just sorry you got caught." I take a confrontational step forward and Beth steps backward, lip quivering. "I'm not stupid, Beth. I doubt you were ever going to tell me."

"I . . . I . . ." Beth stammers, frightened eyes blinking. Her lack of denial is enough to confirm my suspicions.

"I work so hard, day and night, to put you through school and give the both of us a life we deserve because God knows Dad's too busy screwing up his next marriage to really give a shit about us," I say, aggressively edging toward her until Beth's back bumps against a tree. "And you just throw everything that I've done for you back in my face? Just like that?" She hasn't said a word, too stunned to speak, so I throw another question at her—one that I'm fairly certain I already know the answer to. "Are you still seeing Jax?"

Beth looks away guiltily.

"Wow." I exhale. "That's a new low even for you."

"You don't understand, Sienna. I—I love him," Beth says.

"Oh, you love him. Yeah, that totally excuses everything." I laugh bitterly, rolling my eyes. "Come on, Beth. Are you seriously that naïve?"

"I know how it sounds but . . ." Beth murmurs. "I can't walk away from him, Si. He cares about me."

"Oh, he better, because you're dead to me. Both of you are." Anger thrums through me, blisteringly hot. "I don't care if you love him. Or if you just wanted to sleep with him. I care that you *lied* about it and did it as if I didn't mean anything to you," I say, sucking an unsteady breath into my mouth. "You think that I can ever forgive what you did? If you really think that, then you really don't know me at all."

I'm too disgusted with her to say another word. A small crowd has now formed, with students whispering among themselves as to what's going on. I'm certainly not here to put on a show. I don't have time for it. But just as I'm about to turn my back on Beth, a hand clings to me.

"What do you want me to do, Sienna?" She looks at me with so much desperation that I feel the grip on my anger momentarily slip. "Do you want me to kneel and beg for forgiveness? Do you want me to break up with Jax?"

"You still don't get it, do you?" I shake my head in disappointment, wrenching my hand away from her. "I don't want you to do any of that. I don't even want you to leave him. I just want you to see what you've lost *because* of him."

And with that, I turn on my heel and leave.

EIGHT

For the rest of the day I let the confrontation between me and Beth play in my head. Guilt chafes at me at how small I know I made her feel. I never liked fighting with my sister. Even when we were kids, I couldn't bring myself to get angry at her if she did something to upset me. There was enough animosity around the house as it was that I wanted to protect her more than I wanted to pick fights with her.

Perhaps she was counting on my anger to pass just as easily as the other times.

I shake my head silently. As harsh as my words were when I wielded them in the courtyard, it was well-deserved. Especially after telling me that she's still seeing Jax.

Beth can do whatever she wants with him. As far as I'm concerned, they belong together.

In the fiery, blazing pits of hell.

Perhaps I can just ignore her for the rest of my life. It'll be difficult to navigate around the awkwardness if we bump into each other around campus or our once-a-month family dinner with our dad, but I'm sure I'll get used to it. Denying Beth the attention she craves will serve as sufficient payback, I suppose.

But with Jax I need to hit back harder. Bolder. Play the only game that he's ever taken seriously, more so than his own life—the underground.

I remember mocking him about how obsessed he was about it when we first started dating, and he looked at me dead in the eye and said *You can laugh all you want, princess, but in the underground, you fight to* survive. *It's a sick, twisted microcosm of life. Except there's only one difference. Life can fuck me over time and time again, but in that cage, I control all the elements. I control whether I win or lose. And there's no better fucking feeling than that.*

God, I really hope he leaves that final fight against Kayden on a stretcher.

It's almost evening by the time I'm finished with classes. I steal a quick bite to eat from Caffeinated before rushing over to Breaking Point to meet Kayden. When I saunter in, I pass by a group of guys throwing practice jabs at each other on the mats and weave through the impressive display of modern gym equipment on my way to the large cage sitting in the middle of the gym. The cage is empty with the exception of the half-naked tattooed man I'm training with today. He has his back to me, busy strapping on his gloves. Blood red, to keep with his brand.

"You're late," Kayden calls, not bothering to look over at me.

"Yeah, I know," I say in defeat, dropping my bag on the

outside edge of the cage and bunching my hair into a slick ponytail.

I purse my lips as I sneak another glance at Kayden. He's practicing a couple of shadowboxing movements to get some momentum going. His tattoos shift every time he makes a jab-cross combo, and his baggy shorts inch down, resting hazardously low on his hips, making no attempt to haul them back up. I have a feeling it's on purpose. When he feels me staring at him, he pivots toward me, and a mischievous grin twitches on his lips, causing his dimples to pop.

Ahhhhh shit.

Those dimples. I'm fairly certain they exist on men for the sole purpose of torturing women. And it's working *too* well.

"How long have you been training today?" I say, clearing my throat along with my dirty mind.

Kayden's arms fall limply to the sides. "Two hours so far. Ran three miles today, worked on technique, and ended with half an hour on the bag."

"Good. I see you're sticking to my schedule."

"Oh, I wouldn't dream of crossing you," he murmurs. "We're easing into it today, right?"

"You wish." I slide into my MMA gloves and head up the stairs and into the cage. "We're sparring today. During these first few weeks we'll be working on getting you into good shape for the knockouts. Based on the tentative schedule you sent me, it's unlikely you'll be encountering Jax during those rounds so that's good. I have a feeling they're hoping you'll end up in the finals against him because it'll rake in a large audience. So let's not focus on him just yet," I explain, and Kayden nods in understanding. "Our main focus is to close the gap in your game and increase precision. You'll be fighting against other fighters roughly in your weight category, so upskilling what you already know will be enough to get you through the semifinals. Later, we'll zero in on what kind of skills you'll need to equip yourself with during your fight against Jax. Fighting against him is a completely different ballgame, so I hope you'll be able to keep up. But for now, I just want to see what you've got."

"That's fine with me. I've been practicing all day," Kayden says, a dangerous glint in those grey eyes. "Meanwhile, I heard that you got yourself into a fight of your own today. With Beth."

"How the hell do you know that?" I chuck my towel on the floor.

"Some dude recorded it and it went viral on Twitter. Guess who sent the link to me," Kayden tells me lightly, and I roll my eyes. I love Brent but he is such a superspreader of gossip. I usually don't mind it when he's blabbering about other people's business but I feel uneasy when the news involves me. I don't care if that makes me a hypocrite.

"Word travels fast, huh?" I say, placing my hands on my hips. "It wasn't a fight. Just a very heated argument that resulted in her on the brink of tears."

"That's harsh."

"That was *necessary*," I correct him. "And she's still seeing the bastard even after I found out about it. Shows me just how sorry she is for what she did."

"At least with whatever happened, someone gets to be happy. You clearly aren't," Kayden notes distinctly.

"Do I detect some judgment there?" I wrinkle my nose at him. "Because if I recall, it is you who is also benefiting from this deal. How about let's keep both our noses where they belong. I don't judge you for fighting in the underground and you don't judge me for wanting to watch my ex burn."

"Fine," Kayden mutters tightly.

"All right," I say in finality, easing into a stance. He does the same. "Less talk, more work."

Kayden launches himself at me.

His fists fly toward my face and I block his first few hits fairly. When his guard is open, I send a jab his way but he slips it quickly, immediately weaving to the left. He sends another fist toward me but before it can reach me, I jump back and whip my leg to throw a roundhouse kick. He winces when it makes contact but isn't the least bit unhinged.

Kayden retaliates by shooting toward my lower body, hooking one arm underneath my leg and forcing me off balance, sending me crashing to the ground. Then he rolls on top of me, using his weight to cage me in, but I'm lighter and faster, and I know how to use that to my advantage. Before he can force a submission, I pull his arm behind his back and catch his leg with mine, sending his shoulder painfully to the ground.

The sudden jerking movement causes Kayden to falter for a split second. Which is all I need to trap his arm and get my legs wrapped around his neck in a triangle armbar. Next thing I know, Kayden is tapping the mat furiously as I start to pull on his arm.

"*Ah!*" He grunts in pain as he feels his tendons start to strain. "All right, all right. Get off of me."

"Come on. You can do better than that," I purr, climbing off the mat and reaching a hand out to him. Kayden appears shell-shocked, looking at me with astonishment.

He barely shakes off the previous sparring session before declaring, "*Again.*"

And we're both on the move. Kayden strikes first but I duck quickly under him and send an uppercut at his jaw. He shakes my blow off and when I go in for a left hook, he pulls his arm up to block the hit. I plow forward, driving Kayden on the defensive with a flurry of blows; he staggers backward trying his best to fend off my attacks.

Kayden tries for a kick and I intercept it, going in for a takedown, but he manages to regain his balance by digging in his back foot. My muscles strain against his weight, trying to get him on the ground, but he maneuvers himself in a way that hooks his arm over mine and sweeps me to the floor. I immediately try for another armbar but this time Kayden is ready. With a heave, he hauls himself up, muscles straining as lifts my lower body off the mat. My legs are still wrapped around him but he slowly leans his full weight into me, putting pressure on my neck. I struggle against him restlessly, trying to wrestle free from his grasp, but all my attempts are rendered futile, no match against his ferocious size.

Kayden releases his hold on me. I roll away from him and rest my arms on my knees, gasping for breath.

"Not bad," I wheeze. "But you only won that because you used your weight against me. If you were fighting against any other guy, they might be able to get out of that fairly quickly."

A confused look. "I thought you told me to do better."

"If that's you doing better than we're both doomed and I might as well find someone better to take Jax down," I say.

He narrows his eyes. "That's not fair."

"I didn't say I was going to be fair," I reply fiercely. "You want me to coddle you or push you to win? Because I can't do both."

A muscle ticks in his jaw. He forms into his fighting stance, fire lighting up in his eyes.

"Again," Kayden rasps. "I can do this all night, Lucky."

There's something about the way that he won't back down despite me putting him down like that that I find endearing. Most fighters would lose their cool or get defensive and yell obscenities at me. So I respect that Kayden can take whatever I dish out to him.

"I'd like to see you try, Killer." I hold my fists up. A crooked smile graces my lips.

He barrels toward me with a roar. I block his advance. He retaliates.

We do it again.

And again.

And again.

***

By the time we're finished with our sparring session, my stomach is begging for me to fill it with a proper dinner. I don't usually get this hungry after a workout but my session with Kayden had taken quite a toll on my energy.

This man is relentless. Every time Kayden loses a fight,

he shakes it off quickly and tries again. When I scrutinize his movements, he digests my advice and tries to do better in the next round. Toward the end of the session, it's harder to get Kayden to give up. He's still losing more times than he's winning, but he's finally depending on his skills as a talented fighter rather than relying mostly on his weight to crush me. I think he would have wanted to keep sparring if I hadn't thrown the towel in and called it a day.

I'm shoving my gloves into my bag and hauling the strap over my shoulder when Kayden emerges from the showers, his dark hair curling with dampness, beads of water falling past his eyes. The number of people in the gym has dwindled as it approaches closing time, so I take it as my cue to leave.

"I'm gonna head out," I announce to Kayden. "Dying to get something to eat."

He purses his lips, worry clouding his expression as he debates whether this is a good idea. It's cute that he thinks I can't handle myself out there if anything were to happen.

"You sure? It's getting late and there's nothing really good around here," he says. Then he adds, rather quickly, "I'll cook you dinner."

My ears perk up. "Seriously? You would do that for me?"

"Sure. What are you craving?"

"Pan seared fois gras topped with caviar—"

"Seriously," he mutters, throwing me a warning look. "What are you craving that I can *reasonably* make?"

"I'm good with any kind of pasta you can whip up. And it better be healthy if you're eating too. With lots of lean meat."

"Yeah, sure. Give me a couple of minutes to pack up."

"Fine."

I wait for Kayden by the entrance, trying to tame my hunger by scrolling through my phone, preparing my next cheesy pickup line for when I see Brent tomorrow in class. When Kayden finally emerges, he jerks his head in the direction of his truck and I follow his lead.

The ride is mostly silent because we're both slumped from exhaustion. There's nothing much to say. Or perhaps it's more like I don't know what to say to him. I've never met a person I felt like I was walking on eggshells around. It feels like every time we're together, I might just set Kayden off with one wrong word. But at the same time, during those few rare moments when he lets his guard down, there's a kind of genuineness there that softens me and makes me feel all gooey inside.

When we arrive back at the apartment, Kayden heads straight to the kitchen. He already has a bunch of sauce jars and vegetables laid out in front of his chopping board by the time I get into a fresh set of clothes and join him. When he flips the stove on and chucks the pasta into the boiling water, I'm already salivating.

"How long is it going to take?" I whine, tapping my fingers at the edge of the kitchen counter impatiently. "I'm so hungry I could rip off your arm and eat it."

"You can try but I don't think it's going to be nearly as tasty as this dish."

"Fine," I mutter scornfully. "You've got fifteen minutes before I go all *World War Z* on you."

"Calm down, Lucky. Patience is key."

"Well, I'm training you, aren't I? I have a feeling I'm gonna need a lot of that in the upcoming weeks."

Kayden angles his body to face me and lifts his wooden spoon. "Hey, you gotta admit that I held my own pretty well against you," he says gruffly. Then he shrugs, pivoting back to the stove. "It's actually a shame you don't fight in any promotions, because you're good at what you do."

I draw my lips together, contemplating. I've never allowed myself to consider fighting MMA outside of training. It's something that has never been of interest to me. Training with clients have been all I've ever known since I got certified, and it's a comfortable space for me to be in while juggling school, work and my sister.

"That's not my fight," I explain, resting my back against the sink. "I like helping people get where they need to go."

"How about the underground, then? Less commitment, more cash."

My mouth pulls into a frown. There's no denying my distaste for fighting in the underground. Even when I was dating Jax, the unregulated, debased nature of it was difficult for me to get behind. The only reason I put up with him fighting there was because he was too stubborn to be convinced otherwise.

"No thanks. I respect the competitive nature of the sport. Not so much the underground." I shrug. "But hey, if for some superfluous reason, I have to face a jacked-up dude in a greasy basement somewhere, you know you'll be my . . . well, I don't know if you'll be my first call but you'll be *a* call."

"So you think that I'm fighting for superfluous reasons?" Kayden asks, gesturing for me to move aside so he can strain the pasta over the sink.

"That's why most people fight in the underground. For

money, gore, fame, or all three. They don't care about the sportsmanship. The spirit of being a professional athlete."

The corners of his eyes crinkle slightly as he studies me. "Interesting. You know, for someone who dated an underground fighter for three years and is currently training another one, you seem to have a weird problem with it. And with me being in it."

I pause for a moment, not realizing that I've been putting a lot of judgment on him for fighting in the underground. But I doubt it's for the reason that he assumes it is.

"Fine." A defeated sigh leaves me. "You really want to know why?"

"Yes."

"It's because it's clear you don't belong there. You don't deserve to be fighting there because the underground's *beneath* you," I tell Kayden sharply, my words clanging through the kitchen. "It's not because I think you're more skilled than anyone who's ever entered that cage. Though I admit you're pretty good. You and I both know that a lot of people who join those fights are not entirely good people. Some have done horrible things to people who don't deserve it." My gaze drops to the floor as I begrudgingly admit, "And I don't know you that well, but I have a feeling you're not like them."

He lets out a bitter laugh.

"Well, you're wrong about that."

My instincts push me to ask him what he means by that, but I hold my tongue instead.

It's none of your business, Sienna. Things between you and him are complicated as it is.

"Here you go," Kayden says as he scoops the pasta into

two bowls and hands one to me. "Creamy pesto chicken pasta. I told you it wouldn't take long."

"Thanks." We take our seats opposite each other at the dining table and I scoop the pasta into my mouth ravenously. I let out a moan. "This is *amazing*. Totally worth not severing your hand for this."

"I'm glad that you like it." Kayden watches me as I continue to gobble up the rest of the dish. A disgusted look crosses his face. "Jeez, you'd think with the way that you're eating that nobody's ever fed you. Did Jax not cook for you?"

"Actually, he did," I deadpan. "I hate to burst your bubble, but he treated me fairly well. Right up till the cheating part, anyway."

"Did he ever apologize to you?"

"No." My breath feels tight against my chest. "Because I don't think he's sorry. And it wouldn't matter anyway, because I would still want this. To get back at him."

Kayden is silent for a moment. His jaw clenches tight as he takes a bite from his dish. "Why did you love him?" His eyes search for an answer in my face as he seethes. "He's a fucking asshole."

"Not to me." I shake my head. "At least, not in the beginning."

I think back to the times when I was so distressed after an argument with my dad and Jax would scoop me into his arms and console me by convincing me that the world just wasn't ready yet for what I had to offer.

You're a fucking hurricane princess, Sienna, he'd whisper. *And one day, you're gonna make the world tremble underneath your goddammed feet.*

I liked what Jax brought out in me. He taught me compromise was never an option, that I should embrace the darkest, twisted parts of me, even if no one else could understand them.

And I liked knowing that he was the only one who ever could.

"Jax was always kind to me," I point out. "And he helped me work through a lot of stuff with my parents splitting up and my mom moving away," I murmur, pushing the pasta in my bowl around with my fork. "I wouldn't be the person I am today without him."

Kayden shrugs. "That doesn't sound like love, Sienna. Sounds more like gratitude to me."

I wince as he strikes me with his candid observation. I don't know why, but the words cut into my skin deeply, and my body tightens with offence, propelling me out of my chair.

"I'm done," I snap, trudging to the kitchen.

Regret immediately seizes Kayden as he bolts out of his own chair and tails behind me. "I'm sorry. I shouldn't have said anything."

"You don't know anything, okay? Stop assuming what Jax and I had wasn't real," I mutter as I drop my bowl into the sink so hard that I'm pretty sure I crack it.

Kayden gulps, staring at me with fear. "I never outright said that."

"Well, you implied it!"

"Okay, I'm sorry." His tone is soft and apologetic as he tries to calm me down. "Of course what you had with Jax was real. Or else you wouldn't be going to such great lengths to get back at him." He inches closer to me, hesitating, before placing a soothing hand on my shoulder. I'm startled by the gesture but I don't pull away. I don't want to. His remorse spreads from his hand to my chest and all my anger toward him begins to dissipate. His hand trembles as it moves farther up my shoulder, and it's like it's itching to reach out to cup my cheek, but to my disappointment, he holds himself back. Instead, he says, "I don't know what I was saying, okay? Maybe I'm just tired. I won't assume those kinds of things about you anymore, I promise."

His throat bobs as his body writhes with guilt, and I feel instant regret for going off on him like I did. I know it's a harmless observation, and yet something about it rattled me deeply. But I can't stay angry at him for long.

"Yeah." I nod quietly. "All right."

Relief floods Kayden's face and he drops his hand from my body. I feel empty now that his touch is gone.

"Okay," he whispers. "Let me help you clean up."

We settle into sharing dish-washing duty in silence. Every so often, Kayden glances over at me to make sure I'm okay. I'm not sure if I am.

A new heaviness settles across my chest. I shouldn't have gotten that vulnerable with him. Who is he to assume what went on between me and Jax? He hates Jax's guts, so of course there'd be bias in his observation. And as much as I despise Jax, I *know* I loved him. I wouldn't have stayed by his side for that long if I didn't. I wouldn't burn with outrage at the mere thought of him.

And yet, despite it, it's hard to keep Kayden's words out of my head.

When we're done cleaning everything up, I dry my hands with a kitchen towel and drag myself to my room. I'm too exhausted to think about this right now.

"Hey, Sienna?"

I turn back and lock eyes with Kayden.

He hesitates, mouth quivering, before blurting, "I'm sorry you're hurting inside."

I feel all the air leave my lungs. Shit, I definitely shouldn't have let my guard slip tonight. And now he knows that what happened between me and Jax is still a raw, open wound.

I should feel uneasy about it. But I'm not mad that he knows. I get a feeling that he'll be the last person in the world to ever judge me for what happened.

"Kayden—" I rasp.

"Good night, Lucky," he murmurs, heading to his own room. He clutches the door hard, before offering a sad, gentle smile.

And then he shuts the door, leaving me utterly speechless.

NINE

"You know, when Beth told me yesterday what happened between you two, I was stumped." My dad is berating me over the phone this morning.

I yawn as I prop myself against the bed frame in a sitting position, mentally beating myself up for mistaking my ringtone for an alarm and picking up the call. Ignoring all his calls these past few weeks had proven to be successful thus far, and I had intended on continuing the streak, but I guess that's all gone out the window now.

"To say that I'm disappointed in you would be an understatement," he continues.

I peek at my phone screen and groan. It's way too early for this. I can already feel a throbbing headache forming, which typically happens when my dad decides to check up on me.

My dad and I have a very rocky relationship. He's pretty much lost all sanity since my mom and him split up, remarrying three times in the short span of the past three years. And, suspiciously, to mostly wealthy heiresses as well. His last one was to a two-time widow with a fortune the size of Daniel Kerrington's father's. I can only imagine how she got all that money.

My dad's carefree nature toward marriage has always irked me, given that he never tried hard enough to mend things with my mom. I know my parents weren't perfect, but their marriage had always been solid. So when my dad suggested divorce to my mom, it came as a huge shock to the whole family. My mom was shattered but ultimately agreed to the divorce, and decided to move out of the country to find some closure from it all.

Giving up is second nature to my dad. His other failed marriages have only served to prove my point. Ergo, he doesn't deserve my respect, nor do I think he ever will.

"Okay . . . " My voice trails off, unsure of what else to say on the matter.

It's clear he's fishing for an apology. Well, tough luck because he's not getting one from me. I'm not sorry for what went down between me and Beth. She deserved to be called out for her selfishness.

"You aren't even going to try to explain yourself?" he demands. I hate it every time he takes that tone with me—as if he's the least bit capable of being a good dad.

"There is nothing to explain," I reply, gripping the phone tightly. "She had an affair with my boyfriend and I told her off. End of story."

"Did you really have to do it in front of everybody? She was absolutely mortified afterward."

"Okay, first off, she confronted *me* in public. And I didn't say anything to her that wasn't a lie. Secondly, you talk about Beth as if she's not nineteen years old and can't take some heat from her sister. Heat that was rightfully deserved." It baffles me that my dad continues to defend her. But I guess I shouldn't be surprised; Beth can do no wrong in my dad's eyes. A muscle ticks in my jaw as I strangle the phone with my grip. "Come on. She did tell you she slept with Jax, right? You know—the guy you absolutely *despised?*"

Just like how my dad has never approved of anything I've done, he's also never been the biggest fan of the boys I brought home, which had been sparse to begin with. And when I first introduced Jax to the family, a few lines of conversation between him and my dad was enough to seal my dad's hatred for him. Since then, I never let the both of them be in the same room together for the fear that they'd butt heads.

So it's ironic now that he's trying to defend my sister dating him. A classic tell of who's my dad's favorite.

"Look, I'm not trying to excuse what she did with him." He lets out a sigh. "But at the end of the day, she's still your sister."

"Yeah, that's not gonna work on me. Just because she's family doesn't mean she gets a pass for being a terrible human being." Annoyance climbs up my body. "And by the way, you of all people shouldn't be lecturing me about keeping the 'family' together."

I hear my dad's sharp intake of breath, indicating that he's tired of me constantly bringing this up. "Sienna, I'm sorry. I don't know how many times you want me to say it," he says. I can picture him massaging his temple with his fingers, something that he does when he's getting really frustrated with me.

"I only bring it up because you're being a hypocrite right now. So excuse me when I choose not to listen to your advice. That's just like listening to Hannibal Lecter on how to be vegan." I shoot out of my bed, chucking my blanket away.

"This blame game is getting really exhausting, Sienna," he says. "We're talking about you and what you did to your sister. You know she's hurting."

"Well, some things are just unforgivable, Dad," I say dryly, digging my teeth into my bottom lip.

He pauses for a beat, then lets out a defeated sigh. This is usually the point in our conversation when he's at his wit's end but won't let go of the chance to slip in another generic piece of fatherly advice. And sure enough . . .

"You're going down a dangerous path, Sienna," he warns me. "You need to let all that anger go or you'll never be able to move on."

"Yeah?" A humorless laugh leaves me. "Well, maybe I *don't* want to move on."

And then I hang up and drop the phone on the bed.

This is exactly why I dread talking to my dad—because I know that regardless of what Beth has done, he'll always see me as an irrational, volatile person who only serves to invite chaos to the family.

It makes me wish mom was still around. She has always understood me, more than Dad ever tried to, and I miss her company terribly. Last summer, I had the chance to visit her in Rio and it was the most magical time of my life. We hit the best dance clubs, drank our livers to death, and passed out on every beach in the city.

I don't get to see her as often as I'd like, but I'm happy that she's thriving down there. We still talk whenever we get the chance, and sometimes on FaceTime I see glimpses of sorrow in her eyes when I mention Dad, and I know she misses him. Wishes that they were back together. I hate that he won't ever discuss it.

I hop into the shower to wash off the conversation and slip into some comfortable clothes. After deciding that a nice, tummy-filling breakfast is in order, I head out of my room. Taped to my door is a note, and I peel it off, scanning its contents.

Out for a jog. Don't follow.
—Kayden

At least he's leaving notes now. Although they're not very nice ones. I chuck the note into the bin and pass through the living room. Rustling sounds drift from the kitchen and my entire body stills.

If Kayden's out, then who the hell is that?

Retreating to my room, I snatch the golf club stashed under my bed for emergency situations and grip it tightly as I slowly creep back into the living room. Whipping it back, I slowly inch closer to the kitchen, preparing for a nasty confrontation. A blonde-haired man has his back to me as he rummages through the kitchen cabinets.

Shit. He's looking for things to steal!

The thought immediately kickstarts my impulses as I dart into the kitchen and swing the golf club at the intruder, aiming straight at his head. I wince when it makes contact with a loud thud.

"Ah *fuck*!" The man drops all the food he's holding and groans in agony, his hands flying over his head.

"Hah! Take that, thief!" I yell, reeling the golf club back for another hit. "Don't steal our shit!"

"What the hell—" the man rasps, holding his hands out in surrender before the weapon can descend on him. "I'm not a thief, you psycho!"

I stare at him, puzzled. Brent bolts out of the washroom when he hears the commotion and his jaw drops as he tries to register what's just happened.

"What the hell is going on here?" he says, horrified.

"This guy broke into the apartment!" I raise my voice, swinging my head in the man's direction. The man who is now on the floor, yelping in pain. "Give me your phone! I'm going to call the cops."

"Oh my God. *No*." Brent says frantically, reaching out to grab my wrist before I do anything else stupid. "He's our friend."

I glance over at the man, then back at Brent, confused. "He's not my friend."

"He's mine and Kayden's friend," Brent clarifies.

"What?" Kayden has never mentioned him before. "But—" I stop abruptly and narrow my eyes. "Who let you guys in?"

The man glares at me. "We have the keys, idiot."

I snatch my wrist away from Brent, glaring daggers at him. "Why do you have the keys to our apartment?"

Brent shrugs. "Because Kayden trusts us? And sometimes we hang out here when he's not around."

"Well, I live here now too! You guys can't just barge in like this whenever you please!" I jab a finger at the not-thief, feeling absolutely mortified. "And *you*. I could have killed you!"

"You almost did." He wheezes, and Brent has to help pull him up from the floor.

"I'm so sorry," I mutter, and shuffle to the refrigerator, trying to shake off the shock. "Let me get you an ice pack."

I'm going to kill Kayden for not telling me about this. He could have at least warned me that his friends can come and go as they please.

"We're sorry. We did text Kayden to let him know we were coming over. I guess you didn't get the memo." Brent follows me into the kitchen, looking remorseful.

Of course I didn't get the message. One second Kayden and I are having a heart to heart and next, he's completely icing me out.

It's always one step forward, two steps back with him.

I blink at the stranger. "I really am sorry for hitting you, uh—"

"Evans," the guy says smoothly. "Although you may know me by other aliases on campus: Mr. Drop Dead Gorgeous, Bachelor-I-Wanna-Bone . . ."

"Oh God. You're one of those." I groan.

Brent rolls his eyes. "Don't mind him. He has an ego the size of Europe."

Evans clicks his tongue. "How else am I going to mask my deep-seated insecurities about my own masculinity?"

"Well." I give a shrug as I hand him an ice pack. "At least you're self-aware about it."

Brent rolls his eyes. "I liked you a lot better when you were on the floor groaning in pain."

"Wow. Way to be sympathetic to my plight." Evans sends a dirty glare Brent's way as he moves the ice pack down his head to where I hit him. He winces when it makes contact with the most sensitive part of his skin.

"Can I please have the keys back?" I extend my palm toward Brent, my voice terse. "Because I really think that it'll be better if you knock on the door before you make yourselves at home. And that'll make me feel a lot safer living here too."

Brent shakes his head vehemently. "No way. Kayden's my brother. I need to check up on him from time to time."

"But it's weird that you guys can barge in anytime that you want. I live here now," I protest. "I'd like to have the keys back." I lunge forward to grab them from Brent's grasp but he recoils away from me, grinning.

"No can do, Sienna," he tells me. "But shall I propose a truce?"

A sigh pulls itself out of me. "On what grounds?"

"That we'll use the keys for emergencies only. Anytime we just wanna chill here, we text you *and* Kayden first."

I bite my lip in contemplation. I guess it wouldn't be very nice of me to take away their key privileges considering I just moved into the apartment.

"Fine," I snap. "Only emergencies, you got me? As in, someone catches on fire kind of emergency. Not because you want to raid our kitchen for food." I cut a glare at Evans.

"Sorry, we ran out of Cheetos in the dorms. And Kayden has a ton of them in his hidden stash," Evans says innocently, returning my scowl with a sheepish smile.

The sound of the front door opening announces Kayden returning from his jog. The grey shirt he has on is drenched with sweat, and when he steps into the living room, confusion whips across his face when he notices the golf club resting against the dining table and an injured Evans sitting beside the assault weapon.

"What the hell?" Kayden hisses out.

"You have an evil roommate, Kayden!" Evans moans as he shoots out of the chair and rushes toward Kayden like a preschooler tattling to his teacher when the kids in the class aren't treating him right. "She just whacked me on the head for no goddamned reason!"

"Oh, for fuck's sake." I mutter a string of curse words under my breath. "I genuinely didn't know who he was. And this all could have been avoided if you'd told me they were coming over. I thought they were robbing the apartment."

"Who the hell robs an apartment in broad daylight?" Kayden demands. "You should have known they were my friends."

"Was I supposed to just read your mind?" I shoot back defiantly. "Or perhaps I should have read the text you sent me telling me that they were coming over. Oh wait, I *didn't* because I guess you conveniently forgot to press Send."

"I'm not in the mood for this, Sienna. Just drop it." His expression is fierce when he snaps his gaze at his brother and his friend. "Evans, Brent. *Leave.*"

Brent drops his arms to his side. "What?"

"I'm heading to the shower," Kayden grumbles.

"But—" Evans start off.

"*I said leave,*" Kayden barks.

Then he proceeds to slam the door to his room behind him. The entire apartment falls into an uncomfortable, scratchy blanket of silence.

"Okay, what the hell was that?" I say to Brent, jolted by Kayden's sudden outburst.

"And that's why we have the key," Brent says miserably. Evans slumps back into his chair. A frown forms on Brent's lips as he glances at his friend, who looks really dejected at being kicked out of the apartment. "Kayden gets that way sometimes."

"What? Seriously?"

"Everyone has their bad days." He shrugs. "Kayden has more than most."

Oh. Right. Brent had hinted this to me when we met in the underground. I just assumed that whatever Kayden's going through, it wouldn't affect what we have.

"I get that, Brent. I really do. But just because he's dealing with something doesn't mean he has to take it out on everyone." I say, frustrated.

I'm tired of not knowing where I stand with Kayden. Sometimes I think that we can get along, maybe even develop a friendship of some sort outside of our trainer-trainee relationship, but it's looking like it's going to require more patience and effort than I thought. Both of which I'm quickly running out of.

"I need a break. I did not sign up to deal with his mood swings," I mutter to Brent as I snatch my keys and purse, lying on the table. "Call me when he finally gets his shit together."

I stomp out of the apartment and brush past the door, not pausing to lock it behind me. Doesn't matter. Brent has the keys anyway.

The last thing I hear as I charge into the elevator is Evans screaming at the top of his lungs, "Why is everybody so goddamned angry today!"

TEN

When I arrive at Breaking Point after my classes to join Kayden for his afternoon session, he still has the whole brooding thing going on, choosing to outright ignore me.

I'd been looking forward to sparring with him today, needing to pour all my stress and frustrations out after a grueling five fours worth of lectures. But as soon as I see him—darkened eyes looking anywhere else but at me, facial features irritable—all the excitement drains from my face.

"Are you finished?" I ask Kayden as I grab the boxing pads from the shelf behind me. He's seated on the floor beside the cage, taking forever to wrap his left hand, drawing out the simple action like he wants to stretch out the tension as long as he can.

"Do you need help?" I throw another question at him, my patience wavering. "Kayden?"

He just grunts.

"Okay, what the hell is your problem?" I snap at him.

This time, Kayden finally looks at me.

"I don't have a problem."

"Of course you have a problem." The aggravation in my voice is difficult to keep at bay. "What happened? I thought we got along just fine yesterday. We had a good time training together. Did I do something wrong?"

"Sienna," he says in a warning tone. "I'm not in the mood."

"You're never in the mood." I almost want to laugh. "Look, if you want out of this deal we have—"

"I'm considering." Annoyance infuses in his eyes, dark and fierce.

Are. You. Fucking. Kidding. Me.

"All right, that's it." I throw the pads to the floor and jab a finger at him. "You think you can do this without me? Think again. I *beat* you yesterday. Which means you probably won't even last thirty seconds in that cage against Jax. It makes me wonder how the hell you managed to be a runner-up in a competition like this, because you must be fighting against amateurs." I blow out a breath, trying to thin out my anger, but the action only serves to fuel the feeling, like a bellows against a fireplace. "I don't know what happened between last night and this morning, but this *can't* continue. At least not in that cage. I did not sign up to work with someone who doesn't treat me with civility. I deserve to be treated with respect."

He clenches his jaw tightly, as if trying to keep all of his emotions from spilling out of him.

"You don't know what I'm going through, Sienna," he says through gritted teeth.

My mouth tightens. A part of me feels guilty for being so hard on him. But he's gonna need a massive wake-up call and if I have to be the villain and break it to him, that's more than fine with me.

"You're right. I don't know what you're going through," I say, my tone softening. "But I believe you're better than just beating yourself up about it. You know what makes a person a fighter? It's not the number of punches he can throw or how long he can last in a cage. It's when he shows real courage and strength to overcome his battle wounds. You have scars, Killer. Own up to them. Otherwise, I don't know what the hell we're doing here."

He doesn't say anything for a while. He merely remains silent, pondering what I've said. Instead of waiting out the awkwardness, I turn my back on him, snatching the pads off the mats and making my way back to the shelf.

"Go home, Kayden. Take the rest of the day off. If you still want out, I'll leave your apartment first thing in the morning," I mutter.

I turn to see if he heard what I said, but as I look around I notice that—

He's already gone.

One step forward, two steps back.

***

When I realize he's not coming back, I sigh in defeat and plunge my hand into my bag, beside the bench, to grab my phone. As much as I'm frustrated with Kayden right now, I still wonder if he's all right. If what Brent said about him is true—that he needs to be checked up on because he gets this way a lot—then I'm worried that he's not going to be able to do this with me.

I can only hope he'll get out of it. He needs a strong, focused mind if he's going to fight in this competition. Otherwise, he's only going to set himself up for failure.

I need to talk to someone. My first instinct is to call Beth, because she's usually the person who can help me rationalize how I'm feeling. She can always bring calm to the storm, and is willing to talk through it all until I've got a clear mind again.

My finger hovers over her number, itching to press it, but I can't seem to swallow my pride. A deep frown tugs on my lips at the thought of not being able to call her whenever I want anymore—not when the yearning of her comfort comes with the fresh scars of her betrayal.

Instead, I dial Brent's phone number and wait for him to answer. If there's anyone who understands what I'm going through with Kayden, it'll be his brother. When he picks up, his smooth voice immediately puts me at ease. "Hey, Sienna."

"Hey," I say. "Is Kayden with you?"

"No. But he texted saying he's gone out to cool off," Brent tells me. "He'll be fine."

I let out a sigh of relief. "I don't know what to do, Brent."

I'm used to training with guys who commit to the fight. MMA is not only a sport; it's a consistent and steadfast lifestyle. If my students can't get used to that, then there is no space for them here.

"Cut him some slack," he says. "I don't think he's used to someone like you."

I raise a quizzical brow. "Someone like me?"

"Who pushes him. Makes him confront things about himself that he doesn't like to think about." He pauses for a beat to let those words sink in. And sure enough, my heart does a mini-somersault in my chest. "But don't worry. Give him some time to adjust. After today, he'll realize how badly he treated you and he'll be sorry about it. Trust me."

"I don't know . . ."

Trusting seems hard when it has to do with Kayden. But then again, trusting is hard when it has to do with anyone right now. Every time I decide to put my faith in someone, I end up losing more of it.

I let loose a breath. "No. I think I'm gonna stay. Work out the frustration."

"Okay. You know I'm here to talk if you need someone."

I bite my lip in contemplation. Talking it through seems futile when there's a punching bag a couple of feet away from me waiting to get brutalized by my fists.

"Maybe some other time," I say in a rush. "I gotta go."

As I hang up, I drop the phone on the mats. I need to stop shadowboxing myself into this ridiculous mental corner. There's no use getting this worked up over a guy I barely know.

If Kayden's interests no longer align with mine, he needs to tell me soon, because my patience is paper thin. Nothing is going to get in the way of me seeing Jax lose everything he holds dear.

Pinching my gloves off the floor, I strut over to the punching bag.

ELEVEN

Much to my annoyance, the animosity between me and Kayden has yet to fizzle out the next day. So I choose to look forward to something else, since I refuse to let him sour my mood. Alex and Cara asked if I wanted to join their walk to campus in the morning, and for a moment I considered asking Kayden to drive me there instead, but then I remembered that he's still a piece of shit so I didn't bother.

After managing to squeeze in a quick coffee break at Caffeinated, I spend the next few hours drowning in lectures and seminars, trying to pass the time by replying to all of my unanswered text messages. I get a brief text from my dad and let out a sigh when my eyes glaze over it: *I'd like to see you this weekend. Let's talk.*

I stare at the words again, debating whether it's a good idea to go home. I haven't been back in months, instead choosing to pour all my focus into training with Julian and on my assignments. It did help that Jax was also there to keep me company in those moments when it felt like I needed to keep myself busy. Because keeping busy is the only way I can feel sane. And after the whole Jax and Beth thing, I've never felt like I needed to cling to that feeling more.

So instead of replying, I shut off my phone and return my attention to the human nutrition science lecture, deciding to make a decision about going home later. Within the first five minutes of the class, as the lecturer drones on about nutrient classification and the basics of digestion, I conclude that it's going to be a rather dry module, like the other ones I'm taking this semester. While I've been tempted in the past to switch to an alternate degree, I always end up justifying my need for this particular one since it might give me an edge when applying for a masters in athletic training after I graduate. And it'll make my résumé look great when Julian starts looking for someone to run his gym after he retires.

It's another full day of classes today and I'm really tempted to put myself out of my misery by faking a terrible illness, but if I do, that would mean I'd have to return to the apartment. And that would mean I would have to see Kayden, something that I'm not in the mood for right now. At least Brent is with me for the last couple of classes, to ease the suffering. We've had our best cheesy pickup line track record yet, with a total of twenty-one rolled out back to back during one lecture.

When we're dismissed from our last lecture of the day, I rush out of class and zip through the streets to UFG before Julian has my ass for showing up late to work again.

"I'm here, folks!" I announce cheerfully as I saunter into the gym, a little out of breath. Julian, perched in his office as usual, glares at me through the window. His legs are crossed casually over his desk and he has a book in hand as he watches me enter the room to make my presence further known.

"Well, better late than never." His face is set in a bored stare.

"Well, a wise person once said a queen is never late. Everybody else is simply early."

"You are not a queen, Sienna. So shut up and just get to work, please." He gestures lazily toward the young, dark-haired man waiting by the benches, who is already padded up with boxing gloves, ready and eager to train. "Brandon is waiting for you to do drills."

"Right. Gotcha." I smile sheepishly and make my way to the lockers to drop off my stuff.

Then I get down to business, Fa Mulan style.

Brandon is a timid seventeen-year-old kid I've been training for a couple of months now. He's one of the few who keeps coming back to train with me, and I'm pleased to say that he's getting much better. His plan after graduating is to work toward going pro one day, and it's my job to show him the reality of how gruesome professional MMA fighting can be.

"Jab, cross, jab." I hit him lightly against the head with my pad. "You're too far away. And you dropped your right hand. *Again*," I order, and Brandon surges forward, eyes laser focused on the pads as he drives his fists toward them. But he doesn't notice his feet aren't planted firmly on the ground. I do, and take the opportunity to hook my leg onto his, causing him to stumble. "Be aware and connected to every part of your body. *Again.* Jab, cross, jab, hook, hook—come on!" I bark as I tap him on the head, then hold the pads up again. Brandon, unrelenting as he rises from the ground, drives toward me again, his fists perfecting the combination. "*Better.* Jab, cross, jab, hook, hook, body, body, jab, cross, jab, hook, hook, body, body—*yes.* You've got it."

Through the beads of sweat coating his entire face, he musters a smile. I hold up one of the pads so he can high-five it. "You're getting better. I like the attitude. Tomorrow we'll work on Muay Thai. Keep up the energy and the next session's going to be a breeze."

"Thanks, sensei." Brandon grins, unstrapping his boxing gloves.

"Wow, Sienna Lane giving compliments," someone says from behind me. "And here I was thinking they didn't exist in your vocabulary."

I whip around to see Kayden walking toward me, his shoulders squared. The strain between us is back, wafting through the air and causing the other fighters in the gym to send curious glances our way.

"I only give them out to fighters who deserve them." My mouth flattens. "And those who pay me."

From the corner of my eye, I can see Brandon's questioning gaze as he wonders which category he belongs to. I merely smile back at him.

Amusement coats Kayden's face as he watches me. "Fair enough."

"What are you doing here?" I ask.

He pauses, hesitating. Hands shoved into his pockets uneasily.

"I came to apologize."

I'm listening.

"I treated you like shit and I'm sorry," he mumbles, his eyes dropping to the ground, unsure of himself. The discomfort that coils around his words makes me think that this might be one of the rare times he's apologized. "I'm not saying this because I need your help to win that championship. I really do mean it."

"If you knew you were wrong, why did you flip out on me, anyway?" I ask him. "Is this about not being able to trust me?"

"No. I do trust you." Kayden releases a shaky breath. "I just don't trust myself around you."

"Kayden . . ." My breath hitches, heart buoying at his unexpected honesty.

"Look." He lets out a rugged breath and lifts his head, his gaze connecting with mine. "You *scare* me, Sienna."

I blink at him, dumbfounded. *What is he talking about?*

"After that night . . ." he says, his throat constricting as he tries to get the rest of his words out. "When I clearly crossed a line with you talking about Jax and I pissed you off . . . it freaked me out. I don't want to hurt you, okay? In or out of that cage. That's the absolute *last* thing I want to do."

His words are an unexpected lightning bolt zipping through my body. So he's cold with me because it's easier to close himself off than to hurt me? I should find it flattering that he would put my feelings first, but really, it only serves to heighten my curiosity about what happened to him in the past.

"You're ridiculous, you know that, Kayden?" I step

forward. "You can never hurt me. If you think that I'd ever let you do that, then you'd never be more wrong about me."

"Trust me, I'm way past underestimating you now," Kayden says, his dimples peeking out when his lips sneak upward.

My heart leaps out of my throat. Damn, I really missed that smile for sure. And those goddamned dimples.

"I just don't know how to act around you, Sienna," he says, his voice rough.

"Just be yourself," I remind him. "Well, a less shitty version of yourself."

A low laugh. "I'll try."

"So, you're going to let me train you again? We're going to make this deal work?"

Kayden nods confidently, truth beaming in his eyes. "Absolutely."

"Good. Because you need to focus. Knockouts are in two weeks and we gotta get you into prime shape. I can't have you being hot and cold with me anymore. You need to be ready for this. Mentally and physically. Otherwise Jax *will* kill you."

"I'm in, Lucky," he says with utter conviction. "I'm all in."

"You better be," I say, glancing at my phone for the time. "I'm just about done now. Meet you at Point in ten minutes? If you get there first, I want you all stretched out because I'm going to work you so hard tonight that you won't be able to walk tomorrow."

Kayden swallows hard. "You are?"

It suddenly hits me how my words sounded to him.

"That's not what I mean—" *Oh God.* I feel my cheeks

explode with heat and I look away swiftly, wanting to die of embarrassment. "For fuck's sake, just *go*." I dismiss him.

Kayden hoots with laughter as he heads to the exit. He looks over his shoulder, another dimple-laden grin gracing his lips, and says, "Glad to have you back, Lucky."

"You, too, Killer."

I can't help the smile sneaking across my lips as well as I watch him leave.

One step forward, no steps back.

***

"Maddock is a wrestler," I tell Kayden as I gesture for one of Breaking Point's fighters, Declan, to get into the cage. He was one of the only few left in the gym and graciously agreed to do a sparring round. He's also a decent fighter, and the perfect candidate for a situational sparring session because like Maddock, he's a fan of wrestling takedowns. Declan and Kayden knock fists with each other before taking their places on either side of the cage, easing into their proper stances. "Which means, during the knockouts, once he gets you on the ground, you're done for. So there's only one thing to remember and that is to not let him clinch you. Stick and move, and don't let him get close. Ready?" I yell, eyes darting back and forth between Declan and Kayden. They both nod. "Go."

Kayden bursts with energy and precision as he pounces on Declan.

"Be aware of your footwork." In the cage, I hover over them like a referee would as they trade blows with each other. My hands are clasped behind me as I watch the fight, observing Kayden's movements closely. He's testing Declan to see if he can find an opening. Good. "Keep your defense *impenetrable.*"

Kayden backs off, arms up guarding his head as Declan lunges at him in a forward grapple. He almost gets caught but bounces away on the balls of his feet while throwing a variation of jabs, forcing Declan to dodge quickly.

"Here's a rule for any fight: while you're studying your opponent's moves, he's likely doing the same to you. You need to switch it up so he won't be able to get the better of you. Keep him guessing *all the time*. It's likely Maddock will fall into your trap since he's always been somewhat of a meathead, and since I just said that advice aloud, I'm sure Declan is taking it right now and switching up his moves. Yep, just as I predicted."

Declan strikes, surprising Kayden with an unorthodox high kick to his forearm, shattering Kayden's defense like a Roman phalanx. Kayden narrowly evades another attack heading straight for his nose.

"Give him an opening to take advantage of as he tests you," I order as Declan aims for Kayden's face again and Kayden jerks back. "*Mislead* him."

Declan hammers Kayden with more high kicks, forcing Kayden to block each unrelenting one. Kick. Block. Kick. Block.

"And when he finally takes the bait . . ."

Kayden's movements are slow, the attacks taking their toll. He flinches to his left, moving to block another kick aimed straight for the side of his face.

" . . . you go in for the kill."

But with an unexpected burst of movement, Kayden ducks under Declan's kick and pushes into an uppercut, which connects, stunning his opponent. Kayden doesn't relent, moving into a flurry of combos that Declan tries his best to block, but he gets disoriented and Kayden's surprise overhand catches him on the side of his head, throwing him to the floor.

"Get him on the ground," I bark, pumping a fist. "Aim for his head—yes! That's right—"

Kayden straddles Declan, raining down blows as Declan's defense finally falters.

Declan meekly taps out.

"Good work, boys." I give a slow clap as Kayden helps Declan off the ground. They knock their fists together as an acknowledgment of no hard feelings. "Let's take five then we'll go for another round."

I hop out of the cage. Kayden follows after me, He picks his towel up off the ground and wipes the sweat pouring down his face, then walks over to me wearing a tired but triumphant smile. It's nice to see him feeling proud of himself. He deserves it. I chuck a water bottle at him and he snatches it, squirting water into his mouth greedily.

"I can't believe you were gonna back out of this deal," I tell him. "Did you see yourself almost get crushed there?"

"Fair enough. You really are working me hard." He grins and throws the bottle back to me. I catch it with a strong grip and kneel on the floor, rolling the bottle toward my gym bag, beside the benches.

"Speaking of working, I might not be able to make

Friday's training session," I say quietly as I pull myself back up so our faces are level with each other. "I'm being summoned back home."

A curious brow. "Oh?"

"Yeah. My dad wants to see me," I say. "I think he wants me to clock in some good old family bonding time."

"Sounds like fun."

"Pretty sure it's gonna be dreadful," I say, sifting hand through my hair. "I could stay," I blurt, desperate for him to plead for me to train with him so I can get out of it. "We've still got a lot of work to do, so . . ."

"Don't worry. I think I can survive a day without you," Kayden notes, his tone growing serious. "And I do think you should go home. Family's important."

"I know." I let out a long sigh, plopping myself on the bench and resting my elbows on my knees. Kayden joins me, taking the empty space beside me and angling his body toward mine.

"You need a lift back home?" He offers. "I can drive you."

"No. Don't worry about it. I'll figure it out." I wave a dismissive hand. "Plus, you need to train tomorrow. And I won't have you skipping it for my sake."

"You're just as important," he murmurs. My eyes widen at the comment, and he suddenly looks flustered. "I'm just saying, if you need any support . . ." He quickly backtracks but it's too late.

My attention rockets to his face. "Have you gone soft on me, Killer?"

"I . . ."

A smirk climbs onto my lips as he gets more unnerved

with each second. I jump out of my seat, humor seeping out of me. "I told you I'd wear you down."

"My defenses have never been more up," he replies coolly as he rises from the bench, fists clenched, and arms propped up in front of him. "Impenetrable, even."

"Liar."

Laughing, I drive a mock jab-cross at him. He blocks it easily, completely leaving his left flank exposed so I dive toward him. But I realize too late that it's a setup when he grabs my arm and twists it so my back collides with his chest and uses his other arm to cage me, putting me in a lock.

I can't believe it.

I actually took the bait.

"I never lie, Lucky," he whispers, lips grazing the shell of my ear, his breathing rough and uneven. "Only mislead."

Holy shit.

My pulse gives an unsteady lurch as Kayden feathers my face with the back of his hand, the weight of his touch pressing deeply on my skin and warming my entire face. I feel the muscles of his body contracting, like he's struggling to restrain himself from what he wants to do with me. All the words that I wanted to say before have completely dried up in my throat at the possibility that he might just lose control and take me right then and there.

And I'm not sure if I'd even stop him.

Suddenly, as if the fire flaming underneath my skin had seared him, Kayden releases his hold on me. He rubs his hands together and takes a nervous step back.

"See you back in the cage," he mutters, and I drop down to the bench, utterly dazed.

TWELVE

Before leaving the apartment today, I leave Kayden a note. I've got another full day of classes and coming back before going over to my dad's isn't really an option, so I'm probably not going to see him until tomorrow evening. It's weird that I feel sad about it, since it was only yesterday that I was doing everything I could to avoid him. I wonder how I'm going to feel about him next week.

Kayden has already gone out for his morning jog, so I scribble my message across a torn piece of paper, dropping it on the counter and dragging the paperweight over it.

See you Saturday. Don't get yourself 'killed' while I'm gone.
—Sienna

I think I've been spending way too much time with Brent. Having this kind of humor does not bode well.

When I'm done with my last lecture of the day, I head

straight to the bus stop, tugging along a small duffel bag filled with all the necessities for my one-night stay at home. It's particularly cold out today, with the snow billowing down and catching on my hair and eyelashes, so I shrink into my turtleneck to save myself from the assault.

On my way out, I spot a familiar-looking man with an unusually large bump on the top of his head. He has his back to me as he presses a brunet girl against a tree, his lips molding greedily against hers. A knee wedges between her legs and his hands glide down her body shamelessly, exposing her skin. It looks like I've just stepped into what appears to be the beginning of a sloppily executed porno scene.

"Real classy, Evans." I clear my throat.

Evans whips his head back and smiles when he notices me, red lipstick smeared all over his mouth, looking all Joker-like. It's oddly unsettling and humorous. He's surprisingly well dressed for a college student: a double-breasted tan overcoat on top of a grey sweater with a collared shirt peeking out at the top. And to tie the whole look together, a matching grey, wool scarf hangs loosely around his neck. I admire his commitment to style, since most of us here are too lazy to put in that much effort.

"Didn't have time for a dinner date and roses. I've got an assignment to cram out in the library today," he replies smoothly as he adjusts himself.

I narrow my eyes at his hookup. Her shy eyes lift toward me and she gives me an awkward wave.

"Looks like that's not the only thing you're trying to cram," I say flatly.

Evans scratches his head sheepishly in reply. He turns to the girl and leans in to plant a swift kiss on the square of her lips. "You can go now, honey."

She pouts at him. Her fingers tug on the hem of her top and her other hand smooths over her incredibly tussled hair. "But we were just—"

"See you around." He dismisses her absentmindedly, already turning his back on her and walking toward me. I watch silently as the brunet frowns and kneels down to grab her stuff. I hope she's okay. She doesn't seem to have taken the rejection lightly. My gaze flickers back to Evans and he points a warning finger at me, like he somehow has the ability to hear all my thoughts. "Don't judge me."

"Too late. Already judging."

Evans loops his arm over me and pulls me closer to him as we start walking. I'm surprised by his affection because the last time we met, I wasn't exactly the friendliest.

"Do you do that a lot?" The question slips out of me as I notice the girl scuttling in the opposite direction from the corner of my eye.

"When I'm stressed, yeah," he says, then gives me a knowing look. "You want in, huh? Schedule's pretty full right now, but maybe I can try to squeeze you in on Thursdays after my lunch break."

"How generous," I deadpan. "Thanks but I'm good. I'm too busy and you're not my type."

"Just because I'm not an underground fighter with issues stemming from long-lasting trauma doesn't mean I can't rock your world, Sienna." He grins at me sillily. "Although I might be tied with Kayden. He doesn't fuck around a lot but rumor has it he's a beast in bed—"

I push his arm away and pick up my pace. "I really don't want to hear it."

"Of course you do. You like the dude." Evans breaks into a light jog as he tries to keep up with my long strides. He does a surprisingly good job at it, though his breath starts to come out in short, tight spurts after a while. "Also, I figured I owed you that teeny piece of information since you caught me balls deep in my favorite pastime. Look, can you do me a favor and not tell Brent about this?"

I stop in my tracks abruptly. My head swivels toward him, curiosity getting the better of me. "Why does he care?"

He avoids my gaze, eyes dropped to the ground.

"Just don't tell him," he mumbles, voice soft and small.

Something about the way he says those words makes me realize that he's scared. But I'm not about to pry into his business; we've all got our secrets to keep.

"Don't worry, I won't," I say. "I have someplace else to be, Evans. If there isn't anything else?"

Evans's face lights up. "Where are you going?"

"To my dad's."

He raises a curious brow, expecting me to elaborate. I don't know why I feel compelled to give him my life story, but I have a feeling if I don't, he'll keep asking me questions.

"My parents are divorced. My mom has been traveling around Brazil screwing random guys while my dad's getting it on with wife number oops I don't give a fuck."

I expect Evans to be baffled by my response, but he just laughs.

"Nice." He grins widely. "You need a ride? I could sure use the procrastination."

"You and your dick can fuck off—"

"No, I mean *literally* drive you." He *tsks*, giving my chin a flick with his finger. "You have a dirty mind, Sienna."

I slow down my pace and hold a hand out in front of him. "Are you serious about giving me a ride? Because I hate to take the bus."

"Sure." He sidesteps me, taking the lead this time, and gestures for me to follow him to the parking lot. "Don't worry. I'll make it worthwhile."

We walk together for a couple of minutes, a comfortable silence stretching between us. The sun hangs low in the sky, about to make its descent past the horizon, which means I'm going to be late to dinner. Again. I don't usually like to be tardy, but it's hard to be on time to anything when there's a million things to juggle, like school and work and training Kayden.

When we're finally in his car, Evans hands me his phone and I punch in my address for navigation. Two minutes later, we roll out of the parking lot. I go for some light, friendly chatter to pass the time during the drive to my dad's. If Evans is going to be coming around the apartment a lot with Brent, I should at least try to be friends with him.

"So, what do you do?"

"Girls. Boys. Anyone I'm attracted to," Evans replies smoothly.

"I mean what's your major."

"Business," he says flatly. "Boring stuff, but anything to please my parents. Not like that really matters, anyway, because of, you know, said 'doing' of both girls and boys." There is a noticeable lack of enthusiasm in his voice.

His response makes me frown. "I'm sorry."

"Don't be. I'm not. At least, I try not to be." His gaze is solemn when he looks at me. "You're lucky. At least straight men are the only problems you have to deal with."

I think about Jax and how polarizing he made me feel. Our relationship wasn't perfect, but it certainly was fiery and thrilling. He made me feel good most days, but always managed to level it out with the bad days. I always thought it was worth it, though. Perhaps it wasn't to Jax.

And then there's Kayden, in some ways a complete antithesis to my ex-boyfriend. Kayden has a tender heart and a kind spirit—if not a little tainted from the darkness that he seems to carry around with him. And despite him being hot and cold with me, it's getting much harder for me to stay away.

"A hell of a lot of problems they bring, though." I give a cold shrug. "Not sure if it's worth the trouble."

Evans sends a comforting smile my way. "If it's any consolation, I think Kayden is worth the trouble."

"You're just biased because he's your friend."

"Maybe, yeah," he says. "But the fact that he's been so dismantled by you and yet still wants you to be a part of his life is something completely unheard of."

I want to tell him that the only reason why I'm a part of Kayden's life is purely professional. Though I'm not sure I still believe it. The weird feelings I get makes it so confusing to be around him. I simply can't afford to think about them any deeper, especially when I just got out of a three-year relationship in the worst possible way.

When we finally pull up at our destination, Evans whistles at the huge, sprawling mansion in front of him. It has a loud, French aristocratic feel: a gazillion windows lining every available wall, gaudy gold trimmings, and a driveway so wide you could fit a dozen cars in it. My dad has always longed for the pristine, upper-class fixtures to complement the wealth he's accumulated through his divorces. It's a shame he doesn't have the taste to back it up.

"Holy shit," Evans swears. "You're like 90210 rich."

"I'm not. My dad is," I say as I climb out of the car and come up from behind to take the rest of my stuff from the trunk. "The alimony from his three previous marriages paid for all of this. So I wouldn't exactly call him entrepreneur of the decade."

"Sienna." My dad bursts from the door, clad in a gold Versace shirt and a pair of khakis with pockets lining every inch of them. His outfit screams *I'm going through a midlife crisis*. It honestly baffles me how he's been able to court all these women with his God-awful sense of fashion.

"Thanks for the ride," I tell Evans as I tap on the hood of his car.

"Anytime." He winks at me before pulling out of the driveway.

My dad's lips make a flat, disapproving line when I walk up to him. He eyes the distressed black denim jacket that barely covers my gym attire, along with my battered training shoes.

"You didn't have time to change into something a bit nicer?"

"This *is* nice," I insist, narrowing my eyes. How does a black tank top and gym tights not constitute as nice? "It's what I wear all the time."

"Right. I suppose it's because of your fighting job." My dad pauses, allowing the discontentment to reach his eyes. "Well, I'm sure we have something better for you to change into in the house," he says, though a little uncertain. He places a hand behind my back and guides me inside. "Come in. Let's get the festivities under way."

***

After setting my bags in the guest room and changing into a clean-cut baby-pink flare dress my dad brought for me, I linger around the living room for a while, eyes scanning the newly added furniture. There's a couple more expensive-looking paintings on the walls, inside thick intricate frames. Flowers are perched on every available surface imaginable, scenting the room with a sickly, funeral home–like smell.

I miss the modest suburban home where we used to live before my parents separated. We had a lot of good memories there. Beth and I sharing a small bedroom, bunking in each other's beds and gossiping about which of the two of us had the best chance at the cute transfer student's heart (we decided we both had equal opportunity to strike since I sat beside him in homeroom but Beth was in Model United Nations with him). Then, waking up the next morning with Mom downstairs in the kitchen, a warm smile on her face, cooking up another batch of waffles for us because Dad had already eaten the first round. The three of us making a mess in the kitchen trying to help her prep, making us late for school.

This new house just feels too sterile. A neat façade on the outside but a lifeless carcass inside.

"Sienna?" A soft, squeaky voice sounds from behind me.

A groan rips out of me. I should have known coming here would mean I'd have to face her. She's standing by the doorway leading to the kitchen, and I try to side step her but she won't budge.

"Get out of my way, Beth," I snap.

"No." She shakes her head. "Jax told me to stand up for myself."

"So you do everything he tells you now?" I reel back, choking back a dry laugh. "Right, I almost forgot about your goody-two-shoes act. It's hard to still see you that way."

Her eyes flicker with hurt. "What's it going to take to get you to forgive me?"

"Nothing. Like I said before, you're dead to me."

I make another attempt at escaping again but she blocks me with her arm, covering access to the doorway. I cut her an annoyed glare.

"Please. I want to try to fix this," Beth says.

"Beth," I hiss. "If you don't get out of my fucking way—"

"Hello, girls," a strong, feminine voice sounds soothingly from the other side of the doorway. "What's going on here?"

"Hey, Alyson." My sister drops her hand, addressing the woman's presence with a tight smile. "Don't worry about it."

Who the hell is *Alyson*?

I nudge Beth aside and step into the kitchen, coming face to face with a dark-haired woman. She doesn't look older than twenty-eight, which is concerning considering my dad's pushing forty-five this year. She has a slender figure, accentuated by a classy red peplum dress. The muscles on her high cheekbones strain as she welcomes me with a kind smile.

"Sienna." She ropes me into an unexpected hug and I wince in discomfort. "Nice to meet you. Your dad told me so much about you. I have a feeling we're going to be the best of friends."

I pull away from her just as quickly, eyeing the huge diamond ring resting on her finger. It winks under the harsh kitchen lights. My gaze bores into hers. "Somehow, I doubt that."

Alyson's smile wanes but she doesn't let my comment faze her. Instead, she merely forces her smile wider.

"All right, let's get on with dinner, shall we?" She links her arm with mine and Beth's and ushers us to the dinner table, where a feast awaits.

I peel my arm from Alyson's and take my seat opposite my dad, while Beth makes herself comfortable in the seat next to me. My dad rises from his seat and kisses Alyson on the cheek before pulling out her chair beside him.

When we're all seated, my dad clears his throat, excitement thrumming through him as his gaze flickers toward Alyson. "So, Alyson, darling, would you like to tell them the big news?"

A bright smile graces Alyson's face as she turns to us, leaning into my father's embrace lovingly. "Your father and I are engaged to be married."

"Wow! Congratulations, guys." Beth reaches a hand

across the table to clasp it around Alyson's, beaming with joy for her. I wish I could harbor the same feeling, but it feels like my body has completely hollowed out upon the confirmation of their engagement.

My dad notices the shift in my mood. He sighs, reaching out to offer a comforting hand. I don't take it. His arm retreats as he tilts his head modestly at me.

"Sienna, I want you to know that it's different this time around. Alyson is an amazing woman. She's smart and beautiful and she makes me smile all the time, and I know she'll make a wonderful stepmother to you," he says, eyes darting to both me and Beth. "To the both of you."

"What fun," I deadpan. "Add her to the three other stepmothers I've had over the years and I've got myself one for every season."

Dad's lips quiver at my sarcastic comment. "Sienna, it would be nice to have your blessing."

Blessing? Seriously? After everything he's done?

"It's difficult for me to do that when you keep letting me down, Dad," I snap back at him, letting the words ripple across the room with a strained, ugly feeling.

Dad's eyes flood with guilt.

"Your father's a very nice man," Alyson says, trying to quell some of the tension. "He's not the same man he used to be."

"Oh? And you think you know him better than I do?" I lean back against the chair, folding my arms across my chest. "How long have you known him? A couple of months? Surely that's not enough time to know what you're getting yourself into."

Silent tears threaten to spill from my eyes but I hold them back while I struggle with my keys outside the apartment. My hands are shaking so much that it's hard to even fit the key in the lock. Eventually, I get so frustrated that I fling the keys at the wall, desperate to relieve some of the anger building up in my chest. They clash against the surface and skid across the floor.

The door to the apartment opens hesitantly and Kayden's large form appears in front of me.

"Hey." A perplexed look forms on his face. "I thought you weren't supposed to be back until tomorrow."

"Can I come in?" I ask, tears swimming in my eyes.

The anger that I once felt is gone, now replaced with guilt. My heart aches so much that it feels like it's slowing my heart rate down.

Kayden's expression crumbles.

"Of course," he says softly, opening the door wide for me. When I set my bags down, he inches toward me, a look of worry plastered on his face. "Sienna, are you okay?"

"No," I croak, the tears starting to spill from my eyes. I try to wipe them away but they fall endlessly, flooding me in my own hurt and pain. "I fucked up, Kayden. I really fucked up this time."

He closes the remaining space between us and slides his huge arms around me, crushing me against his chest.

"Hey," he murmurs, his voice soft and filled with concern. "Lucky . . ."

For once, I let him hold me. For once, I allow myself to cry into his shirt, feeling like I'm so small in this huge world.

For once, I allow myself to be vulnerable.

"Sienna." Beth gapes at me. "She's family now."

"And what do *you* know about family, Beth?" The question slices through the room like a sharp blade, startling Beth. "Alyson deserves to know that our dad has been jumping from marriage to marriage without a care in the world. She deserves to know how much pain he put Mom through until she had no other choice but to move away just to get away from it all."

"Sienna, stop this. Why do you always try to ruin what's supposed to be a good moment?" A muscle feathers in my dad's jaw as he tries to keep his anger in check.

Unfortunately, I don't possess the same kind of restraint.

"Because unlike you, I can't keep pretending that this *works*. You think this is a normal, functioning family? My sister is a boyfriend-stealing backstabber who shows little remorse for her actions and my dad is a useless deadbeat who constantly judges me for what I do while he does nothing to earn my respect." I whip my face to him in resentment. "Clearly nobody's gonna tell you the truth here, so I guess I should be the one to do it. You act like you can mend our broken little family with a bandage of superficial marriages, but let me break it to you: *it's not gonna work*. And now, when I see you with her—" My gaze cuts to Alyson briefly. "I think you're a big coward. You hide behind these women to replace whatever you lost a long time ago. And that was us. Me, Beth, and Mom. We stood by you. And you took us for granted. You *continue* to take us for granted. You're a sad, sad coward and I really fucking *pity* you."

My dad slams his fist against the table, the last of his patience shattering.

"Get out." He sneers, pointing to the door. "Get *out*!"

"Gladly." I launch out of my seat and trudge out of the dining room to snatch the rest of my things.

THIRTEEN

I feel defeated as I ride the elevator back up to the apartme with my bags, feeling the shame from what occurred over dinner form into a massive lump in my throat.

I'm not proud of the things I said to my dad. I'm *especiall* not proud of the things I said about his engagement to Alyson. Sometimes, I just wish he'd put the same amount of effort he gives to whisking these women off their feet to giving a damn about me and Beth. Because the truth of the matter is that he doesn't. He only calls when it's convenient for him or when he wants to pull this kind of shit.

That's why I refuse to take his money. I worked hard to get where I am now, securing a job at UFG to help pay mine and Beth's bills. I stopped depending on my dad completely after that, knowing all too well that he's not going to change.

I wish I could force myself to feel otherwise.

I wish my dad would give me a reason to believe in him again.

***

It takes me another hour to get myself cleaned up in the bathroom and to gather myself. My eyes feel so swollen that I can barely open them. I wash my face for the fifth time in the sink, forcing myself to stay awake because I know I don't deserve to sleep through the hurt that I knowingly caused myself.

When I return to the living room, Kayden is waiting by the couch, concerned grey eyes tracing my every movement. He gets off the couch as I approach him, my arms hugging myself tightly to keep the rest of me from falling apart. I'm not sure how I feel about losing it like I did earlier tonight in front of Kayden, but I do feel embarrassed about it now. I know he won't hold it against me, but it still feels weird knowing that I broke down in full-fledged ugly sobs in front of him.

I've never been comfortable crying in front of anyone before. *When you show them how you hurt, they'll find more ways to hurt you,* Jax used to say to me. Any weakness that I had—in or out of that cage—he taught me to keep them closely to myself. He sure did for his own. He's never been the type to let me glimpse his vulnerability either. I used to think that was what made him special, that his invincibility was his greatest weapon.

But I never thought I'd be on the receiving end of it, too, where he'd completely shut me out and leave me in the dark.

Throughout the three years we were together, I don't think I ever heard him say I love you in a truly genuine way.

Perhaps he perceived saying those words as another form of weakness.

Or perhaps he simply didn't understand the concept of love.

"Look . . ." I tell Kayden hesitantly. "It'll make me feel a lot better if we just forget this ever happened."

He releases a tortured breath, scrubbing the side of his jaw. "I wish I could. But I can't let it slide because of how much it affected you." A deep pause. "What happened at your dad's place?"

"Let's just say I shouldn't have gone." My voice quivers as I lean against the couch. "You know, I tried so hard to keep my family together. Maybe it's about time I stop trying."

"I know how that feels," Kayden mutters quietly, eyes swimming with agony. When I raise a brow, wanting him to elaborate, he shakes his head and looks away.

Frustration nips at me, but I pull myself back from prying any further. I need to respect the boundaries we've set up. It's better to have them. Every time his gaze sweeps over me, it makes me feel even more exposed than I already am.

"For what it's worth, I'm sorry that things between you and your family are so strained," he murmurs, head tilted toward me.

"It's been broken from the start. It's my fault for having any expectations in the first place," I say, my breath tight in my chest. I brave a steady hand through my hair. "I'm just tired of feeling like things are beyond my control. This thing that we have, this deal—" I swallow hard, feeling my throat getting clogged up. Understanding dawns in Kayden's eyes.

"I know. I won't let you down." He nods thoughtfully, rife with pointed determination. "I need this win just as much as you do."

"Then let's train," I order, extending a hand to him. He eyes it cynically. "Get up."

"It's late," he reminds me. "Breaking Point is closed."

"That's fine. We don't need a gym," I tell him, a smile sneaking on my face. "I have an idea."

***

I lead Kayden upstairs to the rooftop of our building. Alex told me about this place earlier this week, citing it as one of her go-to make-out places with Daniel when her place feels too claustrophobic with Cara and Simon around. I push through the door, careful to jam a brick in the opening to keep it from shutting behind us.

"Nailing your footwork is the best way to offset someone bigger than you, like Jax. You need to be quick and light on your feet all the time. Good footwork will also be handy when you're against a Muay Thai fighter or a wrestler," I say as I drop my duffel bag on the ground. Kayden stands around awkwardly in his fleece hoodie, battling the blistering cold. "You get good at building balance and controlling your distance, it's an easy ride to claim that championship."

I grab a soccer ball from the bag, resting it on one side of my hip, and then sling a timer around my neck. "We're gonna do some kick-ups. All you have to do is keep the ball up and moving. Don't let it drop to the ground. No hands or you start over. I'll be timing you."

Kayden looks at me like I just told him to jump off the building.

"What?" He gapes at me. "Are you kidding me?"

"Nope."

He blinks dumbly at me. "This is a soccer exercise."

"It's also a great exercise to improve your balance and coordination. Which you need."

Kayden's gaze flickers to the ball and then back to me, eyebrows descending low on his face. "I probably won't be able to do more than ten seconds."

"That's a shame. I was only gonna let you go to bed if you hit a minute. So I guess you should start soon if you don't wanna freeze to death on this rooftop."

He shakes his head. "This is ridiculous. There are footwork drills for this kind of thing."

"Julian used to swear by it. He was a soccer player in college before he turned to fighting. And there's a reason why he's one of the most decorated MMA fighters," I tell him confidently. Kayden still looks unconvinced, though. I shrug nonchalantly. "If you're not keen, we could try something else. Like ballet. Though I would recommend we get a pink tutu and ballet flats for the full effect—"

"Fine. Give me the ball."

I throw Kayden the ball and he seizes it midair with his hands. Giving the ball a light bounce with one hand, he tries to catch it with his feet. He manages to bob it from one foot to the other twice before it hops away from him.

"Give it back." I sigh and he throws the ball back at me. "You're kicking it up too high. Try to keep it around waist height," I instruct as I show him how it's done. Tapping the ball as lightly as I can with either side of my feet, I make sure to keep it low enough that I don't lose control but high enough to get some momentum.

He grunts and tries again, kicking the ball upwards with his feet. Each time, he loses his balance after a couple of seconds and the ball bounces away.

"Your feet are too pointed. Connect with the ball on the forefront of the foot." I do a slow pace around him as Kayden attempts it another time. The ball flies past his head and lands on the other side of the rooftop. He grunts irritably as he goes to retrieve it. "Stop kicking it so hard. You're not trying to score a goal here. You wanna be tapping the ball upward lightly."

Kayden releases a frustrated breath but continues with his third attempt.

"There you go," I say as he keeps the ball going with his feet. This time, he manages to balance it better, the ball moving along his feet in a light and rounded manner. "Yes. That's it. Find the rhythm."

Kayden looks up at me, his lips twitch upward at my encouragement. But that one second is all it takes for him to lose his footing. When the ball rolls away, he swallows his annoyance before looking at me expectantly.

"How long was that?"

I glance at the timer.

"Nine seconds."

A loud groan.

I wrinkle my nose at him, a challenging gleam in my eyes. "You're gonna quit on me, Killer?"

"No," he says unflinchingly, already moving to retrieve the ball again.

For the next hour, I perch myself on the edge of the railing while Kayden tries to get a consistent rhythm going with the ball. I can't help but snicker every time the ball flies away from him. I've lost count of the number of times I've had to reset the timer for him to start over.

By the end of the hour, Kayden finally manages to get past thirty seconds. Not quite the victory he'd hoped for, but when I read his latest timing to him, he lets out the loudest howl of joy and plants a huge kiss on the ball. I force myself not to cringe because *ew, dirt,* but it makes me happy when I see him swelling with pride at his accomplishment.

"Let's call it a night," I declare.

Relief slackens Kayden's impressive shoulders and he joins me by the railing, hopping over it and allowing his legs to dangle in the air, like mine. Above us, the sky is a blanket of darkness, with not even a wink of a star in sight. The temperature has dropped within the hour, but the adrenaline from practice has warmed both of us up enough to keep us from feeling like we might get frostbite from being out here.

"Hey. I'm sorry I couldn't make it to a minute," he says to me apologetically.

"It's fine," I tell him, both of my hands gripping the railing on either side of me as I turn to face him. "It's not about perfecting the move. It's about being aware and connecting yourself to every part of your body, especially to your feet. You're not gonna win against Jax in a punching contest. He packs too much weight behind his punches. The strategy is to be agile on your feet, then find the right opening to take him down."

"Good strategy," Kayden notes with an agreeable nod.

I can't keep myself from staring at him. The winter chill has begun to dry the sweaty mess of his dark, wind-tussled hair. His eyes are closed and he inhales deeply, as if allowing the wind to carry all his thoughts away. I've never seen him look this calm before. It inspires a warm feeling in my chest.

When his eyelids flutter open again, his eyes are bright with curiosity.

"Is it true that you did ballet?" he asks softly.

I bite my lip, debating whether I should share this piece of information with him. But it doesn't bother me if he knows, so I cave.

"Yeah. When I was in middle school," I explain. "My dad was the one who got me into it. Said it would help me achieve some much-needed poise and grace. He pulled me out once he found out to get good at ballet you have to develop a lot of hard muscle." My lips flatten at those memories. It feels like a lifetime ago when my life didn't revolve around fighting and Jax. "It did help me ease into MMA better, though. Taught me a good deal about balance and coordination. I don't think I'd be nearly as good a fighter as I am now. Which, ironically enough, is a nice middle finger to my dad."

I wonder if what my life would be like if I'd just shaped myself into who my dad wanted me to be. Maybe there would be less animosity between us. A part of me wishes I could be more like Beth—sweet and compassionate and demure; who fits into the mold in every way possible.

"Keep with fighting. It's what you're good at," Kayden says with an easy grin, echoing the words I said to him back at me. My heart does a little victory lap around my rib cage at the sight of his dimples. He rubs his hands together, eyelids dropping before rising back up to my face again. This time, there's apprehension in them. "I—uh . . . I'm really sorry I'm a pain in the ass most of the time. You're a good trainer and you deserve my respect. Which you have."

His sincerity warms my heart, the heat spreading across my neck and up my face. I like this new side of him. Despite our rocky start, I'm glad to know that we're on the same page with this deal. And about damn time too.

An unwitting smile touches my lips as I close my hand over Kayden's, sealing our comradery.

"Then let's kick some ass together, shall we?"

FOURTEEN

Tonight is the night of the knockouts. It's crazy, but I don't feel nervous about it. Perhaps it's because we've been training our asses off for the past week, helping Kayden hone his strengths while keeping him sharp and fit.

We've fallen into a nice little routine. Every morning Kayden and I make sure to go out for a run together to build up his cardio, every few days pushing ourselves to go another half mile. We've reached six miles so far, making it all the way to Trinity Church and back. Afterward, I'll head to campus while he does his own strength exercises or works the bags, and later, when I have the time to swing by, we'll either practice striking and grappling or do a couple of sparring rounds in the cage to work on fixing his imbalances.

And on most nights, we make a habit of practicing his ball kick-ups on the rooftop. There's been a massive improvement since Kayden's first time. He's incredibly proud of the fact that he can now easily do about fifty seconds, which has also helped bolster his confidence.

Now, a few hours before the fight, we've parked ourselves in the kitchen, finishing up the last of the prep meals we had stocked in the refrigerator. In the living room, Brent and Evans huddle over the dining table, having a heated debate over who gets the last slice of the pizza they ordered.

"You ate the last two. I think I deserve the last slice." Brent reaches over to grab the pizza but Evans slaps his hand away angrily.

"Come on, Brent. You're not being fair. This one has *extra cheese!*"

"Yeah, that's why I'm claiming it."

Brent reaches for the slice again but at the last second, Evans snatches the entire box off the table.

"*My precious,*" he hisses.

Evans and Brent spend the next minute having a glaring contest. It's long. *Strangely* long. I force myself to look away, feeling like I'm witnessing something I shouldn't be witnessing.

Instead, I turn to Kayden, gesturing to his best friends. "Tell me again: Why do you still keep them around?"

"Stepbrother. So by default, he has to stay." Kayden nods at Brent while forking some chicken into his mouth, though his gaze flicks to the friend beside his brother in reassessment. "I'm reconsidering Evans, though. But as you can see, making new friends isn't exactly my thing."

"And whose fault is that? Most of the time you look like you want to bash people's faces in if they try to come within a mile radius of you."

He shrugs uncomfortably as he sets his plate down on the kitchen table. "Can we talk about something else?"

"Why? Do you feel uncomfortable talking about your lack of friends?" I tease him and his entire body tenses, broad shoulders squaring. "Does it force you to think about your inability to keep them around because you're just so cold and aloof all the time?"

Kayden leans in closer, his voice going husky as his callous stare pins me down. "Why do you always have to do that?"

"Do what?"

His hot breath is right in my ear. "Challenge me."

Holy shit. That really shouldn't have turned me on. But it did and now, I want more of it.

"Because I like getting you all riled up," I say, pursing my lips. "Your ears get super-red when you're pissed at me, and I think that's kind of cute—"

He stalks away from me and into the dining room, muttering curses under his breath. My hands fly to my face to try to soothe the heat spreading across my cheeks.

Simultaneously, everyone's phones buzz with an incoming message. It's enough of a distraction for Brent and Evans to drop their argument. I straighten up from leaning against the kitchen counter as my eyes scroll through the contents of the message.

"Franklin Park Zoo bear cages?" I say.

"Yeah. Shouldn't be too far," Kayden notes, sliding his phone into his back pocket and pinching his car keys off the dining table. "Let's go."

"Give me a second," I say as I cross the kitchen into the

living room and with a quick hand, snatch the last slice from the box that Evans is carrying. I smile widely as I take a huge, satisfactory bite from it. "Okay, now we can go."

Brent gapes at me. Evans drops the empty pizza box, chest heaving as if it takes every bit of effort to reel in his rage.

Kayden just shudders with laughter.

***

The air is charged with excitement and scented with sweat, blood, and beer the moment we arrive at the abandoned bear cages. It took us a while to get here because they're situated in the middle of the woods and we had to walk on foot. When we arrive, two enclosures greet us, both overrun by nature, with vines and scrub crawling over the grey stone walls. At the very top of the stone frame of one of the enclosures is a carving of two bears facing off against each other—a fitting image for the savagery about to take place tonight.

Toward the middle of the main enclosure there is a huge, shallow, circular pit, which I assume was once a water bath for the bears that used to be kept in the dens here. Now it's being used as a makeshift cage.

Spectators are packed so tightly into the place that it's hard to even move around. Somehow, people have managed to climb over the walls, making themselves very comfortable at the top for a prime view of the cage. Breaking Point must have paid off the park rangers to host the knockouts here because there are a good few of them stationed outside, watching everyone closely as they enter.

On the way in, I pass a huge poster taped flimsily on one of the stone walls. I snatch the poster and scan it for Jax's face amid the roster of men fighting tonight, and a smug smile tugs on my lips when I spot him.

Let the games begin.

Chucking the poster aside, I veer off to the smaller enclosure where most of the fighters are mingling, preparing for their fights. Kayden leans against a railing in a shadowy corner, watching everybody with critical eyes. When he sees me heading toward him, those same eyes soften.

"Before I forget," I say, one hand rummaging through my bag and pulling out his red robe, "Found this in the dryer. Thought you might need it."

Kayden takes the robe from me, breathing a sigh of relief. "Thanks."

I watch him stare at the robe for a couple of moments. "You wouldn't be 'Killer' without it," I murmur.

He smiles.

I help him adjust the robe, sliding my hands over the back of his body as he puts it over his sculpted physique. He gulps when my fingers make contact with his skin and I look up to see him staring boldly at me. My hands drop to my sides and a deep sudden ache passes through me. We're barely inches apart and I've never wanted to be this close to anyone before.

"What are you doing to me, Lucky?" He drops his voice to a whisper.

I can keep the butterflies out of my system if I can avoid seeing the greyish hue of his eyes or the strong shape of his mouth. I let my gaze drop to my shoes. At least he won't be able to see how much of an effect he's already had, how much my entire body trembles and yearns for him with just a thin string of words.

I clear my throat and take a step back.

"It looks ugly on you," I say.

He chuckles.

"It's time," I say, glancing at my wrist but finding that there's no watch. I pretend to be picking at a scab instead to hide my embarrassment. "Good luck, Killer."

"I don't need it. I've got you."

I think my heart just flew out of my chest and landed on Mars.

No. I can't let myself get affected like this. I'm here for one reason only, and that is to watch Jax fall. Kayden is just a distraction and he needs to stay that way.

It takes every bit of willpower I can muster to walk away from him. When I return to the main enclosure, I squeeze through the crowd, making a beeline straight for Brent and Evans. Brent catches sight of me and waves me over.

Soon, the blare of the horn interrupts the chatter and the crowd erupts into cheers. People bump their fists in the air in anticipation as the announcer jumps into the cage with a roar, his face painted like a grizzly bear and his entire body sloppily slathered with brown dye.

"First rule of the underground: you don't talk about the underground!" The announcer yells, mimicking Tyler Durden from *Fight Club*. "*Nahhh*, who am I kidding? Of course y'all gonna talk about it because it's gonna be maddafakkin' *SIIIIICK*!!!!"

Another round of cacophonous cheers and hoots from the crowd.

"All right, let's get on with it!" He yells. "Three weeks. Sixteen fighters. Who's gonna leave crawlin' and who's gonna leave the ultimate *CHAMP*? Place your bets *right now* and ladies and gentlemen, let the knockouts *BEGIN!*"

Throughout the next hour, fighters take their turns battling it out against each other in the cage. Most of the fights are gruesome. The spectators at the front get speckled with blood and sweat that aren't their own, but they cheer anyway, greedy for more of the gory sport.

Some fights lasted longer than others. Others were bad. One of the fights had both fighters holding their positions, too scared to hit first, instead choosing to circle each other to buy time. It drew out like this for five minutes, with water bottles and trash being thrown into the cage by aggravated spectators trying to get them to do at least something.

The rest of the fights were mediocre at best. Straightforward jab-crosses and kicks, shitty footwork, and a permeable defense, which leads a predictable tap-out position on the ground. All of them truly amateur fighters. The only saving grace for the spectators was the gruesome carnage of broken bones, blackened eyes, and gnarly, wounded flesh.

As the announcer crawls into the pit for the seventh time, my heart hammers wildly against my chest in anticipation when he declares the next two fighters entering the cage.

"Fighting Maddock West tonight is everyone's favorite . . . Kayden 'The Killer' Williams!"

I suck in a breath. I watch the crowd part for him as Kayden heads to the cage.

Oh my God.

There.

He.

Is.

It's only been an hour since I last saw him but my breath still catches at the sight of Kayden as he parts the crowd. His dark hair gleams with sweat and his face is mean. Tenacious. Laser focused. When he climbs into the pit, he removes the robe and tosses it to the side, and lean muscles stretch under his tattooed skin when he flexes, causing all the girls in the crowd to go mad with fangirling shrieks.

Kayden's eyes search the crowd, and when they land on me, he smiles. I give him an encouraging nod, trying my damnedest to ignore the whirlwind of butterflies erupting in my belly.

Shit, I really am screwed.

He doesn't rip his gaze away from me. Instead, he looks at me like he's searching for something. A sliver of emotion, maybe. Big mistake. Because when the fight starts, Maddock pounces on Kayden, catching him completely off guard.

Kayden tries to hold his defense steady while trading blows with Maddock. Right off the bat it's intense, the thuds of Maddock's hits reverberating through the pit. But punch after punch Kayden's defense still holds firm. I beam with pride.

"That's right! Wait for the opening!" I yell at him.

Frustration lines Maddock's face. He steps in for a body lock but Kayden is ready for it. He times the counter with a brutal high knee, catching Maddock on the chin for a split second before dancing away.

Maddock growls, clenching and unclenching his jaw as he repositions himself. I see Kayden's right leg flex as he shakes it.

He must have overstretched himself going for that high knee, I worry. Maddock, seeming to have drawn the same conclusion, goes straight into a kick at Kayden's leg.

Absorbing the blow, Kayden unleashes his own flurry of punches, which Maddock blocks deftly, then strikes at Kayden's thigh again. Unwavering, Kayden continues his barrage of jabs, forcing Maddock to focus on his defense, but something's wrong. Kayden's starting to favor his left side, his right leg obviously hurt. He dips to go for an overhand. Maddock sees it coming and readies to block it.

Almost too obvious, I note.

But then Kayden turns it into an *explosive uppercut* instead, coming up to ram Maddock on the chin.

Bam! Maddock crumples to the ground. Out cold.

"Yes!" I holler, beating both my fists in the air when Kayden's announced the winner.

He beams with joy, body swinging around to find me in the crowd again. Almost immediately, he's whisked away so the next fight can start. He gives me a hard nod toward the other enclosure, signaling that he will meet me there. I push a thumbs-up forward before squeezing out of the crowd, excited to celebrate this win with him.

Just as I'm about to break free from the mass of people, a strong hand clamps around my wrist.

"*Hey!* What the—?"

I whip my head back, ready to curse out whoever has the nerve to touch me unwarranted like this when my gaze meets an instantly recognizable pair of dark eyes.

"Rude of you to leave without saying hello, don't you think, princess?" His deep voice sends a rush of goose bumps down my arm. I brave a steady breath.

"Hello, Jax." I say.

FIFTEEN

It feels strange, staring at Jax amid the colliding bodies moving against us. The more I look at him, the more it feels as though rest of the world has crumbled away, with only the two of us at the center of the universe, anchoring ourselves together. I don't know why I thought he'd look any different than he did two weeks ago, when really it's only my perception of him that has changed.

That golden mess of hair I used to love running my hands through is now tainted with Beth's fingers. Those lips I could never stop kissing are now scorned from peppering kisses down my sister's jaw and all over her body. Those eyes that I could get lost in for hours, have never looked so callous. Bile rises in my throat but I swallow it, careful not to show him that his mere presence has already begun to do its damage.

"Did you see me fuck Jorgen up? KO'ed the guy in thirty seconds. Broke my previous record," Jax says, a smug smile tugging at the corners of his mouth. He's half naked, as usual, with his black robe falling past his arms carelessly, revealing a body packed with steel-hard muscle and boasting a golden-tan skin tone.

I snatch my hand away from his grasp. "I wouldn't know, Jax. I haven't been keeping track."

"Then why are you here?" Jax's eyebrows knit in confusion.

I roll my eyes, already tired of this conversation, knowing that there's nothing that he can offer me. Not even an *I'm sorry.* I spin around and start to walk away from him. Naturally, he doesn't like that.

"Hey, what are you doing?"

"What does it look like?" I push myself out of the crowd. "Getting away from you."

Jax places a strong hand on my shoulder, trying to slow me down. "Why?"

"Why? Are you serious?" I whip back around, incredulous at his ignorance. "Or did you forget the tiny little fact that you fucked my sister?"

Jax's eyes flicker for a moment—guilt, perhaps—though I can't be certain because when he blinks again, the emotion is gone.

"That was a mistake."

"Yeah, I'm sure it was when you accidentally found yourself inside her. Repeatedly."

I almost want to laugh at his absurdity. Surely he can't be this dense. Or perhaps he thinks he can throw me a bunch of lame excuses and I'll take him back anyway. Wouldn't be the first time he overestimated my loyalty to him.

Jax clamps his mouth shut tightly. His eyes scan the

crowd before he takes another daring step toward me, then dips his head low. "Look, is there somewhere else we can talk?"

"I'm not going anywhere with you," I snap, moving away from him.

"Wait, come on," he pleads. "At least give me a chance to explain myself."

"Too bad. You lost that chance the moment you decided to *cheat on me*."

"I didn't think, okay?" He snaps, letting out a slow, tortured breath. "I fucked up. I get it." The sharpness in his tone has dissipated, replaced by a distinctive softness. "I still love you, princess. I always have."

His earnest expression tells me that he's dead serious. It makes me want to laugh.

"Oh yeah? Tell me how you can love me and go behind my back and pull this shit?" I accuse him, jabbing a finger at his hard chest. "You lied to me. You've been doing that to me for three years, and that's all you know how to do to me, you fucking psychopath."

"Tell me, how did I lie to you when all I've ever tried to do was get *real* with you?" He grabs my finger, pacifying my aggression by closing my hand into a fist with his own, his fingers brushing over mine. I'm startled by how familiar it feels. "I was the only person in your life who gave a shit about you. Cared about what you really wanted to do when your family didn't. I was the only one who helped you harness that anger inside of you and made you who you are today. I fucking *love* you. I wouldn't have done all that for you if I didn't."

I blink at him, willing myself to believe that what he's saying is a lie, and yet, this is the only time I've ever felt like he was telling the truth.

Or he *believed* he was telling the truth.

I let my hand fall to my side.

"Then why did you do it? Cheat?"

"Because . . ." Shadows darken Jax's eyes. His fingers drift through his sweat-slicked hair. "Things got way too serious between us. And I got scared, all right?"

Scared. After three years of dating. Yeah, that sounds about right.

"And now your feelings have changed?"

"It was a wake-up call." His gaze slides over me, a scrap of modesty in it. He reaches forward to caress my cheek, sliding his thumb over my skin. And for a second, I let him. Because damn does it feel good to feel his touch again. "I want you back, Sienna. I'll be better for you, I promise."

And there it is again. More empty promises.

Promises that I told myself I'll never fall for again.

"You're a joke." Anger wends through my chest again and I pry his hand off of me. "Do you take me for a fool? I know you're still seeing Beth."

A muscle leaps in his jaw. "She means nothing to me."

I try to force my rage down but it won't go easily. Not when Jax just admitted that he slept with my sister *just for the hell of it.*

And the worst thing is, she doesn't even know.

Oh Beth, what have you gotten yourself into?

"Then why are you still seeing her?" I demand.

"I don't know." He shrugs nonchalantly. "She was there

when you weren't. And she's just . . . easier. Naïve."

"Wow." I whistle lowly.

The fact that he uttered those words about Beth that easily is revolting. I wonder what she would think if she heard him speak about her like that. The thought makes my stomach churn with disgust.

"I'll end it with her," he tells me, desperation edging his voice. "Just say the word."

"You do whatever you want." I wave him off, no longer wanting to continue this conversation. At this point, I've been gone way too long and I don't want Kayden to be worried. "Just don't do it on my account. I don't care what happens to yours and Beth's epic love affair."

My reaction is not what he was expecting, because as I walk away from him for the third time, he's hell bent on following me.

"We're not done here," he yells. I continue to ignore him, reaching the entrance of the enclosure. Jax raises his voice again. "*Princess!*"

"Don't call me that!" I snarl at him, my last bit of patience shattering like glass under the highest frequency. "I am *not* your princess! You no longer have the privilege of calling me any of your *stupid pet names!*"

"Princess." He ignores me, stepping to the side to hinder my path. His stubborn resolve would be endearing if he had tried to fight for this relationship before cheating on me. "I'm gonna ask again: If you're not here for me, then why are you here?"

"It's really none of your business," I merely say.

"That's where you're wrong. *You* are my business.

Whether you like it or not." He edges closer. "Tell me. Why come here if you weren't looking for me? You were never the one to indulge in the underground."

I don't know why, but I just laugh. A low, agonizing laugh that rips out of me as if I've been keeping it buried for a while now. His self-serving desire to want me to be with him despite still actively sleeping with my sister. Him thinking I'm here because I want him back.

This is Jax. The real him.

Conceited. Egotistical. Sets fire to everything he touches and just leaves it to writhe and burn. There isn't any other way for him to function otherwise.

I can't believe it took me this long to see it. I had allowed myself to get swept up in blind devotion all these years, hoping that he could be the man I'd always wanted him to be, that I didn't stop for a moment to dig deep into the man he really is.

"You know—" I start, clicking my tongue. "I used to love you so much, Jax. I stood by you for three years like a stupid, loyal lapdog. And you did nothing but throw my love back in my face, you ungrateful asshole." I hold his gaze, chin tilting high and shoulders squared. "You think you can sleep with my sister, fuck me up, and get away with it? Not a chance." Taut silence hangs between us for a moment, before a slow, cruel grin spreads across my face. "I'm here because I'm going to make sure this year's tournament is going to be a very memorable one for you."

Jax's mouth tightens. "What the hell are you talking about?"

"I think I'll just save the killing for the Killer, don't you think? After all, that's his specialty," I tell him, leaving him to connect all the dots on his own.

"You wouldn't." His face is a violent outburst of temper when my words trigger his suspicion. His fingers curl into fists, knuckles going paper white. "Sienna, don't you dare!"

"Just fucking watch me," I hiss before striding away from him.

***

Once I manage to squeeze out of the main enclosure, I notice Kayden heading straight for me. His body shudders with relief as he approaches me.

"Where the hell did you go?" Kayden asks. "Brent and Evans were looking all over and they couldn't find you."

"I got held up."

"By what?"

A slight pause. "By Jax."

When he registers the name, his grey eyes infuse with rage, dark and wild and fierce.

"Where is the bastard?" He demands, his head already swiveling around, eyes scanning the sea of people in front of him. "Tell me."

"Don't." I shake my head adamantly, not wanting his animosity toward Jax to lead him astray from our real goal. "Tonight isn't the night. Save it for the cage." I step toward him, tilting his face towards me as I search for any sign of injury inflicted during the fight against Maddock. "Are you hurt from the fight?" I scan the whites around his eyes to make sure they aren't bloodshot, then the rest of his face for any wounds that'll require stitching. Much to my relief, he looks better than most fighters after their fight, save for the bruising on his legs and arms. I make a mental note to make sure he runs an ice bath when we get home to help with the soreness.

"No, I'm fine," Kayden insists. "I'm worried about *you*. Did Jax hurt you?"

"No, he didn't. We just talked."

He swallows hard, eyelids fluttering closed. I'm not sure if he's relieved or angry.

"What did he say?"

"Doesn't matter. The only thing that matters is that we win," I tell him urgently. "He knows we're working together now and that you're a real threat. So he's going to try to use your weaknesses against you. What we have to do is get ahead of them so we can get ahead of *him*," I say sharply. "So what are they?"

Silence descends on us. He glances away briefly, avoiding my gaze. He looks almost sad.

Eventually, he sighs. Relenting.

"You."

"What?"

His breathing is ragged and his voice is strangled when he whispers, so softly that nobody else but me can hear it, "My weakness is *you*, Lucky."

My heart inflates like a goddamned helium balloon.

"There you are. We've been looking everywhere for you." I hear Evans approach, pulling us both out of the trance. Brent sticks beside Evans, body tensing and eyebrows dipping low with concern. "Knockouts are over. Let's scram before the cops arrive."

I nod silently. As the four of us join the line of people exiting the park, Kayden's hand brushes against mine and I close my eyes briefly, remembering the words he just uttered to me. They circle my heart and fill it with warmth, and deep down I know that his feelings are not unrequited.

I think you're my weakness, too, Kayden.

SIXTEEN

When I wake up the next morning, Kayden's words continue to simmer in my mind. I can't stop thinking about it . . . about him—and the fact that we might both be in this deeper than we'd like to admit.

Needing to take my mind off of him, I flip over to the other side of my bed to check my phone. The loud searing blast of light hits me and I groan while my eyes adjust to the brightness. I sift through the messages and emails that have been left unopened since last evening and find that there's an unread email from my dad. When I check it, I notice it's an e-vite.

Mr. Jacob Lane and Ms. Alyson Elizabeth
are delighted to invite you to celebrate their marriage
on the 19th of March at The Dane Estate.

A silent groan rises from my throat.

I guess I should have known this was coming despite me blocking it out of my head these past few days, but now, looking at this e-vite makes everything more real. It's bad enough that this is going to be my dad's fifth marriage, before I even get married *once*, but the timing of it isn't the most convenient since the wedding is being held a day before the finals against Jax. Which just serves as a distraction that I don't need.

When I check today's date on my phone, my mood takes an even bigger downward spiral.

February 14.

Great. Just what I need.

Everyone getting all loved up on Valentine's Day. Including my dad and his new fiancé, no doubt celebrating their upcoming nuptials.

I've never been the type to really do the whole hearts-and-flowers thing on Valentine's, but I did try to make an effort to spend time with Jax whenever the occasion rolled around. It was important to me that we did, since it was one of the few times that made me feel like we were a couple. For our first Valentine's Day, he took me out to an Italian restaurant and kissed me under the stars. Our second one was spent making love under the duvet the entire night. And as for tonight, I had been planning on making him a fancy three-course meal that I remembered trying hard to ace last month.

I guess that's not going to happen now.

Truth be told, I don't think I have much desire to spend the day with Jax. In fact, this is the first time in the past two weeks that I don't yearn for him like I used to. Yesterday's confrontation with him really put a lot of things into perspective for me.

Perhaps what I do yearn for is the feeling of being in love, the feeling of having someone you can depend on everyday and share your life with. Because I don't think I miss Jax's love, since it's evident that he had very little to offer to begin with.

I guess I just miss being in a relationship.

I'm going to need a distraction if I want to get through the day so I head out of my room to see if I can find anything that'll spark my interest. It's still early in the morning— eight thirty to be exact—and there's no note on the kitchen counter, which means Kayden is sleeping in.

Good, I think to myself. *He deserves a rest day after last night's fight.*

I stare at the nearly barren living room, stripped of any character. It's obvious it's to serve a particular purpose. If Kayden ever needs to disappear, he can do it without anyone knowing that he was ever here.

Running my fingers over the walls, an idea forms in my head.

I know exactly what I'm going to do today.

Snatching Kayden's keys off the table, I set off.

***

I return with several cans of paint from Home Depot. When I've set all the cans down, Kayden appears from the doorway of his room, shirtless and only in his navy-blue boxers, displaying his perfectly chiseled and lean abdomen. Even when he's not flexing his muscles, his body is an amazing sight—one that I rush to mentally capture in hopes of running my hands over it repeatedly in my dreams.

"Morning," I say in a light tone.

Kayden yawns and eyes the cans of paint I've placed to the side.

"What's all this?" He asks curiously, his voice heavy with sleep.

"Oh, I went on a little shopping spree," I tell him, sauntering over and dropping the car keys in his hand. "Thanks for lending me your truck."

"I didn't lend you my truck."

"Whatever."

He tosses the keys on the table, watching me curiously. "Where did you go?"

"Went shopping. Bought myself this cute top," I say, pinching my new lavender blouse. A nice statement piece given the ocean of black in my closet. "And I got myself a cute little manicure too." I wriggle my freshly painted nails in front of Kayden's face.

"Now I'm upset you didn't invite me out. Would have loved a French mani," Kayden mumbles.

"Help me with these." I drag the cans over to the kitchen.

Instead of offering aid, he simply stares at the paint. "What are we going to do with these?"

I grin wolfishly at him. "We're painting your apartment today."

A pause that seems to stretch on for miles. Followed by—

"Not a fucking chance."

"Come on," I whine, like I've just been told I can't have candy for breakfast. "This place is miserable."

"But I like it the way it is."

"You've been living here for so long now," I protest. "Don't you think it needs to look more like your home?"

"Why do you care?" Kayden demands.

"Because!" I retort. "I just do, all right? I just care. I care about you and I want this place to look more like *our* place than a dungeon. I care because I'd rather do this on Valentine's Day than lock myself in a room thinking of what I'd be doing if I was still in a relationship."

I stop to catch my breath and I see Kayden's eyes flood with sympathy. He stares at me, long and hard, flattening his lips into a thin line.

"Today sucks for you, doesn't it?" He murmurs.

"Yeah," I say quietly. "I need of get my mind off of it, that's all."

Kayden offers me a sympathetic smile.

"Okay. Fine." He gives in. "Maybe you're right. This place does look like shit. I hope you bought paint rollers."

Shit. I can't believe I spent three hours at Home Depot only to not buy paint rollers. "Um . . ."

Kayden's eyes flutter closed, trying to process my stupidity.

"What kind of person buys paint but not paint rollers?"

"I forgot! I was too busy figuring out all the colors I wanted to get," I say defensively, resting my hands against my hips. "Do you have any?"

"Does it look like I paint shit around here?"

Damn, Killer, a simple no would have sufficed.

"Fine," I snap, not wanting to continue this argument. I'm on a serious mission today, and I'm not gonna waste time arguing. "Give me your keys. I'll just drop by Home Depot again—"

"Nah, I'm just joking. I think I have some in the bottom drawer."

My hands fall limply to my sides. I stare at him, incredulous.

"I'll get you back for that," I say determinedly.

A smug smile slants across his face.

"I'll go get the tarp," he muses.

Half an hour later, we've moved the little furniture we have to my room temporarily and covered the entire living room with the tarp. I've changed into a high-school art smock and an old pair of shorts. By the time Kayden has put on some clothes, I'm already opening the can of my selected shade of paint.

Kayden's face twists with disbelief when he peers into the can. "You are *not* painting my apartment that ghastly shade of yellow," he says strictly.

"Why not?" I whip around to face him with a pout. "Does it not remind you of sunshine? Could help warm up that dead soul of yours a little."

Kayden rolls his eyes at my comment and lifts the paint roller from the floor. He does a slow walk along the cans of paint lined up in front of him, a finger tapping lightly against his jaw in contemplation as he deliberates which color is the best. Eventually, he leans forward to dip his roller into the crimson and lifts it back up. "How about red because you've been a pain in my ass lately?"

"You wish." I click my tongue, dipping my roller into a pastel-blue shade. "Maybe a bit of blue because you need to *chill*."

He lifts a brow. "Oh, I need to chill? Says the girl with the revenge quest." He flicks his roller at my direction, the sudden movement sending paint splattering all across my neck and chest. My mouth drops open when I press my hands against my chest, my palms now smeared with red paint.

"Are you kidding me?" I scowl at him.

"That—that—I didn't mean to do that," he mumbles, trying to stifle a smile at the same time. *Oh, it's on.* With a wicked grin, I push forward and sweep my paint roller across his chest. The blue paint drips down his shirt, pooling at his feet in a big puddle. When he lifts his head, his eyes connect with mine in a cold, deadly sweep.

"Sienna," he says, his voice low and threatening. "You did not just do that."

"I believe I just did." A coy smile dangles off my lips. "What are you gonna do about it?"

"Come here," Kayden growls, shooting toward me.

I laugh, circling around him as he chases me around the living room, his paint roller lashing forward to try to get to me. I duck under the ladder, sliding over to the other side but as if Kayden had anticipated the maneuver, he catches me by surprise by picking up one of the paint cans and splashing it all over me face-first.

I let out a yelp, slipping in the excess paint all around me and tumbling to the ground. Kayden hovers over me, a victory laugh ripping out of him as he continues to drip the remaining paint all over my body.

"Stop!" I wheeze, shielding my face. "All right! I'm sorry! Just stop . . ."

When he's done, he tosses the paint can aside. With the remaining energy I can muster, I snatch his hand and yank him to the floor with me. Kayden lets out a yell as he clatters to the ground, splattering himself with the same paint he got all over me.

We're both drowning in crimson.

The side of Kayden's large body is now pressed against mine as he props himself up on his shoulders. All the laughter dies down when we realize our faces are inches away from each other. His grin has disappeared, replaced by an unreadable, tense look. His throat bobs as those smoldering eyes trace me, his fingers reaching out to wipe the splashes of paint from my face.

"Sienna." He breathes my name, a tortured yet hopeful sound.

With just a whisper of my name on those perfect pair of supple lips, my body shifts gears. His face is so close now. My breathing hitches as his thumb floats to my mouth, gliding across bottom lip. I start to lose all train of thought, now squirming with anticipation. When he tries to pull his hand away, I wrap a hand around his wrist, my willpower taking a nose dive as I beckon him not to stop.

My gaze unwittingly falls to his lips.

If I just lean in a little more, I can end our agony—

No. Not like this.

The thought alone snaps me back to reality. I shouldn't be allowed to want him like this. It's too selfish.

Not when I'm still trying to get over Jax.

Kayden's not a distraction. Nor would I ever want him to be.

And the last thing he deserves is to be treated like a rebound.

I let go of his hand and pull away from him. And he doesn't stop me. I yank my knees together, hugging them, and Kayden edges away, running his shaky fingers through his hair. He doesn't look at me. I know if he did, I would glimpse a swirling pool of pain.

"We should get more paint," I suggest.

"Yeah," Kayden says, his voice dry. "We should. After . . . after I get cleaned up."

He looks like he wants to say more and I watch him expectantly, waiting for the next string of words to leave him. But instead, he clamps his mouth closed, hauls himself to his feet, and walks to his room, slamming the door shut after him.

I let out a defeated sound.

One step forward, ten steps back.

SEVENTEEN

The rest of the afternoon was spent in silence, finally finishing what we started and painting the rest of the walls. After replacing the tarp we had dirtied with some newspapers that we found near the elevator, we eventually settled on a color we both liked—lilac for the accent wall and a muted beige for the secondary walls. When we're done, I take a step back and wipe away the thin sheen of sweat on my forehead. The paint job was decent; though it probably would have looked a lot better if we hadn't made such a mess of it before this.

"Looks all right," Kayden comments as he descends from the ladder, taking a couple of seconds to admire our effort.

"Do you like it?" I ask.

He glances at me, eyes softening. "Yeah. I do."

A pleased smile crosses my face. At least I know that today's activity benefited him just as much as it did me.

Kayden's phone rings, jerking his attention away. He lifts the phone to his ear to answer. "Hey, Brent," he says. A long pause as Brent explains something to him I can't quite make out. "Oh yeah? Sure, I'll ask her and let you know. Bye."

"What did he say?"

He slides the phone back into his pocket. "There's a knockouts after party at a club tonight. Brent and Evans are thinking of going. They asked if we'd like to join."

"Sure. Why not." I shrug. "Unless you wanna stay in."

He shakes his head. "I'm game if you are."

"Then let's go."

I dash into the bathroom to take a long shower, scrubbing the rest of the dried paint from my hair and body. Once I'm freshly cleaned, I slap on some makeup and rake through my closet for something decent to wear. My closet isn't exactly the most versatile; most of my clothes are sportswear. But after a couple of minutes of searching, I finally find something suitable: a sleek black halter minidress that I'm sure will look good with a pair of faux leather boots.

By the time I'm out of my room, Kayden is leaning against the wall in the hallway, wearing a plain black shirt and jeans. It's a simple outfit, yet he looks devastatingly handsome in it, complementing his clean-shaven face and neatly styled hair. I've never seen him look this well groomed. Most of the time he's a sweaty, but hot, mess. I can't tell which I like better, but this new look is a nice change from the usual.

When he finally notices me, his eyes widen as he drinks in my entire form. Color blooms on my cheeks as his eyes dip from my face down to my chest, pausing for a moment at the exposed skin peeking out of the dress cutouts at the sides of my abdomen, traveling to my legs then all the way back up again. When they return to my face, his eyelids flutter closed and he inhales a ragged breath.

"Is something wrong?" I ask.

"No. Not at all," he mumbles, and beckons me with a nod. "Let's go."

When we get to his car and prop ourselves in our designated seats, Kayden turns to me from the driver's seat. He leans forward and presses his hand to my cheek, his eyes shining bright. I hold my breath, wondering what he's going to do.

"You're catastrophically beautiful," he blurts before releasing his hold on me and turning the ignition.

I fall back in my seat, desire exploding in my stomach as those rough words hit me.

Holy shit.

He's going to kill me, isn't he? With his beautiful words and kind stares and big, gentle heart. He's truly going to be the death of me.

We ease back into a welcoming silence, ignoring the heat festering between us. I still don't know what to make of it. I've known him a few weeks but I've never wanted anyone more in such a short period of time. I just want to replay Kayden's words in my mind repeatedly so that I never forget them. *Ever.*

When we finally make it to the club, I spot Brent and Evans together, waiting in the long line of busty girls and overeager men. There are a couple of fighters I recognize from the day before; it's rather easy to spot them what with the cuts in their eyebrows, puffy eyes, and large purple bruises across their arms.

"Damn, Sienna." Evans whistles lowly as I approach them. "You clean up well."

"I can't believe this is how we're spending Valentine's Day," Brent mutters, his glasses getting fogged up by the smoke wafting from inside the club.

"Why not?" Evans questions. "The people here are hot."

Brent glares at him, his irritation silent. "The line's moving. Let's go."

We wait in line for another half an hour before the bouncer finally lets us all in. The second we're inside, Evans vanishes into the massive crowd, trailing a group of girls making their way to the dance floor. Brent, seeing this, stalks the other way, heading straight for the bar. I follow after him, concerned.

"Hey, are you okay?" I ask.

"Yeah. Fine," Brent mutters, agitated. He tips his head to the bartender and the bartender nods back, signaling that he's next in line. "Never been better."

"You know you can tell me anything, Brent. I'm always here for you if you need me," I say, nudging his shoulder with mine. "Does it have anything to do with Evans?"

A muscle pops in his jaw at the mention of Evans's name. He visibly swallows, adjusting his glasses on his nose. "That obvious, huh?"

I nod slowly. "Let me guess: it's complicated?"

"Yeah. A little."

"Well, you're in luck. I'm well-versed in the subject," I say, remembering my own perplexing situation with Kayden. "I'm all ears if you want to rant."

Brent inhales deeply, tapping his finger on his chin in

contemplation. "I've had a crush on him since high school. It was a one-sided thing and I didn't really think too much about it. But these past few months he's been flirting back a lot and it feels like he has feelings for me. But I know it's hard for him to admit those feelings. You know that he's terrified of his parents, right?" His eyes flicker to me and I nod silently. "He likes to put up a façade sometimes and pretend that nothing ever gets to him. But deep down, it really affects him a lot."

Huh. Evans and I would be great friends.

"How about you?" I prod, shifting the attention to his plight worriedly. "Does it affect you?"

"My parents have always been cool with it," Brent explains. "Even Kayden. Though I'm not entirely sure if he knows about me and Evans." He lets out a long sigh. "I don't know what to do, Sienna."

"If you want my advice," I say, pressing my back against the bar and resting the back of my elbows on the surface, "maybe you guys should have a talk about it. Get everything out. I don't want to see you unhappy because both of you are too stubborn to admit your feelings for each other."

"Mmmm." Brent hums. "Speak for yourself, Sienna."

Ah shit. Of course.

I clutch a hand over my chest. "Touché."

The bartender finally reaches our corner to take our order. I raise my eyebrows at Brent. "You want a shot?" I offer.

Brent is silent for a beat, thinking. "Make it three. Each. Because we're gonna need all the alcohol we can get if we're going to survive the night without getting laid."

When the shots arrive, Brent and I clink our glasses against each other's and down our shots. Brent lets out a gurgling laugh trying to finish his last shot, spitting some of the liquid on me. It splatters across my dress.

"Ew, gross!" I slap him on his shoulder. He just laughs even harder.

I watch from the sidelines as more people pack the dance floor, sweat-covered bodies pressed tightly against each other. Kayden seems to have completely disappeared, nowhere to be seen. I wonder if he's just as affected by what happened between us this morning as I am.

The techno music eventually gives way to a slow-tempo ballad. Brent and I let out a collective groan when the DJ, perched in the booth, lifts his microphone and says in a deep, raspy tone, "This one's for all your lovebirds out there. May there be a lot of lovin' and grindin' for y'all tonight."

Aw, jeez.

I watch Kayden appear from the sea of bodies, his eyes darting around as he looks for us. He appears uncomfortable, like he'd rather be anywhere else. I don't know why he wanted to come since this clearly isn't his scene to begin with. He's silent for a moment when he reaches me.

"You wanna dance?" He looks almost embarrassed to be asking me. It makes me smile a little.

"Sure. Lead the way."

He extends his hand to me and I take it, allowing him to pull me onto the dance floor. I cut a glance back at Brent at the table, who wriggles his dark eyebrows back at me knowingly.

When we've found a small space amid all the other

couples, he pulls me closer to him. We sway back and forth a little and I rest my head against his chest. I've decided that while I like him as he is most of the time—that impressive, admirable strength and the raw masculinity he radiates whenever he strikes a brutal punch—I much prefer this gentle, delicate side of him. It's a breath of fresh air.

With a quivering smile, Kayden twirls me around and a laugh bubbles out of me when he dips me low, strong arms tightening around me, before pulling me back up for another effortless twirl.

"Damn." I whistle lowly when I'm pressed up against him again. My hands glide up his chest and rest on his shoulders. "I honestly didn't know you had it in you."

"It's probably that soccer exercise," Kayden winks. "Got the footwork down."

"Glad to know all those nights on the rooftop have paid off."

The DJ cues another slow song, so we stay locked in like this—arms entwined around each other. Being in his arms has never felt so right; I've never felt like I belonged anywhere else but in them. His hands trace the curve of my spine, the heat of his touch searing my skin through the fabric of my dress.

"Hey . . ." Kayden whispers. "Can I ask you something?"

"Of course. Anything."

"There's a reason why we didn't kiss this afternoon, isn't there?"

I'm taken aback by the bluntness of his question. Not a lot of men I know would approach something like what happened –or to be more specific, what *didn't* happen–in such a direct manner. It makes me like him even more.

"I respect you, Sienna. You know I do," he tells me. "I respect you enough to give you your breathing space. Jax was a huge part of your life. As much as I hate his damn guts, I'm not here to further complicate things for you." His mouth drops into a frown. "So, perhaps we shouldn't be doing anything."

I relinquish a sigh but nod in understanding anyway. He's right. We shouldn't continue to flirt and tease each other like this, not when we have enough of our own issues to deal with. Besides, getting involved with each other would make our deal much more complicated than it needs to be. And I don't think I'm ready to open that can of worms.

And yet, neither of us lets go of the other.

"Look," I start, "let's just forget about the whole thing and dance. Pretend for three minutes that we aren't carrying all this baggage with us. Pretend that it's just you and me. And nothing else. Maybe that's what we deserve. At least for the remainder of this song."

"Okay." Kayden whispers. I press my cheek against his chest, hands clutching his shoulders, and he lets his chin rest on top of my head.

Despite the harsh spotlights blasting down on us, everything else feels like swirl of haze. Kayden lulls us to the low tempo of the song, rocking side to side lazily. My body infuses with sadness when I think that this is going to be the closest we'll ever allow ourselves to physically be to each other.

My gaze stretches to the swarm of couples crammed around us, and in the distance, I notice Brent and Evans packed together in a small pocket in the crowd.

I can't make out what they're saying to each other, but the conversation looks intense, with each of them throwing angry words at the other. Eventually, Brent stops, drags a frustrated hand over his mouth while Evans continues talking at him, and just when the conversation picks up its intensity again, Brent clutches a fistful of Evans's shirt and kisses him deeply, shutting him up.

Huh. I guess the liquid courage gave Brent the impulsiveness he needed.

"Hey, look at them go." I nudge Kayden, pointing in the new couple's direction.

His jaw drops.

"Did—did you know?" He asks me, the shock still jolting through him. His alarmed gaze flickers from Brent and Evans back to me again. "Oh my God. Are they . . . ?"

"I don't know, either, buddy." I tap my hand lightly against his chest. "But it sure looks like that has been going on for a while."

Evans's shock has completely dissipated and he leans in to Brent's bold advance, kissing him back just as fervently. Their union feels like a huge sigh of relief after all the pushing and pulling between them. It feels too intimate to watch so I turn my attention elsewhere to give them the privacy they deserve.

"I can't believe it." Kayden gapes, unable to shake off his bewilderment. "My brother and my best friend."

"I think it's kinda cute," I say. "You're not gonna go over and confront them, are you?"

Kayden scrunches his mouth in contemplation.

"Don't be an asshole. Let them have their moment," I insist. "And we can have ours."

He stares at them for a moment longer, having an internal debate with himself, before caving in to my suggestion.

"All right." He yields.

And we let the rest of the night carry our thoughts away.

***

Half an hour later, we manage to pry ourselves off the dance floor. Kayden exits through the door at the back of the club, opting for some fresh air, and I grab another drink since the last round of alcohol has fizzled out of my system. I prop myself in an empty booth by the washrooms, casually sipping my piña colada to pass the time. A couple of minutes later, I spot Brent and Evans emerging from said washroom, hands linked tightly together.

They come to a halt when they catch me staring.

"So . . ." I begin casually, eyeing their clasped hands. "I'm guessing you two sorted things out?"

"Yeah," Brent says sheepishly. "Any chance you can not tell Kayden about it?"

"I think he already knows."

"Great," Evans wails, throwing his hands up behind his head. "I'll be immigrating to Canada if anyone needs me."

I think there's something so comical about Evans's easygoing nature getting demolished in fear of not knowing what Kayden might to do to him the second he finds them together, even though I'm certain that Kayden would want nothing but the best for both of them.

"You're his best friend," I coax, twirling the straw casually with my finger. "You'll be fine."

"I'm his *best friend*," he echoes in a wildly panicked tone. He drags his hands through his hair, pulling at it like he has half a mind to rip it out to make himself feel better. "Which means he'll kill me with his bare hands if he has the chance."

"Where is he, by the way?" Brent searches the crowded space.

"He went out for a bit," I tell them, peeping over my phone to look at the time.

Whoa. It's already been twenty minutes since I last saw him. Worry knots in my stomach at the thought of him running into some kind of danger. I propel myself out of the booth and toward the exit I'd seen him go through. Before leaving, I spin towards Brent and Evans.

"I'll be right back. Stay put," I order.

When I'm outside, a dead end greets me to the left, forcing me to make a hard right and go around the corner, which leads me to a dirty alleyway. It's cold, clammy, and misty, and it takes me a while to waft through the fog to see anything at all. But as soon as I do, what awaits me on the other side immediately puts me in panic mode.

I retreat quickly behind the wall and peek over instead to watch the confrontation unfold.

"You know when my girlfriend said she was slumming it with you, I didn't think she was actually serious," Jax says, irritation flickering in his eyes as he and a few other men close in on Kayden.

Kayden doesn't appear the least bit intimidated, scoffing at Jax's attempt to frighten him. I look around frantically for anything that can be of use to get him out of this situation.

Nothing but barbed-wire fencing, a ton of littered cigarettes, and resting beside one of the dumpsters sits . . .

A crowbar.

Bingo.

"Don't you mean ex-girlfriend?" Kayden says with a lifted brow. "It's not my fault you couldn't keep your dick in your pants. Cheating on someone with their sister is a new low, even for you, Deadbeat."

Jax's eyes flare with unbridled fury.

"Where is she?" He demands, head swirling around. "I'm not gonna cause a scene if you just give her back to me."

"She's not mine to give, nor is she yours to take," Kayden says, his voice firm and ringing with reassurance. "Stop treating her like she didn't decide to leave your sleezy ass on her own."

"She's *mine*," Jax declares. "Day or night, she belongs with me. And she's coming back with me tonight. Tell me where she is, and I promise I'll keep the fight between us in that cage. You don't want to get in my way, Killer."

Instead of caving, Kayden hoots with laughter, making a mockery out of Jax.

"Wow, I think I'm really going to enjoy fucking you up in that cage and taking that championship away from you." Kayden stalks toward Jax until he's a mere foot away from him. Protective anger rears up in him as he seethes. "There's no way I'm *giving* you Sienna. She's her own person and she can make her own choices. But I know for a fact that she's better off by my side than yours."

"She will never love you like she loved me," Jax retorts. "I was everything to her."

"Please," I call as I swagger toward Jax and his goons, my hand swinging the crowbar effortlessly. "Don't make it sound like you were *that* special to me."

All heads whip in my direction. Jax's dark eyes soften when he sees me.

"Princess," he breathes, already striding toward me.

I haul the crowbar up over my shoulder, ready to aim. His entire body freezes at my weapon, staying put where he is. He lifts a fist, signaling his men to do the same.

"Stay away from Kayden or I will *splatter all of your fucking brains out with this*!" I yell in a frenzied temper as I dart in front of Kayden protectively, wedging myself between him and Jax's men. "I'm not afraid of you. Or your *goons*!"

Gales of laughter fly out of their mouths.

"You think I'm joking?" My eyes flash with warning. "All right. Fine. Don't believe me. Why don't I give you two options here? Option one: get the fuck out of our faces and disappear. Or option two: stay *RIGHT HERE* and be my fucking piñatas!"

Low murmurings pour from Jax's men. But nobody dares to shout an answer, not even Jax himself, who looks like he's internally debating whether to take my physical threat seriously.

"*DING, DING, DING!*" I say manically. "Time's up! I think I'm gonna go with option *two*!"

I swing my crowbar back to gain momentum and right before I swing it back, Jax interrupts me, holding both hands up in surrender.

"All right, fine." He urges me. "If that's what you want, we'll go."

"Leave us alone," I demand, leaning against the crowbar like a walking cane. "Our fight is in that cage, four weeks from now. I'm not in the business of fighting you here. It's too merciful for you. You deserve to have your ass savagely handed to you in the cage while everyone there watches, hungry and chanting for your blood."

"I love it when you talk dirty to me like that, princess." He purrs at me, a tongue sweeping over his teeth. A hand rubs over his chin as he contemplates my words. "All right. I'll play your game. It's certainly more intriguing than the one me and your sister play."

At the mention of Beth, the outrage boils over and I spit at his feet.

"Go to hell, Jax."

He isn't the least bit disgusted. In fact, it further serves to spur him on.

"Mmmm." Jax presses his lips together, edges curling upward smugly. "I'll be sure to meet you there, princess."

And he gestures for his men to retreat. When they've finally disappeared from the alley, I let my shoulders slump with relief. I immediately rush over to Kayden.

"Hey," I say, consumed with worry. "Are you okay?"

"Yeah, I'm fine. Don't worry about it," Kayden tells me. "You're not hurt, though, right?"

"No." I exhale. I look at Kayden and shake my head in disappointment. "I can't believe I left you alone for twenty minutes and you've already gotten yourself into trouble."

"Hey, I was minding my own business when they ambushed me," Kayden says defensively. "I can't believe you did that. Not that I needed your help, but thanks."

"You always need my help," I tease. "Kayden, the damsel in distress."

He grabs his chest in mock pain as if I shot him. "Please. My masculinity is already fragile enough as it is."

Relief floods my core knowing that Kayden left the fight unscathed. I shouldn't have underestimated Jax in thinking he wouldn't give us any trouble outside the cage, especially after letting it slip that Kayden and I are working together. It looked like there was a real possibility of Jax beating Kayden up right then and there. The fact that he retreated peacefully is suspicious at best. It's clear that Jax doesn't do anything without an ulterior motive.

The game between us has only just begun. And it looks like we're both in it for the long haul.

Which means I have to stop getting myself distracted and get focused.

"Let's go, Killer," I urge him, a hand extended toward the exit. "Valentine's Day is over."

EIGHTEEN

The next two days whiz by pretty quickly. My courses have begun to pick up pace, with many assignments pouring in, and their demanding deadlines give me little to no rest. Cara helped me prepare a meticulous schedule that outlines my time for these two weeks down to the minute so I can keep up with all that I have going on with Kayden and my students, while still squeezing in time to finish my assignments. Most of the time, it feels like I'm running a never-ending marathon, but the adrenaline from my training sessions with Kayden has helped keep my momentum going.

Our workout sessions continue to remain consistent—with Muay Thai, boxing, and grappling to help Kayden nail his moves and maneuvers, and full body conditioning sessions to get as strong as possible and increase his endurance. A mixture of bodyweight exercises and weight training work Kayden's muscles enough to keep his body building core strength.

Today I've arranged circuit training to work on his endurance—a total of six exercises, ten reps each, as many rounds as Kayden can do in forty-five minutes. With the number of sparring sessions we've been doing lately, I thought this would be a nice break for him. But from the looks of it, Kayden would rather get smashed around in a cage for hours than push himself to do another rep.

"Come on. You're dying on me here," I snap impatiently, circling around him as he finishes his triple jump rep across the finish line. "Keep it up. You're falling behind."

"I'm *trying*." He pants as he moves on to the next exercise.

"You've got one minute left. You can do ten more reps," I urge Kayden as I bend down slightly, resting my hands on my knees so our gazes are level with each other. He grunts as he lifts the ball, then goes down again and drags himself back up for a pull-up. He looks like he's about to cave in at this rep. I try to keep his spirits high with a motivational saying. "'Build aggression to the point where pain no longer matters.' There's a Julian quote for you."

"Oh yeah? It's not working," he says as he gets up, a little out of breath. He picks up the ball, jerking his head at me. "What's a Sienna quote then?"

"Don't quit, don't split, and don't bitch."

"How inspirational," Kayden deadpans as he throws the medicine ball over his shoulder, repeating his movements.

Two more reps. Then one more. Much to his relief, the timer in my palm beeps and I jam the button to reset. "All right. Time."

Kayden immediately drops the ball and collapses.

"Ten rounds," he says breathlessly, inhaling through his

mouth as he stares up at the ceiling defeatedly. "Look at that."

"See? Easy stuff," I tell him as I head to the bench to pick up his water bottle, then walk back and set myself down beside him, thrusting the bottle at his face. "Rest up. Here's some water."

He takes it more than willingly. "Thanks."

I watch Kayden silently as he guzzles the water, allowing a bit to dribble down the sides of his mouth. It's nice to see him unwinding like this, when I've worked him to the point where rest feels like a vacation.

I feel his eyes on me as he towels himself off. It feels strange whenever we look at each other; despite the fact that we've openly admitted our feelings for one another, it's not nearly enough to ease the longing and pining. Every single time I catch him staring at me, it's so electrically charged that my body feels like it needs to get extinguished by a fire brigade.

I clear my throat, desperate to rid myself of these thoughts since I'd already promised myself not to entertain the possibility of being something more to Kayden. Pulling my knees up, I rest my arms over them and say, "So . . . semifinals against East Lee."

Kayden throws the towel to the side and crosses his legs. "Yeah."

"You'll be fine," I say confidently. "Lee has a tell. He's got a habit of telegraphing with his feet. When they point left, you know you're expecting a left throw. Same for the other side."

Kayden quirks a brow. "Huh. I never noticed."

"Yeah." I nod. "Everybody has a tell if you look hard

enough for it. Jax doesn't think he has any, but he does. He doesn't do it all the time, only when he feels like he's losing control in the cage. When he's locked in and his defenses are up, he'll move his right leg back slightly to turn it into a front kick. Saw it happen twice when he used to spar with Julian. And I saw him do it again when he fought you last season."

"Hmmm. Interesting," he says, leaning back and resting his upper body over his propped hands. "How about you? What's your tell?"

"I don't think I have any. Or at least any that I'd want you to know about."

He pauses for a beat. Then a slow, knowing smile lines his mouth. "I think I know what they are."

"Surely you haven't fought me enough one on one in that cage to know my tells," I scoff.

It seems impossible that Kayden would know because I don't spar with him, usually opting to have another male fighter help out during the session so the fight will be fair.

"I'm not talking about inside the cage, Lucky. I'm talking about outside of it."

My eyebrows dip in confusion. "I don't think I follow."

"Come on. Your mask is immovable in that cage but outside of it, it's pretty easy to tell how you're feeling," he notes. When I give him a blank stare, Kayden fires back a look that says *Seriously?* He leans forward, cupping his knees. "Every time you bite your bottom lip, it means you're completely spaced out and lost in your own thoughts. Most likely thinking about your family. When you press your hands to your face, it means you're frustrated at yourself and you don't know how to let the feeling out," he says matter-of-factly. My mouth gapes at how much he's been memorizing me. Just like how I've been memorizing him in that cage. Kayden pauses momentarily, head dipping down. His mouth tightens, as if he's unsure about what he's going to say next. When his head lifts again, those grey eyes look tortured. "And when you look at me with your lips pursed, you're thinking about what it'd be like to . . ."

Kayden stops. I nudge him with a nod, egging him on.

"To what?"

He shakes his head, waving me off. "Nothing. Forget I said anything."

I inch toward him, curiosity taking reign. "Come on. Tell me."

"When you look at me with your lips pursed . . ." he murmurs, suddenly going shy. "I—I think you're wondering what it'd be like . . . to kiss me."

His words snatch all the breath out of my chest. I look away, uncertain of how to react.

"That's bullshit." I shake my head in dismissal. "I don't do that. I don't purse my lips."

He looks at me, amused by my defensiveness. A forced smile climbs onto his face.

"You're right. You don't," he says. "I was just messing with you."

I can only nod. I don't want to stick around here anymore if he's going to say stuff like that to me. My heart can only take so much from him.

"We should get going," I mutter softly.

"All right. Come on," he says, already pushing himself to his feet.

Kayden extends a hand to me and I take it, forcing myself up, but I stumble a bit, stabilizing myself by pressing my hands on his chest. Kayden's entire body goes stiff the second my skin touches his. I look up and catch those intensely dark eyes staring down at me, an unreadable expression crossing his face. We're so close to each other, our faces mere inches away. A heavy breath reverberates from me, shivers flying up my spine as our eyes lock for way longer than they're supposed to.

I pull back abruptly. "Um."

"Yeah." He looks down, clearly embarrassed. "I'm gonna take a shower."

I nod wordlessly, watching him grab his towel that was chucked to the side on the floor and head to the showers. He mutters something under his breath but loud enough for me to catch what he says.

"Preferably a cold one."

I purse my lips.

Goddammit.

***

I have another late-night sparring session with Brandon at UFG before I have a long, noncancelable date with my research papers in the library tonight. When we're done, it's twenty minutes to closing and I'm famished from not having had enough time to grab a quick dinner before the session started. I'll probably just grab something from the vending machine on campus later.

When I emerge from the locker room after packing up, Julian appears from his office. He doesn't seem happy at all;

his forehead is creased and his mouth flattened into a tight line, eliciting a nervous feeling in my belly.

"Get in here," he barks.

I loop my bag around me and hurry into his office, shutting the door behind me. He hovers over his table, drumming his fingers impatiently against the surface. I eye the fresh doughnut sitting on the plate beside him, which is left untouched.

Oh no.

My gaze swings back up. "What's up, Jules?"

"Your father's fiancé says she can't reach you."

"What?" I ask, drawing my eyebrows low on my face. "How do you know that?"

"Because she has been calling the gym incessantly, asking me for your training schedule," he says pointedly. "And I told her I couldn't disclose that information in case you wanted it to be kept private."

"Thank you." I breathe out in relief.

Julian and I may have our differences, but I know at the end of the day, he's got my back.

He shakes his head, indicating that he's not done. "So she's been showing up every hour today to see if you're around. She just said she's outside right now," he adds nonchalantly. "I told her to come in."

I take it back. I hope he chokes on his doughnut and dies.

"Julian, what the *hell*?"

"She sounds like she wants to connect with you, Sienna," he says. "I know you have your issues with your dad. But she seems nice and wants to make things work with you. And I think you should."

I wince at the irritation spiking in my body. He's crazy if he thinks he can make that decision for me.

"No offence, Jules, but that isn't exactly your call to make."

"No offence, Sienna, but you need to sort your shit out soon. You're too unhinged right now for me to consider you taking over the gym after I retire," he retorts. "I have high hopes for you because you're good at what you do. You're one of the best trainers I've ever seen, hands down. And that's why I need you to work through your own issues before I can even think about handing over the keys."

I force my mouth shut. Is this how he really sees me? *Unhinged*? I know I'm not exactly the most rational person ever, but I would think that with what I've been going through, I've been coping fairly well.

I can't believe he's going to dangle ownership of the gym over my head like a carrot on a stick just to force me to do his bidding.

"This is blackmail," I state.

"It's motivation," he corrects.

Motivation my ass.

Making an annoyed sound, I shove the door a little too hard on my way out.

As I cross the length of the gym, I spot Alyson eyeing all the equipment as she strides toward me. Her hair is swept neatly to the side and she's wearing a burgundy off-shoulder bodycon dress with a matching Prada bag perched on her arm and a pair of heels. They dig hard into the mats when she walks over them.

"Oh, how cute," she says when she stops beside one of

the punching bags and knocks a playful fist on it.

Oh boy.

"Alyson," I say flatly. "To what I owe the pleasure?"

She seems shocked that I'm even speaking to her. "Sorry. I didn't know how else to reach you. You wouldn't answer my calls, and nobody knows where you live now. This was the only place that your father mentioned that you would be."

I eye her critically. "So your plan was just to ambush me at my place of work?"

"I'm sorry. I know it's weird," she says, embarrassment floating up her face. "But I wanted to ask if you were coming to the wedding. You didn't respond to the e-vite."

"I'm pretty sure me not responding automatically implies that I'm declining the invitation."

"Oh, I see." Alyson's expression crumbles. "Look can we talk somewhere else? Have you had dinner? I'd love to take you out."

If I hadn't been burned by the many women who have been in her place before this, I'd think her gesture to reach out to me was adorable.

"Look, Alyson," I start off, resting a hand over my hip. "I appreciate you trying to make the effort. I really do. But it's hopeless. You're not the only woman my dad has been with who has tried to take on a maternal role and wanted to create a 'bond' with me. And don't get me wrong, I've tried to make things work with them on my end too. But they don't stick around long enough, and I somehow end up being disappointed every time. That's why I've stopped trying. I'm sorry, but my answer is no."

My words echo through the empty gym and Alyson shifts uncomfortably. She's silent, biting her lip in contemplation as she wonders what she's going to say next, her heels rocking back and forth against the mat. She turns around halfway and just when I think she's going to just give up and leave me alone, she pivots back to me, her face wrought with determination.

"I know your dad hurt you, Sienna," she says sympathetically. "And I know better than to pretend that his previous divorces didn't leave huge scars in your family. But you must know that I really do love your dad. And he's trying to change. It might not seem like it, but he is." Conviction rings in her voice as she continues. "I'm not planning on leaving. I know there's a lot of trust between us that needs to be built and I'm willing to make it work. Because I care about you, Sienna, and I think if you gave me one chance, you'd really see that."

I let the words parse slowly in my head. Maybe she is telling the truth about her and my dad. And yet I can't help but cling to that familiar cynical feeling just so I can keep my heart away from the prying hands of people trying to take it away from me. I put a lot on the line when I choose to care for people, and somehow, I'm the one who always gets burned.

It's hard to trust anyone when the pattern of behavior has already been laid out.

And if there's one thing I can trust, it's consistency.

"We're having a bridesmaid dress fitting in two days. It'll be nice if you could come. I've ordered a dress for you anyway, in case you change your mind," Alyson says with a faint smile. Again, I don't respond. She pulls out a pen and notepad and scribbles down something before tearing the paper off and placing it on the bench beside me. When she senses that I don't have anything else to say to her, the smile on her face disappears and her head dips slightly in an apologetic manner. "I'm sorry about coming here. I'll get out of your way now. See you around."

I watch her wordlessly as she disappears the way she came, the doors closing after her.

Sighing, I stare at the piece of paper left on the bench, my eyes scanning the details she'd written. It's the location of the bridal store along with the date and time of the dress fitting.

I scrunch it into a ball with my hand and toss it into the trash before leaving.

NINETEEN

Midterms are happening soon, which means on top of the busy schedule I already have, I've got to somehow cram exam prep into it as well. The last thing I want to do right now is study, but I know if I slack off with my academics, I'm going to regret it later.

Any spare time I have is now spent living in the library studying with Cara. Though I have to admit that those sessions haven't proven to be particularly fruitful due to her rather tempting offers to get me to screw exam prep and pass time at Caffeinated with her.

I knew I should have picked Alex to be my study buddy instead.

Slacking off with training isn't exactly an option either. Semifinals are two days away, and while I'm confident Kayden can kick Lee's ass, he's still not in the prime shape I need him to be in for his fight against Jax.

And that's the most important fight of all.

I'm planning another gruesome sparring session soon. I hope Kayden's ready for it. I know he will be. He always takes everything I dish out to him. And I need to see that attitude now more than ever.

Back at the apartment to grab all my training gear from my room before darting over to Breaking Point, I'm interrupted by unexpected rattling from the kitchen. *What the fuck?* My eyes grow wide with alert. My first instinct is to grab the golf club but I squash the thought down, not wanting to repeat what happened two weeks ago. This time, I dart towards the my intruder with my guard up, but when I recognize who it is, I drop my fists, an annoyed expression drags my entire face down.

"Seriously, Evans? I told you the spare key is only for emergencies."

Evans whirls his head back, pausing the rummaging he's doing in my cabinets. He already has a few chips stuffed in his mouth. When he sees me, he crunches them and swallows. "This *is* an emergency."

"One day I swear I'm gonna take your key privileges away because surely breaking into my apartment to steal Pringles is a violation of the treaty me and Brent agreed to a month ago."

I watch him as he drops his hands from the cabinets and rests his palms against the edge of the counter behind him. He looks distraught, his eyes squeezing shut and his chest breathing heavily. I edge closer to him with concern.

"Are you okay?"

"Nope." He shakes his head, eyeing the keys looped across my finger. "Where are you going?"

"I've got a session with Kayden at Point," I say, going to retrieve my gym bag sitting on the sofa and slinging it over my head. "What's up?"

Evans pauses. Presses his lips together thinly.

"Tell him you can't make it."

"Uh . . . I don't know if I can do that. Semifinals are this weekend."

"Please," he says desperately. "I'm in distress and in severe need of retail therapy."

Guilt nips at me for bailing on Kayden at the last minute. I'd been hoping to see him since I haven't got a chance to catch him all day. But I'm pretty sure he'll understand if I skip today's session to console his best friend. Besides, the past week has been hectic and I'd be lying if a half-day out with Evans doesn't sound appealing. I'll just make sure to catch up with Kayden later.

"All right . . ." I say, dropping my bag on the dining table. Evans's face immediately lights up. "But Kayden's not going to be happy about this."

"Kayden's not happy ninety-nine percent of the time anyway, so I doubt it'll make a difference."

"That's fair." I shrug. "I guess I'm down for a closet revamp."

"Cool. You need it, anyway. You have a fifteen-year-old emo kid's closet and that's not okay. You're better than that." He clicks his tongue and I gasp at the insult.

Surely my closet isn't that bad. Sure the color palette's a little darker than most, but that's just because I own twenty black sports bras and leggings. It's not that I'm opposed to color; athleisure is just easier to match when it's all black.

Evans pushes himself away from the counter and loops an arm through mine, dragging me out of the apartment.

"I get to pick all your clothes today," he declares cheerfully.

I arch a brow. "You're paying for them, too, right?"

He sends a glare at me.

"Don't push it."

***

As I predicted, Kayden wasn't exactly happy about me skipping training this close to the semifinals, but after I explained to him how distressed Evans was, he was more than willing to let it go. Evans and I ended up making a quick stop at a drive-thru for a much needed ice-cream run before hopping over to the mall.

To my disdain, Evans proceeds to drag me to every single store that features a mannequin in their storefront, throwing me a heap of clothing to try on. I oblige him because it seems like he needs the distraction. And if trying on a gazillion dresses will get him to chill out, then I'll gladly do it.

"Remind me to never to go dress shopping with you ever again," I moan.

"Come on," he insists. "Red is totally your color."

"That's what you said about blue. And gold. And green," I say begrudgingly as I slip into the red dress. Out of all the dresses I've tried on today, I think this might be my favorite. It's a sleek midi dress with a ruched detail on either hip, and it's made from a stretchy, breathable material, making it easy to get it over my body. When I'm done, I push open the door to my dressing room and step out. "Here. How do I look?"

Evans is lounging lazily by the velvet chaise, aggressively dog-earring a men's fashion magazine as if it's his own. When he realizes that I'm out of the dressing room, his head lifts slightly and a wry smile tugs on his lips when he sees me in the new outfit.

"Ravishing," he murmurs, eyes scrolling up and down the length of my body. He clicks his tongue in approval. "If you walked into the apartment wearing this, Kayden would tear it off of you the second he saw you."

"Probably not worth the purchase then," I say amusingly as I glance at the whopping eighty-dollar price tag strung over the side zip. Dropping the tag, I lean a lazy arm over the frame of the dressing room and ask, "So . . . are you gonna tell me what's been happening with you or are we gonna skirt around it like the problem isn't there?"

Evans sighs, setting aside the magazine. He drops his legs onto the floor and rests his elbows over his thighs.

"Fine. If you must know, it's about me and Brent." He speaks in a defeated tone. A hand sifts through his mess of blond hair. "I really like him, Sienna. And this past week of being with him has been the most amazing week of my life." He drops his gaze to the floor, pausing before adding, "But my parents are coming to visit me tomorrow. And I'm not sure if I should tell them anything about it. I don't know if I even *want* to because I know they won't be happy about it." He lets out a frustrated sigh, burying his face in his hands like he just wants to shut off from the entire world. "And I know, I *know* I should embrace what I have with Brent and I shouldn't let my parents' approval dictate who I love and all that shit. But they're my *parents*, you know? And they support me financially too. So it makes everything so fucking stressful. I just don't know if I'm brave enough to go through all of that. And . . . I know no matter what decision I choose, I'll end up hurting someone in the process."

My lips pull into a frown at Evans's tortured expression. It is a rather tricky and difficult decision. And it clearly must have taken a lot for him to admit that. What a different man sitting in front of me today than the one I met two weeks ago.

I saunter over and sidle onto the chaise beside him, hoping I can provide some form of encouragement.

"I know how it feels to have a strained relationship with parents," I say, clamping a hand over his shoulder. "You're right. It's not an easy decision to make. It's going to be one of the toughest decisions you're probably going to have to make. I'm not gonna tell you what to do, but I just want to say that I'll support you no matter what you decide. But it's your life, Evans. You should be able to live it however you want to. I just don't want to see you sacrifice something so special with Brent and be unhappy for possibly the rest of your life. You might just hate yourself even more for it. And while you're a pain in my ass sometimes, I quite like you the way you are right now." I grow silent for a second, a half smile growing on my face. "You're brave enough, Evans. You just haven't had the chance to test out that bravery yet. I know you have it in you."

Evans looks at me with the most earnest expression. He nods at my advice, silently mulling over my words.

Eventually, he lets out a long breath and hoists himself up from the chaise, leaning a hip against the armrest.

"Thanks. That means a lot," he says hoarsely. "Though I don't know why I'm getting advice from a girl who seems to be doing the same thing as me—hiding."

My eyes grow big at the sudden shift in conversation.

"That's not fair," I say with a flicker of surprise. "And we're not talking about me. We're talking about *you*. Let's continue with that."

"Ah, deflection. That's a sign of hiding you know."

"I'm *not* hiding," I say defiantly.

"Come on. Really?" He lifts a brow in amusement. "Everyone who has seen you and Kayden together knows that there's something going on here."

I clamp my mouth shut. Surely it isn't that obvious . . . right? It's been hard trying to suppress the feelings I have for him, but are they really that evident? I think back to Kayden's words the other day at Breaking Point: *Your mask is immovable in that cage but outside of it, it's pretty easy to tell how you're feeling.*

I shake Evans's observation off, pushing off the chaise and beelining straight for the dressing room again. "Trust me. I assure you nothing is going to happen."

Evans just stares at me, writhing with humor. I shut the door then peel off the dress I have on and slip into the next one hanging on the rack.

"Come *on*. Everyone sees the way he looks at you. And you him. You guys are not fooling anybody," he says, his voice echoing through the dressing room. "I like that you're able to look past his flaws and see the good in him. But you aren't going to do a damn thing about it because you're afraid of how he makes you feel."

"You have no idea what's going on between us." I shake my head, stepping out and presenting what I'm wearing to Evans, giving a little twirl. "How about this dress?"

"Pass," he comments in a bored tone. I frown at him then disappear into the cubicle again, slip out of the dress, and loop it over the hanger. I do the same to the rest of the dresses that I tried on and have been piling on the floor. "And what exactly *is* going on between you?"

"I know he has his own shit to deal with, and I try to be understanding about it. But I can't be with someone who has secrets, Evans," I explain, peeking through the door and staring right at him, voice constricted. "I've been hurt badly by Jax. And it's not just because he cheated on me. I gave him the best three years of my life. *Three years*. And I'm starting to doubt that he really loved me at all that entire time. That's not something I can get over quickly."

The Beth and Jax thing has taught me that everyone has masks. Jax had his. And Kayden does too. What if that secret is the thing that will shatter his? Would I like the real him underneath?

Evans pulls the door wide open and I stumble back.

"But that's what falling for someone is, right?" He says, his head tilted to the side. "You gotta be vulnerable to *get* some vulnerability back. You just need to be patient with him. When he's ready, he'll tell you." Evans extends his hand to me, palm out, nodding at the large pile of clothing that I'm balancing on one arm. "You just need to trust him. And in return . . ." When I pass him the pile, he hands the bag that

I left sitting beside the chaise back to me. "He'll trust you."

"Trust." I choke back a laugh as I snatch the bag from him, a little too roughly. "Every time I do that, I somehow always end up hurt and fucked up. Maybe I'm just not good with emotions. They're messy."

"I think you're confusing them with your wardrobe," he jabs back as we walk out of the dressing rooms. I roll my eyes. A bored sales rep waits by the entrance, and when she spots us, extends her hands to receive all the discarded clothing. Evans, unsure of whether he should just give the entire pile to her, angles his body to me. "Do you know which one you want?"

I pluck the red dress out of the pile. "I think I'm gonna get this one."

"Perfect. It's my favorite too," Evans says, dropping the clothes into the sales rep's hands and patting his own hands on his jeans to find his wallet. "I'll get it for you. As a gift."

"Sweet," I coo. Evans slings an arm around my shoulder and pulls me close as we navigate through the maze of racks to get to the counter. I drop my head against his shoulder, liking this new bond. As much as I loathed being Evans's mannequin for the day, I really did enjoy getting to know the man behind the player archetype that he clearly likes to box himself into.

"So are gonna take my advice?" I ask. "Are you going to trust your feelings for Brent and embrace them, regardless of what your parents might think?"

"Only if you learn to trust your feelings for Kayden and embrace them, regardless of what Jax did to you," Evans says.

I look away. "I don't know, it's a bit too soon for that."

"Fine," he says. "Baby steps then. Trusting is a process. So just learn to trust *someone*."

I chuck him my dress. "Do you count as someone?"

"You should not trust me. I'm such a bad gossip." He takes the dress gladly and slaps it onto the cash counter along with his credit card.

"You and Brent truly belong together," I mutter under my breath.

TWENTY

I don't know why, but Evans's advice sticks with me throughout the next day. Maybe it's because I've been feeling guilty about how I blew Alyson off. She seemed nice—nicer than the rest of Dad's previous wives, anyway—which makes it even worse. I know she didn't deserve me being so cold, and to be honest, I think I'm more upset at my dad than with her.

Trusting is a process. So just learn to trust someone.

Alyson should be given a fair chance, irrespective of my dad. I promised Evans I was going to put my faith and trust in someone, and maybe she's just the person to do that with.

And maybe that's why I'm here, standing in front of the bridal shop, debating with myself about whether I should go in. I don't know why I'm hesitant now, since an hour ago, I was more than willing to set aside my ego to call my dad and ask for the bridal shop address.

Fortunately for me, the decision is effectively stolen from me when Alyson spots me from the inside. She scutters over in a modest white midi dress with a pink sash that says "Bride To Be" in gold. She throws open the door, eyes lighting up in excitement, and ropes me into a big hug. I pat her on the back awkwardly.

"I'm so glad you could make it!" She beams at me.

She grabs my hand and drags me into the shop where there is a large sofa with several women squashed together, chattering excitedly and clinking champagne glasses. When they spot me, they shoot up from their seats and smile brightly at me in greeting.

"These are my bridesmaids." She gestures to everyone as she pulls me along the line of women.

"Nice to meet you girls." I wave a small hand at each of them.

"You're gorgeous!" One of the bridesmaids gasps as her hands cup the blades of my shoulders, her eyes trace the length of my body. "And so *toned!*"

"Sienna is an MMA trainer. And a very good one at that." Alyson shares proudly. She pulls me from her bridesmaid's grasp and hauls me in the direction of the changing room. "Go on in. I'll bring you your dress."

I wait for Alyson in one of the cubicles, sitting on the stool while clicking my feet together. A few minutes later, she slips through the crack in the curtains into the cubicle, and grins when she shows me the dress.

"Thought you might like this," she says, propping the dress over her arm. "Classy. Sleek. A little sexy. The perfect dress for my perfect bridesmaid."

It's beautiful all right, no question. It's a burgundy satin cowl dress with a modest slit down the side; the fabric looks soft to the touch and the cut of the dress would probably be flattering on my body shape.

"Wow, you really outdid yourself," I say in awe as I take the hanger from her, careful not to drape the bottom of the dress on the floor. "This is really pretty."

"Glad you like it," she murmurs, smiling at my approval of the dress. "I want you two girlies to shine just as brightly as the other bridesmaids on my wedding day."

Girlies?

Beth pops her head into the changing room. "Hey, Sienna."

Of course.

Alyson's gaze zips between us. Sensing the tension, she pulls open the curtain to let herself out. "I'll—uh, leave you two alone."

Beth steps into the room. I ignore her, looping the hanger over the hook to keep me busy. She pouts at my silence, her hands linked tightly together. "Please. You can't stay mad at me forever."

"I think you underestimate how long I can hold grudges."

"But you gave Alyson a chance," she asserts.

"That's different. She didn't sleep with my boyfriend, Beth." I snap my head toward her, irritation prickling my skin.

"Look, I'm sorry. I really am." A frown curves over her mouth. "The past few weeks living without you have been hell. And I . . . I really miss you."

The irritation momentarily dissipates and I bite my lip, preventing the *I miss you too* from slipping out of my mouth. Because it's true. As much as I hate to admit it, I've been carrying around a deep ache in my chest ever since I moved in with Kayden. I've never gone this long without talking to her, and it feels like a part of me is missing when we don't. But my pride has already set up camp in that gap, rendering it difficult to admit all those feelings to her.

"Then you probably shouldn't have done what you did," I mutter.

"I'm really sorry, Si." She rushes toward me wearing those sad eyes. "I can't help it. I just . . ." She braves a shaky hand through her hair. "I love him. I know it's senseless and stupid to love him but I do. And he loves me too."

Oh God, not this again.

"I assure you, he does not," I tell her sharply. "He's a vindictive, manipulative asshole and he'll ruin you. Just like he ruined me."

Beth shakes her head timidly. "He's kind to me."

"They always are. In the beginning."

"He's different," she insists.

Why is she so stubborn about him?

Though I guess it makes sense—I was the same with Jax all those years ago too. To me, everything he said was pure witchcraft. He could have told me he was a serial killer and I probably would have been fully committed to a murder spree with him.

"What kind of spell does he have you under, Beth?" I ask, and she looks away, mashing her lips together in annoyance. I grasp both her arms and force her gaze to meet mine. "Listen to me: Jax is not who you think he is. He's just using you. I saw him at a fight and he admitted it to me. Right after he declared his love for me and begged for a second chance. He might have you believing that he loves you and wants to be with you, but they're all lies. That's *all* he's capable of doing: lying."

Beth wrenches my hands from her and covers her body with her arms, shielding it from me. "That's not true."

"Fine, don't believe me. Your loss," I say dryly. "I'm just trying to protect you."

"I don't need your protection." She snaps back.

"Oh really?" I say with loud huff. "I haven't seen you around campus for a while now. I'm guessing you've been skipping classes? What's Dad going to think about that when he finds out?"

"Like you said before. Dad doesn't care about us," Beth says quietly.

"He only cares about me when it's convenient," I correct her. "But he cares about *you*. And he wants you to do well in school."

"I haven't been going because I've been busy."

"With Jax no doubt," I mutter.

Hurt crosses her eyes.

"Stop it, Si."

"No, I won't," I say, wrought with determination. "I'm *not* going to stop because you aren't seeing past him and his lies."

"Well, that's for me to decide, isn't it?" Beth counters.

"Oh, for the love of—" I tear my hands through my hair, frustrated. I just can't get through to her.

I don't even think there's a way *to* get through to her. She's going through the same thing I did years ago, and I know there was no way anyone could have talked me out of loving Jax then. Not even my friends or family. I held on because I was so sure that nobody else could see what I saw—that *they* were the ones who were blind, not me.

"It's useless trying to convince you," I say, spinning away from her and toward the full-length mirror. "Please go."

This time, Beth doesn't put up a fight. I watch her in the reflection as she lets out an aggravated huff and retreats from the changing room.

When I emerge from the cubicle a couple of minutes later, Alyson rises from the chair, noticing my distraught expression.

"Sienna? Is everything okay?"

"The dress fits. Can't wait to wear it on the wedding day," I say flatly, holding the dress out to her. Alyson takes it hesitantly, her eyes oozing with concern. My gaze flickers to Beth, who's standing awkwardly next to the sofa, then back to Alyson again. "I can't stay for the rest of this. I'm not feeling well. So I'm gonna split."

Her face drops in disappointment.

"Oh, all right then."

Guilt snakes around my throat. The point of me coming here was to try to be open minded about her being a constant presence in our family and trying to form some kind of relationship with her. I can't let it end like this. I won't forgive myself if I do.

"But let's have lunch sometime," I offer instead. "You know where I work."

Hope returns to her eyes. She nods in agreement. "I'd like that very much, Sienna."

As I retreat from the store, I stop in my tracks abruptly,

the ugly feeling of leaving things with Beth in such a harsh way gnawing at me like a leech. I need to do whatever I can to help her get out of her delusion. Even if she won't listen to me. Even if she dismisses me. Maybe if she hears my advice enough, she'll start to let those words in.

Before I can think twice about it, I twist back and trudge toward her.

"Beth, whatever you do, please don't let Jax burn you," I say to my sister. "He's done his damage and look how I turned out. Whatever you do, don't let him *win*."

***

By the time I make it up the elevator to the apartment, I'm mentally exhausted. Hearing Beth talk about Jax roused such a temper inside of me that had been difficult to keep in check. And the worst part is, I let Alyson get caught in the middle of all of this drama. It definitely disappointed her that I couldn't stay longer for the bridesmaids' fitting but she did seem understanding of my plight when I left. My excuse was flimsy at best but she knew not to press me about it. And I'm grateful for that.

Which reminds me of something else I have to do.

I slide my phone from my pocket and shoot a text to Evans when I reach the outside of my apartment.

Trusted a person today. Baby steps. You owe me

Barely ten seconds later, my phone pings with a reply.

My debt's already been paid

No. Way. Him and Brent? I type back frantically.

What do you mean? Parents???

Came to visit today. As I predicted, it didn't go well

I frown at his text. I know all too well how disappointing parents can be.

I'm sorry

It's fine. Decided then and there that I wanted to be in control of my own choices. So I took your advice and told them to shove it. And then . . .

A couple of seconds later, he sends a picture. I open it and a wide smile forms on my lips. It's a photo of Brent and Evans lying on the couch together eating chips, with Brent's head on top of Evans's chest. They're smiling up at the camera. The contentment and happiness that they feel radiates through the picture and unfurls across my body.

I'm happy for you two. My two favorite people. Let's celebrate after semifinals

<3

I turn to the side, my gaze stretching as I think about the two of them finally allowing themselves to be together, no longer having their problems tying them down. I wonder if it's even possible for me to experience that. I don't exactly carry the lightest of baggage.

"What's got you smiling, Lucky?" Kayden says as he leans against the door frame. He's staring smugly at me. "I take it today went well?"

"Shit." I let out a yelp, almost dropping my keys. "You scared me."

"Saw you standing outside for ten minutes. Thought you needed a little refresher on how to open the door."

"You were peeping at me for ten minutes? And there you were just a few weeks ago accusing me of being a stalker."

Kayden opens his mouth to protest but no excuses leave his mouth. I push past him to get inside, grinning as he locks the door behind us.

"So bridesmaids' dress fitting," he prods eagerly.

It's cute that he's curious about everything that goes on in my life. I oblige him most of the time. But that's more than I can say about him when I'm the one doing the prodding.

"Yeah, it was a disaster. Beth was there. And that's all you need to know. I don't really want to get into the details," I say as I fall onto the couch, relieved that I'm home. Kayden follows, making himself comfortable in the available spot beside me. I use the opportunity to shove my phone screen at his face. "But look what Evans just sent me."

Kayden takes the phone in his grasp, squinting at the screen. "Wow," he says with a twitch of his lips. "I'm glad they made up. Brent's a good guy. And they deserve to be happy."

"Glad to see that you're easing up on your best friend and brother dating."

"They're good for each other," he notes distinctly. "So you'd really rather not talk about bridesmaids' dress fitting? I've been hoping for something juicy."

"Nope. I'm not caving. Deal with it."

"Fine," he grumbles.

"How was training today?" I ask instead, clearing a couple of the empty mugs that are strewn across his newly purchased coffee table. I had him pick one up the other day because I was sick of not having a place to eat food when I want to watch TV.

"It was all right," Kayden answers, crossing his legs

casually as he watches me amble to the kitchen to put the dishes in the sink. "Probably would have been better if you were there."

I turn my head, wearing a funny smile. "You can just admit that you missed me today, you know."

"All right." He gives in, staring back at me with an amused smile of his own. "I did miss you. And I'm happy you're back."

"Glad to know that I'm appreciated around here," I say, pretending to wipe sweat off my forehead like I'm really working hard to wash these dishes. "I'm starving. And I'm done with the prep meals. Please make me some fresh food."

"Fine." He picks himself up off the couch and joins me in the kitchen. He pries open the refrigerator door and hauls onto one arm several containers of ingredients. He slaps them onto the counter and turns to me. "Today on the menu we have chicken breast, cherry tomatoes, brown rice, and broccoli with minimal seasoning."

"I hate eating clean with you," I moan.

"Come. Cook with me." He gives the sleeve of my shirt a hard tug. "So you can make some yourself when I'm not around."

"Now why would I do that? You're my very own personal chef."

He gives me a *really?* look and I sigh, wiping my wet hands on the kitchen towel. I should probably start helping around, since lately he's been cooking all my meals. To be fair, he's always the one asking if I need to be fed, and after a full day of classes and a couple of training sessions at either UFG or Breaking Point, I usually jump at the offer.

"Fine. I'll help," I say, giving in. "What do you want me to do?"

"I'll give you something simple. The only thing you need to do is cook the rice." He opens the top cabinet and hands me the packet of rice with a knot tied at the top. "I'll handle everything else."

Ten minutes later, I'm staring silently at the rice cooking in the tiny pot, waiting for the water to start fizzing with bubbles.

"This is boring." I pout childishly, my attention moving to Kayden, who has taken the noble task of pan frying the mixture of broccoli and chicken cubes. "Can we put on some music? Give me your phone. I want to judge your Spotify." He nods, grunting at the phone he's left beside the stove. I reach for it, inputting the password he recites to me, and scroll through his playlist. I snort loudly when I see what's on his most played. "Oh God, Guns N' Roses? You're so basic."

"Says the hardcore Ed Sheeran fan," he fires back and my body freezes. *How does he know that?* "Yeah, that's right. You're not very discreet when you sing in the shower."

"What?" I pretend not to be embarrassed. "'Shape of You' helps me lather, rinse, and repeat."

"You're kidding." He hoots a laugh, covering his face with his hands out of shame for me. "If you like that trashy song, I think I'm entitled to a little Guns N' Roses."

"All right. If you insist," I say, a ridiculous smile forming on my face when I press Play on "Sweet Child O' Mine." And in my most villainous voice, I hiss out "Dance for me, monkey. Dance!"

"I mean, if you say so."

Kayden does a little awkward body wriggle followed by a moonwalk. Although he's been getting better at his footwork, I can't say the same about his own dance moves. He's so bad it looks like he's trying to be bad on purpose, but he's really *just that bad*. I try to hold my laugh in but that only lasts for five seconds before a stream of laughter bursts out of me and I'm bending over, my hands clutching my knees.

"Oh God," I say, grinning as a tear breaks free from my eye. "You're adorable, Kayden. Like a little puppy."

"*Oof.*" He clutches his chest as if he's in pain. "Way to bruise my ego."

"It's a compliment." I defend myself.

Kayden shakes his head. "A compliment is when you brag about how ripped a guy looks, how he makes you wanna throw yourself at him, how big his dick is—"

"And how can I possibly say that when I've never even seen Kayden junior?"

"Kayden Junior? *Junior?*" He stares at me like I just insulted his entire family lineage with those words alone. "I assure you, Lucky, there's nothing junior about it."

I merely smirk. "I guess I'll never know unless I see it."

"Maybe you will, maybe you won't," he says, his voice low and coarse.

We're staring at each other now, our bodies so close that I can feel his body heat. Kayden's gaze dips slightly, landing on my lips, and like a fool, I lick them, tongue stroking my bottom lip slowly. *Yeah, I'm totally seducing him back and I'm not even being subtle about it.* He sucks in a breath through his teeth. His eyes—now darkened to an almost smoky charcoal color—return to my face, weighted with so much lust that makes my heart feel like it's about to have an aneurysm. I'm suddenly aware of the swelling of my breasts, the loud *thump, thump, thump* of my heart and my breath coming out in heavy, unsteady spurts.

Do not purse your lips. I repeat: DO NOT purse your lips—

It is only the unexpectedly loud crackle of the pan that forces us out of our trance.

"So, um." I step back, forcing my gaze away from him. "Food."

"Right. Food." He clears his throat and returns his attention to the stove.

We stew in the awkward silence for a good few minutes more until lunch has been cooked, then silence ourselves some more as we sit opposite each other at the dining table and munch away, our eyes never leaving each other. I can't seem to look at him for longer than a couple of seconds before feeling the sensation of my cheeks turning pink.

What. Is. Happening?!

When we're both done with lunch and the dishes, Kayden clears his throat and announces, "All right. I'm gonna hop in the shower real quick."

"Cold?" I blurt before I have the chance to stuff the word back in.

His unflinching gaze snaps to me.

"Hot," he says, a dangerous glint in his eyes. "Steeping, scorching *hot*."

I think my underwear just disintegrated.

"I'm . . . gonna take a nap before our session tonight," I mutter quickly before hurrying to my room.

When I've changed into a more comfortable T-shirt and shorts, I fall into bed and try to get some sleep. It's been an exhausting first half of the day and I'm dying to squeeze in a bit of rest before a grueling one and a half hours of drills tonight.

Just when I feel like I'm starting to doze off, I hear Kayden step into the bathroom and shut the door behind him. And before he hops into the shower—

He blasts "Shape of You" from his phone.

I turn over in my bed, unable to stop the silly grin blooming on my face.

Fuck me.

I think I'm falling in love with Kayden.

And the worse part is . . .

I don't want to stop.

TWENTY-ONE

Saturday arrives and Breaking Point is closed for the semi-finals. Spectators pile in from the back exit, eagerly waiting to get their cut in on the fighters who are gonna survive to-night. The four of us split, with Evans and Brent headed to the deck while Kayden and I head to the back corridor to prep.

Fighters lurk all around us, doing their prefight rituals; some of them are listening to music or resting, while others are shadowboxing in the corner to get their adrenaline going. Kayden just leans his hip against the wall, huge arms crossed over his bare chest as he watches them with critical eyes.

Jax is nowhere to be seen, as usual. He despised hanging with the others, always under the impression that he was above everyone else, hating the thought of exposing any possible weaknesses he had.

"Why don't you have a ritual?" I ask as I approach

Kayden with the boxing wraps. "Hands out. "

He obliges me, extending one hand, palm up, and allowing me to wrap the tape over it.

"I do." His gaze slides to me. "I just try not to think too much."

"But that's a default." I go over his knuckles a couple of rounds just for safety, strap it into place on the wrist, then repeat the same process on the other hand. He stretches his hands to get a feel for the tension and then drops them to his sides. I take the opportunity to prod him again. "How about all that other weird shit? Like slapping yourself? Withholding sex? Tweaking your own nipples?"

The corner of Kayden's mouth kicks up at my suggestion. "Tweaking my own *nipples*?"

"Georges St-Pierre. Said it helped bring him good luck."

A low rumble vibrates from his throat.

"Whatever gets him the win, right?" He says, watching me as I take a step back. He nods to me, beckoning. "What was Jax's?"

I bite my lip in contemplation. "I don't think I should say."

"Why not? Does it involve you?" Kayden's eyes flare with alarm. "It was copious amounts of sex wasn't it? He seems like the kind of guy who would do that before a fight. Come on, Lucky. Tell me."

"I won't because I'm not in the business of getting you fired up against him tonight," I tell him. "You gotta focus on Lee."

"Come on," he whines playfully. "If you don't want to tell me, just blink once for yes and twice for no."

I shake my head, feigning a ridiculous smile. As much as I find the jealousy endearing, there are more important matters at hand.

"Let it go, Killer."

"Fine," Kayden mutters.

"Remember. Look at his feet to know how he'll throw."

He nods. "I'll find you in the crowd."

"You better."

And we leave it at that. When I return to the front where all the action is about to happen, I spot Brent beckoning me over. I squeeze through the sweaty bodies, bumping into several bookies still trying to catch last-minute bets.

The announcer does his usual prologue, announcing the four fighters taking the cage tonight, starting with Kayden and East's fight. Both fighters emerge from the shadows, taking their places on opposite sides of the cage. East does a little show on his own, forming his hands into claws while emitting predatory bird noises from his mouth.

The crowd roars in anticipation, chanting "Killer! Killer! Killer!" repeatedly as Kayden walks over to his side of the cage. He isn't showboaty tonight. He's serious, urgent in the way that he moves as he shrugs off his robe and gets into his stance.

A shiver runs along my spine as the women all around me shriek and hoot eagerly at him. I glare at one of them a couple of feet away from me and shouting at Kayden to *something* her up in her *something* and she will *something something* to him tonight.

I'm guessing she wasn't inviting him on a very friendly outing to catch a Boston Bruins game.

217

"Hey!" I jerk my head in her direction, jealousy getting me right in the gut. "*Beat it.*"

The women stares at me blankly before muttering how crazy I am and walking away.

Calm down, Sienna. I try to convince myself. *You can't get jealous. He's not yours.*

Kayden's gaze scans the crowd, his eyes searching the sea of people for mine. When he finally sees me, he casts me a crooked smile, and my heart leaps out of my throat and into the clouds.

Kayden redirects his focus back to the cage. He circles East, his face is as fierce and predatory as that of a mountain lion hunting his prey. East wastes no time in diving in first, going straight for a kick to Kayden's ribs. Kayden sidesteps him only to catch a spinning kick from East on the rebound. Kayden recoils, shrugging off the blow and countering with a classic jab-cross-hook combo. East blocks the first two punches, and ducks under the third, slightly shifting his left foot forward.

There's that tell, I think to myself.

Kayden notices it, too, because he's ready for East's right roundhouse. In an expertly choreographed counter, Kayden catches the fighter's kick, gives it a hard tug to unbalance him, and pulls him in closer into Kayden's real attack—a reverse back elbow crunching into East's face.

Now on the offensive, Kayden surges forward, body ringing with smooth confidence.

From the corner of my eye, I spot Jax on the top deck of the building. He's right at the front and has some wriggle room to pace around as he watches the fight. Then, slowly, as if he can sense exactly where I am in the crowd, those dark, cunning eyes zero in on me.

A deadly smile coils around Jax's mouth.

I force a tight smile back, along with two middle fingers shoved in his direction before turning my attention back to Kayden.

He's looking straight at me, his momentary lapse in concentration giving East an opening as he sweeps Kayden's legs out from under him. They both collide on the ground.

"Focus, Kayden!" I yell, snapping his full attention back to East.

Right on cue, Kayden manages to get East straight into his closed guard and locks him into an armbar from the bottom position, then pulls hard.

East taps out meekly.

The audience is bleeding with cheers and chants as Kayden is declared the winner.

When he's quickly whisked away, I crane my neck to see where he's going and if I should go and find him.

"Kayden?" I shout as I watch him get swallowed up by the crowd. "*Kayden!*"

It's difficult to hear anything in here but somehow, he does. His head whips back to me, desperate eyes seeking me out as he pushes through the other way to get to me. But before he's able to reach my corner, the host cuts in with his microphone to announce the next fight.

"The moment you've been waiting for: your reigning champion, the savage of beasts, Jax 'Deadbeat' Deneris!"

Jax barrels through the crowd like an animal as he pumps his fists in the air. The crowd goes berserk at his entrance, hands reaching out to touch him like he's some kind of God who just ended world hunger.

"*DEAD-BEAT! DEAD-BEAT! DEAD-BEAT!*" They chant like zombies.

When he finally climbs into the cage, his opponent is looking impatient. Fists ready in front of them, stances formed and the second the bell rings—

BAM! Jax lands a forceful punch straight on his opponent's face and he collapses.

There is a loud, collective gasp from the crowd.

"Oh *shit*!" The announcer yells. "Ladies and gentlemen, I think we have a TKO!"

Murmurs and whispers emit from the crowd, with people in the back pushing us closer to the cage to see what has happened.

Meanwhile, the man in the cage doesn't move. He just lies limply on the floor while Jax beats his fists, basking in the victory of his knockout.

***

"Holy shit!" Brent clamps a hand over his mouth.

"Is he dead?" Evans gasps in horror.

Two in-house paramedics rush into the cage. One of them checks for a pulse on the fighter's neck. The audience falls into an eerie silence as we wait. My heart thunders against my chest, nerves spiking in anticipation. What if Jax did kill that guy? It would be unbelievably tragic—

But at least he'll end up in jail.

That's better than any kind of revenge that I'd ever come

up with. And the best part is I wouldn't even have to do a single thing.

No, Sienna. You're sick. You want him dead just so your ex can go to prison? What kind of person does that make you?

I suppress a shudder at those twisted, corrupted thoughts. Purging them from my mind, I shove my attention back to the paramedics, waiting impatiently for any kind of signal from them. And I'm not the only one; it feels like every person in this basement is holding their breath for a good outcome.

Finally, the paramedic raises a thumbs-up. A wave of relief sweeps through the crowd.

Jax spins in Kayden's direction. He points to the limp body then to Kayden, and grins maliciously, as if saying *That's gonna be you soon.*

I whirl around to find Kayden's expression going completely rigid. He shoves his way out of the crowd and disappears in the direction of the exit. I follow him, matching his pace so I don't lose sight of him, and when I'm out of the gym, I find Kayden pacing back and forth on the sidewalk anxiously.

"Kayden." I step into his path and hold him steady, clutching his shoulders. "Kayden, calm *down.*"

He pushes my arms away in frustration, raising his hands to cup the sides of his head. "I can't beat him, Sienna. I can't. Did you not see what just happened?"

"Yes, I did," I say. "But you'll be fine. You won against Lee."

"Yeah. Barely. I made some sloppy mistakes in there," Kayden says, his throat clogging up. The vein in his forehead pulses when he squeezes his eyes shut. "I just couldn't focus."

"Why?"

His eyes slowly peel open. They are now bright with tenderness as they roam my face. "You know why."

I step back, swallowing hard. *I guess I do.*

This has *to end. Get him to focus, Sienna!*

"Okay, listen to me," I snap. "This is *exactly* what Jax wants: for you to get scared. Let's not give him the satisfaction. I have faith in you. But you need to have faith in yourself, otherwise it won't work and this deal will be for nothing."

Kayden doesn't answer.

He devours my eyes with his own, wanting badly to believe me, but it just doesn't quite reach him. I know him enough by now to anticipate that when he's in doubt, he retreats. He's going to go back to his hiding spot and shut me out.

I'll be damned if I let him do that to me again.

I'm not giving up on him. Not now, not ever.

"You're stronger than that, Kayden. And you. Can. Do. This," I say, pinning his eyes with distinct focus. "You're not going down without a fight. I won't let you. Okay? Everyone's out there fighting for something. You must be too. What are you fighting for? *Who* are you fighting for?"

His expression falters. "Sienna . . ."

His body stiffens in discomfort, denoting a sore topic, and I know better than to push him. In the end, I decide to drop it. "It's okay. You don't have to tell me. But at least let me ask you this: Is it still worth fighting for?"

No muscle in his face reacts to my question. He's immobile, swimming in his own thoughts.

Eventually, he lets out a slow, long exhale.

"Yes."

"Good." I sigh in relief. An idea rings through my head. An idea that might cost me my job but I have to at least give it a shot. "I have an idea. But it's gonna take some convincing."

"What are you talking about?"

"You need someone who has fought Jax before. And won," I say, pressing a hand against his back to guide him toward the truck. "Let's go."

***

"No." Julian roars, hitting a fist on the table. "Absolutely fucking not."

"Come on. Just hear me out." I plead with him.

I have to admit, this is probably not the best time to have this conversation. It's past midnight and Julian was in the midst of locking up the gym when I dragged him back into his office and caught him up with what's been happening with Jax. I told Kayden to wait outside while I tried to reason with my boss.

So far, it's not going as well as I'd hoped.

"I *did* hear you out, Sienna." Julian shakes his head. "And I'm not doing it."

"Why not?"

"Why?" He echoes sharply. "For starters, I don't train anymore. It's not worth it. Not after Jax when he bailed. Two, I have a gym to run, so I've got my hands full already. And three: I don't fuck with the underground. If I get caught training someone associated with it, we could lose the gym.

And you can say good-bye to you running it in the future."

He snaps his chair back under the table and tries to leave the office but I block his path, holding my hands out in front of me.

"Okay, I get all that, Julian, but I really do think it's worth the risk." I plead with him. "It's only an hour or two every day. You can train Kayden after hours if you don't want anyone knowing that he's training here. It's worth it, Jules. He's one of the best fighters around and you know that. And he can take down Jax. Don't you want that?"

Julian sucks in a breath through his teeth. I can tell I've hit a nerve. "Why the hell would I want that?"

"Because you're still angry that he bailed on you," I tell him. "I know how that feels like. And I know it hurts like hell."

"Oh no. You don't get to play that card with me. I'm not like you," he shoots back, and his words dig into me, twisting my insides. "I don't like to hold grudges. And . . . I've let it go."

There's a slight falter in his words that I cling to, using it as ammunition. It's the only thing I've got.

"Come on. You've always been salty about Jax. And I get it. He was your golden boy. You trained him in hopes he would go pro and bring recognition to UFG, but instead he *abandoned* you and threw it in your face by going under too," I say, and Julian grows quiet. Contemplative. For a second there I think I might just convince him, but as he releases a sigh and opens his mouth to answer, I can tell I'm about to lose him. "Okay, fine. Don't do it for revenge. Do it for me. Do it for my *sister*. I don't know what he's doing to Beth but I know he's still with her. And I can only imagine the damage. I don't want her to end up like me. He needs to be stopped, Julian. *Please.*"

Julian senses my distress. His eyes soften with sympathy.

"And what are you gonna do if I don't agree to help you?" He asks pointedly.

"I guess I'll continue training him at Point."

That stirs up his temper again.

"That's where you've been this month? Are you *kidding*?" His eyes flare with contained fury. He starts pacing back and forth behind his table, then grips the back of his chair hard. "Look, the last thing I want to do is to dictate what you do during your free time but you do realize you training an underground fighter there could potentially get people talking about you and your ethics, right?" He mutters a string of curse words before hissing, "You're fucking killing me, Sienna."

My heart aches to see just how frustrated and angry he is with me right now. I've never been shy about pissing people off, but Julian hasn't given me any reason to do that to him.

And yet, I still don't stop with the hounding.

"My reputation has already been tainted by associating myself with Jax before this. And this time is no different," I explain. "I'm sorry, but I have to do this. You know what Jax did. I need to see this through. And it's only for another three weeks, I swear. And after that, you don't ever have to see Kayden again if you don't want to."

A muscle twitches on Julian's face. He grits his teeth, probably hating himself for what he's about to say next.

"All right, fine. I'm doing this because I care about you." He cuts me a cross look. "But you have to listen to me: after this shit, after you get what you want, I want you to *stay out* of the underground. It's not healthy for you. And you're a good trainer. I don't want your reputation tarnished just because you're dealing with them. So promise me you won't go back after this."

Julian has never asked me to do anything apart from work obligations. So if he's asking this of me, I know he's only looking for my best interests. I do want to strengthen his trust in me and make him proud someday.

"I promise," I say, nodding vigorously. "I won't let you down."

Julian lets out a defeated sigh. "Tell him to get in here."

I push past the door and hold it open to let Kayden in. He shoots up from the bench eagerly and saunters into the office.

"Sir," Kayden says with a kind of modesty that I've never seen in him before. He extends a hand to Julian. "It's an honor to meet you—"

"Yeah, yeah, whatever. Just sit the fuck down and listen to me, boy." Julian gestures to the chair and Kayden plops down submissively. "We train before and after hours, six days a week. Six in the morning and ten at night. You arrive and leave through the back door and you leave nothing behind. I don't want anyone here knowing I'm affiliated with an underground fighter. You understand me?"

Kayden gulps. "Yes, sir."

"Tell me, what's your reason for wanting to take down Jax?"

"I just need to," he says.

Silence.

I meet Julian's gaze with a shrug. "He's doesn't like to share much."

"No shit," he grunts. "All right. Keep your reasons to yourself. As long as you give me your commitment and leave your ego at the door. Because for the next three weeks, I'm gonna break you."

Kayden leans forward, resting his arms over his thighs. He looks up at Julian with determined grit. "I can take it."

"We'll see about that." Julian huffs. "Six o'clock tomorrow. If you're late, we're canceling the whole thing and you fend off Jax on your own."

"Got it."

Kayden spins back and sends Julian a ridiculous military salute. Julian rolls his eyes, fighting off a small smile slanting across his face.

TWENTY-TWO

"What kind of sloppy offence is this, Killer?" Julian spits out as he lands a solid kick to Kayden's arm, weakening it. As Julian reels back, exposing his midsection, Kayden dives in but not before Julian slams a Muay Thai clinch into place, locking his arms around Kayden's neck. Kayden struggles to get free as Julian slams his knee repeatedly into his torso, eliciting an agonizing groan from him.

Just as Julian is about to kick in for the fourth time, Kayden launches a straight punch at him, trying to catch him off guard, but Julian easily dodges. Retaliating, Julian launches a vicious low kick at Kayden's knee, but at the last second, Kayden reels his leg back and goes for a front push kick, throwing Julian back. I smile to myself, pride bursting from within me at that good footwork. They scramble into position again, a thick sheen of sweat already covering their ripped bodies.

I'm watching from the sidelines, shoving a torn piece of

doughnut into my mouth and chewing with delight. If I'm waking up at six in the morning at least it'll be to see two half-naked dudes going at it with each other in a cage.

Kayden's eyes flicker briefly toward me. I raise him a thumbs-up and he smiles briefly through the sweat. A tired but rugged smile pops one of his dimples.

Ah fuck.

Sadly, the smile is short lived when he spots Julian barreling toward him.

"Focus!" Julian yells, snapping Kayden's attention back.

They trade blows a few times, both expertly dodging and landing hits in the right places. Kayden anticipates a blow to the head, defenses going up quickly, but—*too late*! Julian feints and takes Kayden down, scrambling into position. Immediately, Kayden covers his face with his arms as Julian pounds on him from above.

"What are you doing?" Julian yells. "You're not getting out of this position by doing this kinda bullshit."

Kayden grits his teeth in pain, his arms absorbing the blows as he struggles against Julian. He's reaching and grabbing for anything of Julian's but is unable to find the opening. Eventually, after making way too many hits to the head, Julian pries himself off of him.

Kayden drops his head to the ground in defeat.

I scramble toward him, snatching a towel and a bottle of water from the benches before climbing into the cage.

"Here," I say, passing him the items. Kayden sprays half the bottle of water over his face and sloppily cleans it up with a towel.

"What the hell have you been teaching him?" Julian cuts

a glare at me. "He barely lasted a couple of minutes in that cage."

"I taught him all that I know from you."

"Which is surprisingly little for someone who's been working here for years now," he mutters, throwing his gloves to the ground. He turns toward Kayden. "You have potential, kid. I see it in you. But it's like you're not completely in it. You're distracted. Stop fighting with your heart and start thinking with your goddamned mind instead."

Kayden merely groans, pulling his arms over his eyes.

I squat on the ground so I'm eye level with him. "Kayden, you need to listen to him."

"I'm trying," he says sharply.

"Not nearly enough," Julian says, wiping sweat off his brow. "Getting out of that mount was difficult, yes, but not impossible. You just have to retain your focus and find the weakness. Lesson number one: you always have more control of the situation than you think. Get into position again. I'll show you."

Kayden throws the towel and bottle to the side and lies on the ground. Julian straps his MMA gloves on and climbs into position, hovering over Kayden.

"Your first instinct should be to get some kind of upper body control. Use your legs to bump me and make me base out. Your opponent—me—will be off balance now." Kayden does what Julian says then locks his ankles together around Julian's legs. "Good. You come at me from an angle, not straight on. I'll be resisting, which means you have to switch to either side of my body to gain the upper hand. Disengage. Use your hips to escape to the other side and re-entangle. Now you've got a good opening to attack."

He struggles against Julian, jerking his body side to side while retaining a firm defense. As Julian predicted, he has the upper hand now. If Kayden can keep his opponent busy enough, he might just be able to get out of that grapple.

Julian pushes off of Kayden. "See? You can fucking do it. So why don't you?"

Kayden pulls himself into a sitting position, resting his arms over his bent knees. His gaze slides toward me briefly before falling back to the ground again. If you weren't paying attention, you'd hardly notice it. But Julian does.

Julian trudges over toward me and pulls me to the other side.

"What the hell did you do to the guy?" He demands.

"Nothing." I knit my brows in confusion. "What are you talking about?"

Julian sighs, rubbing a hand over his mouth. I have a feeling I'm not going to like what he has to say. And sure enough . . .

"I need you to leave."

"You're kicking me out?" I say, baffled. "Why?"

"You motivate him." He nods in Kayden's direction. "I know you do. Hell, if you weren't here, he'd probably do a lot worse. That boy has a heart of a lion and you *live* in his heart. So I need to see him spar when you're not around." He notices my fallen expression and adds, "It's not permanent, Sienna."

As much as I want to stand here and argue with him, deep down I know Julian's right about this.

"Fine. I get it," I say. "I'll go."

I feel both Julian's and Kayden's gazes searing my back as I head to the benches to grab my things. Kayden climbs out of the cage and jogs over to me. He presses a hand on my shoulder to still me, shaking his head.

"I don't like this," he says. "Don't go."

"It'll only be for a while," I assure him, looping my bag over my body. I pat his arm reassuringly. "You got this."

"Come on, kid," Julian calls, waving him over. "Let's go again."

Kayden looks torn, his gaze flickering back and forth between me and Julian. Eventually, he relents, walking back over to the cage as he lets me go.

***

I have to admit, it feels weird not having anything to do while Kayden trains with his new trainer. I feel replaced, and I know I don't have any right to feel that given that I was the one who recommended him to Julian in the first place, but it's unsettling no longer having this purpose that's been keeping me going for the past few weeks. So it's hard to focus on anything else while I try to imagine how Kayden is doing without me. No doubt he's in far better hands with Julian taking over, but I wish I was still there with him, offering some of my input alongside Julian's.

And to be honest, I just want to see Kayden. I hate that I already miss him. It's an odd feeling to have for someone I've adamantly decided to chuck in the friend zone.

Needing a break from boring solitary midterm prep in the library for an upcoming paper later today, I pop over to Brent's dorm room before lunch. Evans is already there, having slept over after pulling an all-nighter in the library. Brent looks tired too, if the stacks of revision papers and notes cluttering his desk is any indication. They had been relieved to hear I was stopping by so they could catch a break along with me. I let both of them talk about their spring break plans, which consist of a luxurious staycation at a suite at the Ritz-Carlton with a reservation to a French fine-dining restaurant.

"How do you have the funds for this?" I ask them, tossing one of Brent's throw pillows in Evans's direction.

Brent and I are both sitting cross-legged on his bed while Evans takes his place on the desk chair, reclining it back and resting his head on it. He catches the pillow midair and chucks it straight at me, landing it in my lap. I plant my elbows firmly on it, hands cupping my chin, leaning forward.

"He's a trust fund baby." Brent answers the question for his boyfriend, propping his arms behind him.

"Well, not anymore." Evans corrects his boyfriend, misery coating his face. "Remember that day when my parents came to visit and I told them I was seeing Brent?" I nod in remembrance. "As I expected, they threatened to cut me off if I don't break up with him."

"Shit. What are you gonna do?" I ask.

"Well . . ." Evans starts, wriggling his eyebrows in a scheming way. I already know this is gonna be good. "They gave me about two weeks to do it before all my cards stop working. So I just transferred most of the money over to an independent savings account and I'm planning to blow a good chunk of it to get back at them. Hence, staycation. Among other things."

"Oooh. Sounds like fun," I say with an easy grin. "You should make a bucket list of things to do and cross off every one of them before you hit the end of the two weeks."

"See, this is exactly why we claimed you to be one of the gang," Evans says, already tearing a piece of paper from Brent's notebook and picking up a pen. "Should we do an out-of-town vacation next? Oooh, how about Paris? I've always wanted to see the Eiffel Tower and eat baguettes."

"Come on." Brent groans, pushing himself off the bed and snatching the paper from Evans's grasp. "That was part of my physics notebook! And I hand numbered each page with ink too!"

"B, you're being ridiculous. It's just a page." Evans snatches the page right back. "I'll buy you ten more notebooks later, how about that? I'll even buy you one from Paris as a souvenir. Although you might want to get better souvenirs in Paris. You know what? I'll just buy you a whole bookstore in Paris just because I *can*."

My phone alarm buzzes in my pocket, and I slide it out to check the time. "While I'd love to stay for this riveting conversation, I've got a seminar in ten minutes," I say, shooting off the bed and pressing a light kiss on Brent's cheek. "I'll see you around. Have fun on the staycation."

"Wait!" Evans's scream echoes down the hallway as I make an exit. "What about my kiss on the cheek?"

"Have *B* give you one instead!" I holler, poking fun at Brent's new nickname.

***

As I'm heading over to Caffeinated to grab myself a panini sandwich for lunch, Cara shoots me a text.

Paint ball this Saturday! Daniel, Alex & Simon are in! Bring Kayden along?

I type back. *I'll ask him and let you know.*

I'm not sure how I feel about taking a day off from training to play paint ball. But then again, I'm certain that Kayden will be grateful for the break, given how hard Julian pushed him today. I remember it being the same with Jax when I was still learning how to fight. Long, hard hours of sparring and honing technique. My body was consistently marked with bruises from being knocked around so much, which sparked a lot of arguments with my dad.

Sometimes I wonder what life would be like if my mom had stayed in Boston. Would I have turned to fighting? Would I have turned to *Jax*? Both things felt like comfort after the pain of my parents' divorce and my mom's subsequent abandonment.

I'm certain, though, that life without fighting would indeed feel empty, like a piece of my soul would be missing if I didn't have it. There's just something intrinsically human about the sport. You get hurt, you pick yourself up and you try even harder again. There's no room for giving up.

When I finish today's midterm paper, I almost weep out of relief. I have three more papers scattered throughout the week, but I've done enough prep work for those courses to enjoy a little breather today. It feels weird not having a place to go. I'm usually rushing off to a training session with a client or with Kayden. But I don't have any sessions today, and trainings with Kayden I can no longer do. And those are really all I have.

Luckily, I'm not alone in my misery. Because less than an hour later, Kayden strolls into Caffeinated, looking as beaten up as a foot soldier coming home from war. He doesn't even bother to wipe the rivulets of sweat that pour down his face and neck, which soak the front of his shirt. When he spots me sitting by the window, he drops into the seat opposite me, defeat slacking his impressive shoulders.

Damn, Julian wasn't kidding when he said he was going to break him.

Kayden and I stare at each other silently for a couple of beats.

I look him up and down. "Do you want to talk about it?"

"Not even in the slightest," he mutters, reaching forward to steal my coffee cup and taking a huge swig of it. He hasn't had any sugar during the four weeks I've been training him, and I want to tell him off for doing so right now, but I decide to let it slide. After the day he's had, it's the least I can do.

"How was your paper today?" He asks.

"It was all right. I'm expecting at least a B on it," I inform him with a bored stare. Then, remembering Cara's standing invitation, I propel the question toward him. "What are you doing this Saturday?"

"It's my day off."

"Perfect. We're going paint balling, then."

He slides the cup—now mostly empty—back to me, wiping his mouth with the back of his arm. "You serious?"

I nod in confirmation. "Cara invited us."

He gives me a perplexed look. "Who's Cara?

Right. I don't think it's ever come up in any conversations that I'm friends with the neighbors he turned down multiple offers of civility and friendship from.

"Our neighbor." I take a sip of the coffee, pausing. "And my friend."

Kayden doesn't even take a moment to think about it. "No."

"Come on," I whine. "I know you don't like making new friends but they're a fun bunch. I think you'd really like them."

Deep down, I'm not actually convinced of that. But I'm certainly not going to go to a paint balling event where I'd be a fifth wheel. That's every single person's nightmare.

Kayden squints his eyes. Still uncertain.

"More than I like Brent and Evans?" He asks in a hesitant tone.

"Well, I don't know about that." I shrug, leaning back against my seat. "But they're just as fun, I promise."

Kayden leans forward, tenting his hands together across the table. A muscle twitches in his jaw as he stares at his hands. "I don't do well with people, Lucky. You know that."

"Pretty please?" I say with a pout. "You owe me for Julian."

Kayden tips his head back, coughing out a strained laugh. "Owe you? I've never felt this beaten down in my life." His darkened gaze pinpoints mine when he says, his voice a little scruffy, "You should be *punished* for Julian."

"Oooh. Punished, huh?" I wriggle my eyebrows teasingly. "I like the sound of that."

Kayden lets out a frustrated sigh. "You know that's not what I mean."

"You know, between you and me, I do like the occasional spanking—"

He hisses out a string of obscenities.

"*Sienna*," he warns in a dangerous yet tortured tone.

When I look up at him, his eyes are molten with desire. I force myself to look away, feeling stupid for threading that fine line again. But at the same time, I *wanted* it. And I knew exactly what I was saying and the kind of reaction I'd get.

My mind can't help wondering what Kayden would be like in bed. Would he be tender and kind, like during those moments when he'll do anything to put a smile on my face, or would he be rough and possessive, like his sculpted physique and intense gaze suggest? Callous hands pressed up against my skin, tongue sweeping over the bottom of my lip teasingly, hand clamped around my neck as he rams into me like the blazing force of the nature that he is—

Stop thinking about him like that. You don't deserve to.

"I'm kidding. You're so uptight sometimes." I clear my throat, wanting to change the subject. "For what it's worth, I am glad that you prefer my training sessions to Julian's."

Kayden shakes his head. "Be careful, I never said that."

"Oh trust me, you didn't have to."

My eyes scan his body again, scrolling up the bruises on his arms. Kayden smirks, his broad chest heaving from the movement.

"Let's go home," he announces. "I reek."

"Yeah, you totally do," I say with a grin while sliding out of my seat. "You want anything before we go?"

"Probably just a chilled bottle of water," he says, grabbing his wallet out from the side pocket of his black joggers. He opens it to pull out a ten and a picture falls and skitters to the ground.

"Hey, who's this?" I bend down to pick up the picture.

It's frayed at the sides and folded over many times, with huge creases running across the paper. But the image of the girl is still as clear as day—a pretty dark-haired teenage girl beams at me, showing a beautiful set of braced teeth. She looks about thirteen or fourteen. And she has the exact same pair of grey eyes that Kayden has.

He snatches the picture roughly from me. "Nobody."

"Doesn't seem like nobody to me."

"Just drop it, Sienna," he snaps.

"Kayden, wait—"

He doesn't hear me. Or he chooses to ignore me. Whatever the case is, he's already storming out of the café.

I squeeze my eyes shut and release a shaky breath, already mentally slapping myself for my own stupidity.

One step forward, ten steps back.

TWENTY-THREE

During the next few days Kayden avoids me like the plague. Predictably so. He's been leaving the apartment early and coming back at a ridiculously late hour, and while I've tried to wait up for him, I somehow always end up falling asleep on the couch before I can ambush him. Though I always find a comfortable pillow nestled under my head and a cozy blanket wrapped around me to keep me from freezing.

It's a nice gesture, but it would have been nicer if Kayden would just *talk to me.*

I get it. I overstepped his boundary. But I genuinely didn't mean to, and if I could just get on speaking terms with him, at least he'd know that. But since I'm still getting the cold shoulder from him, the guilt that I feel has slowly been chipped away, replaced by the frustration of him icing me out when things get difficult in our . . . friendship. Or whatever the hell this is.

I try to not let it get to me since I've got more important things to focus on, like finishing the term with a good GPA. When I'm finally done with my last physics paper on Friday, Brent and I have a little celebratory lunch at the school cafeteria, though it is really so we can compare our exam answers. I was reassured knowing that most of our answers were similar. I wish Kayden could have joined us, but it seems like he still needs his space.

Up until now, I was fully convinced he wouldn't even show up to the paint ball arena today. I even left the apartment without him, choosing to carpool with the rest of them. It's about a thirty-five minute drive from here to Tewksbury where the arena is situated, so I doubt he'll want to make the drive to a place where he'll be spending time with a bunch of strangers.

So imagine my surprise when ten minutes before our match, a mysterious man in a helmet, black sporty jumpsuit, and loaded PCP paint ball gun joins us by the bleachers beside the entrance to the arena. When he peels his helmet from his head, I immediately shoot up from my seat.

"I didn't think you were gonna come," I breathe.

Kayden nods, balancing the helmet on the side of his hip. "I didn't want to leave you alone."

"You must be Kayden!" Cara steps in front of me, extending her hand. "I'm Cara."

Kayden presses his lips together thinly. "I know who you are."

She blinks in confusion.

"I mean—" he says quickly. "You're the girl who keeps trying to invite me to things."

She glances away, pink tinting her cheeks. "Yeah. Sorry about that."

"It's fine." He scratches his head, guilt flickering in those grey eyes. "I'm sorry that I was rude to you then. I wasn't in the right head space."

The smile returns to her face. "I'm just glad you're here. Come on, you can wait with us."

She guides Kayden to the bleachers where our group's bulky forms have crowded the available space, leaving the other participants no choice but to stand around awkwardly while they wait their turn. It's spring break weekend, so people have been coming and going all day. Most of them are young teenagers, crowding around the entrance as they wait impatiently for their turn to enter. The perimeter of the arena is sealed with corrugated metal, preventing us from passing time by watching other people have fun; the only hint of excitement is the sound of far distant war cries and whizzing pellets.

Daniel's eyes sweep over the length of Kayden's huge arms in awe. "Your tattoos look cool, man." He compliments Kayden.

"Thanks," Kayden says with a slight pause. "I'm looking to get inked next month. You wanna come with? Maybe you can get one yourself."

"Seriously?" Daniel asks, excitement lighting up his face. "Hell, yeah."

"You'll look ridiculous with a tattoo, Daniel," Alex chimes in.

"I let you get a dog," her boyfriend counters. "Even though I didn't like it."

"That's different. Our dog is adorable," she says. "I doubt your tattoos will be that cute."

"You have a dog?" I scoot closer to her curiously. "You know we aren't allowed to keep pets in the complex."

"Yeah. His name is Ace. And please keep it on the DL." She pleads with me. "We were visiting the shelter the other day and we couldn't resist."

Daniel rolls his eyes. "You mean you couldn't resist. *I* resisted. Heavily."

"Yeah, but you were outnumbered three to one. Perks of living with two extra roommates," Alex says, sending a cheeky wink my way. "Ace is great. He drools all over the carpet when he sleeps but he's adorable. Such an angel."

"That demon?" Daniel rasps. "He ate my underwear and took a shit in our room."

Kayden and I both let out a laugh.

"All right, everyone, listen up!" The man who had previously helped us get into our suits and load our paint ball guns appears in front of us. He's a brawny man with a scraggy beard, his already tired-looking eyes wrecked even further from having to chauffeur teenagers into the arena all day. "Team leaders, gather up front. Pick your teammates and let's get going. You guys are up next."

Simon leaps from the bleachers and heads on up front to stand beside Cara while the rest of us huddle together opposite them.

"Simon goes first," Cara announces, beaming at her boyfriend.

Simon wastes no time to make his first pick. "I choose Kayden."

Kayden, unable to register the shock of having been picked first, takes a couple of seconds before a small smile breaks across his face. He shuffles in Simon's direction, giving him a casual fist bump along the way.

"Du-uude." Daniel sends a deadly glare to his best friend. "Where's the *loyalty*?"

"Relax, I'll pick you next round," Simon says smoothly.

"In that case," I say, raising a hand, "I'll be on Cara's team."

"All boys versus all girls. Seems fair," Alex deadpans as I take my place among the two girls.

"Relax. We have Sienna. She's like ten guys rolled into one," Cara says, beaming. Then she spins toward me and leans into my ear. "*Pssst*, you think I can get away with punching people in this game?"

"I think it would be to our team's expense."

"Right. Just checking," she says, trying to seem casual about it, though she's unable to fend off the annoyance washing over her face. "Daniel ate my leftovers yesterday and I was hoping for payback."

A small laugh leaves me. I can only imagine how living with three other roommates, all with wildly different personalities, would be. Thankfully, I don't really have to worry about that with Kayden. We're fairly responsible when it comes to maintaining the apartment together while mostly keeping to ourselves.

The rep unlocks the wooden gate for us and we stream into the arena. The forest is thick with trees and shrubbery, with all kinds of wooden barriers and bootleg landmarks erected all around the place. Almost immediately the boys make a beeline for the opposite side of the arena. I begin to make a visual sweep of the place so I can form a strategy.

"All right, girls, listen up," I announce, holding my arms out to form a huddle with Alex and Cara. "I think they're heading for the fort on the other side of the arena. That's most likely gonna be their base of operations so I say we head there for a flash attack."

"That seems like suicide," Alex notes cynically.

"That's what we *want* them to think. But really, it's a distraction," I explain.

Cara gives me a look. "What do you mean?"

I proceed to tell them the rest of my plan. By the time I'm done, Cara and Alex stare at me with newfound awe.

"You're fucking brilliant, Sienna," Alex says, clapping her hands together slowly.

"That I am." I wink at her. "All right. Let's get moving quick."

We start trekking, with Cara taking the lead. Moving through the arena without being seen is harder than it would seem despite all the trees, so we make sure to stop at a small pool of water to paint some mud on our faces and stick twigs in our hair to better camouflage ourselves. As we trudge along the path, careful to align ourselves behind the barriers along the way, the fort slowly comes into view.

"Get behind here!" Cara orders when she reaches a dirt-beaten car partially submerged in the ground.

We run up to her and I inch toward the edge of the vehicle to take a look at what lies beyond us. The fort is just a few feet away and sure enough, three shadows are seen moving about in flashes through the tiny open window.

I raise an eyebrow at the girls and they nod wordlessly, both of them moving to either side to cover my right and left flanks. I thrust my arm upward, fisting my hand, before counting down from three. *Three . . . two . . . one . . . go!*

With a roar, we burst out from behind the car, painting the fort walls a new shade of red. We manage to fire off another round of paint before I hear vague shouts from within the structure.

"*Get down!*" I hiss to Alex and Cara.

We duck back behind cover as multiple pellets splatter against the car's metal frame.

I venture a peek, slowly poking my head up to see Kayden's eyes flash from the open doorway of the fort. Suddenly, something whizzes past my ear and splatters on the tree behind me.

"*RETREAT!*" I yell, waving them over to my area.

We scramble backward, maintaining cover fire as more and more pellets whiz past us, thwacking the trees. Once we're safely in the tree line, we break into a dead sprint toward our objective: the fort on the other side of the arena.

We keep running, guns tucked tightly at our sides. Soon enough, the pellets stop coming and I breathe a sigh of relief as we reach the fort. I nod to my teammates, and the three of us split up. Cara takes a left flank, Alex heads straight to the right, and I take the fort. I push through the fragile wooden door that is barely hanging on its hinges and duck below the side window, careful not to make any kind of noise that will draw attention.

The sound of something scraping against the outer wall jolts me to my feet again. I aim my gun, gaze darting all around me. I hear nothing for a moment but my breathing, and after about a minute, just when I think I'm in the clear, I feel the barrel of a paint ball gun dig into my back.

"Drop the gun," Kayden orders.

***

"You really think I wouldn't figure you out? That your ambush at the fort was a distraction to get me here so I could be bait for when Simon and Daniel come crawling?" Kayden huffs as he pushes the barrel harder against my skin. I make a soft yelping noise. His mouth is right at my ear now, warm breath tickling the curve of it. "*Mislead*. That was your first lesson to me. You're unpredictable, Lucky, but even unpredictability has a pattern of behavior."

It should have occurred to me that Kayden would figure me out this easily. We've spent the past few weeks training together, learning and memorizing each other's movements for the sole purpose of breaking each other. He knows me just as well as I know him.

Well, *almost*.

"If you knew my plan, then why are you still here?" I say, eyeing the window above us. Nobody from the outside, not even the girls, will be able to see what's going on in here, which puts me in panic mode. I'm all alone in this, and for the first time in a while, I don't know what to do. Maybe there's nothing else I can do. Perhaps Alex and Cara might still be able to win this if Kayden takes me out now.

"Thought I'd give you what you wanted," he explains nonchalantly. "But just so you know, once I pull this trigger, a signal from me is all it takes for the boys to finish Alex and Cara, who, if I recall correctly, are waiting on either side of the fort, ready to pick Daniel and Simon off."

A bolt of fear shoots through me at the mention of the girls.

Okay, maybe it'll be better if I'm still in the game.

I try to mask my unease by straightening my back. "Then the ball's still in my court, don't you think? My girls still have the element of surprise since Daniel and Simon's only route here is through the clearing."

"I guess it depends on who gets to signal first," Kayden replies smoothly. "And from the looks of it, that'll probably be me."

Damn. I hate that I love how smug he looks knowing he's bested me. Maybe I should just give him the win so I can see the arrogant side of him come to life. I've really been missing that side of him. Along with every other part of him. His dimple-laden smile, his deep, husky laugh, which always seems to warm my insides, his intense eyes watching me with unabated hunger whenever I flaunt my body in a way that a friend *definitely* shouldn't . . .

I guess the past few days of not seeing him hasn't been particularly easy on me.

"Hands up," Kayden orders. "I'm asking nicely."

"All right, all right. Fine." I relent, allowing the gun to clatter to the ground and hauling my hands over my head in surrender as I turn to face him.

But not before dropping to the ground and using a leg to sweep Kayden's legs out from under him.

He falls on his back, sending dirt in the air upon impact,

and instinctively loosening the grip on his gun, which gives me the prime opportunity swiftly grab hold of both mine and his guns and spin them toward him.

Kayden lifts his hands up in surrender, fear striking him in a way I've never seen before.

"Hands up," I tell him, my chest heaving. "I'm asking nicely."

His gaze drops to my chest, sucking in a breath as he watches the steady rise and fall of my breasts as I try to stabilize my breathing. His eyes zip back up to my face, voice dropping low. "You won't do it."

"You didn't either. And look where you are now. Completely and utterly at my mercy," I say with a villainous edge to my voice. "But since you spared me before, I'll be fair. We're both stuck here as bait anyway, so we might as well wait it out and see which team picks each other off first."

Kayden recites a string of obscenities under his breath before going silent again. His gaze zeroes in on the guns I have aimed at him, and for a moment, I seriously think he's gonna fight me for them. But eventually, he lets out a conceding sigh and musters a tight nod. I throw both the guns as far as I can across the room and sit down beside him. We huddle in the corner, out of sight of any outside intruders.

I pull my knees together and rest my left cheek on them, facing away from Kayden. "And now the waiting game begins."

We spend the next minute sitting together in silence, focused on listening for any movements outside. I've no idea where Simon and Daniel are, but I'm certain they're still waiting for Kayden's signal. I wonder how long it'll take for them to realize that it won't be coming.

I cut a look at Kayden. He's breathing hard, sweaty from all the running and sabotage from earlier. He notices me staring and wipes the sweat with his hand silently. I've almost forgotten how he looks since I've barely seen him this week. I stare at him longer than I would ever allow myself to, taking in his alluringly taunt eyes, lips that look pillowy soft to the touch, and that subtle five o'clock shadow that shades the top of his mouth and along his jaw.

A thick air of tension settles between Kayden and me, the reality of not speaking to each other for days becoming too palpable. And yet, no matter how many times we've been through this—him completely icing me out—I still put up with it. It's stupid and I probably would have left a long time ago if it wasn't for the fact that I'm falling irrationally in love with this man.

"Look, I'm really sorry for getting mad at you about the picture the other day," he murmurs, slicing through the silence.

I guess we're having this conversation now.

"That's okay," I say softly. "If anything *I* should be the one to say sorry. I shouldn't have pried. Clearly that was a sensitive thing and I shouldn't have looked at the picture."

"It's not your fault." He shakes his head, leaning his head against the wall. "It's just that you caught me off guard. And I shouldn't have been pissed at you for being curious."

I nod silently, wanting to end this back and forth of taking responsibility for what had happened. It seems meaningless to continue because I know he'll be insistent on letting the blame fall on him.

I scoot over and lie against his shoulder, my arm brushing against his. Making another bold move, I spread my palm over his hand tenderly, to ease some of the guilt he's feeling. He slides his hand out from under me and uses it to link our hands together, his fingers curling into mine.

When I look up at him, his eyes are heavy with pained affection for me.

"Why do we keep doing this?" Kayden breathes.

"What do you mean?"

"I don't know. This." Aggravation creases his forehead. "We said we were going to stop this. Just be platonic. And then we hold hands and we touch and we have these moments. Moments that feel like something more."

My lungs empty at his acknowledgment of what's been happening between us. I try to keep my expression vague but it's difficult to keep a mask on when he's allowing honesty and vulnerability to pour out of him like this.

"Sienna, it's like I'm addicted to you," Kayden says, spilling more of his thoughts out loud. "You're the first thing I see when I get into that cage. The last thing I think about before I go to sleep. I seek you out in the darkest days and I miss you when you're not around. I think about what it'd be like to kiss your lips and every other part of your body. I want to feel you bare against me in bed. I want to say many things to you . . . things that I can only dream of saying to you." His husky, rough voice sends a shiver racing through me.

I don't say anything. Because he's just stolen all the words that I've been too afraid to say to him. He drags his fingers lightly over his bottom lip, and when he catches me staring at them, he drops his hand.

"I don't think I can just be friends with you." Sadness softens his voice. "But it's not that simple for me. Not when I can't give you everything you deserve."

"Don't say that," I whisper. "You are everything that I want, Kayden. *Everything.*"

"But you know it's hard for me to open up about what happened. I'm scared that you're not gonna want to be around me once you find out—"

"It's okay. You don't have to tell me," I murmur with a strained smile. I close my hand over his shoulder, eyes sliding over his. "Your past is in your past, and it doesn't define who you are. I know it doesn't because I can tell you're a good person. I've known it ever since I met you. And it's okay. Forget what you think you owe me. I like you as you are right now."

Relief flits through Kayden's expression. He studies me through the dark, and a deep, yearning ache passes through me as I realize that I've not been alone in trying to restrain my own feelings.

"What do you want?" He asks, his voice barely a whisper.

The air, which a couple of minutes ago was heavy with awkward tension, now pulsates with a new kind of energy. A sensual and lustrous kind. And I welcome it, exhausted from holding my feelings captive for such a long time. I don't know how long I can keep going at this without bursting at the seams.

Kayden gently puts his fingertips on my jaw and turns me toward him. His face is so close to mine that I can smell the saltiness of his breath. Heat rises in my body and I'm certain I can feel my head pounding from the deafening sound of my heart thundering against my chest.

He knows my answer to his question.

He *knows*.

And so I deliver.

"This." I grab a fistful of his jumpsuit and catch his lips with mine.

TWENTY-FOUR

When we kiss, everything tumbles away—the guilt, the concern over what's going to happen next—and the world around us becomes small and inconsequential compared to what's happening in the moment. I claim Kayden's mouth, tongue sweeping over his skillfully and eagerly, with one hand resting against his cheek. Just as I'd always imagined, his lips are heavenly soft, like the lightest, fluffiest kind of whipped cream you could ever imagine. My hands tug his jumpsuit hard as I try to capture him, all of him, because just having his lips isn't enough to quench my need for this man.

More. I want more.

Kayden's rough hands slide up my shoulders to my neck and along my cheeks as he kisses me back with equal fervor. I smile against his lips, my heart inflating at the certainty that he wants this just as much as I do. He coaxes my lips apart, slipping his tongue inside my mouth to taste me, and I gasp when it gently caresses mine. Pleased with my response, a low rumble vibrates in his core and he takes it upon himself to haul me onto his lap and crush our chests together, deepening the kiss.

Holy shit, his lips should have come with a warning sign, like a *proceed with caution because you can't handle this*! Because when Kayden drags his lips from my mouth to my jaw, I swear I could combust into flames right here and now. I let out an unexpectedly loud moan, which summons a teasing laugh from the back of his throat. He grips the back of my neck and sets a wide pathway of kisses from my neck all the way to my collarbone. If it wasn't for the thickness of these jumpsuits, I'm sure he would've tried ripping it off of me to get to every other part of my skin.

When he brings his face up again, he captures my lips for the second time. *Oh God, yes.* Tongue sweeping against my bottom lip, hands climbing over my frame and pillowing my back, our lips folding over each other's in a satisfying, unshackled release, finally allowing this moment we'd been dreaming of.

Kayden pulls away from me enough that the tip of his nose touches mine. His grey eyes are heavy with need.

"That is the best thing that's ever happened to me," Kayden whispers before trailing his nose down to nuzzle my neck. I gasp when he dips his head, sucking the skin right above my collarbone—

The sudden explosion of gunfire ringing from outside the fort immediately jerks us out of our trance.

What the hell is going on?

Kayden and I exchange confused looks. The realization that we're still in the middle of a death match sinks in and we pull away from each other, in agreement that we should do the honorable thing and help our teammates.

In a flash, we immediately scramble to retrieve the guns discarded on the ground and then jump to our feet. I'm the first one out of the fort, with Kayden tailing close behind me, paint ball bullets ricocheting all around us in the clearing.

It's then that I spot the absolute bloodbath laid out in front of us: Cara holding a paint-splattered Simon captive against her, him wheezing for air as she strangles him with her gun, and Alex pinning Daniel to the ground, savagely catapulting paint across his chest while Daniel just takes it, too exhausted to fight back.

My mouth hangs open in shock. *Holy shit.*

I guess they really didn't need me at all to finish the boys. Pride sprouts across my body as there's something so empowering about watching Alex and Cara completely annihilate their boyfriends.

Well, time to do the inevitable, I guess.

"Sorry about this," I mutter as I turn to Kayden and splatter red across his chest.

And just like that, the game is over.

"We did it!" Cara and Alex scamper toward me, hollering a victory cheer and roping me into a huge group hug.

Kayden, looking bruised and beaten, bleeds red paint from his chest. Daniel and Simon amble over to him to make sure he's okay.

"Well, *that* wasn't part of the plan," Cara says as she pulls back my hair, eyeing a certain spot on my neck.

I press a hand over where she's looking and feel the tenderness over my skin. *Oh. That.*

I guess kissing in the middle of a paint ball game wasn't exactly the brightest idea but I don't regret it one bit. I hope Kayden doesn't.

"Damn, and he got you real good too," she says, inspecting the hickey closely.

She tries to touch it but I swat her hand away.

A slow clap emits from the trees as the paint ball rep who'd ushered us in earlier slowly comes into view. "Good job, red team! And as for blue team . . ." He shrugs sympathetically. "Well, better luck next time."

"Come on, buddy," Alex says as she beckons Daniel to walk with her. She looks him up and down and says, "You look like shit."

"No thanks to you," he replies flatly. "I seriously can't believe you emotionally blackmailed me into winning. *'Come on, baby, you can't kill me! What kind of boyfriend does that make you?'*" Daniel mimics in a falsetto voice not even remotely close to Alex's.

"Hey, Sienna wasn't gonna come save us since she was too busy fraternizing with the enemy. So I had to take some drastic measures, all right?" She says, looping an arm over her boyfriend, but not before turning around to send me a sly wink. I roll my eyes.

Cara and Simon reunite in front of me as well and I slow down my pace to match Kayden's so we can have some privacy. When he sees me, a ridiculous smile forms on his beautifully sculpted face. He shoves his hands into the pockets of his jumpsuit, meeting my gaze with a shy, uncertain look.

"So the kiss . . . ?" His voice trails off as he waits for me to finish the sentence.

"Was part of my villainous plan to leave you vulnerable so Alex and Cara could pick off their boyfriends in a badass way that James Bond would be jealous of? Definitely not. That's way too evil." I shake my head.

He stops abruptly in his tracks. "It was real, then?"

"As real as it can ever be," I whisper, looking up at him with renewed affection.

A slow smile spreads across Kayden's face. He reaches down to entwine his fingers with mine and gives my hand a tight squeeze, reaffirming his feelings for me.

"Good," Kayden says, pleased. "Let's go home then."

***

When we've parked, Kayden helps me out of the truck and tugs on my hand, leading me to the stairs rather than the elevator. He's in a rush and I'm all for it. We're flying up and up and up, my legs barely catching up as he propels me forward, and I'm so breathless from how fast we're going that by the time we reach our door, my knees feel like they're about to give out. But I refuse to let something as insignificant as lack of oxygen keep me from what I think is about to happen.

When Kayden produces the apartment key from his pocket, I've never felt more relieved.

The door gets unlocked.

He steps in.

I step in after him.

We look at each other, our eyes clouded with lust.

We haven't even been in the apartment for five seconds before Kayden steps forward and devours my lips with his.

Neither of us can keep our hands off the other. He cradles my face with his huge hands as he invades my mouth, just like I'd fantasized him doing. I don't think I can ever get enough of kissing this man. Pandora's box opened the second our lips touched in that fort, and I don't ever want to go back to the time when I didn't know how it felt to be kissed by him.

Our bodies ripple against each other with urgency. I wind my arms around his neck as he peppers sweet kisses down my face onto my body, prompting a moan to tear out of me. I bring his face up with my hands so I can kiss him again, this time with more need and desperation. We probably reek of sweat and paint but it doesn't matter. Nothing matters.

All that matters is him. This. Us.

Kayden slides his hands down to cup my butt and in response, I curl my legs around his hips and circle my arms around him, allowing him to take me anywhere he wishes. I hope he knows where I want us to go. I wonder if he can feel the erratic pounding of my heart against him. I can certainly feel his.

Kayden continues kissing me as he walks over to his bedroom, only pausing long enough to kick the door open.

It doesn't budge.

He kicks it again. Still nothing.

I laugh against his lips. "Here. Let me."

I reach down to cup the doorknob. I give it a little twist. The door creaks open.

He groans, blushing from his failed attempt. "Well, that was a total fail."

I lean into his face, my nose grazing his. "A-plus for effort."

He chuckles, meeting my lips for another kiss. His stubble is a teasing scratch against my face, inviting a trail of goose bumps across my arms.

My legs are still wrapped around him when he kicks the door closed behind him. He carries me to his bed, laying me down softly. I've never known of such gentleness, and for that reason alone, I feel even more turned on than ever. A smile tugs at the corners of his lips as he climbs over me, one leg wedged between both of mine.

I want to touch him so fucking bad. My hands go everywhere—brushing against the long curve of his shoulders, fingers dancing at the back of his neck, tugging on his messy, sweat-coated, dark hair. Kayden's hands do the same, skimming under my black tank top and slowly slipping the material up over my toned stomach until it shows a hint of my bra. He grins at my half-clothed state of disarray, pressing a tender kiss on my belly.

I don't let him linger for too long, flipping us over so I'm on top this time, my legs straddling his hips. Slowly, I peel off my shirt and unclasp my bra, my eyes never once straying from his. He watches me, in awe at my naked form. Then he closes his eyes and breathes in once, twice, like I'm some miracle he thought he was never going to have.

When Kayden finally opens his eyes again, he cups the back of my head and pulls me down to his face, claiming my lips with a soft kiss before moving down to latch onto my neck, worshiping the skin there. His hands travel to thighs, the lightest of touches threatening to skyrocket me off his lap. I let out a whimper as they slowly make their way up my body, reaching over to cup my breasts. His fingers graze my nipples lightly, building delicate pressure over them as he rolls the hard peaks between his fingers. The sensation makes my eyes flutter open and closed, and my breathing growing increasingly uneven.

I arch my body against Kayden's restlessly when he replaces his fingers with his mouth. When he sweeps his tongue, hot and wet, over the first nipple, I could just die then and there. Every swirl of his tongue sends an explosion of pleasure shooting across the spectrum of my body. Holy shit, if this isn't the most exquisite form of torture, I don't know what is. When Kayden lets his teeth graze over the other sensitive bud, another breathy moan leaves me and he groans in response, the sound escaping me completely undoing him. It's enough for him to flip us around, push me down on the bed and climb over me again.

"You have *no* idea what I want to do to you right now." His voice is rough and needy, full of arousal.

Desire explodes in my stomach as those words hit me. I level my gaze with his. Challenging him.

"Show me."

A tortured groan. "Best damn words I've heard all day."

The wicked gleam that enters his eyes tells me that I'm going to like what's going to happen next. He slides farther down the bed, helping me wiggle out of my leggings and underwear. When I'm completely naked before him, he sucks in a tortured breath.

"You're so beautiful," Kayden whispers. "This beats all the fantasies I've ever had about you, you know."

My cheeks turn crimson.

"Do you know how many cold showers I've had to take to get you out of my mind? More times than I can count on one hand," he murmurs. "But I can't forget you, Lucky. *Never*. You've sewn yourself into my brain. Embedded yourself in my heart. I'm a goner. A fucking goner."

I close my eyes because I want to replay those words over and over again.

When I open them again, I see Kayden smiling down at me and I return the expression, red tinting my cheeks.

I help him out of his clothes, unbuttoning his jeans and tugging up his shirt, then toss the fabric aside to the tangled heap of clothing by the edge of the bed. I gasp when he's completely naked before me. He runs a thumb over his lip when he looks down at me. He looks so sinfully indulgent like this. That incredibly chiseled, rock hard abdomen that I've spent all our training sessions trying not to ogle, except now I can. *Shamelessly*. Even better, I allow myself to travel my excited gaze down to his navel, skimming along the hard V line of his thighs, then trailing the light sprinkling of dark hair leading down to his—

My pulse explodes into a gallop.

Holy fucking hell.

I was *way* off about the Kayden junior thing.

I've never been more wrong about something in my entire *life*.

"Damn," I whistle lowly. "You really weren't lying."

Kayden replies with a shy but hearty smile. Damn, even when he's trying not to be cocky, he's cute.

I slide my lips over his, humming with anticipation.

The next few minutes are a blur of moans, kisses, sweat, and hands. Wild sounds tear out of me, as ragged as my breaths. He doesn't stop touching me. *Everywhere.* Stroking my breasts, sliding over my belly . . . and then his hand between my legs, feeling the heat and wetness pooling between them, fingers rubbing over my clit in a delicate and skillful dance.

I sigh against him, feeling a strong pressure in between my thighs. I'm completely at his mercy and for once, I don't wish to do a single thing about it. My teeth dig into the back of my arm to prevent myself from moaning too loudly as he continues to ravish me with his oh-so fucking talented fingers, circling over the bud and sending spasms up my body. When he slides two fingers into my opening, I bite down onto my arm hard, so close to being undone.

His fingers continue to plunge in and out of me in a steady rhythm. Just when the pleasure gets too unbearable, Kayden slowly removes them from between my legs. I laugh, relieved, wanting my first orgasm with him to be when he's inside me. And sure enough, it seems like he feels the same way. My body pulses with excitement. He looks nervous. I am too. But I know we both want this.

"I want to make love to you right now," he murmurs to me.

Those nine words are officially my new favorite words ever.

"Will you let me?" He searches my face for answers.

"Yes," I rasp.

Kayden reaches into the top drawer of his nightstand to grab a condom. I watch him, writhing in anticipation as he rolls in onto his cock and adjusts himself between my legs. My heart almost flies out of my chest when he lowers his strong body over mine and presses against me. He fills me up slowly, inch by inch and when he's all the way inside, his eyes gaze over me with worry as he forces himself to remain still.

"Are you okay?" He asks.

"Never better." I nod, claiming his mouth with a sweet, loving kiss.

Kayden smiles against my lips and begins moving again, caging me with his thick arms. Beads of sweat dot his forehead. I adjust my hips, allowing my body to get used to the length of him. The pressure is intense, but exquisite. As he moves inside me, a relieved sigh leaves my lips as all those weeks of dancing around our desires finally comes to a swift end.

I can't believe I've managed to hold off being with him like this for this long. I mentally slap myself for being this stupid, because having his body against mine is simply the most natural thing in the world.

I wrap my arms around his neck, ankles digging deep into the edge of the mattress as his cock plunges into me, connecting our bodies. The muscles in his neck strain, as if he's fighting to keep himself from losing all control. But I don't want him to fight it. I want to see him fully unleashed, like I've never seen him before.

Sweat prickles on both our bodies, sticky and salty. Heavy breaths fall into the air. Skillfully, Kayden rotates his hips to switch up the angle, and my eyes roll at the new, mind-numbingly divine sensation that hits that deep spot inside me. I gasp, pushing my hips into his eagerly to capture more of the sensation.

"Does that feel good for you, baby?"

"Yes," I moan.

"Good." His thumb caresses my bottom lip. "Because you might want to hold on."

The air pulsates with energy and desperation as he rams into me with increasing speed and my arms cling to him for dear life, my body flexing against his to meet every powerful and fluid thrust. The feeling inside me builds, and my inner muscles ripple around his cock as an orgasm becomes imminent. I dig my fingers harder into his back, trying to hold on to something, *anything*, so I won't lose all sanity.

When the pleasure escalates to a crescendo, my body shudders with ecstasy. Kayden's eyes are dark with satisfaction as he watches me completely unravel under him. He doesn't stop moving, though; he fills me up again and again, calloused hands lifting my hips higher. I wrap my legs around his body and the new angle completely shatters the already waning sense of control that he had been clinging to.

"Fuck," he hisses as he pushes into me a final time, swimming in his release.

I join him with another unexpected orgasm of my own, the sight of him losing it inside me sending another burst of pleasure spreading through me.

Then we're falling, the passionate haze slowly retreating until we collapse on the bed, completely spent. Kayden glances over at me, looking tired but content.

"Come here," he says, barely a whisper.

Afterward, we lie together, wrapped up in the sheets, with our legs entangled. I lean into his chest and Kayden folds his arms over my frame, nuzzling his nose in my hair.

I angle my head to better look at him. His eyes are closed. I realize that I've never seen him like this before. So peaceful. I like that I'm the only person who gets to see this side of him. He's giving me a small piece of himself, and I like it.

"Lucky," he mumbles, snuggling closer to me.

I'm not sure what tomorrow will bring us. Our future is uncertain, but I'm grateful for this night to lose myself in him. We both needed this.

Regardless, I cocoon myself in Kayden's arms and let sleep overtake me.

TWENTY-FIVE

I stir sometime before dawn. It's still dark outside, with cracks of orange and purple bleeding into the horizon as the sky prepares itself for daylight. As I clutch the sheets tighter to my chest, I'm suddenly aware that I'm naked.

Last night's memories float back to me like a nearly forgotten dream. I remember how rough Kayden's hands were when they roamed over my body, how he kissed me until my lips were numb and tender, and how earth shattering it was when he gifted me orgasms that left me in fragments. We were in and out of sleep for a few hours, each time waking up and craving more from each other. It was beautiful, kind, unspoken in the way we moved against each other, as if we needed any more convincing of our affection for one another.

I never wanted the night to end.

But the question still lingers at the back of my head: Does he regret it now?

I know my answer. What happened last night was exactly what I wanted.

I turn over to his side and notice the absence of his body next to me. My heart drops, a nervous frown marring my lips. The clothes that were lying on the floor are now in a pile inside the laundry bag beside his door.

I leave his room, popping into mine quickly to slip into some clothes before peeking into the living room. Sure enough, I find Kayden sitting on the couch, his huge arms rested over his thighs and his head dipped low. He looks deep in contemplation, frustrated almost. Like he's having an internal battle with himself and losing.

I don't know if I should go over to him. I'm scared that I won't like what I'll hear if I do. But I don't want to go back to my room. I need to know where we stand.

I clear my throat, announcing my presence.

Kayden whips head up, an emotionless expression on his face.

"If you regret it . . ." I say, my throat constricting at the words that are about to leave me, "we can pretend that it didn't happen."

He looks at me, incredulous.

"You think I regret it?" He whispers. "Sienna, I've been dreaming of being with you like that for ages. I don't regret it one goddamned bit."

I hug myself with my arms as I approach him. It's a little cold with the wind drifting into the living room from the open window. He makes space for me on the couch and when I'm seated, he drags the throw blanket over my body to keep me warm. I peek a glance and notice that he's staring at me, his expression a mixture of sadness and surprise. Like he can't quite believe that I'm still here. And to be honest, I feel the same way about him. I figured he'd bolt by now.

We lean into each other on the couch. He takes my hand in his and places it above his heart.

"Feel this," he says, his voice strained. "You *own* my heart. Every single heartbeat is for you."

I gulp, my lips trembling.

What have I done to deserve all these beautiful words?

I force myself to look away from him, feeling the tears spring into my eyes. I hold them in because I don't really want to cry right now.

"What are we doing, Kayden?" I whisper.

The question ripples through the room, exposing the complicated nature of our relationship.

"I don't know." Kayden shrugs, rubbing his hands together. "I woke up early because I needed to think about us. What we did last night kept replaying at the back of my mind and I realized that I don't want just one night with you. I want all of them."

Delightful shivers fly up my spine.

"And if I want that, it means I have to be honest with you," he tells me. "Yesterday, you said my past didn't matter. That you only cared about me as I am now. But I care. I care about what you think of me. And if I want to be with you, you have to know who I am. All of it. Even the ugly parts."

I take his hand and link our fingers together, giving him a reassuring squeeze.

"I'm here," I whisper. "And I'm not going to leave."

He pauses, swallowing hard. He struggles to find the

right words to tell me. My heart quickens, almost afraid of what he's going to say.

Kayden draws in a slow, uneven breath as he gathers his thoughts.

"The girl in the picture is—*was*—my sister, Clarissa," he says shakily. "And five years ago, I killed her."

My stomach completely hollows out.

He must have noticed my discomfort because he frowns deeply but pushes himself to continue.

"Let me start from the beginning. A few years ago, when I was sixteen, my parents died." A muscle ticks in his jaw when the words leave him. "I was making a lot of stupid decisions back then. Acting high and mighty. I got really drunk at a party one night and just wanted to get home, so I called my parents to come get me. Told them to take the shortcut that went through some cliffs." His voice takes on a faraway note. "It was raining pretty bad and the police officer told me they lost control of the car and flew off the cliff."

"Oh my God." I clamp my hand over my mouth.

"We had no one else. Clarissa and I. No relatives, no family. Nothing. We had no way to support ourselves financially, other than the little inheritance we received from our parents. And we both knew what awaited us if we got absorbed into the foster care system. So me and Clarissa decided to make a run for it together. We spent the next few months living in crappy motels. Those were tough times, but they were happy ones too. And we were determined for it to stay like that. But of course, after a while, the money began to dwindle and we were running out of options. So, to keep us afloat, I resorted to street fighting." A frown touches his mouth and I lean back against the armrest, realizing that that was the genesis of him dipping his toes into the underground. "I found out I was really good at fighting, and winning paid the bills. I didn't like hurting the people I fought, but I didn't want to disappoint Clarissa more. She wanted me close, and I promised myself I'd do anything to uphold that. To protect her from anyone who could separate us. We kept bouncing around while I fought in illegal fight clubs a few times a week, earning just enough to jump to the next place and evade childcare services all over again. Even though our situation was shitty, at least we were together. And that was all we both ever needed."

I nod quietly, empathizing with where he's coming from. Everyone who fights in that cage has their own battles to overcome, and it seems like Kayden's was a hell of an uphill one. I can't imagine what his life was like then—being a teenager and already feeling like he had to do anything necessary to survive, even if it meant breaking the law.

"We thought we were so smart, that we had actually bested the system. But of course, it didn't last. Eventually, we did get caught and thrown into foster care. The day it happened, my heart fucking shattered. Seeing Clarissa get whisked off like that, it was the most difficult thing I had to witness. And knowing that I let her down . . ." Kayden snakes a hand along his jaw, attempting to ease the strain building there. "Anyway, I was adopted by Brent's parents because his mom was my social worker and they took me in because she was good with bad kids and was sympathetic to what I had been through. And Clarissa . . . she, um . . . she got this couple." His hands begin to shake and I reach over and cover them with mine. He inhales deeply, as if trying to breathe in some courage, before resuming. "They seemed fine on paper but in reality they were *really* good at hiding their abuse. I was only allowed to see her once every few weeks, but every time we had our visits my suspicions grew. Her weight dropped and there were bruises under her sleeves." His voice wobbles, each word singeing his tongue as it leaves him. "It was karmically unfair. That I got adopted by the best family in the world while Clarissa had the worst. Every day I felt like I was living in my own version of hell, watching them kill her slowly. And there was absolutely nothing I could do about it."

Fury simmers in the pit of my stomach at the thought of his sister being isolated and assaulted like that. It's sickening. How cruel do you have to be to inflict pain on *children*? I don't even want to think about what I'd do if Beth had to endure all that.

"I had Brent's mom report it to the authorities, and pushed for the case to be urgent. But the police handling the case didn't want to hear any of it because when they went to investigate, they found no evidence of abuse. I tried to get them to listen but they said I couldn't be trusted because I'd tried to dodge child services with Clarissa, and they saw my complaints as another attempt to flee with her again. That didn't stop me from being vocal about her abuse, though. And by the time they even considered reopening the case again . . ." Misery burns a path down his throat as he croaks, "Clarissa's adoptive parents had already killed her."

My eyes flutter closed, my chest tightening from what I've heard. To think that he might have been able to prevent his sister's death if he'd had more time—it's no wonder Kayden has been suffering from such massive guilt even all these years later.

"It didn't take too long for those monsters to get thrown into prison and make headlines," he tells me. "At least they're behind bars now. But it's not enough to bring her back."

I frown, remembering that I heard about a couple who'd killed their adopted daughter. It had been big news for a while. But it never occurred to me that the girl had been *Kayden's* sister.

Kayden's eyelids hang low over his irises, the emotional turmoil he has to undergo to tell this story already beginning to take a toll on him. Tears flood his beautifully broken face and I lean forward, wiping my hands across his cheeks.

"That's me. I'm a killer," he says in finality.

The words ripple through the air and crack my heart wide open. I hold back the tears edging my eyes because I need to be strong for him.

"Kayden," I say, shaking my head adamantly. "That's not true. You can't blame yourself for that."

"Why not? Because of my mistakes, I set off the chain of events that left them all dead." He slants his head at me, an edge to his voice. He tears his gaze from me, opting instead to stare straight ahead at the blank wall beside the television. "After that, it was all downhill from there. I got so fed up with living that I considered ending my own life. But I didn't, because I deserve to be punished for what I did to them, and if that means condemning myself to an empty, soulless life, then so be it. That's the *only* thing I deserve.

"That's why I continue to fight in the underground.

Fighting is the only time I ever let myself feel anything, even if it's just pain," he explains. "I use the money for food and other essentials. Then I donate the rest of to charities and shelters working to end these kinds of injustices against children." His fingers curl into fists, knuckles going pale. Raw determination flows from his eyes in the form of his tears. "So no one will ever have to endure what Clarissa did."

Suddenly, everything that I'd once found confusing about him now makes complete sense. The reason his apartment was barren when I arrived. Why he dropped out of college. Why he never got a better car even though he could well afford it. Every choice, every decision he has made up until this point has been to justify why his life isn't worth living.

If only he could see just how fucking special he is; how his life *does* matter. To me. To Brent. To Evans. To his family.

"You asked me why I fight." Kayden's head tips toward me. A small light flares amid the darkness that shades his eyes. "I fight for her. *Clarissa.* I fight for the life she never had. Taking down Jax is taking down a version of myself that got her and my parents killed. At least it would make their lives matter more."

I nod thoughtfully. As twisted as it sounds, I get it. After the shit that he's been through, I understand the determination to make meaning out of something that is as debased and cruel as his family's deaths.

Outside, the sun has fully risen in the sky, shading Kayden's wounded face with the soft yet radiant glow of morning light. He stares at the sky for a moment, quiet and thoughtful, as he basks in the sounds of birds chirping and leaves crinkling against each other in the trees below our apartment. He wipes the remaining tears coating his cheeks and sniffs before turning his attention to me again.

"I know this is a lot to take in," he says roughly. "I failed my parents. I failed my sister. I don't deserve to be with you."

I shake my head in disagreement. He still has no idea, does he? That nothing would ever make me choose to leave him. I'm in this too deep now.

"Kayden, I'm so sorry that you had to go through that. I can't imagine how it all felt," I whisper, hands sliding over his shoulders to clutch them. "You're a selfless and courageous person. I have always thought that about you, and while what you just told me is incredibly sad and tragic, it doesn't disprove any of it. If anything, I'm more proud of you than I was before."

He stares at me silently, looking unconvinced by my words.

"You're not leaving?" He asks hesitantly.

Cradling his face, I lean forward, mouth finding his in a reassuring, tender kiss.

"I'm not going anywhere," I murmur against his lips, conviction ringing in my tone. "And hopefully neither are you."

The corner of his mouth inches up, and it's enough for him to sling an arm around me and pull me toward his body. We lie on the couch together, his arms cocooning mine, and remain like this as the time ticks by, searching for solace in each other's pain.

TWENTY-SIX

I can't possibly fathom the kind of suffering Kayden had to go through to be here today, to lose his entire family and then to feel like he was responsible for their deaths. I'm surprised anyone could still possess such kindness and humanity in them with that kind of harrowing past. I wonder how he finds the courage to keep going and not lose himself in the void.

Perhaps sometimes he does lose himself. Whenever his eyes take on a faraway light, plunging deep into thought and the memories of his trauma, or when he's swarmed with self-loathing and hurt. In those moments he slips further and further away from me, and I'm left just praying and hoping that he'll eventually drift back to shore.

I hope one day he'll be brave enough to trust me to help him carry the burden.

At some point during the early hours of the morning Kayden let me peel him off the couch and lead him back to his bed. As we lie together, he loops an arm around me to bring me close to his body and pulls the blanket up so we're nestled in our own warmth. He smiles down at me through his dried-up tears—a faint wounded, yet hopeful, smile—and relief overflows in my chest knowing that he has found emotional release in sharing his story with me.

"I'm sorry for not telling you sooner," Kayden says, his voice coming out hoarse. He strokes my hair with his hand gently. "I don't like to talk about it. It brings to the surface a lot of emotions that I don't usually like to feel."

"I get it. There was some heavy stuff." One of my hands drifts across his abdomen. I tilt my head up, lips pulling into a frown. "And. . . I'm sorry too . I shouldn't have been so hard on you before. You didn't deserve it."

His mouth thins, like he doesn't quite believe me. "You don't think I'm a terrible person?"

I hoist myself up, pushing onto my elbows so I can properly look at him. "What? No, of course not," I tell him reassuringly. "I've known it from the start that you're a good person, and I still believe that you are. And as much as you've convinced yourself that you're to blame for all that happened to your parents and your sister, it's not true. Not to me. Or Brent. Or Evans. I'm sure of it. You can stop blaming yourself for their deaths."

"I'll try, but it's a feeling I've been accustomed to for so long now. It's hard to will myself to stop feeling like that . . . but I'll try." His mouth puckers into a frown. "You know, there's still time to leave in case you change your mind. I won't stop you."

"I'm not leaving and I meant it. And you know I don't

change my mind about anything," I say urgently, mushing his face between my hands. He stares back at me, wide eyed. "I'm all in, Kayden. So if I let go of you right now, will you stop telling me to leave?"

Slowly, he nods.

I release my hold on him, and he immediately tackles me into a fearless, sweeping kiss. A laugh escapes me as I snake my arms around him, my eyes fluttering closed as he drags his lips from my mouth to my jaw, then all the way down my neck.

He pauses at the place above my collarbone, brushing away the hair sticking to my skin, and a smirk snaps onto his face.

"You have a hickey," Kayden notes.

"Yeah, I do." Heat diffuses into my cheeks. "From paint ball."

His fingers dance lightly over the spot where they hickey is, as he stares at it with utter fascination.

"I've never given anyone a hickey before," he admits.

"I hope I'll be the only one you'll be giving hickeys to." I poke his chest, the possessiveness rousing in me.

He chuckles, a deep rumble from his throat. I love it when he laughs. It's the most delightful sound in the world.

"Oh, Lucky. I plan on giving you much more than just hickeys," he murmurs seductively, and I groan, my mind already wandering with the possibilities of his statement.

I wonder what he plans to give me. Orgasms? *Babies*? I hope he doesn't mean the latter. I'm all for option one, though.

Kayden ducks his head again and presses a lingering kiss

over the hickey, then brings his lips lower and lower until he's at the curve of my breasts. I'm panting beneath him, my hands digging into his hair, silently begging for him to travel farther down.

He helps me out of my shirt and I oblige him willingly, lifting my arms to let him discard the fabric. He sweeps a thumb over his bottom lip, lustful eyes tracing the length of my body, and I whimper from the ravenous sound that leaves him, like I'm the best thing he's ever seen in his whole damn life.

"Take off your shirt," I say, giving a tug on the edge of Kayden's shirt.

"Yes, ma'am."

He does a mocking bow at me before grabbing the hem of his shirt and pulling it off in one skillful sweep of his hand, arm muscles coiling with the movement. *Holy shit, that was sexy as fuck.* In his reveal, he displays his familiar set of broad shoulders that frame his huge chest and a perfect set of abs that I can't seem to stop staring at.

I stare up at him. "Kiss me."

Kayden's lips sweep against mine gently at first, stroking my bottom lip with his tongue teasingly before slipping into the seam of my lips. I sigh against him, feeling like the only place where my mouth fully belongs is on his.

My eyes flutter as his hands roam the length of my figure, setting all my nerve endings on fire. When he adjusts himself on top of me, his body dipping to the side to get on his elbows, a glimpse of his back shoots a wave of guilt through me.

"Wait. Turn around," I murmur, worried. Kayden looks

at me, confused, but does what I say and turns his back to me. A hand flies to my mouth to cover up the horror settling into my expression. "Oh my God. I'm so sorry."

A crease digs into his forehead. "Why? What's wrong?"

I scoot over to the side of his bed, picking up my phone from the nightstand and snap a quick picture of his back. "Look," I say when I show him the picture his muscled back, now scuffed with long red marks.

"Oh, that." Kayden doesn't look the least bit fazed, which is surprising to me. "What? You think I mind this?" I nod and he smiles, taking the phone from my hands and setting it to the side. "Nah. It doesn't hurt. I love the claw marks. They're so fucking *sexy*."

I bite my lip. "What if people see them? I'm sure the guys at the gym aren't gonna be as forgiving."

"I don't care. Let them," he drawls, climbing back on top of me. "Let them see what you've done to me. You've claimed me, Lucky. I want everyone to know that."

I stifle a laugh with my hand. I guess boys will be boys when it comes to championing claw marks. "You're crazy."

"Only when it comes to you." He looks down at me, his thick eyelashes hooding his mesmerizing eyes. "You drive me insane, Sienna. But I don't care as long as you'll have me."

My heart balloons into the clouds.

"Kayden, is that an offer for me to be your girlfriend?" I whisper.

He nods, a blush forming on his cheeks.

I flick his nose with my finger. "You're adorable."

He rolls his eyes at my comment but is undeterred in his quest to get a straight answer from me.

"So is that a yes?"

"No. That's a *hell, yes*," I say instantly.

The smile that he returns at my confirmation threatens to break his face. His nose grazes my neck as he brushes his lips against the sensitive skin there. A pathetic whimper leaves me at his superpower ability to undo me like this with *just* a kiss.

"Be careful what you're agreeing to," he murmurs against my skin. A wave of arousal swells inside me as his palm brushes against my nipples. His eyes connect with mine again, a smug look on his face as he watches me fall apart at his touch. "I won't be the most patient boyfriend. I'll want to fuck you every chance I can get. And I'm not afraid to beat up any person who hurts you. Anyone who hurts *my* Lucky deserves to go through me and my fucking fist."

There's that protective, possessive edge in him that I crave. I love that one second he's the most gentle, loving giant and the next he's dominating and fierce, staking his claim over me. I like that I don't know which side of him I'll get.

"Do you understand?" He says roughly as his demanding eyes meet mine. My core swells with heat at the primal edge that contours his face. "I want you in any way I can get you and I'm not going down easy. Not after the night we spent together, not after what I told you, and certainly not after everything we've been through."

His words speed up my already racing pulse.

"Yes, sir." I salute him, like he'd done to me earlier.

He nods, satisfied at my answer. "Good."

"So are you gonna keep true to your promise?" I say

teasingly, arching my back to tease him with the sight of my bared breasts. "About fucking me every chance you get?"

Kayden's gaze falls to my chest, eyes narrowing with sensuous desire. He sucks in a forceful breath as if trying to contain himself.

Fortunately for me, all that restraint gets thrown out the window when I purse my lips.

A ridiculously boyish smile enters his face.

"Fuck, yeah."

And then he wastes no time in discarding the rest of our clothes and ravishing me.

***

It's been an hour since our lovemaking session. Neither of us wanted to leave bed, still too engrossed with exploring the other's body as much as we could before we have to fall back into reality and get back onto our usual routine again.

I get hungry after a while, so I creep into the kitchen to grab Kayden's hidden stash of cookie dough ice cream at the back of the freezer and jump back into bed. It's been a while since either of us had anything remotely unhealthy, and since I'm no longer his trainer, I figure I'll just let this one moment of indulgence slide.

We're both still naked, neither of us really bothering with clothes because of how accustomed we are seeing each other this way. I especially like stroking the perfect specimen of manhood between his legs whenever I feel like it, rousing a lusting temperature inside of him every time I do so.

Neither of us have looked at our phones all morning,

nor do we plan to. We both want to stay in our little bubble, at least for a while longer.

Now, Kayden is lying at an incline on the side of his bed while I set my head on his torso, my disgustingly greasy hair splayed over his skin. He doesn't mind it one bit, even though I've insisted on tying it into a bun. I think he likes pulling on it when we have sex.

"How about this tattoo?" I whisper, leaning over to trace the tattoo on his left shoulder blade. It's a small inscription that reads "I did not weep; within, I turned to stone."

"When did you get this one?"

"After Clarissa died," he tells me. "It's from Dante's *Inferno*." When I make a face, he lets out an embarrassed chuckle. "Cheesy, I know. It was the first piece of literature I read in school, and I don't know why, but the words always come to mind when I remember how I felt about her death."

I nod silently, fingers brushing over the words again like I can somehow feel his agony by touching it.

"What about this one?" I say as I point to another spot across his abdomen. It's a tattoo of a little butterfly—not quite something I'd imagine Kayden ever getting. So far, every ink he's ever gotten has had meaning to it. I wonder if this one also has links to his past. "Does it stand for hope or something? A new life reborn?"

"I wish it was that deep." He scoffs. "You don't want to know."

"Try me."

He grows quiet, debating whether it's a good idea to say anything. But eventually, he concedes with a sigh.

"It was stupid, okay?" He prefaces, stroking my back

lazily. "Evans and I were very drunk one night after a bender and he suggested something that *may* have sounded appealing at the time."

"No," I whisper, feeling like I know exactly where this is going.

"Yes," he grumbles, and my mouth falls open in shock. "We got matching friendship butterfly tattoos."

I explode into fits of laughter. Kayden rolls his eyes, pink rushing to his face in embarrassment.

"But why didn't you remove it?" I ask, unable to keep the grin off my face.

Kayden shrugs. "I don't know. I've never gotten a tattoo removed before."

His body shifts as he twists toward his nightstand, where we'd placed the tub of ice cream, grabs it, jabs a spoon into the soft cream, and sticks it into his mouth. There's something about the way Kayden licks the back of the spoon, tongue sweeping over it like he's savoring every last sinful drop, that gets me fucked up. So far he's had that wicked tongue on all parts of my body now, except for the spot where I crave it the most.

Though a little part of me tells me that he's holding the best for last.

My eyes fixate on his tattoos, and I squash the dirty thoughts wandering about in my mind again. My finger swirls around his chest as I stare at them in fascination. Tattoos have always intrigued me. I've rarely seen a fighter who hasn't been inked in all the years I've done MMA. It almost feels like a rite of passage into the sport.

"Maybe I should get a tattoo," I tell him, pointing to the

area on the inside of my arm, below my wrist. "Right here."

Kayden follows the direction of my finger. He cocks a wary brow. "You sure? Skin's pretty tight here. It's the most painful area to get one."

"I can take it. Plus, I think it'll be nice. Just a simple one."

"What do you want to get a tattoo of?"

"Maybe . . ." I blurt out the idea off the top of my head. "Your initials."

He blinks at me, as if he didn't quite hear me right.

"My initials," he echoes skeptically.

I gulp hard, wishing I could retract what I just said. It does sound pathetic when I replay those words back in my head, since it has only been a few hours since we decided we were officially in a relationship.

"Yeah . . . maybe not." I say, immediately backtracking on my suggestion. "It was a stupid idea. Forget I ever said anything."

"No. It's not stupid." Kayden shakes his head, easing my worries. "Lately I've been thinking of getting one too. I want the word *Lucky* right over here." He takes my hand in his and presses it over the skin of the only space on his chest that isn't inked.

The place above his heart.

I trace my finger lightly over the empty space and his eyes follow the line of movement.

"It might be too soon," I admit quietly. "To get each other's names as tattoos."

"Perhaps," he says thoughtfully. "But maybe it doesn't matter. I don't ever want to forget this. I want to remember you—everything about you. I want to remember what it's like to be with you. It doesn't matter if in five or ten years we're just a memory to each other. When I look at your name on my heart, I want to remember that you once had it. And I once had yours."

I stay quiet, inhaling in his beautiful words. Somehow the thought of this thing with Kayden being temporary fills me with sorrow. But I know he means well. He's just stating the truth.

Sometimes couples don't stay together.

I don't know if that will be the case with our relationship, but I really hope not. This thing between us *is* special. Kayden is the only person who can make me feel like this. He makes me cry from laughter and soothes me afterward with gentle words of expression. He makes me want to get a tattoo of him and stay in bed with him all day, floating in his featherlight kisses. He makes me feel cared for and protected and leaves no room for doubt.

But the best thing is that he makes me feel like we're true comrades, walking into battle with each other knowing that we're going to give it all that we've got.

Kayden's finger floats to my mouth and traces the outline of my lips. "What are you thinking about?"

"You," I say with tender smile. "And how amazing you are."

"Huh. I like this new side of you," he notes, stifling a smile of his own as he leans back against the bed frame. "Dishing out compliments like this. It's so refreshing."

"Well, don't get used to it. I might decide to stop being nice again."

Kayden frowns at my warning.

"Hey, that's no way to treat your boyfriend," he murmurs, flipping me onto my back. Warm lips brush the side of my throat and I let out a moan. "You give and you get, Lucky. Give me nice and loving Sienna, and I promise I'll return the favor. Tenfold."

"That's ambitious," I note dryly.

"That's a *promise*." He corrects me, his warm body sliding down mine. His head is now nestled between my legs. "How about I give you a little taste?"

When his mouth lands on the spot where I want him to the most, I lose all ability to speak and comprehend complex sentences. *Oh. My. God*, The first flick of his tongue almost sends me shooting out of the bed. I feel his breathy chuckle against my skin as his hands clamp down on my legs to calm my hips from rocking too much. But it's hard to keep my cool when he has a godlike tongue.

"Keep still, baby," he whispers as he pulls away from me, rubbing circles over the swollen bud with his thumb. A playful gleam ignites in his eyes. "I'm not done with you yet."

He doesn't give me any time to respond, instead, going back down and latching his mouth on the sensitive skin. He teases the seam with his tongue before plunging inside me again. My hips buckle as he fucks me swiftly and hungrily with his mouth, using his thumb to rub my clit for that extra shot of pleasure flying through my body.

"Oh God," I moan. "Kayden . . ."

Kayden continues his torture, his tongue sweeping in upward vertical strokes, then horizontal, then circular; the constant switching up of patterns has me teetering on the edge. Each time, when he feels like I'm on the verge of an orgasm, he pulls back and teases me elsewhere—a frustrating yet mind-scrambling experience—but I'd be lying if I said I didn't enjoy the challenge.

I thought having Kayden inside me was the best that it could ever get but *boy*, was I wrong.

Kayden's tongue truly has a mind of its own as it wreaks havoc all over my pussy, applying pressure to the most sensitive parts without it feeling too overwhelming. I moan loudly as he pokes at my clit, swirling and flicking, building potent, reality-bending pleasure, and just when I think it can't get any better than that, an unexpected finger plunges into me and I gasp so hard that I'm certain I've inhaled all the oxygen in the room. As Kayden's finger rocks inside of me at a steady pace, I feel the wave of my orgasm about to crest, and I'm waiting for it to arrive, to shatter all over me—

Suddenly, the door to Kayden's room flies open and I scream like a banshee, immediately pulling the covers up to shield myself.

"*FUCK!*" Brent yells, looking like he's just witnessed a gruesome crime scene.

Kayden is still beneath the sheets, a huge lump in the sea of white. When he finally emerges, poking his head up, his first instinct is to cover me with his body.

"What the fuck, Brent?" Kayden screams.

"I'm *sorry!*" Brent wails, hand flying up to cover his eyes. "Got back early from our staycation and I was in the area so thought I'd chill here for a bit to catch last night's hockey game. And then I heard noises from your room . . ." His fingers part slightly, allowing a peep at Kayden. "Did you just . . . and you were . . . and she was . . . oh God, I swear I didn't mean—I didn't know you guys were—"

"*Get out*," Kayden growls.

He doesn't have to say it twice.

"Got it." Brent rushes out, slamming the door behind him.

My entire face is rife with embarrassment, knowing that he just saw me and his brother in bed. Together.

How the hell am I going to face him today?

Once he's gone, I scramble to grab my phone. And sure enough, there are eight missed calls from Julian and three from Brent. Also a couple of messages from Alyson asking me if we're still on for lunch.

Shit on a brick. I completely forgot about that.

I return to my usual position and find Kayden still kissing my thigh. I nudge him away reluctantly with my foot.

"You should go," I tell him, trying to sound serious. "You're late for training with Julian."

"But I'm not finished with breakfast yet." He groans, casually swiping a finger over my opening.

"As much as I want to, it can wait." I drag one foot over to the other side so I can sit at the edge of the bed. "You know Jules hates tardiness. Plus, I've got a lunch date with Alyson in the afternoon."

Kayden makes a sad sound of protest, like a schoolboy who's just had his television privileges revoked.

"All right," he grumbles after he notices that I'm not going to budge on this.

I lean back to brush my lips over his to comfort him. Almost instantly, his shoulders sag as he leans into my kiss.

289

"But after I'm done, I'll come find you?" I whisper against his lips.

My words earn a smile from Kayden. "You better, baby."

TWENTY-SEVEN

As I step foot into Caffeinated, I have only one mission. Brent had unsurprisingly scrambled out of the apartment after he got kicked out of the room by Kayden, but that didn't stop me from tracking him down via his Instagram to our favorite coffee spot. And as expected, he, Evans, and Cara are lounging at one of the tables outside the cafe, all wearing smiles as they chat lightly with each other. I made the mistake of introducing Cara to them a while back and now they can't stop hanging out with each other.

I stomp over to them, anger singing in my body. Cara, who's sitting at the edge of the table, notices me, and her expression turns wary. She nudges Brent, who's midway through eating his tuna sandwich, on the shoulder, and he whips his head around. Fear immediately seizes his entire body, already knowing why I've come.

"Key," I yell as I approach him, sticking my hand out. "*Now*."

Brent swallows his bite. He lays his sandwich down on the table with shaky hands. "Sienna, what a nice surprise—"

"I'm *not* fucking around," I snap impatiently. "You broke the treaty."

Brent doesn't think twice about it. He releases a conceding sigh and reaches into his pocket to dig around for the key. "Dammit."

Evans, who is seated opposite him, cuts a glare at his boyfriend as Brent drops the key into my palm. "What the hell did you do?"

Brent looks down at his sandwich shamefully. "I walked in on Kayden giving Sienna h—"

"Hockey tips," I interject quickly. "We're going for a lesson down at Lowell this weekend."

None of them look like they're buying my story one bit. Evans and Cara jerk their heads to Brent, whose face has turned as red as a fire truck.

A look of disbelief crosses Evans's face when he swivels back toward me. "You and Kayden *hooked up*?"

"Well . . . yeah," I admit, voice softening for a moment. "It was supposed to be a private and intimate moment until Brent showed up."

Brent throws his arms up in aggravation. "For the last time, I'm *sorry*. I swear I didn't know you guys were doing it."

"You should have been to paint ball, Brent. They were all over each other. Making out in the fort," Cara mentions casually, uncrossing and crossing her legs. "If the other team wasn't about to ambush us, they probably would have done it right then and there."

I scoff at her accusation. "I have way more class than that."

Cara turns in Brent and Evans's direction, her shoulder shrugging. "Maybe you guys shouldn't have gone to the Ritz-Carlton. Then you wouldn't have missed out on all of this."

"You kidding me? It was an amazing weekend. Screw our friends," Evans mutters, reaching over to grab Brent's sandwich to steal a huge bite. He leaves a measly little piece for Brent to finish, earning him a death glare from its owner. "That two-hour spa was insane. I would sell both my kidneys to go back there."

"If you didn't have your kidneys, they'd be massaging a corpse," Brent says matter-of-factly.

"So how was it?" Cara jerks her head in my direction, a barely restrained smile on her lips. "The sex?"

"Oh my God, I don't wanna hear it!" Brent cries dramatically, his hands flying up to cover his ears. Evans lets out a breathy chuckle.

"Relax. I don't kiss and tell," I say.

A pause. Cara swings her attention to Evans, then to Brent, and then back to me.

"Tell me later?"

I nod, fighting a smile. "Tell you later."

Evans scoffs loudly at me, mouth falling open in betrayal. *I can't believe you*, he mouths to me.

"All right," I announce, glancing at my phone to check the time. "I'm late to meet Alyson for lunch."

Somehow everything feels like a drag to get through until I get to see Kayden. It's odd to feel like this about a guy again, and I don't know if I like it or not. Feeling like you're being consumed by one person feels great—sensational, even—but also dangerous at the same time.

Evans folds his arms over the table, laying his head over them and looking up at me casually. "Oooh, besties with the stepmom now?"

"Not really." I shrug. "But she's actually not that bad."

It's true. Ever since the bridesmaids' fitting a week ago, I've tried to make a habit of helping Alyson out with small bridesmaid duty stuff, like helping her purchase decorative items for the reception and picking out wedding shoe options. It's the only way I know how to bond with her, since we're still only a foot deep into this friendship, but it surprises me that I genuinely enjoy talking to her, which makes me certain that our upcoming lunch appointment will be a breeze to get through.

I bid good-bye to my friends, already making my way to the bus stop where Alyson will be picking me up. But before I get too far down the walkway, I hear Cara racing toward me, her heels clicking fast against the hard pavement.

"Hey, Sienna," she says, a little out of breath. She clutches her folders tightly to her chest. "I just wanna say that I'm happy that you and Kayden are together. It's way overdue at this point."

"Thanks," I say warily, wondering if she ran all the way here just to say that to me. "I guess."

"But . . ." She's quiet for a moment, hesitating. "I just hope you know what you're doing. Brent told me about your two-person fight club against your ex-boyfriend and it just got me a little worried." She drags a hand through her thick strawberry-blond hair, face growing serious. "Kayden seems like a genuinely good guy. And I know you mean well. I just don't want to see anyone hurt because of this."

Her advice makes me frown slightly. I guess I hadn't thought about what happens with the underground now that me and Kayden are romantically involved. We were so wrapped up in each other this weekend I didn't really want to deal with it.

But Kayden and I are professionals. I'm sure we'll be able to work it out. As far as I know, the deal between us still stands.

"Relax. I think it'll be fine." I reassure her with a laugh to ease the mood. "Don't worry about it, Cara."

"All right," she says unconvincingly. "If you say so."

I watch her walk away from me, and when I reach the bus stop and wait for Alyson to pick me up, I can't help repeating her words in my head.

***

Lunch with Alyson was great. It ran a little longer than I had anticipated since neither of us really wanted to end our conversation. I can't remember the last time I had so much fun on one of these obligatory get to know your future stepmother lunch dates that were typically orchestrated by my father—but this time, the conversation felt light and natural.

I get what my father sees in Alyson. She's so genuine in the way that she holds herself and cares for others that it's difficult *not* to like her. She's also an eager listener, prodding me about school and my job, and even taking the time to learn more about MMA before our lunch so she could better understand me and what I do. I didn't have the heart to tell her when she started going on a tangent about the latest UFC fight that I didn't even catch the match.

Afterwards, since I had time to spare, we spent the next few hours doing some shopping. I helped Alyson pick out a cute headpiece to go with her wedding dress. We ended up staying in the boutique until closing time since neither of us could make up our minds between the celestial crystal headpiece or the baroque tiara. Alyson caved and bought both anyway, deciding that she was just going to wing it and make a decision on the day itself.

Later, I had her drop me off at UFG. I promised Kayden I'd check up on how he's doing. Finals are next week—much closer than I realized with all that's been going on—and I'm starting to feel really antsy. But when I breeze through the doors of the gym, the feeling recedes once I spot my two favorite guys battling it out in the cage.

I watch as Julian and Kayden fight each other expertly, challenging each other with a series of moves and countermoves that leaves them both frustrated and breathless. After a series of skillful grapples, Kayden manages to pin Julian in an immovable lock, forcing Julian to give up. Kayden climbs off his trainer and pumps one first into the air, letting out a victorious roar.

The laugh that escapes me unintentionally announces my presence in the gym and Kayden's attention immediately whips to me, a beautiful, excited smile forming on his face. He scrambles out of the cage, pulling off his MMA gloves, and with little effort sweeps me up in his huge arms and spins me around, exhilaration bursting out of him.

When he puts me down, warm lips brush against mine in greeting and I smile against them, winding my arms around his body. He tastes salty from the sweat, but I don't mind it one bit.

"Hey, Lucky," he breathes, hands sliding down to pinch my butt. I make a weird squeak that I've never once heard myself make and slap his hand away playfully.

In the cage, Julian just stands there, both arms resting on his hips as he shakes his head.

"Nauseating. That's what you both are," he grumbles.

Kayden laughs, a deep husky rumble that tickles my core.

I pull away from him and strut over in Julian's direction.

"How's he doing?" I call.

"Pretty good. I made him do extra strength work today since he missed our first session in the morning." Julian hops out of the cage, pulling off the wraps secured to his hands. "Just mostly trying to keep him sharp and focused."

Kayden comes up behind me and does a little shadow boxing combination. "I'm at the top of my game," he declares confidently.

"Yeah, we'll see about that," I say, and Kayden shakes his head, feigning a smile.

Julian, looking like he's completely over the both of us, shuffles to his office to wind down from the session. Which leaves me and Kayden alone in the gym.

He nudges me on my shoulder. "How was hanging out with Alyson?"

"Great," I say, following him to the bench where most of

his stuff is at. He plops himself down. "Bonded over our love for *Gilmore Girls*. Told her about the Jax-Beth drama. I think she might have called Beth a bitch at some point after I told her what she did, but I might have heard it wrong. If she did, I think we're gonna get along just fine."

"It's nice to see that you're spending time with family," Kayden notes thoughtfully. "Even if it's one out of the whole bunch."

"Yeah, well." I give a cold shrug. "I didn't exactly have many great options to choose from." My gaze pivots to Julian's office, where he's busy cleaning up his desk. "At this point, Julian's probably the closest thing I have to a dad."

Right then Julian lifts his head to peek at us through his window and I send him a cheeky wave. Julian glares back and shuts the blinds to his office.

I face Kayden. "He loves me. He just doesn't want to admit it."

"He does," Kayden says with a hint of a smile. He takes a swig from his water bottle before lowering it and resting the bottle on his thigh. "He raves about you all the time when you're not around."

"As he should." I flip my hair confidently.

I edge closer to Kayden and he curls a finger around one of the belt loops of my jeans and tugs me to him.

"You reek by the way," I say as my head dips down to take a huge sniff. I make a disgusted face. "You need a shower."

"Take one with me," Kayden murmurs, hooded eyes sweeping over me as he lifts the hem of my shirt a little and presses a lingering kiss on my bare stomach. I gasp at the sensation, my breathing becoming shallow as he continues to sweep the pads of his thumbs over my bare skin.

I jerk my head at Julian's office. "What about Julian?"

He tilts my chin toward the exit, where Julian just slammed the door shut on his way out.

"Does that answer your question?" He tells me, swinging me up on his arms and hoisting me over his shoulder.

"You're insane!" I squeal, hitting him on his back with my fists weakly. "Put me down. *Now.*"

"Come on. Ease up a little," Kayden coos as he carries me into the men's showers. He puts me down and nudges me into the tight space. "Relax, just get in with me and . . ."— he follows me in and shuts the shower door behind him. A hand clamps around the knob as he continues his sentence— ". . . get real *wet.*"

He twists the knob. Water rains down around us.

I laugh incredulously as the steady stream of water soaks through our clothes, making them cling to our skin. Before I can even mention that I didn't bring a spare change of clothes, Kayden pulls me in for a hungry kiss, devouring my lips with his. A low, pleased growl runs through his chest as he tilts my head to align our mouths better.

Yeah, okay, fuck that then.

Feeling his warmth in my mouth just as our bodies touch sends a rush of exhilaration down my spine and into my core. I find him irresistible like this, especially when he's all hot and bothered from training. I want so badly for him to use the same aggression he showed to Julian on me, except this time all over my fucking body.

"I want you," I whisper, peeling off my shirt and helping him out of his, along with both of our pants.

I toss the rest of our clothes onto the shower floor and kick them to the corner so they won't be a hindrance later on. I don't think I'll ever get used to seeing Kayden's naked body. Long, powerful, not even an ounce of fat on him, just thick and heavy muscle cresting and contouring his body. He's undeniably ripped and gorgeous—and all *mine*.

"You have me," he murmurs back, hands sweeping over the curve of my breasts as his mouth returns to mine, forcing my lips apart with his tongue. The aching need building between my legs intensifies.

The kiss is hot and heavy, mirroring the state of the shower room as it overflows with steam. Pleasure skates up my spine as his mouth travels down the curve of my jaw, down my neck, peppering a trail of searing kisses along the way.

I pull back from Kayden far enough to reach one hand down and grasp his erection, and I stroke him, applying pressure to the most sensitive parts. It's a struggle, with him being so damn big in my hand, but I make do, taking the spurts of breath coming out of his mouth as an indication that he's enjoying this. And *holy shit*, does he enjoy it. He leans in to my movements, pushing his cock into my hand like he can't get enough of it. I tighten my grip on him, applying even more pressure on the base of his cock, making sure to get back at him for the torturous head session he gave me this morning.

Steam permeates the air, now opaque with a thick grey fog. It's getting hard to see anything, even Kayden. But my grip on him is solid, pumping him in long, hard strokes, and just as I feel him trembling, close to losing himself, he wraps a firm hand around my wrist.

"*Stop*," he commands.

"But, Kayden—"

"Turn around. Face the glass."

Holy shit. I love controlling Kayden.

He flips me around then presses both my hands against the glass. I feel his presence leave for a couple of seconds as he goes to retrieve a condom from his pants. He sheathes himself with the rubber and settles behind me. Then he guides his cock into me, plunging straight into my opening.

I'm certain the moan that shoots out of my mouth could be heard from space.

Another desperate noise tears out of me as Kayden rocks his hips into me, rough hands pinching my skin. My hands try to cling to anything, my wet palms slipping against the glass with every thrust. Kayden, noticing my struggle, lets out a low laugh and covers my hands with his, the pressure enough to keep both our hands pressed together against the wet panel without falling.

My God, even when he's fucking me like the unbelievably potent force he is, he's able to find tenderness and affection in the most intense moments.

"Kayden," I whisper, my head twisting back toward him, frantically seeking his lips. I need his taste in my mouth. Now.

Kayden obliges me, meeting my lips with his own, his tongue plunging mercilessly into my mouth. He's deliciously primal and rough, but loving at the same time. Pleasure shoots across my nerve endings he grabs a handful of my hair and tugs until my throat is exposed to his mouth, allowing his lips to graze the exposed skin there. I arch my body against him restlessly, desperate to meet his every kiss and every hurried thrust.

Not even the heavy pounding of water against our skin can drown out our moans. My legs struggle to keep me standing from the sheer pleasure of Kayden having his way with me like this. He's desperate and rough and overpowering, every muscle in his body tightening and squeezing as he keeps fucking me. I feel almost smug that I've done this to him, his curses and groans filling my ears as his movements grow uncontrolled.

"Fuck, baby . . ." He grunts.

Kayden grabs my hips for dear life as he rocks into me, and all I can do is whimper and plead with him *to keep going, please, Kayden, you feel so fucking good* as he fills me up so perfectly, each long stroke intensifying the ache inside me, until I'm no longer panting but screaming for release.

"Kayden . . . I—"

I can barely get the words out before all the tension built inside me explodes, an orgasm rippling through my body like a flash flood, drowning me with a huge wave of pleasure. Joining me, Kayden's fingers dig into my hips hard as he slams into me one final time, breathing hard against me as his entire body convulses in release.

Just as I think we're finished, he whips me back around to face him, caging me in with his arms on either side of the glass. I straighten up, my heart hammering wildly against my chest as the water continues to thunder down on us, the heavy patter of the shower not nearly enough to keep us from drawing together.

"We're not done here, are we?" I say, my mouth so close to Kayden's.

His husky laughter tickles my lips as one finger tickles my chin.

"What do you think?"

The knowing smile I return to him is the only answer he needs before he hoists me up, allowing me to wrap my legs around his waist for round two.

TWENTY-EIGHT

The next few days feel like a weird fever dream of distractions—amusement park dates, rough kisses, and amazing sex. I didn't know I could enjoy someone's company to the point where I'd be addicted to it. And I am. Addicted to Kayden.

The only time I'm not with him is during his training sessions with Julian, which I've now been permanently banned from. Julian thinks I'm a major distraction and I can't blame him. Kayden can't keep his attention on his opponent long before his eyes search for mine. And while it's flattering, I certainly don't want to be the person who costs Kayden his championship.

But apart from that, I like the moments we have. I finally got him to leave notes more frequently for me around the apartment before he leaves for a training session. He always signs it with a "<3," which is sweet. And when Kayden gets back home, we stay up late, lying in his bed, while he tells me about his family. How his parents used to be. How sweet and amazing Clarissa was. I wish I could have met her. From the stories he's told me about her and her funny, spunky, wise beyond her years nature, I think we would have gotten along well.

I tell him about Beth too. I have been seeing her around campus more often recently, and I wonder what's been going on with her. A part of me wants to approach her since I'm still worried about her, but every time I build up the courage to try, I find myself hesitating, unable to keep my anger from overshadowing my guilt. The calls and texts from my dad to make up with her haven't exactly helped the situation since I have a stubborn habit of not doing what my dad tells me to do.

He did take it as a small win that I finally decided to RSVP yes to the wedding. But I'm only doing it because I like Alyson and want to show my support for her. And I guess if she loves my dad, it means there's at least *something* in there that's worth loving. Even if I can't see it.

All I really care right now is Kayden. Seeing him is more than enough to reel me back into a happy, contented state.

We usually take turns on whose bed we're going to be sleeping in every night just to keep things fair. Tonight, Kayden sits up against my bed frame while my head rests in his lap as I churn out an assignment on my laptop. I can feel him watching me as he plays with my hair lazily. I pull my attention away from the laptop and look up at him, smiling and catching one in return.

He's so beautiful like this. His black hair is an adorable mess from the many hours I spent running through it with my fingers. I suddenly envision myself tugging on it again while I let him have his way with me. I wonder if he shares the same sentiment I have right now.

"What's up?" I whisper as his eyes continue to roam over my face.

"Come visit my parents with me this weekend," Kayden blurts.

"What?" I shut my laptop and pull myself off his lap to really look at him. "Really?"

"Yeah," he says, uncertainty washing over his expression as he realizes how unsettled I look. "Is everything all right?"

"Yeah. No . . . I don't know." I let out a sigh, dragging a hand over the side of my face. The thought of visiting his parents make me nervous. Really nervous. "Look, it's bad enough we're missing one day before the finals for Alyson and my dad's wedding. I just don't know if we have the time to spare. You need to train."

"Come on, it's my family we're talking about." He arches an eyebrow. "I know it's bad timing but I gotta go home. Brent's bringing Evans as well, and it's a big deal to him. So I thought I'd bring you, too, because you're really special," he says, his voice drooping with tenderness, which makes me feel even more guilty. "Plus my adoptive parents have been good to me. And I really think they'd like you."

"I don't know . . ." My voice trails off. I pull my knees toward me, wrapping my arms around them. "We've only been together for less than a week."

It sounds unnecessarily cruel when I admit the fact out loud, but isn't it the truth? Everything suddenly feels like it's getting really serious, which prickles a nervous feeling in my system.

"Yeah, so?" Kayden's face falls slightly but he tries to cover up the disappointment of hearing those words with a strained smile. "We've known each other longer than that. I think we're actually kind of overdue for a meet-the-parents session."

I bite my lip in contemplation. I guess he's right in a way. It does feel like we've known each other longer since we see each other every day and are also living together.

And yet, I still don't give him an answer. I know I should tell him what he wants to hear and I don't know why I can't. A hesitant feeling tugs at me, and I feel bad for even feeling it.

Kayden lets out a frustrated sigh when he notices my silence. "It's only for one weekend, Sienna. What's the big deal?"

"I'm sorry," I mutter, pulling my knees together to hug them. "I just want to set our priorities straight."

Instead of agreeing with me like I'd expect, he narrows his eyes at me in odd suspicion. "Is that the *only* reason?"

Somehow, that rouses annoyance within me. I straighten up on the bed.

"What's that supposed to mean?" I glare at him.

Kayden forces himself to look away.

"Nothing."

I frown at his answer. Surely it's something. This is the first time all week that he's been frustrated with me and I want to know what's up with him.

"No, seriously. If you want to say something, you can say it," I tell him.

Kayden hesitates. Instead, he rubs a hand over his mouth and releases a strained breath.

"I'm just saying that if you're worried about training, don't worry—I've got it covered," he assures me in a serious tone. "Saturday is supposed to be rest day anyway. And I'll make sure to squeeze in a session or two on Sunday when we get back."

Somehow I doubt that that's what he was going to say but I don't push him because I don't want to make a big scene. This was supposed to be a normal, casual night, and now everything between us feels rigid and tense.

"Okay. You just have to keep focused," I urge him, scooting over and cupping his face between my hands. "Seriously. You have to win, okay? This is what we've been working toward. So we gotta finish this."

He nods wordlessly, his hands coming down on my wrist.

"Lucky, I won't let you down."

"All right." I nod back, dropping my hands to my lap. I let out a sigh, dipping my head low as the nerves continue to wreak havoc inside me. "You're right. I'm just nervous."

I don't elaborate because I don't exactly know what I'm nervous about. The upcoming fight against Jax? Meeting his parents? Perhaps both.

"There's nothing to be nervous about." Kayden pulls me into his lap so I'm straddling him. He pushes my hair back behind my ears and slides his hands down my face. "I'll protect you if anything happens. I'll always protect you."

I nod with a small smile. "I'll always protect you too."

Kayden brushes his lips over mine in a pleasantly loving kiss. I lean into him, craving the warmth of his body and the closeness between us that I can't seem to get enough of. The hard muscles of his chest relax beneath me when I press a light hand against them. His tongue sweeps against mine tenderly as his fingers outline my back gently, a silent declaration of just how much he cares and wants me. When we pull away from each other, we're both breathing hard, staring into each other's eyes.

"So we're good?" He whispers, tilting my head with his index finger to level his gaze with mine.

"Yeah," I say quietly. "We're good."

If meeting Kayden's parents will make him happy, then I'll gladly do it. I want to be there for him and I want to show him that I care. After everything that we've been through, we deserve to be happy for once, and I'm not going to let this gnawing, terrible feeling ruin the both of us.

Even if somehow, it feels like it's already beginning to do its damage.

***

On Saturday Kayden and I load all our bags into his truck before driving it over to the dorms to pick up Evans and Brent. When we pull up at the entrance, Evans shows up with enough luggage for a two-week vacation around Europe.

"What the hell is in there?" I look at him curiously as he tucks in the handle to his monstrously sized luggage. He struggles to lift it into the truck bed, so I just nudge him away, preferring to do it myself. I haul it into the space with little effort. "You know we're only staying there for one night, right?"

Evans blinks at me. "I have a lot of skin care."

Brent, who drops his duffel bag beside the luggage, pats his hands together and shrugs. "He really does."

"All right, fine," I say, snapping the tailgate into place. I walk back to the front door and Brent intercepts me quickly, laying a hand over the door.

"I call shotgun," he announces.

"No way." I nudge his hand away. "I was sitting here just now."

Brent narrows his eyes at me. "But I'm the brother."

"And I'm the girlfriend," I say defiantly.

"It's only been a week. Who knows how long you'll stick around after," he mutters.

Beside me, Evans makes an *oof* face. I ignore him.

"*Excuse me*?" I say incredulously, my hands flying to my hips.

Brent swallows hard at my response but tries to look unfazed.

"Cut it, the both of you," Kayden snaps from the driver's seat. He leans back, arm slung over the front seat headrest. He casts me a sympathetic look. "I'm sorry, Sienna. Brent gets a bit weird with shotgun. You mind taking the back?"

"Fine." My face twists into a scowl as I look at Brent, prying the backseat door open a little too hard and climbing into the truck. "As long as you watch yours, Brent, because I'll be coming for you. You better be sleeping with one eye open."

"He rarely sleeps with me around anyway," Evans says with a sly wink.

Kayden pulls us out of the parking lot. Brent loads up some Guns N' Roses and we let the song fill up the silence in the car.

I think back to the last time I visited home—that disastrous family dinner when my dad announced his and Alyson's engagement. I hadn't heard from him about visiting home again since, despite Alyson nagging me to do so. He's probably still angry at me for what I did, so I don't blame him for not reaching out. Maybe I should just be the bigger person and reach out first.

Yeah, I don't know. My ego isn't quite ready for that step just yet.

I do wonder how my dad would react if I brought Kayden home. He'll see us together anyway at the wedding, so I wonder if he'll approve. Given my track record of dating underground fighters, probably not. But my dad was right to be wary of Jax, viewing him as a terrible influence on me. I probably should just have listened to him. If I had, we all wouldn't be in this mess.

"Is there anything we should know before meeting your parents?" Evans asks as he reaches over to the front seat to steal Brent's phone to switch up the song playlist.

"Well, Pat's the tougher critic but she usually means well," Kayden explains, casually gripping the wheel with one arm. "But other than that, they're both pretty cool."

Brent turns behind to look at me, neck craning. "When you and Jax were dating, did you visit his parents?"

"Once." I shrug. "But he was always private about his family. Maybe he knew we weren't going to last, which is why he didn't really bother."

"I'm glad you didn't go back to him." Kayden glances at me in the rearview mirror. "At least that'll take the guilt off of me when I bash his face in next weekend. Which, speaking of finals . . ." Kayden's voice trails off, uncertainty lacing his tone as he faces Brent. "If you could not tell Pat and Elijah about it, that'll be great. I just don't want them to worry."

"Aw, come on. You know I can't keep secrets." Brent moans. "And also, I already told them."

"*Brent!*" Kayden scolds.

"I'm sorry," Brent cries, guilt reddening his face. "They wanted to know what you were up to. They're not gonna be angry at you, you know that."

"Somehow, that feels worse," Kayden mutters.

"It's okay because he's gonna win that fight," Evans says confidently, turning to me. "Jax is gonna be like *pow-pow-pow!*" He does a jab-cross combo at me and I laugh at how sloppy it is. "And Kayden's gonna be like the fuck you don't." Evans reels back in slow motion, *Matrix*-style as he pretends to dodge a few blows.

Sometimes, I wonder if he's a ten-year-old stuck in a grown man's body.

"Spot-on impression, Evans," I deadpan.

Evans lets out a chuckle, then jabs at me—for real this time, his fist making contact with my forearm. Evans winces when he makes contact against the skin, fist reeling back in pain.

"Fuck. That's all muscle," he says incredulously as he shakes off the pain.

From the front, Kayden looks at me proudly in the rearview mirror again, as if saying *That's my girl*.

"Of course, what did you expect?" I tell Evans.

A challenging gleam hops into his eyes and he punches my forearm again, harder this time. It causes a sting to shoot down my arm. Evans pulls back, looking smugger this time around once he catches me wincing at the pain.

"Okay, now you're just asking for it," I mutter, pushing the sleeves of my top up my arms.

And then I plunge forward to tackle Evans.

"Help!" Evans pleads as I dig my arm against his neck while wrestling him into a grapple by trapping his hands. "B, help me!"

Brent merely chuckles, deciding instead to stare straight at the road. "You brought this upon yourself."

I finally have him pinned, with his face smashed against the seat while I hold him captive from the top. Evans struggles relentlessly against me, trying to pry his hands free from me but I hold him steady, deciding I'll at least torture him like this for a couple more minutes.

"Hello!" A dark-haired woman pries open the backseat door, forcing me to realize that the car has stopped. She's in her midforties, her complexion fair and her cheeks rosy, with her eyes bulging out of their sockets when she catches at me and Evans together.

The shock of seeing the woman I'm supposed to impress is enough for me to momentarily lose focus. Evans takes that as an opportunity to writhe free from under me, the sudden movement causing me to stumble forward and fall onto the gritty road face first.

Well, shit.

"Hi, Mrs. Jacobs," I say shamefully.

TWENTY-NINE

Once I've awkwardly dusted the dirt from my jeans, I gawk at the house in front of me. It's a modest two-story suburban home with a rustic red brick exterior, surrounded by a white picket fence and a sprawling green yard boxed in by tall, luscious trees. It reminds me a little of the house my family used to live in before the divorce. Kayden's family house seems like a far cry from my dad's loud mansion. It feels like a real home.

The interior of the home is lovely, with dark wooden floors and a myriad of psychology and sociology books displayed on floating bookshelves along the hallway. Pictures of the happy family of four line the walls, along with medals won by Kayden and Brent during high school. I smile to myself at the thought of just how much the Jacobs really value and appreciate mementos of their kids' childhoods, and embracing Kayden wholly as one of their own. With what he endured with his parents and Clarissa, it's nice knowing that he was well taken care of and supported by his new family.

"Oh, you don't need to do that, Patricia," I call after her as she drags mine and Kayden's bags into the house. I catch up to her and give the duffel bag a little tug. "I can bring those up myself."

"Nonsense. You're our guest." She shakes her head fervently, a warm, nurturing smile gracing her face. She nudges me aside so she can take the stairs. "I just hope you guys are hungry because I prepared some food outside."

Kayden trails in after me, carrying Brent's and Evans's bags with little effort. He sets the bags by the foot of the stairs and makes a sharp left, peeking through the sliding doors that lead outside to the backyard.

"Hey, what's up with the feast? Are we expecting more people?" Kayden prompts.

"Your mom just wants you guys well fed," Kayden's dad, Elijah, says as he pops out of the living room and shuffles into the hallway, his hands clasped behind his back. He tilts his chin in Kayden's direction, eyes growing sharp. "Especially *you* since we heard you're going to be fighting next week."

Kayden blinks hard, then just as he's about to open his mouth to respond, Brent swoops in in a wildly panicked tone. "We should unpack!" He exclaims as he pushes Kayden quickly up the stairs. I follow behind them, the floorboards creaking with every step I take as I ascend. By the time we reach the top, Patricia is already in Kayden's room, unloading our bags inside.

"Once you're settled into your rooms, come down for some food, all right?" She props herself in the doorway, beaming at me with a friendly yet evaluating expression on her face. "I'm looking forward to getting to know Sienna."

I force a smile back.

As she disappears back down the stairs, Kayden closes the door. I wander into the heart of his bedroom, looking curiously around the space. It's a standard boy's room, with pale-blue walls, matching colored sheets and pillows, and movie posters plastered across his walls. His closet is small, creaking open to reveal a half dozen boxing wraps littered across the floor and a pair of dusty red gloves hanging on one of the hooks behind the door.

My gaze catches the few photos perched on his desk, and I walk over to lift one of the frame. Both boys are in their high school graduation robes, posing together outside the school. Kayden wears a shy, heavy-lidded smile on his face as he loops an arm over Brent, who leans into his brother's embrace eagerly. It's an adorable picture, one of the rare ones that I've seen of Kayden smiling and looking at ease.

"Look at you and Brent," I say, cradling the frame and angling it in Kayden's direction. "So cute."

"Yeah. You know we didn't really get along at first," he says as he walks over to take the picture from me, staring at it with a glassy expression. "It was weird getting a new brother when Clarissa was so far away from me. But he really helped me out when I was spiraling after her death. Helped me get through some of the trauma."

He sets the frame down, pressing his mouth tight as he slips into the memory. I embrace him from behind and press a light, soothing kiss on his shoulder.

"I'm glad he was there for you," I murmur.

Kayden turns around so we're chest to chest. His hands are warm and steady press against my back.

"Thanks for coming home with me today." The genuine delight in his tone immediately puts me at ease. "Did I tell you that you look beautiful today?"

"Only today?" I tease.

"Yesterday, today, tomorrow, every day," he whispers, his desire-thickened voice dancing with purpose over my skin.

His eyes soften as he leans down and presses his lips over mine with feathery tenderness for a couple of heartbeats. The pressure is soft, yet laden with so much meaning and affection the feeling makes my entire body sing with purpose.

"Kayden?" I pull away from his lips enough to run my thumb over the stubble shading his jaw.

"Mmmm?" He hums lazily as he dips his head down to my neck.

"As much as I want to continue this, we should really head downstairs," I whisper. "Before your mom barges in and asks what we're doing."

"I hate it when you're right. She'd actually do that." Kayden nuzzles my neck, inhaling my scent like he wants to imprint it into his brain permanently, and plants a kiss on the hollow behind my ear before pulling back and weaving his fingers through mine. "Let's go."

***

When we finally pull ourselves downstairs, Evans and Brent are already outside with Elijah and Patricia. Elijah is stationed at the barbecue pit, expertly grilling some hot dogs. Kayden's mother really spared no expense with the vast spread of food. Pistachio cake, miniature lemon tarts with some kind of compote, along with other savory bites like kebabs and tuna casserole.

When we're able to join the party, Patricia scoops some of the casserole onto a plate and holds it up in invitation for Kayden, wriggling her eyebrows.

"I'll pass." He shakes his head, shoving his hands deep into the pocket of his khaki shorts. "I'm supposed to be eating clean until the fight."

"But it's your favorite," she notes with a frown. "You and Brent used to beg me to make it for you every day for school."

"Fine. I'll have a bit," he mutters, pinching some off the plate. Patricia's face lights up in delight. "But no hot dogs for me," he warns, pointing to his dad who's just about to offer him a freshly made hot dog right off the grill.

Elijah gives a disappointed head shake and hands the plate to Brent, who gladly takes it.

I settle into the unoccupied seat beside Brent and grab a plate, helping myself to the food. Despite my lack of hunger, I'm afraid I might lose approval points from the Jacobs if I don't eat something.

"So, Sienna . . ." Elijah nods toward me as he pokes the hot dogs around with his spatula. "What do you do?"

"I'm an MMA trainer," I say, collecting a few lemon tarts on my plate. "In fact, I used to train Kayden."

"That's impressive." He cuts a glance at Kayden, who stands uncomfortably beside me while he chews his casserole. "How is my boy in the ring?"

"Good," I say with a smile. "One of the best fighters I've ever had the privilege of working with."

"She's exaggerating." Kayden waves a dismissive hand.

I look up at him. "You know I don't exaggerate."

Patricia presses her lips together, hands resting on her hips as she looks at me. "Don't you find it such a gritty sport?"

"I suppose it is," I say with a shrug. "But it's also the purest form of combat. It takes a lot of mental and physical strength to do MMA. And I think it should be celebrated because of that."

"MMA maybe. Debatable. But the underground can hardly be called a sport," she says with a scoff. "Do you fight in the underground, Sienna?"

"No, I don't."

"Good. At least you're not in the business of associating yourself with an illegal syndicate like Kayden over here," she mutters as she begins to clear the empty plates scattered across the table. "You know, I still don't understand why you keep doing this to yourself."

Brent chews silently, sensing the awkwardness that has arrived with this new topic of conversation. Evans bumps his head down and stuffs the remainder of his casserole into his mouth as silently as he can.

"Patricia," Elijah warns. "Not now, please."

His wife ignores him. Cuts a narrowed glance at her adopted son.

"I'm sorry, but you know I have to say something. You know Eli and I try to be supportive of what you do, Kayden," she says sternly. "And we try hard to understand. But it's getting harder for us to stand idly by while you fight these men for money. Especially when we've given you plenty already."

A muscle tenses in Kayden's jaw as his gaze dips, looking down at his feet. "You know it's not about the money."

"I know, but that doesn't make it any less wrong." Patricia swivels her head to me, a slight edge to her voice. "What do *you* think about it, Sienna?"

Fuck.

The entire family is now staring at me expectantly, waiting for my answer. It swamps with me unease and I gulp hard, scrambling to search for the least wrong answer.

My voice feels tight when I finally speak again. "I, um, I have my own reservations about the underground, but I think if that's what he wants to pursue, I—I won't stop him."

Patricia's frown deepens, dissatisfied with my response.

"Well, I disagree with that," she replies, her face set in a tense countenance.

I suck in a breath to ease the tightness clutching my chest but it only serves to strengthen its place even more.

Kayden is right; Patricia really is a tough critic.

While the group chats for a while longer, I excuse myself and bring all the dirty plates into the kitchen. Making myself useful is always a great way to get out of an uncomfortable situation.

I'm a few minutes deep into scrubbing the dishes when someone comes up beside me and takes the plate from my hands. I spin around to look at who my new companion is.

"I apologize if I came across as harsh on you, Sienna," Patricia murmurs, her expression sincere and remorseful.

Now I feel guilty that *she* feels guilty. I mean, she's his mom. Of course she has his best interests at heart. I'm not going to fault her for that.

I plant my attention back on the dishes. "That's okay. I know you care about Kayden and you only want what's best for him."

"I can sense that you feel the same too," she notes thoughtfully, picking up a sponge herself and rubbing it over the back of the plate. "Kayden has always been troubled. Don't get me wrong, I don't mind him fighting. It's just, what he's doing in the underground and you encouraging it . . . it feels dangerous."

"I understand why you worry," I say, biting my bottom lip in contemplation. "If it makes you feel any better, I won't let anyone hurt your son."

Patricia drops the sponge into the sink and pats her hands dry on her apron, shaking her head.

"That's not why I worry, Sienna."

A confused look passes over my face.

"I don't understand."

She looks around the kitchen, checking for anyone who might be eavesdropping. When the coast is clear, she lowers her head, along with her voice, and meets my gaze with her own, except this time, her eyes are dark with worry. "I'm only saying this because I think you're a good person. And the both of you clearly care about each other a lot. But it's hard to be with someone with the hopes of fighting their demons for them. They've got to do it on their own."

"Oh um . . ." Her words catch me off guard. "With all due respect, I'm not in this relationship to fix him. And I know

Kayden has his issues, but it seems like he's doing really well."

His mood has definitely brightened up when he's around me and he's more open and honest with me than ever before. I definitely sense the change but now, upon reflecting on mine and Patricia's conversation, I wonder if it's temporary. Would he still be that same person if I left?

"Perhaps." Patricia pulls away from me, fiddling with the edge of her apron. "But it's not just him I'm talking about. I'm talking about you too. Seems like you're also fighting a fight of your own."

"Oh," is the only thing I can say as her statement permeates my troubled brain.

Damn, she's good. Of course she is. She's a social worker, she's supposed to be good at reading people. And the fact that she can sense all from one conversation makes me feel uneasy. My body feels helpless against the weight-crushing disappointment, knowing that no matter how hard I try with Kayden's mom, her opinion of me has already been set.

"Excuse me," I say, the feeling of inadequacy and anxiety climbing up my throat and pricking my eyes with tears. I drop my sponge into the sink and scramble out of the kitchen.

I don't want her to see me like this. Or anyone for that matter.

I need to be alone.

***

I decide the best course of action is to hide from the rest of them for the remainder of the day, perching myself on the footsteps of the front door. I inhale deep, steady breaths to get rid of the strain between my shoulders and crammed in my chest. I must have stayed out long enough for my absence to be noticed because the front door wrenches open and a concerned-looking Kayden joins me by the steps.

"You all right?" He asks, looping an arm over me and pulling me into his warmth.

"Your mom hates me." I make a sad noise.

"No, she doesn't," he says obliviously.

"Trust me. She does."

He pauses, concern deepening as his mouth sinks into a frown.

"Did she say something to you?"

Doubt crosses my mind, holding me back from saying anything. As much as I want to tell him what his mom said to me, I doubt it's a good idea. The last thing I want is to drive a wedge between him and his family. Plus, I'm still not sure what to make of Patricia's words. Could she be right about me and Kayden? That we're trying hard to fix each other to no avail?

It doesn't feel like it.

"Nothing much." I shrug instead. Kayden doesn't look convinced one bit. I know he's going to press me about it so I clear my throat and point to his right hand, insistent on changing the subject. "Why do you have the car keys?"

"Oh." He looks at the keys as if he'd forgotten he was holding them. "I want to take you somewhere."

"Okay," I say hesitantly "Where?"

He smiles. "You'll see."

***

"If this is your idea of a date, I think we might have to visit the whole idea of you going to therapy," I mutter, my flats crunching against the gravel pavement heading toward the cemetery.

It's already late evening by the time we arrive, and the dimming sun across the horizon is the only light illuminating our path. So far no bones, which I'm really grateful for.

Yay.

Sienna—1. The dead—0.

Kayden hurls an apologetic look my way as he guides me along the rocky pathway. I swallow hard as my eyes roam the headstones erected on either side of the path. Some of them look centuries old, weather-beaten with much of their carved words now faded away. Others are overrun with grass, shielding the stones from the world, neglected by the families who have long forgotten them by now.

I'm not usually afraid of anything but there's something about being among the dead that really gives me the creeps.

A good few minutes later, we finally come to a halt. It takes me a while to make out what he's seeing until I take my place beside him. His entire body tenses when he stares at the very thing that has haunted him for a long time—his family's graves.

My eyes scan their individual names: Robert, Laura, and finally Clarissa. A sharp pain twists in my gut when my eyes fall on her name. Gone too soon. All of them.

And my gaze pivots to the man in front of me. Kayden.

Marked by tragedy and yet he's still here. Alive and beautifully broken—but still *fighting*. For himself. For the people he loved who aren't here to see his fight.

I read the lovely words carved into their tombstones. I stand there silently, paying my respects to them, wishing I could have met them, sympathizing with the time that was cruelly stolen from them, and lastly, thanking them for blessing this Earth with the wonderful man next to me.

Kayden slides his arm around my waist and kisses the top of my head.

"They would have loved you, you know," he says after a while, his voice strained. "My parents always knew I was going to end up with a spunky girl who could hold her own."

"And Clarissa?" I whisper, looking up at Kayden.

"She said you would be pretty," he murmurs, fingers drifting into my hair. "And you'd probably want to sneak her into parties."

"I would," I say smugly. Then I add, with a tone of sternness, "But no alcohol until she's twenty-one."

"*Oof*, I don't think she'd like that. But she'd probably admire you for being responsible with her."

The conversation falls silent and I let the wind carry it away. Kayden clasps his hand in mine and I let him have a long moment to himself. He stares at the tombstone, despair and ache carved into every line of his face. I let him ruminate on the what-ifs and what could have beens, and I watch his tears fall down his cheeks. I don't tell him that it's going to be okay. Because it won't be, and I know better than to tell him that. Instead, I just let him be with himself in his grief, hoping my presence is enough to bring some kind of comfort.

We stay there for about an hour, and after a while, Kayden tells me that we should go. I nod wordlessly and let him guide me back to his truck. He seems somewhat lighter now, like a huge burden on his shoulders has been lifted. When we're back in the vehicle, he turns on the engine but we don't pull out of the parking lot just yet. He reaches for me, one hand sliding over my cheek.

"Thank you for coming here with me," he says.

"Of course. You know I'm always here for you," I murmur back.

"After what happened with my family, I've barely been getting by, just waiting to join them." His voice wavers, eyes closing briefly before meeting mine again, this time clouded with agonizing affection for me. "But you—you brought me back to life, Lucky. And I'm forever indebted to you."

I'm awed by the way he looks at me, like everything is pitch black and I'm the only radiant light he needs. Smiling, Kayden leans in a little more and captures my lips with his. It is a soft kiss, a kiss that feels like I'm meandering in the clouds with him. A kiss that kick-starts my heart and floods it with bliss. Unspoken words are flying, making my head spin like a turntable. But when he pulls away ever so slightly, his lips still hovering over mine, I'm certain I hear the three words that escape from them.

"I love you," Kayden whispers.

*****

I didn't say it back.

Kayden said *I love you* and I didn't say it back.

What the fuck is *wrong* with me?

He doesn't even bring up the matter the next morning. Not even when we're packing up to leave Elijah and Patricia's home, which makes me feel even more guilty about it. The horrible memory of me saying thank you and pulling him into a hug right after he said those words has been plaguing my mind like a stubborn scar since.

A hug. A goddamned hug.

I laugh to myself at how absurd it is.

Now you're really asking to be dumped.

I wish I said it back. Kayden deserves to hear those words from me. We've been through a lot this past month and a half together, and deep down I know my feelings for him are mutual.

But I can't seem to muster the courage to tell him, not when I've harbored so much distrust for those words because of Jax. Over the three years we dated, I was so sure I loved him and was certain that he felt the same way. But ever since we broke up, I've realized that he never really meant his *I love yous* whenever he said them. He would only say it to appease me or when he felt like he was backed into a corner. I vividly remember times when I'd whisper those words to him in the dark only to be met with cold silence. And when I'd pry about it, he'd tell me to drop it.

I thought I was Jax's only focus. His priority. Perhaps I was none of that and the priority had always been himself. He just hid it from me really well.

How the hell did I put up with that for so long? How did I let him string me along like that for years, allowing him to take advantage of my unconditional love to get me to stay in an unhealthy relationship with him? He made me a docile pet, a willing submissive who craved his love. It fueled my obsession of constantly, always wanting to reach out to him despite him always putting me down.

I'm angry. Angry that I let myself fall into his large pit of empty truths.

I made a promise long ago I was going to get focused. Instead, I allowed myself to be swept away further and further from my original goal—the one that I'd sworn I wasn't going to stop until I achieved.

Jax needs to be stopped.

I won't let him get away with what he's done to me. To many others.

I'm done with waiting.

THIRTY

It's finally the day of my dad and Alyson's wedding. They've chosen a beautiful location—the elegant Dane Estate in Chestnut Hill—probably on Alyson's insistence since my dad has the absolute worst taste when it comes to wedding venues. At his last wedding, he was adamant about a location teeming with gold that made the entire place look gaudy and more like the McMansion he'd moved into.

Regardless, the wedding ceremony was beautiful. I think I might have shed a tear when Alyson emerged in wearing her wedding dress—a long-sleeved A-line style with a gorgeous lace open back for that touch of sensuality—coupled with a long veil and the celestial headpiece that we bought together the other day perched on her head. She looked breathtaking walking down the aisle to my dad, whom I had never seen cry during any of his previous weddings and who was now unable to keep his tears at bay.

Right until then, I had my reservations that this

marriage would last, but as I stood there and watched my dad kiss Alyson, beaming with pride and love for her as they walked back up the aisle together after being pronounced husband and wife, I became convinced that this was indeed the kind of love that my dad had been waiting for his whole life.

As I join the rest of the bridesmaids down the aisle, I catch sight of Jax sitting in one of the back rows, his gaze cutting deeply into me. A slow, malicious smile stretches across his face when our eyes meet. I roll my eyes. At least Beth, who's walking in front of me, doesn't notice anything amiss. Throughout the ceremony, I'd been nothing but civil with my sister for Alyson and my dad's sake, but she has another thing coming if she thinks I'm going to extend the same courtesy to Jax.

A white tent has been erected outside of the estate on the Founder's Lawn to house the seventy-five guests for the reception. Large, lodge-inspired chandeliers droop from the tent ceiling, leaning into the rustic, natural-oak themed decorations that pepper the reception tent. Intricate rose arrangements are perched on every table, paired with mason jars with twinkly lights in them and unique terrarium candles that would put any woman's Pinterest board to shame.

I mingle with the other bridesmaids, greeting all the guests strolling about. Kayden has gone to the bar to fetch us some drinks, which I'm thankful for, since I'm going to need all the alcohol I can get to get through the night. The jazz band that they hired have begun playing my dad's favorite song, "La Vie en Rose," and I groan, already knowing what to expect next.

And sure enough, my dad ambles over to me, a hesitant smile on his face as he extends a hand to me.

"Would you do me the honor of a father-daughter dance, Sienna?" He asks expectantly.

A couple of *awwws* sound from the guests surrounding us, their faces bright with anticipation as they watch us. I nod silently and place my hand on top of my dad's, allowing him to lead me onto the dance floor. He tucks his hands behind my back and I slide my mine over his shoulders as we sway to the lovely instrumental music. I feel the watchful gazes of all the guests as we slow dance, expanding the tightening feeling in my chest.

"You know, if you get married again you might actually run out of cute wedding venues in Boston that you haven't already booked," I note dryly as our bodies sway to the steady beat of the song.

He pulls back enough for me to see the frustration flashing in his eyes. "Sienna."

"Sorry. Force of habit," I mutter. "The wedding's lovely."

"Thanks for coming," my dad murmurs to me in an appreciative tone. "It really means a lot to me."

I stay silent, mulling his sincerity over in my head. It's the first time I've allowed my dad to say something nice to me without spewing something defensive back. I don't want to. And in a rare moment of letting my guard down, I drop my head on my dad's shoulder and cling to his shoulders tightly.

"Alyson's a keeper, Dad," I say, barely a whisper, as I watch Alyson dance with a couple of her bridesmaids, all radiant and full of laughter. "Don't let her go."

"I won't," he says, jaw set at a determined angle. He pauses for a beat, swaying me for another full circle, before speaking again. "Look, I know I'm hard on you most times, Sienna. I just . . . I don't want to lose this family. You, Alyson, and Beth are all I've got. And I know I haven't been perfect. Far from that, actually. But I'm gonna try to earn back that trust, okay?"

I really want to believe him. He's made so many promises over the years that it's hard to keep track of them now. Perhaps it's time for another leap of faith. Because at the end of the day, he's still my dad and I love him. Even though sometimes I really wish I didn't.

"Okay," I whisper.

A slow smile crosses his face and he rests his chin on my head, holding me in a protective and loving embrace, like a father does when his child feels broken.

When the song is over, I smack a kiss on my father's cheek before heading back to my table, where Kayden's seated and waiting for me with two glasses of champagne. I snatch a glass from him and down it in one go. The fizzing liquid burns as it rushes down my throat.

"Whoa, easy there." Kayden peels the champagne glass from my grasp and sets it on the table.

I let out an unceremoniously unclassy burp and laugh to myself at how funny that sounds. Kayden chuckles at my behavior and pulls me into his lap, trapping me in his huge arms, and his lips are suddenly in my ear, gaze matching mine in the direction of Alyson and my dad as they take the dance floor together.

"Think we'll be like them one day?"

I look at him. *Really* look at him.

"What are you implying?" I ask softly.

"You know what I'm implying," he murmurs. "I'm talking about the whole marriage and kids thing."

"Wait a minute." I press a steady hand against his chest. "We're actually having the marriage and kids talk?"

"Why not? Now's a good time as any," he says, taking my hand from his chest and kissing the area below my thumb adoringly. "Weddings get me thinking about these things."

"All right. Let's do this." I crack my knuckles like I'm preparing to throw down. "You actually think we might last and get married?" We're now face to face, unable to wipe the smiles off our faces.

"Hell, yeah." A big, bold grin from Kayden. "We go big or go home, Lucky."

The joy in my heart starts fizzling like the champagne that was in my hand.

"Kids?" I prompt.

"Two. A boy and a girl. I don't care which one comes first," he says without hesitation. "We'll name him Max, after Maximus, because that name is cool. And the girl—Clarissa, after my sister."

My face hurts from smiling. I'm stunned at just how much he's thought about this and the beautiful future he has imagined for us. It's not like I haven't stopped to think about it either; the future has always been something that felt murky and distant, but with Kayden, it has never looked so crystal clear.

"You've thought about this, haven't you?" I whisper, heart swamped with adoration for this man.

"Of course I have," he says, pouring every ounce of affection and love into his words. "I like to think that there is a future for us. I'm not in this relationship to see how it goes, Sienna. I'm in love with you and I'm in this for the long run. If you'll have me, of course."

Kayden's words melt my already fragile heart. I lean forward and brush my lips against his. I still can't speak the words he so desperately wants me to say, but I hope I can show him by kissing him fervently like this—a gasp-stealing, world-dissolving kind of kiss and wrapping us both in a happy, blissful bubble.

Later, he guides me onto the dance floor to join the rest of the guests and engulfs me in his arms as we dance to the myriad of ballad songs played by the band. Even as they play Ed Sheeran's "Give Me Love," which Kayden naturally detests, he still lets me have a go at it, leading him throughout the song and swaying circles with me.

After a while, I excuse myself to head to the bathroom situated inside the estate house. Fortunately for me, it's only a short walk through the garden into Founder's Room—a saving grace for my bladder, which has been holding in five glasses of champagne like a champ. After relieving myself, I step back into the hall leading to the reception tent outside. It's sparse with furniture, with only a few satin-sheeted tables and dusty miscellaneous items from a previous wedding. I begin to make my way back, but my entire body freezes when the silence in the hall is suddenly punctuated by the voice of the one person I definitely didn't wish to hear from today.

"Haven't had a chance to catch you all day. But looking at you right now made the wait worth it."

My expression twists into a scowl. "What do you want, Jax?"

I force myself to look at him. Decked out in an all-white tuxedo and impeccably polished designer shoes, with his blond hair gelled back smoothly in a middle part that I used to beg him to do but that he refused until today. He leans casually against one of the empty reception tables, finger circling the rim of the champagne glass resting in his hand. The warm light flooding from the reception tent through the stone casement windows shades the contours of his freshly shaved face beautifully, but at the same time, illuminates the vicious spark in his eyes.

There's nobody here but the two of us.

My mind immediately starts screaming *danger, DANGER!*

"Where's Beth?" I ask, hoping I can distract him enough so I can slip away.

"Don't know." Jax gives a cold shrug. "But I'm here to talk to you."

"Well, I don't want to talk to you, so scram," I snap back impatiently.

His jaw tenses as he takes in my rejection, as if this is the first time I'm doing that. He strokes a hand down his face but it does nothing to relieve the muscle pulsing in his jaw.

"Do you think it's easy for me to see you out there? With *him*? If you're trying to get back at me for the Beth thing, it's working, okay? I want you back," he says gruffly. I roll my eyes. Of course it's a dick-measuring contest with him. Me being happy with another guy is the only thing that's going to send a dagger straight to his ego.

"How many times do I have to tell you that I'm done with you, Jax?" I seethe at him. "I'm with Kayden now. And unlike you, he's actually good to me."

"Good to you?" He echoes, disgusted at my answer. "What fun is good?"

"As opposed to what *we* had?" I struggle to control my temper. "Me constantly pining for you, begging you for scraps and slivers, and you feeding me just enough to keep me around? And when I thought I deserved more, you got scared and cheated with the *one* person in world you definitely shouldn't have cheated with?" I scoff. "I'd say it's a major step up from that."

"Come on. What we had wasn't all that bad." His eyes flame with heat as he walks over to me, his shoes clacking against the teak flooring. Each step he takes puts me on full alert. "It was us against the world. Two rebel fighters living it up, destroying everything that was in our path and claiming what we deserved. That's you and me, princess. It doesn't get any better than that."

He's delusional. Absolutely fucking delusional.

"You only care about what you want. Not what I want," I spit at him. He's so close that I can smell the expensive Armani cologne I broke my back to get him for his birthday last summer. Everything that he does is intentional, with the end goal being to spite me, and I'm done putting up with it. "And what I want right now is for you to get out of my fucking face."

And then I shove him aside with a shoulder and head straight for the exit.

But of course, Jax doesn't want to leave me alone. He's

truly incapable of doing that if it means backing away from a fight with a bruised ego.

"I'm ready to give you everything you wanted from me." He catches up to me easily because of course he does with his huge frame, falling into step with me with equally determined strides as we weave through the satin-sheeted tables. "I'm ready for a deeper commitment."

I stop in my tracks, feeling another surge of anger bursting from inside of me upon hearing his stupid, vacant words.

"*You had three years to figure it out!*" I'm so pissed off that my whole body is trembling with the force of my rage. My voice is sharp as it rings across the hall and bounces around the oak-paneled walls. "Don't you *dare* insult me by giving me what I've always dreamed of just because I'm no longer yours. You don't really want me. You only want me because I'm with someone else and you can't have me. You always want what you can't have and I'm not falling for it anymore. Remember the promise I made you?" I step closer towards him. "One way or another, I will watch you lose everything in that cage. And I'm gonna enjoy it a lot."

He blinks hard at my words, silent for a couple of moments.

And then he tips his head back and laughs.

I don't know what response I'm expecting but it certainly isn't that.

"Look at you." Jax cocks his head to the side, a mocking smirk growing on his ridiculously smug face. A thumb reaches over to caress the curve of my chin and I flinch, backing away. It makes him laugh even more. "My little firecracker princess. Admitting to enjoying watching people suffer. Come on, can't you see it? We're more alike than you think. Our anger fuels us. Makes us who we are. You can't escape that, no matter how hard you try."

I shake my head, refusing to participate any longer. I have nothing left to say to him.

"I'm done, Jax. I mean it." I don't know why I keep saying it even though I'm aware he's less than capable of holding his tongue when it involves me.

"Come on, Sienna. I've always understood your anger. I've never shied away from it. I *love* it. That's what makes us perfect for each other. We do twisted things and that is exactly why we're good together," Jax drawls, unable to keep the smugness from curving his lips. "You think Kayden is really going to accept who you are? That he's just gonna embrace that side of you? If you really think then *you're* dreaming. I mean, surely he must have said something about it by now."

The blood in my veins goes cold. I reel back from him and look away, hoping that he won't be able to see just how much his words about my relationship with Kayden have affected me.

"Stop it." I scowl at him. "You don't know what the hell you're talking about."

"Oh, but I do. You really think you're going to live your happily ever after with him? He'll never accept who you really are. Who you're really meant to be," he coos, puffing his chest with brazen confidence as he approaches me again, invading the no-man's-land between us. I'm backed into a corner as my back hits the wall, trapped with no moves left to play. "I'll embrace it. I've always embraced it. This petty side of you. The ugly side. That wants to hurt, to see me burn so much that you're here trying to convince me that you no longer care about me rather than dancing off into the sunset with Kayden in that reception tent."

I stumble back at the weight of his words, like he just knocked a deadly punch into my gut, the strength of his blow rattling every bone in my body.

"How about I let you hit me?" He says, a cruel tilt to his lips. "You and I both know it will feel so good. Imagine that, princess—finally getting a taste of that payback for all the shit I did to you." I swallow hard, pushing myself to leave, to *leave goddammit!* "Come on. I promise I won't fight back."

Fear sprouts across my stomach as I struggle to control the rugged, unnerving emotions inside me. I should leave. Push him away and run. He's clearly baiting me and I should extract myself before it goes too far. I really should.

But I can't.

I don't want to.

Because the irrational side of me that's guided by my hatred for this man orders me to stay. To show him I'm not to be trifled with. To play into his little game and find out once and for all who's really the cat and who's the mouse.

"You know I deserve it." He grins at me wolfishly, bracing an arm over my head. Our faces are hazardously close, his hot breath fusing with mine in the air, and just like that the resentment is back as he pulls it out of me again and I'm helpless against him. A wicked gleam glints in his dark, calculating eyes. "I'm a piece of shit, right? I treated you so badly. And I wish I could say that I didn't enjoy myself when

I was with your sister, but that would be a lie. I took my time with her. My God, she was so tight too—"

"I said *shut your mouth, Jax!*" I yell, giving his chest a hard shove.

To the right, the exit door suddenly wrenches open, pulling Jax's attention along with it, which gives me the prime opportunity to escape his gilded cage. Kayden steps into the hall, dark eyebrows knitting in confusion as he stares us both down.

"What the hell is going on here?" He says, irritation flaring at the sight of Jax.

"Nothing. I just told her the truth." Jax shrugs.

Kayden's gaze slides to me. Frown lines mar his forehead when he notices how disheveled I look, angry tears sliding down my cheeks as a result of my outburst thirty seconds ago.

The look he cuts at Jax is bloodcurdlingly *lethal*.

"You hurt her," Kayden hisses.

"No, I liberated her," Jax say acidly. "I told her exactly what she needed to hear: that you and her will never last."

"Jax, for the last time, drop it," I snap, lacing my fingers with Kayden's and tugging him along. "Kayden, let's go."

"You know she's just using you to get her revenge on me, right?" Jax adds nonchalantly. "Everything she's done since we broke up was to get back at me."

The statement ripples through the hall and my stomach hollows out. Kayden's mouth tightens, his eyes leaping to my face. Waiting for me to dispute Jax's accusation.

I open my mouth but no words leave me.

"Oh shit, you didn't know that." Jax places a hand over

his mouth, trying to contain his bitter laughter. "You didn't think she was gonna give up on her fight, right? She's obsessed with me. Can't stop thinking about me getting beaten at the finals tomorrow." His eyes gleam with amusement. I scowl back at him. "This game has always been between me and her. And unfortunately for you"—he gestures a lazy hand at my boyfriend—"you're just a pawn that she's going to get rid of as soon as she's done using you."

Kayden winces. My heart plummets to the bottom of my stomach at how destroyed he looks.

"Jax, *stop it*," I seethe with quiet fury.

Jax, as usual, ignores me. He resumes his taunting.

"Don't believe me?" Jax daringly edges closer to Kayden. The corner of his mouth kicks up. "Fine. Let's end it here once and for all. And see if she sticks around later."

A look of disbelief crosses Kayden's face.

"I'm not gonna fight you here," he says, acknowledging the absurdity of his proposal. "This is a wedding."

"What? You're afraid I'm going to win? Well, you're not wrong." Jax shrugs, doing a slow circle around him. "Face it: I'm always going to be one step ahead of you, Kayden. Always in it for the win. Protecting what's mine." His gaze scrolls toward me. My stomach twists with dread. "You think when it really comes down to it, you'll be able to protect her? Hell, you couldn't even protect your own family. Didn't they all die because of you?"

Fuck.

Every muscle in Kayden's body freezes. He clenches his fists tightly, knuckles going liquid white.

"Yeah, that's right. I know all about you." Jax says,

THIRTY-ONE

Jax stumbles back from the blow, red splotching his face, but he's unfazed by the pain. If anything, he seems to relish it.

With a yell Kayden charges straight for Jax, his eyes blazing with unbridled fury. His tackle connects, sending them crashing through the exit door, both of them now scrambling on damp grass. Jax's smile is savage as he struggles for control, enjoying the challenge.

Sienna, do something! my mind screams at me.

Kayden is on top now, raining punch after punch down on Jax, adrenaline and rage coalescing in his blows. I've never seen him look this enraged before. His eyes are narrowed into deadly slits, his fists ramming into thick flesh and bone with deafening, shuddering force.

Isn't this what I've been training him to do this whole time? To beat Jax? And he's actually doing it. He's winning this fight.

And yet, it feels wrong.

The mental tug of war between what I want to do and what I should do is a nail-biting, gripping match. *Do something, goddammit!* The rational part of my brain jabs at me again. *Break up that fight before either of them regret it!*

But my legs are still glued to the ground.

Jax grabs a handful of dirt and grass and smashes it at Kayden's face, using that as a distraction as he scrambles away and lands a brutal roundhouse, slamming straight across Kayden's jaw.

The force sends him crashing backwards, straight into the reception tent.

Kayden spits out a mouthful of blood, his eyes viper-focused on my ex-boyfriend, barely aware of his surroundings. Jax taunts him, moving his right leg behind him and launching into a front kick. But Kayden, already anticipating it, catches his leg and turns it into a takedown, forcing Jax to lose his balance and ram into the reception table, sending champagne glasses and plates shattering everywhere.

Glass shards crunch under Kayden's feet as he steps over to his opponent, once again on the floor. He brings his fist up for one more blow, but Jax throws an upkick into Kayden's chin, sending him to the ground.

"What the hell is going on?" Alyson yells, appalled at the mess both guys have created.

Jax ignores her. Just as Kayden struggles to get back on his feet, Jax snatches a flower vase off one of the tables and smashes it against Kayden's head, the water mixing with the blood from his split lip. Then Jax grabs hold of him, digging his thumbs into Kayden's eyes.

Kayden struggles under him, roaring in pain, his hands reaching for anything that will help him get out of Jax's grasp. His hand closes over one of the broken shards of the vase and he slashes at Jax's face. Jax immediately releases Kayden and doubles over, hands going to his own face as he feels the blood dripping from the nasty cut searing his check.

Kayden scrambles to his feet and in almost the same breath hooks his arm around Jax's throat, stepping behind him and pulling him into a rear naked choke.

"You gonna kill me now?" Jax spits out in a gurgling fashion. Blood and saliva curdle in his mouth. "I think I might just let you. Show Sienna who you really are: a true killer."

Kayden's bloodshot eyes bulge out at Jax's words. And Jax, despite choking to near unconsciousness, still manages to muster a smug grin, knowing all too well that he's got Kayden exactly where he wants him.

Kayden lets go abruptly, immediately diving to his feet.

He stares at the mess he's created all around him. The ruined reception tent. The shards of champagne glasses scattered across the floor. The seventy or so guests looking at him with shock and disappointment.

Guilt immediately overcomes me. This is all my fault.

And now the wedding is ruined.

"Thanks for showing me your hand, Killer," Jax says with a bone-chilling, bloodied smile. "Looking forward to our fight tomorrow."

Kayden—realizing exactly what just happened—looks at me, face contorting in absolute horror.

My eyes flutter closed in defeat. I can't believe it. Jax got us good. Set the trap up perfectly and we fell right into it, thinking that we had the upper hand.

"I'm really sorry," Kayden blurts, dipping his head humbly at Alyson and my dad, before scrambling out of the tent.

My head whips in Beth's direction, who's helping Jax to his feet.

"Why did you have to bring him here?" I hurl at her.

"I—I didn't know," she stutters.

I don't have time to stick around for the rest of her response. I need to catch up to Kayden before he bails.

Scurrying out of the tent, I sprint through the gardens and to the parking lot where his truck is located, catching up to him just as he's prying the door open.

"Wait!" I yell, desperation leaking out of me like an open, unattended wound.

But he just ignores me. Gets into the truck anyway. I wedge my foot in the door to stop him from closing it. He mutters a frazzled curse and forces himself to look at me.

"You're *not* leaving until we talk this out," I say determinedly.

"Fine. Let's talk," he snaps, climbing out of his truck and slamming the door behind him. "Is what Jax said true? That you're using me to get back at him?"

A knot forms in my throat at the tormented expression of his features. "I thought that was our deal."

Definitely not the answer that Kayden wanted to hear.

His throat bobs in pain. "So all of it, what we shared together, was a lie then?"

"No. Of course it's real," I insist. He scoffs at my answer

in disbelief. Now I'm the one who's frustrated. "I just . . . I didn't expect to fall for you, Kayden. I didn't plan for any of this to happen."

"Well, neither did I! But I thought that our relationship was more important to you than Jax! I thought you were done with him." Hurt crosses his beautiful, sculpted face. His voice drops to a low mutter. "You know what? Perhaps I was right about you all along. You were using me from the start. I was just too blinded by it all to figure it out."

I struggle to contain another rush of anger. There he goes again with his paranoia and doubt.

"You break my heart, Kayden, saying that shit," I say sharply. "If you genuinely think that I've been masterminding a relationship with you from the start, then you really don't know me at all, do you?"

"Then, please tell me. What the hell are we doing here?" He takes a daring step toward me; any closer and we'll be chest to chest. And I wish we could be. It feels like we're drifting further away from each other despite being so close. Kayden's tone grows soft and uncertain. "I know I said I love you, and you haven't said it back, and I would never want to pry it out of you like this but I at least have to know: Do you have feelings for me?"

Sadness nips at my throat at the thought of him doubting me. I did that to him.

I love you, Kayden, I want to say, my entire body wanting to burst forth with the declaration. *I love you, I love you, I love you—*

"You know I do, Kayden," I say despite the strain in my throat. "You have my whole goddamned heart."

"Do I really? I doubt that. Not all of it, anyway. I share it with *him*." He spits out the last word bitterly. "You may not love Jax anymore, but your hatred for him drives everything you do. And unless you let it go, I'll never be a priority."

"That's not true."

"It is. And you know it too." Kayden's Adam's apple bobs as he stares at me again. He lets out another long exhale, pushing his hair back with his hands as he tries to gather his thoughts. When his gaze shifts back to me, his expression is wounded.

"What if I lose tomorrow, Sienna?" He whispers.

I shake my head fervently. The past two months of grueling training has given me enough confidence that he won't lose tomorrow. I have never entertained the possibility of a loss. I don't want to.

"You won't lose."

"I might," he says quietly. "Come on, Sienna. You heard Jax. I just showed my hand. What if he uses that to his advantage tomorrow night and wins that championship?"

I pull away from him, refusing to give him an answer. Because he knows what I will say, and I don't want to show him that he's right.

"You'll hate me," Kayden says with finality. "And I'll hate myself because you hate me. And we're going to tear each other apart."

Aren't we already? I think to myself.

I don't get what he wants me to do here. We both agreed to this deal and it had all been fine . . . until it wasn't anymore. I had always been hell-bent on destroying Jax, and that goal has never changed. I don't understand why, on the day before the biggest fight of our lives, it strikes him as such a huge revelation.

He's asking way too much of me. How can I let all that anger go, just like that? He doesn't understand how it feels to have three years of your life ripped away by someone you used to love so fiercely. He doesn't understand that the vengeful feeling has been festering inside me long enough that it's way too late to be stopped.

"What do you want me to do, Kayden? Just forget about what Jax did to me and forgive him?" Impotent rage burns my throat as I wield my words. "Why should I? What has he done to earn my forgiveness? He's done nothing but lie to me and fuck me and my sister up. You're crazy if you think I'm just gonna bury the hatchet and get all buddy-buddy with him!"

"I'm not saying you should forgive him, Sienna," Kayden says, reaching forward. He drags a hand down my cheek, thumb stroking the skin and I lean into it, almost whimpering from being deprived of his affection during this argument. "But hurting him is not going to heal the pain that he inflicted on you. It's only going to make it worse. And I'm not going to stick around and watch you destroy yourself over this."

The statement clangs through the parking lot, filling the space with dread. He waits for me to speak—to say anything, really—but to his disappointment, I don't. I simply can't tell him what he wants me to say.

The flicker of relief he was holding in his eyes disappears, along with any inkling of hope. He drops my hand and huffs out a dry laugh as he accepts my silence as confirmation of the answer he'd feared all along.

"Got it," Kayden says, wrenching the truck door open and climbing back in, giving me one last look. "Loud and fucking clear."

I say nothing.

I merely watch him soundlessly as he drives off into the night.

THIRTY-TWO

I stayed back to help clean up the mess that Kayden and Jax had left behind at the estate house, offering to pay for any repairs since the brawl that took place was partially my fault. The management wasn't pleased with us but accepted my offer anyway, told me to expect the bill in the next few days, and then proceeded to kick us out of the place to do the rest of the cleaning up themselves.

Dad was livid with me and Beth for what had occurred, considering that the men who had cut short their lovely wedding reception were our boyfriends. After yelling at us for a good half an hour, he went to search for Jax to give him a piece of his mind, only to find that Jax had conveniently disappeared as well.

Seeing as my only source of transport has already left, I opt to take a cab back to the apartment instead. When I arrive home, it's past midnight, and I drag myself to my room, feeling the weight of exhaustion accumulated from today finally crash down on me. Kayden and I had a standing date to share my bedroom tonight, but any plans to sleep in his arms fall right through when I hear light snoring floating from his room.

Instead, I drop onto the bed and bury my face in the palms of my hands. How did we get here? Just hours ago we were good. We were happy. And now I don't even know what we are.

I don't know what awaits us tomorrow. I'm still going to attend the finals. I still want to see Kayden fight. I'm still going to support him no matter what.

Even if he might not want me there.

And even if he despises me.

A fighter never concedes, not even at her lowest point.

***

The most anticipated fight of the season is being held at an abandoned prison camp. Breaking Point sure has a flair for the dramatic, opting to hold the finals in the creepiest of places. I step out of the cab and onto the grounds, suppressing a cold shudder as I pass the graffiti-covered concrete walls and rusted bits of rebar sticking out of the collapsed structure. It doesn't help that the gloominess settling over the sky drops the temperature to one of our coldest nights this spring.

The place is located deep in the forest, shrouded in so much greenery and darkness that I wouldn't have been able to make it there were it not for the trail of people preceding me. I shoot a text to Brent, telling them find a good spot to catch the fight, and wander around the premises looking for Kayden.

I haven't seen him all day. He wasn't in the apartment when I woke up, leaving me to catch a ride here by myself.

I stride toward the solitary confinement cells where I have a feeling Kayden is holed up in, preparing for the fight. I peep inside to find a pair of strong legs dangling from the collapsed concrete roof and haul myself up so I can sit beside him.

My breath stalls in my throat when I look at Kayden. He's a looming, menacing presence—long, sleek body already decked out in his signature red robe, his hands patching up the scrapes on his calloused skin from yesterday's brawl with a pair of dirty boxing wraps. But something's off about him. He's wrecked with exhaustion, despite him getting home early yesterday. His eyes are hollow and the air around him feels strained and rigid.

"Hey," I say, my stomach a stirring pot of shimmering nerves. Only Kayden has the ability to make me this anxious.

Kayden glances over at me, gaze boring into mine, as if he has been expecting my visit.

But he doesn't say anything to me.

I feel the familiar burn of disappointment scorch my chest at his coldness. I guess I should have expected this reaction given how poorly I treated him yesterday. It just feels strange that he's like this. It wasn't even that long ago that we were all over each other, and I already miss us.

"Julian's in the crowd. With Brent and Evans," I say, feeling compelled to slice through the awkwardness. "Said he didn't want to miss this fight."

"That's nice of him."

Then, silence. The only sounds are from the faint rustling of leaves from the trees and the distant cheers of the crowd getting riled up for the fight to begin. From what I can hear already, it's the biggest crowd of the season. All of them waiting to see who's going to emerge victorious tonight.

Deadbeat vs. Killer. Veteran champion vs. trained underdog.

I fiddle nervously with my hands, waiting for Kayden to say something. Anything. But he just leans into the silence, seemingly lost in his own thoughts as well. I want to know what he's thinking about. Is he thinking about the upcoming fight? Is he thinking about me and what's going on between us?

I'm not going to let us end like this. We've barely even *begun*.

"Look, I'm really sorry about yesterday. And how things ended," I say quietly. "I don't exactly know where we stand right now."

His gaze slides to me. Stare pinning me down.

"Where do *you* stand?" He asks me roughly.

I don't know, I don't know, I don't know—

"Kayden, it's only one night." I reason with him. "Everything's going to be over after tonight. And after the fight—after you win—we don't ever have to think about Jax ever again," I tell him, brows descending low on my face. "Don't you want that?"

He shivers, sensing the volatile emotions running through my body.

"Kayden—" I start off again.

"I have to go," he murmurs sadly.

I hold my breath, nodding tightly. As much as I want to keep him here, he's right. I'm taking too much of his time and the fight is starting soon.

"Okay. Fine," I relent.

He doesn't bother to give a reply. My heart sinks when he hops off the roof and moves out of the cell. I follow, trying to keep up with his pace. He walks in fast, huge strides, fists clenched on either side of him as he gets on the pathway leading in the direction of the crowd. But before he makes it to the end, he twists around unexpectedly.

He stares at me with so much intensity it immediately takes me back to the first time he looked at me in the apartment—when everything had been uncertain between us. It still is.

I stop in my tracks. Kayden sprints back to me. My heartbeat turns erratic.

He draws me to him and weaves his fingers in my hair.

"Fuck it," he says and mashes his lips with mine.

I'm so taken aback by his abruptness that my legs almost give out on me the second our lips meet. But he captures my body with his huge arms to steady me, setting aflame every inch of my skin with his tight grip. I cling to him like I've been denied being with him for an eternity, kissing him back just as fiercely. For a moment, everything is right with the world and my shattered nerves begin to heal.

More. I need more.

I make a strangled gasp of delight as his lips glide down my neck, hungrily devouring my skin, like he's finally allowing himself this little moment of greed, to sink into me without caring about the ominous storm hovering over us. I want to take my time with his lips—kissing them, biting them, nibbling them. I want everything I can get from him, even if it's just scraps.

Kayden pulls away from me briefly, nose touching mine. I want to know what he's thinking because I know that there's a million thoughts billowing through his mind right now. My lips part, ready to ask him, but not before he closes his lips over mine again.

This kiss is different. It's slow and delicate, my body weakening from being weighted down with an unexpected, mournful sadness. His hands tremble as they capture my waist, lips pressed against mine sorrowfully, like he wants to draw out this moment as long as he can before the distance settling between us grows wider until it's nothing but a wide, unending chasm.

It's only then I realize what this kiss is.

It's a *good-bye* kiss.

When Kayden tears himself away from me, we're both breathing hard.

"I'm gonna set things right for you, okay?" He presses a light, comforting kiss on my forehead. "For us."

Alarm bells sound in my mind and I rocket out of his grasp.

"What the hell are you going to do?" I demand. But he doesn't give me an answer, already swiveling his body back around and walking away from me with purposeful strides, leaving me completely in the dark. "What—*Kayden!*"

No, no, no, no, no—

He's not going to do it, is he?

I sprint in the direction of the crowd, pushing desperately through the ocean of anxious people to get all the way up front. People are squeezed together so tightly that it's hard to even breathe. The crowd is a ravenous, savage animal tonight, eagerly writhing for blood to soak the cage.

"Ladies and gentlemen, the moment you've been waiting for! D-D-Deadbeat vs. Killerrrrr!" The announcer calls, earning another blast of cheers. "Who will prevail and claim this year's ultimate title? And who's gonna crawl out of this cage tonight bleeding and butchered with broken bones? Wait no longer 'cuz here are your fightersssss!"

I manage to find Brent and Evans by the time I hear the resounding, cacophonous roar of the crowd as Kayden emerges from the shadows. He's stone faced as he circles the cage, giving the crowd a quick, silent wave before taking his place opposite Jax.

Jax raises his fists high, the embodiment of arrogance as he yells and jumps around the cage, riling his adoring crowd up. The "Deadbeat" chant surges and his deadly grin lengthens across his mouth, fueling the exhilarating energy of the masses. The gnarly scar on his right cheek as a result of what happened during the wedding yesterday only serves to heighten the aura of fear around him.

He looks smug as hell. So smug that I wish I could be the one to personally fuck him up in that cage so he'd never be able to make that look again.

The crowd's cheers reach a crescendo as both fighters ease into their stances, waiting for the countdown to the bell. Kayden's gaze swings in my direction, colliding with mine. I shake my head, silently begging him not to do this. His Adam's apple bobs and his eyes flicker toward Jax. They narrow into purposeful slits.

And the second the bell rings, Kayden does something no one but me could have anticipated.

He drops his hand to the concrete floor and taps out.

Outraged gasps erupt all across the camp.

"Did he just—?" Evans stares at the cage in disbelief.

"What the hell is he doing?" Brent yells. "No way he just tapped out!"

Both of them are staring at me expectantly, as if saying *any context right now will be welcome.* But I don't have the answers they're looking for.

This isn't real. This isn't happening right now.

My eyes flutter shut and I suck in a tight breath, forcing my frustrations inward.

I should have known. I should have known this was what he was going to do when I saw his face after he kissed me.

He's really giving it all up. And there's nothing I can do about it.

"And we have a . . . forfeit?" The host's face is a mask of confusion. He scratches his head, eyebrows furrowing low on his face when he snaps his attention to Kayden. "Is this right? Killer, you're tapping out?"

Kayden nods silently.

"*What the fuck?*" Jax screams, gesturing with his arms in aggravation. "You think you're just going to take the easy way out of this?"

"I'm not going to play into your stupid game." Kayden

shakes his head, the exasperation gripping his body causing his muscles to move and tighten. "I'm done with this shit. And I'm done with *you.*"

More gasps. More outrage. More booing.

"Are you for real right now?" Jax fumes.

"Does it look like I'm joking?" Kayden hisses back.

It's pure chaos around the cage. The announcer is trying to get everyone to calm down but the entire crowd is seconds away from turning into a full-blown mob. Some people are already hurling beer cans and cigarettes at the cage. Definitely not a good sign.

Kayden refuses to wait for the referee to call the fight. Cutting one final look at Jax, he turns his back swiftly and heads straight for the cage door. But Jax isn't having any of it. He leaps across the cage to stop Kayden from leaving.

"*Fight me!*" Jax gives Kayden a hard shove, forcing him to stumble back. "Fight me, you fucking bastard!"

But Kayden regains his balance quickly, fire lighting in his eyes.

"No," he roars back, unfazed by Jax.

Jax scowls deeply in response. As if the word doesn't exist in his version of a dictionary.

"You're gonna prove me right and be a fucking coward?" He blasts out.

I watch nervously as Kayden's face reacts to Jax's comment.

He winces at the word *coward* but attempts to shake off the verbal blow, converting it into raw, defiant anger.

"I don't care if I am," he snaps back at Jax, eyes igniting with newfound purpose. A purpose that no longer aligns with mine. "I'm done being a part of this game. It's not worth it. So get out of my fucking way."

A muscle pulses in Jax's jaw, and to my relief, he appears to be debating letting Kayden go. More screams for blood and jeers fly from the crowd as both fighters continue to stare each other down. My body is shaking with nerves at the tension trapping Kayden and Jax inside that cage, amplified by the raging, frenzied crowd.

For a moment, I notice a flicker of sympathy captured in Jax's dark eyes. I know he's capable of feeling remorse. I've seen it before. He just needs to put his ego aside and let Kayden leave unscathed. Let the feud between them die.

Jax just needs to be the bigger man here.

But the crowd is not forgiving tonight. It is a fiery, temper tantrum–fueled abomination finally reaching its crux at the possibility of seeing the biggest fight of the season coming to a disappointing end.

"Come on! The fight is never over!" someone screams.

"You're gonna let him go, Deadbeat? What a pussy!"

"Fight! You useless sack of shit!"

Jax's eyes flare with alarm, the flicker of sympathy leaving him just as quickly as it arrived. His tongue sweeps across his upper teeth as the insults keep coming, causing his massive body to violently shake with anger. I know that look all too well—I became accustomed to it during the years that I was with him—and as a result, a familiar feeling arrives, one of pure dread and fear.

"No. No, no, no, no—" Are the only words I can repeat as the tension in the cage explodes and Jax pounces on Kayden.

Jax is relentless. His fists are everywhere—knocking

into Kayden's face and body like the wrathful inferno that he is. Kayden brings his defense up too late, taking each deathly blow that Jax rains down on him. He doesn't fight back, merely absorbing and blocking the hits with his arms, perhaps hoping that Jax will stop once he gets in a couple of hits that the crowd has been ravenous for.

But Jax doesn't.

And Kayden falters in his stance, his body clashing hard against the side of the cage.

"They shouldn't be fighting!" Brent wails, frantic eyes bouncing from the cage then back to me and Evans. "Why isn't the referee calling it?"

The answer is obvious. I look around and all I see is excitement charging up everyone's faces as Jax continues to pound on Kayden mercilessly. This is what everyone had been waiting for. The brutal, long-standing rivalry finally coming to an end.

But this isn't the fight I wanted.

Not like this.

"Kayden's not fighting back," Brent says miserably.

"He doesn't want to fight back." The words that leave me feel more like a statement than a realization.

I don't know if I respect him for his decision or find it irrational that he's choosing not to fight, especially when his opponent is hell-bent on ripping him to shreds.

Kayden eventually musters some kind of defense, retreating to the side, avoiding a couple of narrow blows here and there, but it isn't enough to escape Jax's onslaught. He falls back into a traditional Muay Thai stance, knee and arms up, forming a wall of joints and bone, but Jax isn't having any of it. With a yell, he slams into Kayden with potent force, knocking them both to the floor.

Kayden tries to shrug him off, eventually managing to squeeze himself out of the grapple, and scrambles past Jax toward the cage door again, but Jax intercepts him, slamming a hard uppercut to Kayden's jaw.

"Fight back, Killer!" Evans says desperately. "Come on!"

I feel the ground beneath me caving in, and I'm drowning in the agony of watching the man I love get brutally beat down like this, at the horrible sight of Jax throwing Kayden around, pummeling his bloody fists into him repeatedly, weakening Kayden even more.

Another fists knocks into Kayden.

And another.

And another.

And each time he doesn't get up. Each time he slumps farther down.

Each time my heart cracks open wider, as sickeningly excruciating as every blow to his ribs.

Kayden is too far gone now. Too incapacitated. His eyes swell to twice their size with hit after hit and blood gushes down the sides of his face. He has lost any semblance of a defense, leaving him completely at Jax's mercy. It's a gnarly and gruesome sight that taunts all the oxygen out of my body as his head whiplashes against Jax's fists and collides with the side of the cage again and again.

This isn't a fair fight at all.

It's an *execution*.

"They need to call the fight. Right now," I say through gritted teeth. "Or Jax is going to *kill him*!"

My desperate gaze cuts to the referee, who has retreated to the bottom of the cage, watching the fight in awe.

Still. Refusing. To. Call.

Kayden's eyes find mine briefly and my heart feels like it's flatlining as gut-wrenching pain continues to slash through every fiber of my being. I can't watch Kayden like this. I *can't*. At this rate, Kayden's lifeless body might be strewn across the floor of that cage and the fight still won't be called. It's unfair. It's unjust.

I'm not going to just stand here and let *my* man get hurt like this right in front of me.

And I'm certainly not going to let him pay for the mistake that led both of us here.

I've got to do something. Anything. I don't know what, but all I do know is that I can't just stand idly by and be a willing witness to a deadly beatdown. My feet are already propelling me forward as I push through the crowd, clawing my way to get to the front.

"What—?" Shock manifests in Brent's expression as he watches me move toward the cage. "Sienna!"

I ignore him; continue pushing through.

"Get out of my way!" I yell desperately to the people in my way. "*Move!*"

The tide of the crowd moves to the momentum of the fight so I lean into it in hopes that the crowd will naturally propel me forward. And it does. The adrenaline swarming in my veins is the last driving force I need to launch myself to the front.

My eyes zip to the cage, blocking out every other sight. The cage door is ajar and I climb the steps, narrowly dodging a couple of security guards on the way, and dive into the cage. I hear screams for me to get back down but I drown the voices out willingly because there's nothing, not a fucking thing in this world that's going to stand in the way of me stopping this fight.

I'm not going to let him die. I'm not going to let him die.

At some point, all my thoughts have shut off. My brain is no longer wired to my body. All I feel is my limbs moving toward Kayden, who's losing consciousness on the ground. Fear floods my entire body like a tsunami as I shield my body over his and lift an arm up before Jax can land another blow—

But I miss.

And he lands the blow anyway.

A right hook straight to my *face*.

The only feeling I remember is the feeling of falling. And an agonizing, soul-ripping cry, "*Lucky!*" as my head knocks against the concrete floor and my body falls limp to the ground.

Followed by all-consuming darkness.

THIRTY-THREE

There are moments in your life you remember vividly because they've made a great impact on you or forced significant change in your ability to see the world and its people.

And then there are moments in your life that you *wished* you didn't remember. That scar your soul in a way, taint it with black, and you try to shut them out of your mind because it's better to pretend not to be aware of them than relive them.

I've had my fair share of either of those kinds of memories.

And somehow, against all odds, this feels like both.

I don't remember much, only catching fragments of what happened after it had all gone down. I remember a pair of huge, safe arms carrying me and handling me delicate care. It's the only time I've ever felt safe during the night. Secure. Like if the darkness swallowed me whole permanently, at least I'd go knowing that I'd been embraced by his sturdy, comforting warmth one final time.

"My Lucky," he had whispered, breathing temporary life into me. "Stay strong for me. You're a fighter. Live for me, baby. Live."

I remember catching a glimpse of his face. Tears sliding down his sweat-covered face, his mouth clamped tight as if trying hard not to let the raw pain he was feeling seep out of him. I remember how broken he sounded. I wanted to cry for what my actions had done to him—what they *continued* to do to him.

Then I remember his warmth leaving me. He let me go and I wanted to reach out to him, call out and plead for him to stay with me. But my voice felt trapped and I was suspended in an in-between, desperately clawing at the surface to break through before the darkness claimed me again.

I wanted to say a lot of things to Kayden. I wanted to scream at him for doing something as reckless as throwing that fight against Jax. I wanted him to know exactly how I felt every time he got hit and punched until he was barely conscious on the ground, how my heart bled for him as he bled on the floor.

I don't regret protecting him in that cage. I know it was a reckless, stupid move to put myself in harm's way like that, and I was certainly aware of the risks the second I decided to do it. Kayden had always had my back—even during the times I didn't deserve it—and it was time I had his. His pain called out to me and I reacted because nothing was worth seeing him get wrapped up in a massacre that he didn't ask for.

When my eyes flutter open after fighting through the disorientation, the first thing I see is the blinding, stark-white overhead lights beaming down at me. My eyes slowly begin to scan my surroundings, taking in the clinical feel of the room. The bare white walls, pale sheets blanketing me, and the wires clipped to my fingers and hooked into the huge machine beside me to monitor my vitals.

My head is resting on a large pillow and when it finally registers that I'm lying on a hospital bed, I immediately get up, but a rush of pain blasts through my head and I groan, squeezing my eyes shut briefly to adjust.

I try not to focus on the pounding in my head and instead move my legs and hands slowly to familiarize myself with my body again. I touch the back of my head, feeling the large bandage wrapped around it.

"Hey," I hear someone beside me whisper. My body surges with relief when Brent brings his seat closer to me and slides a comforting hand over mine. "Take it easy now."

"What happened?" The words rush out of me. "Where's Kayden—"

"Hey, calm down. You need rest." Another voice slides into my ear. I whip around to find Julian leaning against the wall, reaching out to me. "You've been out the whole night."

Beside him, Evans has gotten up from the couch and approached the foot of the bed, his hands clinging to the edge as he watches me, worry filling his eyes.

"I'm fine," I insist, hauling myself into a sitting position. "I just want to know where he is."

"Oh, Sienna," Brent says, like a defeated sigh.

My lip quivers. I know what exactly what that means.

"Tell me what happened, please," I beg.

Brent presses his lips together thinly, gaze flickering to Julian and Evans, who nod back at him in unison.

"All right," Brent says, adjusting himself in his seat.

According to him, after I'd been hit by Jax, Kayden didn't take it well. With a surge of anger-led adrenaline from watching me get knocked out, he went berserk on Jax, charging toward him and accusing him of wanting to get me killed, which in turn got Jax incredibly upset. Apparently, he genuinely didn't see me coming—that hook had been aimed at Kayden, not me, so me getting hurt had not been part of the plan. Which was fair since everything had happened so quickly that even Kayden hadn't realized I had been shielding him until I got hit.

I was surprised to hear that Jax had been incredibly remorseful for getting me hurt, falling to the ground beside me with tears spilling out of his eyes the moment he saw my unconscious body lying on the concrete floor. But despite it being a horrible accident, Kayden refused to let Jax get any closer to me, yelling for him to be taken away from the cage so he wouldn't cause more trouble.

My knockout had finally propelled the referee to call the fight. The crowd had been divided in their responses. Most were sympathetic to the unfortunate situation at hand; others were furious that the fight had ended abruptly.

Kayden had been advised by the medics to call an ambulance since nobody knew how bad my head trauma was. But someone from the crowd warned them that if they called an ambulance, everybody in the camp would go to jail. Kayden wasn't willing to risk another second without getting me medical aid, and since his truck was among all the other cars parked at the outer rim of the camp, he decided to make a run for it and bring me to the nearest hospital himself.

As Brent recounted what happened, some of those memories hurtled back to me. Hearing bits and pieces of alarming conversation between Kayden and Brent and Julian arguing about the best way to handle me, then Kayden sprinting out of the cage with me as he begged me not to quietly slip away . . .

"I can't believe he did that," I say incredulously, sinking back into my pillow. To run as far as he did while carrying another whole person in your arms must have taken a lot out him, since he'd been lying nearly unconscious in the cage before that.

"You know he would have run a goddamned marathon for you if it meant that you were safe," Brent explains.

"At least he made it to the hospital in time. The rest of us arrived shortly after to make sure you were okay." Evans continues on Brent's behalf. "When we asked where Kayden went, one of the nurses explained that after he brought you to the hospital . . ."—he swallows hard, wishing he didn't have to say what I'd already feared—"he chose not to stick around."

"So he's gone?" I whisper, already knowing the answer.

"We don't know where he is," Julian says, sitting by the edge of my bed. He doesn't usually show a lot of emotion, but this time I detect a sliver of sympathy when he looks at me.

"I need to find out," I say adamantly. "He needs me."

Julian shakes his head in disagreement. "He needs time."

"Julian's right," Brent adds, discomfort causing his body to go rigid. "He's not talking to anyone. I would know. I tried calling him all last night and this morning."

I slump in disappointment. I know Brent to be telling the truth. He's his brother; I'm sure he's worried about Kayden too.

"I told you not to fuck with the underground, Sienna," Julian says, his forehead scrunching up in a frown. "Because the underground will fuck with you back. Exhibit A."

"It was a freak accident. Nobody could've anticipated that the night would've turned out like this," I reply quietly, fiddling with the corner of my sheets.

Despite everyone leaving that final fight more or less intact, I still feel unsettled. Anger balls in my stomach— anger I have no right to feel—when I think about Kayden making the decision to tap out without even discussing it with me first, chucking all our hard work out the window.

But I still love him. Still want to see him and make sure he's okay. There are many things that Kayden and I still need to figure out, and I wish he was here so we could work through them together.

"Do you think what Kayden did was right?" I murmur to Julian. "Throwing that fight?"

"No, but I think in his own twisted way he thought it was the only way to help you," he replies honestly, brows twitching together. "I did warn you, Sienna. Your anger is going to be your destruction. That boy will do anything for you, even if it means saving you from yourself."

I don't say anything. Perhaps it's because I'm too

stubborn to admit that I might have been responsible for sending Kayden down this path. Maybe if I did, then last night wouldn't have had to happen. And Kayden and I would be more than fine.

The door to my room opens and my dad sticks his head through. Relief washes over his expression when he sees me.

"Hey, glad to see you're awake," he says, pushing the door open. Alyson immediately rushes to my side while Beth steps hesitantly into the room last.

"Oh, thank God." Alyson exhales, cupping both my hands in hers. She looks like she's been crying; her black eyeliner is smudged a little on the sides. "We were so worried about you."

"We'll give you guys some privacy," Brent announces, shooting out of his seat. Julian nudges Evans along with a hand and I wave good-bye to them as they exit the room.

My dad moves to the other side, occupying Brent's spot, and Beth awkwardly stands beside him, rubbing her hands together, like she isn't sure what to do with them.

"How're you feeling?" My dad asks worriedly.

"All right," I manage to muster. "My head's still throbbing but it's nothing serious."

"Is there anything we can do for you?" Alyson offers kindly, her hand drifting upward to smooth my hair.

"Yeah," I say, propping myself up. "Weren't you guys supposed to go on your honeymoon?"

"You're more important to us than some vacation." She smiles.

It is sweet that they want to make sure I'm all right first. But I'll feel much better if they don't delay their honeymoon for the crazy mess that I've gotten myself into with Kayden and the underground. I know Alyson has been really looking forward to the trip.

"Are you kidding? It's a one week trip around Italy. And I'll be fine. I'll probably be out by tomorrow," I insist, eyes darting between them. "Just go and have fun. You guys deserve it."

A look of uncertainty crosses Alyson's face as she glances at my father.

"You sure, honey?" My dad says with a questioning tone.

"After all that happened with your wedding and afterward . . ." I stomach a shudder at just how much I—along with the guys I've been involved with—put them through. "Yeah. I'm positive."

Alyson and my dad really do deserve a break from this. This has always been my fight to deal with and I hate that they keep getting dragged into it. They don't deserve this and I'm going to do what I can to ensure that they don't have to get involved anymore.

"We'll stay for the night until you get better," my dad declares. "And maybe we'll go in the morning."

"We're just glad you're okay, Sienna," Alyson says in a soothing tone. "I don't know what would have happened if you . . ." She chokes midsentence and I squeeze her hand in reassurance, letting her know that I'll be fine.

"Thanks for making sure I was okay," I say to my family.

I even say it to Beth, who smiles at me with sincerity and relief that I'm safe. And in that moment, I decide to set aside the feud between us and open my arms wide, allowing everyone to come into a group hug. They respond more than willingly, wrapping their arms around me firmly with the intention of never letting me go. Because when everything else in the world feels uncertain and unresolved, at least I can count on my family to stay constant.

***

Throughout the rest of the afternoon, I'm surprised to receive a steady stream of visitors shuffling in and out of my room. Cara, Simon, Alex, and Daniel stop by and bring me some cupcakes to snack on. Cara and Alex spent the entire morning making them, which was a nice gesture, though with just a single bite I feel like I'm halfway to being diabetic. I had to throw the rest of them away when they weren't looking because they simply weren't edible. Their visit still ended up being a good distraction, especially since Simon brought along his Switch so the five of us could play games together while the hours waste away.

When they've left, Elijah and Patricia paid a visit. They apologized for Kayden's disappearance and told me that he had texted them to let them know that he was safe, which I was incredibly relieved to hear.

"You think he'll come and see me?" I ask Patricia. Despite our differences, she knows I care about him a lot.

"Perhaps," she tells me thoughtfully. "If there's anything that I've learned in raising him, it's to never rush him when he's going through something. Just be patient and he'll come around."

I nod silently, wanting to believe her words. But they don't quite reach me.

Maybe because I'm not actually sure he'll come around this time.

Some good news arrived in the evening from the doctor when he told me I was free to go the next morning, but advised me to keep monitoring myself for any side effects from the concussion. Fortunately for me, the only side effect I seem to be experiencing is a mild headache. But I've learned enough from my degree to know that I could have ended up in a much worse state. The power connected to Jax's fist as it plummeted toward me, forcing my head to collide hard with the cold concrete, could have landed me with severe, lasting brain damage that would have ended my MMA training career indefinitely.

I should consider myself lucky to have side stepped a much worse fate.

After checking me out of the hospital, my dad and Alyson offer to drive me back to the apartment . They aren't too eager to leave me by myself but I assure them that I'll be fine and shoo them off to pack for their honeymoon. They eventually decide to take my advice after much convincing and bid me good-bye, promising that they'll text me the minute they land in Rome.

When I manage to drag myself up the complex, I slide my keys out of my bag and unlock the door eagerly. The past two days have just been an avalanche of drama, so it feels good to be back home. At least now I can start the process of returning to some semblance of normal.

But as I step into the living room, the hope for normalcy flattens, replaced with stone-cold dread when the sound of loud, frantic shuffling from Kayden's room drifts into the air.

The door creaks as I push it open, and I see Kayden hauling a bunch of clothes from his closet, hangers still intact, onto his bed. His back is facing me and when I clear my throat, he turns his head and immediately halts what he's doing when he sees me standing by the door. My breath hitches when I notice the huge, dark circles hollowing out his beautiful eyes, dimming out the light in his irises, and his sickly pale skin.

He looks beaten. Defeated. There's a Band-Aid slapped over a gash on his left brow, and his shirt has ridden up to reveal a thick bandage wrapped tightly around his rib cage. My first instinct is to ask him if he's all right, if he sought some kind of medical treatment after the fight, but as if anticipating that I'd ask those questions, he shakes his head, pulling his shirt down.

Silence hangs in the air.

There are many things I want to ask him. The words rush into my mind but I'm incapable of forming them into coherent sentences. I didn't expect him to be here. Brent said he hasn't been back here since I was admitted to the hospital.

I can't believe he's here. Right in front of me.

When I've managed to make my mouth form words, I blurt out all the questions I've been meaning to ask him.

"What are you doing here?" I ask. "Are you okay? Did you know that everyone has been looking for you?"

Kayden doesn't answer me. He doesn't have to. My gaze drops to the duffel bag on the floor that is teeming with clothes, with a few stacks of cash and personal documents strewn around inside. My eyes dart back to his face, which now wears a guilty expression.

"You're leaving," I say with finality.

I try to suck in a steady gasp of air, but he's stolen all the air in the room, right along with my heart, tossing it all in his bag to leave me with nothing.

"I don't . . . I don't get it," I stammer, stepping toward him. "Do you need more time? I get that what happened during the finals was bad, but do you really have to leave?"

So many questions. Not enough answers. I'm searching for them amid the shadows that line his eyes but I'm left empty handed.

"Sienna . . ." Kayden braces a shaky hand over the side of his face.

No. This is not happening. I'm not letting him leave just like that.

"Why didn't you visit?" I ask and he gulps nervously. "You saved my life and you didn't even bother to stick around. If you feel guilty about me risking my life for you then you should stop, because I swear I would do it all over again if it meant that you wouldn't take that deadly hit from Jax.

"I don't understand." My voice is shaky and hoarse. He ignores me, continuing to fold his clothes and stuff them in his bag. I grab his shoulder in an effort to swing his attention back to me. "Help me understand, Kayden. Why? I get that climbing into that cage was stupid but—"

"It's not about that!" He huffs, wrenching my hand away from him. Anger blazes through him in a way I've never seen before, making me flinch. "Sienna, I'm trying to protect you!"

"Protect me? From who?"

"From *me*!"

Kayden's words clang through the room, his torment digging into me deeply.

So *this* is what it's about? That he feels responsible for putting me in the hospital?

Kayden draws out an exhale, allowing his shoulders to sag. "You know why I threw that fight, right? I told you that if you didn't let that anger go, you were going to lose yourself. I thought I could save you from that."

"I didn't ask you to save me, Kayden. I thought we were in this together," I say sharply. "But ever since the wedding, you've been making all the choices without me. Like I'm not even here."

"You chose revenge over me." A pained look flits across his face. "So I did what I thought was right."

"What would've been right was telling me what you were going to do before you went and almost got yourself killed!" I snap at him, my heart pounding fiercely against my chest as the aggravation spreads through the rest of my body. "How was throwing the fight the right decision? And if it was, it should've been *our* choice to make, Kayden. Considering I've been with you on this from the start."

He looks at me with the saddest of eyes.

"If I told you, would you have let me go through with it?"

The dagger strikes deep. I pull my gaze away from him, knowing my answer is exactly what he assumed it would be.

Because Kayden and I both knew what would have happened. We would have had this argument, just two days earlier.

And it would have still gotten us nowhere.

I drag an agitated hand through my hair and gulp down the acid coating my windpipe.

"I thought that victory was important to you, Kayden. I thought we were in agreement on that," I say weakly.

Kayden snakes a warm hand over my cheek, unable to keep himself from touching me. I can feel the volatile emotions radiating from his body as his face leans into mine. The pressure in my gut momentarily turns into flutters as his fingers slide over my skin, but I can't seem to fully enjoy it knowing that him touching me like this is his way of saying good-bye.

"You're more important to me than any other fucking thing in this godforsaken world," he murmurs. He reaches for my hand and takes it in his grasp, lifting it to kiss the inside of my palm. "I live for you, Sienna. Only you."

"Then why are you *leaving*?" I whisper back, choking back a sob.

Kayden takes a reluctant step away. My body shivers at his absence, detoxing from a substance I've been hooked on for weeks. I want him close to me. It's the only reassurance that we're on the same page. Now he feels so far away and nothing—not even me begging—feels like it's going to make the slightest of difference.

A dark look toughens his features as Kayden looks at me again. "I didn't plan for you to get hurt, Sienna. Watching you take that hit meant for me crushed my fucking soul. You can't be with someone who'd put you in harm's way like that."

"You had no control over the situation, you know that."

I rasp. "I made that decision to save you from Jax. I was the one who stepped in to protect you. You couldn't have known I would do that."

"If I didn't throw that fight then you wouldn't have gotten hit by Jax and you wouldn't have been in my arms, unconscious," he fires back. "I wasn't sure if you were going to live or not."

"Of course I was going to live," I say. "I'm right here in front of you now, aren't I?"

"I didn't know that. For all I knew, you were *well on your way to being dead!*" Large tears roll down the sides of his cheeks as he paces around the room. "You can't fathom how it felt when you were limp in my arms. I told you before that the absolute *last* thing I wanted to do was hurt you. Remember that?" I nod silently. His mouth twitches in disappointment. "Well, I did it anyway."

"But you know damn well what happened with Jax wasn't your fault!"

"But *I could have prevented it from happening!*" He slams a hard fist against the table, then grips its edge so hard that I'm certain he's going tear a chunk of it off. A breath drags out of his mouth before his voice grows quiet again. "You're right. You're absolutely right. I shouldn't have gone and thrown that fight without telling you. And the fucked-up thing is that you paid the price for it. Which just shows that I'm never going to escape who I was. I hurt everyone that I love. I'm not going to risk hurting you again. I'm not going to do it."

Raw, unnerving pain rips holes across my chest at the realization that he feels responsible for hurting me because he's convinced himself that everything terrible that has happened in his life is a direct result of his selfishness.

But I wish he could see what I see.

That he's the most selfless, amazing man I've ever known.

"You won't," I say with a determined set to my jaw. "Because it won't happen again."

"It will if I stick around." A crack wobbles in Kayden's voice. "I promised myself that I would protect you and I broke that promise. Just like . . . " He stops himself midway but I already know what he's going to say.

Just like how I broke Clarissa's promise.

"No. Please don't say that." A massive knot tightens around my throat, and I swallow against the painful ache, but it does nothing to relieve it. He shakes his head and shuffles to his bed to resume his packing. I launch myself at him again, my eyes burning with more tears as I try to stop him. "Please. Stop packing and *listen to me*! Yes, you said you'd protect me but I wanted to protect you too! We've got each other's backs, remember? So you're punishing me for protecting you in that cage?"

"I'm not punishing you. I'm relieving you," he mutters, zipping the duffel bag closed and looping the strap over one shoulder.

He walks out of his room. I follow after him, rife with purposeful determination not to let this conversation end. Because if it does, then *we* do too. And I can't even begin to muster that harrowing thought. I just fucking can't.

"STOP IT, PLEASE! Stop talking like that!" I blink back the well of tears threatening to fall from my eyes but they spill over anyway, clouding my vision and making it impossible to make out the features of his face that I desperately want to see. I manage to catch him right before he leaves through the main door. "So you're gonna leave? Just like that?" I ask incredulously. "You're the strongest, most determined person in that cage but when you're outside of it, giving up is like second nature to you. *Why?* Why can't you face me? Why can't you face yourself?"

"I love you, Sienna, with every heart-wrenching bit of me," Kayden says hoarsely. "But I can't forgive myself for what happened."

"But *I* forgive *you*! Isn't that enough?" I fire back, shaking my head. "Don't go."

"Please step away," Kayden says quietly.

"*No.*"

He squeezes his eyes shut, holding his own tears back in. "I'm trying to be a good person here."

"I DON'T WANT YOU TO BE THE GOOD PERSON! I WANT YOU TO BE WITH ME!" I yell with the kind of pathetic desperation I've never experienced before. Because despite me finding weakness in begging and groveling for someone like this, I do know that this is worth fighting for. Kayden is worth fighting for.

I'm shaking so hard when I reach up to cup his face with my hands, searching for any doubt in his eyes that can help me sway him. But Kayden's expression remains passive and it hurts, it hurts *everywhere* because I know he wants to be with me despite him saying otherwise. I *know* it to be the truth, etched deeply in my heart.

"Fight for me, Kayden," I plead. "Please. Fight for us. Just let whatever happened in that cage go. Just let it *go.*"

He looks away, his eyes fluttering shut, each fallen tear a painful reminder that my words don't—*won't*—mean a single thing to him.

"You and I both know it's not easy to just let things go," Kayden declares, tapping on my shoulder to show me that he's giving up the fight. The only fight that *matters*. I shake my head, wishing that this wasn't real, that this wasn't happening right now and my heart wasn't about to crumble into dust and ash.

But . . . I have to face the hard truth.

I've got nothing else left to say that'll convince him to stay. And he won't listen to me otherwise.

And this time, when Kayden nudges me aside so he can leave the apartment, I don't stop him.

I let him go.

THIRTY-FOUR

Hit.

It's been three days since Kayden left and I feel suspended in a never-ending nightmare. I can't stop picturing him standing by the door, looking unfazed by my words, his iron-clad decision to leave repeatedly tormenting me with every step he took out of the apartment.

Hit.

There is not a single trace of him left in the apartment. That was what it was meant for, right? If he ever needed to leave, he could just disappear and nobody would know he ever lived there. He was destined to run. From his past. From himself.

Hit.

He's gone. He really is gone. He hasn't once called or texted to see if I'm all right, and I haven't bothered to reach out either. What's the use of trying to find someone who doesn't want to be found?

Hit.

I want to forget the day I ever met him. I want to forget the way he stared at me like he was afraid of me, afraid of what kind of damage I'd do if I stayed with him.

Hit.

I want to forget that fear turned into adoration when we fought together during our first session, when he was determined to win over me in that cage.

Hit. Hit. Hit.

And most importantly, I want to forget that that adoration turned into something much more sacred.

HIT.

I want to forget our first kiss.

HIT.

I want to forget how breathless I was when he helped me out of my clothes, taking his time with each piece of clothing. Kissing me everywhere like he'd been waiting a lifetime to worship my body. His hands on my skin. Roaming. Exploring. *Loving.*

HIT HIT HIT.

I want to forget the first time we made love and how I wanted to cry from sheer happiness because I knew, I *knew* it wouldn't get any better than that.

HIT HIT HIT HIT HIT.

He loved me. He loved me until he destroyed me. That is the only way I know how to put it. The numbness, the anguish when he stepped foot out of that apartment has eaten me away until I don't recognize myself anymore.

HIT HIT HIT HIT HIT HIT.

I don't want to feel like this, like I'm drowning in a boiling vat of my own pain and suffering, clawing at the surface to get out to breathe because *I can't breathe I can't fucking breathe I need air, AIR please, please, PLEASE STOP—*

Hot tears spill from my eyes when I thrust my hand out to stop the punching bag from knocking me out cold. I rip the wraps from my hands only to dig my fingers through my hair like angry claws. I gasp for breath, wanting to inhale some courage to fight through the pain, to fight through the heartbreak, but I come up short, my body wanting to punish me—rightfully so—for being responsible for the agony in the first place.

Because this has been my fault.

All of it.

I wish I could blame it on anyone else. Jax, maybe. I'd sworn to myself that it was him who had planted that vengeful, wrathful seed inside me and then fueled it when he cheated. But I was wrong.

I did that all on my own.

And because of that, I hurt many people along the way. Even people who didn't deserve it.

I feel broken. Completely and utterly broken.

It will take more than a plot for revenge to put me back together again.

What is *wrong* with me? How did I let my anger get so far that it threatened the best relationship that I've ever been in? Kayden didn't deserve what I did to him. He treated me like a queen and he only asked to be put first, just like he'd put me first. And instead, I let him down, forcing him to give up that final fight against Jax.

I didn't even get to tell him that I love him. I was too

scared to utter those words to anyone because I was stuck on the idea that those I'd put my trust and love in always ended up letting me down.

But in isolating myself from them, I'd only let myself down.

I crawl over to grasp my bottle of water and my phone that are sitting on the mats beside me. The screen lights up to reveal that it's well past midnight now. I haven't been to work for the past three days. Called in sick. At least Julian didn't ask questions. He was aware of what I was dealing with and knew I wouldn't ask for leave unless I really needed the time.

I don't think I've ever allowed myself to mentally steep in my own thoughts for this long before. Maybe it's because I hate being alone with them. They're vicious, only serving to plunge holes into my titanium exterior.

Facing an opponent in the cage has always been as easy as breathing.

Facing myself has always been the hardest fight of all.

"Well, look who it is. Thanks for dodging our calls, by the way. It's not like you have friends and family who worry about you." A deep voice prickles my ear. When I turn toward the source of the voice, my body stiffens.

"Yeah, well I really needed some time to myself," I mutter quietly.

I watch as Evans slips through the back door of the gym, followed by Brent. They drop onto the mats on either side of me, worry sinking their brows on their faces.

I haven't seen anyone since the day I returned home from the hospital. It's not like they haven't been trying to reach out; by now, they've all probably heard about what happened. I haven't been sticking around the apartment much lately, either, because there's too much hurt there, and I need to keep myself distracted from it because that's the only way I know how to keep myself going.

"Sienna, we're really worried about you," Brent says, scooting over to me and bracing an arm over my shoulder.

"I'm fine. I've just been really busy, okay?" I say defensively.

Busy figuring out an antidote to my shattered heart.

"What the hell happened to you two?" Brent whispers.

"He just couldn't forgive himself for what happened during the fight," I tell him, opting to be vague about it. I'm not sure I can live through a retelling of the breakup right now since it's still so fresh. I haven't even recovered from what was said that night.

"He's such a fucking idiot." Evans swears, anger rising in his chest in the form of a huffed breath. "Always thinking he's to blame for everything bad that's happened to the people around him."

I frown at his words, wishing Kayden could have just pushed through the layers of self-loathing and guilt to see that he can't control everything bad that happens around him. And despite my best attempts to get him to realize that, I still couldn't get through.

Patricia was right; the odds were truly stacked against us. We had unknowingly brought our own issues into our relationship, but we decided to fight for it anyway, knowing that it wasn't going to be a fair fight.

And in the end, neither of us won.

"He said that he wasn't coming back, you know," I say, pulling my knees up and hugging them.

"Oh, he will," Evans mutters. "And when he does, he should watch out for my fist."

"Seriously?" Brent asks, appalled. "He's my brother."

"And he's my best friend. I'm sorry. I get that he has issues but skipping town will not solve anything," Evans says sharply. "He's not going to get a very friendly 'Welcome home, buddy' from me, that's for sure."

A warm laugh leaves me.

"I missed your smile, Sienna," Brent says, a small smile gracing his lips.

"Dude, give me a break. I just got my ass dumped," I say.

Hearing myself say that out loud still feels weird. When I was with Kayden, I was so certain that he was going to be my last.

"You know, a breakup doesn't necessarily have to be a bad thing," Brent says, stroking the back of my hair.

"B, all breakups are bad." Evans raises a confused brow. "What the hell are you talking about?"

"Look at it this way," Brent starts off, empathetic eyes meeting mine. "Don't be sad over the fact that you can't have any more wonderful memories with him. Be happy that you got to spend these few weeks making him the luckiest guy in the world. Look back at every single kiss you ever shared with a smile on your face. Remember what it was like to have his heart and be grateful for the amount of time that you had it. Your relationship with him may have ended on bad terms but the time before that was good. *Really* good. Remember those feelings, Sienna. And trust me, you will see this breakup from a completely different perspective."

I gape at Brent, wondering how the hell he managed to recite such beautiful, insightful words to me.

What he said is true. Despite all the ugly, Kayden transformed my life in a way that I didn't know was possible, for the little time he'd been in it. And I love him so much because of it. Every memory we shared is so sacred. I can only hope that one day, I'll be able to appreciate them without the heartache weighing me down.

I have to accept that love isn't enough to hold two people together. Sometimes, real life gets in the way and that's okay. When it does, we have to learn how to let go, not because we want to, but because we have to.

Whether I like it or not, Kayden and I are on different paths now—possibly for the better—and maybe that's something worth finding contentment in. It's my responsibility to try.

"Thanks, Brent." I sniff, feeling the tears well up again. "You're a good friend."

I drag him into a hug. Brent leans into my embrace happily, wrapping us both in comfort.

Beside me, I hear Evans clear his throat. "I believe you've hugged him enough, Sienna."

"Brent," I say. "Can you tell your boyfriend to stop being a possessive asshat?"

"Evans can you stop being—"

"Yeah, yeah I got it," he grumbles. "That still doesn't mean I'm happy about it."

Not wanting him to complain more, I reel Evans into the hug as well. Their embrace provides me with the solace

I long for after three lonely, agonizing days, and I feel really grateful to have their friendship.

"And hey, maybe one day you'll get over him. Maybe you won't. None of us would be able to get over something as huge as what you and him had," Brent tells me earnestly. "In the meantime, you should try to live your life without him."

I nod.

As much as those words sting, I need to hear them.

I'll never know when he'll return. And I shouldn't be pining for him to come back. There isn't any point halting my life for someone else. So I need to move on. I need to find myself without Kayden being a part of my life. And maybe that's just what he needs too.

Perhaps being apart from each other might do us both some good.

Kayden has no doubt given me enough strength to pull myself back together, but I need to test that strength by myself.

"A new beginning, then," I say.

"A new beginning," Brent echoes, nodding.

New beginnings. That sounds nice. I anticipate the process will be tough—painful, even—and it won't always go the way I want it to. But I'm ready. To endure it all. For my own sake.

So I take Brent's advice.

I write myself a new chapter.

A new chapter with a new beginning.

THIRTY-FIVE

The next few weeks aren't as painful as I thought they would be. Brent and Evans's conversation really did help put a lot of things into perspective for me, and I know I need the time to get focused on fixing my own issues—something that I've been avoiding for a long time now.

I decide to follow their advice and move on. Or at least try to. I spend a good amount of time doing a lot of other things apart from fighting, like going on my usual morning jogs to get a healthy dose of vitamin D every day. I've incorporated other stuff into my schedule, like meditating. I never thought in a million years I'd find myself picking up the activity, but it's a good thing for me to practice, especially after a busy and chaotic day. I've also been doing a lot of cooking. When I was living with Kayden, he usually prepared all the food, so it's nice to finally take control of my own meals.

A routine that doesn't involve fighting has brought a nice sense of calm and stability that was long overdue in my otherwise hectic life. I still hit the bags once in a while at UFG when I start to feel overwhelmed again, but at least I'm also able to balance it out with other things now.

Everything finally feels like it's slowly getting back into order.

Well, for the most part. There's something else that has been nagging me still.

Something I've been avoiding for a long time now—and something that my dad has been pestering me about lately.

"Therapy," he suggests, his smooth voice seeping through the phone. "I should have offered it to you back when your mom and I separated, but I didn't think you needed it. I guess I was wrong."

"Dad," I say with uncertainty. "I'm not exactly a big fan of talking to some stranger I barely know about my problems."

"You barely talk to me about your problems, Sienna." A resigned sigh pulls its way out of his lungs.

"That's because I didn't think you'd even want to hear them," I reply dryly. "I always figured you were too busy planning your next wedding and all."

I hear Alyson shout a distant *She's right, though!* through the phone. I love Alyson and how she can joke about my dad's previous marriages while having unshakable confidence that this will be the last marriage he'll ever have. I see how they are with each other, and they're solid.

"But seriously, I think it'll finally allow you to confront all that resentment you've had since the divorce. And maybe also help you move on from your breakup," he advises. I open my mouth, already wanting to protest his suggestion but he beats me to it, adding in a gruff, fatherly voice, "Before you say fighting helps, think again. You were in a toxic relationship for three years with a man who only treated you well when it was convenient for him. And you brought that toxicity into another relationship, which broke the both of you up. Doesn't seem like fighting's been helping you after all."

I snap my mouth shut, his words silencing me momentarily.

Fuck, I hate it when he's right. And I'm usually reluctant to admit whenever he is, but this time, I might be willing to mull it over.

As much as I love fighting and it has proven to be an addictive escape, I'm starting to realize that it has always been just that. An escape. Something that allows me to release all my pent-up emotions but that will never allow me to truly face them in a way that I need.

I'm not going to deny that fighting is still my life. I will never trade it for anything else in the world.

But I can't rely on it to fix everything anymore.

"I know it's scary. But I truly think it'll be really good for you." My dad's voice softens, easing some of my fears.

I continue to stay silent. I promised myself a new beginning, so while it sounds frightening, it seems to be the necessary next step for me right now.

"Fine," I grumble. "I'll do it."

"That's my girl," he says with a light tone, and I can almost picture him breaking into a smile.

And that is the only reassurance I need.

I owe it to him to figure it out. I owe it to my family. Because ever since my parents' divorce, I realize I haven't been able to fully tame the volatility of my emotions. Instead, I placed my focus on other things—like fighting, like Jax. Maybe that's why when I was with him, I felt like I could never stand on my own two feet. I was strong, physically speaking, but mentally I needed him to give me all my validation.

Maybe that was why I was angry when he left me. *So* much angrier at him than I was with Beth. Because I had given him so much of myself that I didn't know how to function with less than what I had.

I'm sure it will get easier. With time.

***

Sessions with Dr. Rosenthal, my psychiatrist, have been easier than expected. I see her about twice a week to reflect on recent events. It's only been a couple of sessions since my first, and I do feel a sense of calm now, with a more comprehensive understanding of myself and why I get reactive in certain situations.

According to her, I possess long-standing issues of abandonment and mistrust, and I lack the self-awareness and motivation to reflect on all my actions, which leads to me closing myself off and using things like revenge as a coping mechanism to avoid processing all the hurt I feel.

Damn, she really didn't have to come at me like that.

But I *guess* what she said makes sense.

I'm going to work on the trust part. If there's a way to kick it, I probably should do it.

And perhaps that is why, two weeks later, when Beth

visits me at the apartment, I don't immediately shut the door. Instead, I hold the door open expectantly, waiting for what she has to say. Which unfortunately, isn't much to begin with.

"Hey," she says.

"Hey," I tell her.

She's a beautiful mess. Her long blond hair is pulled into a scruffy bun, her face pale and stricken with nerves. Her facial features look sharper than usual, like she'd lost some weight, and I'm suddenly worried that she might not be eating.

"Um," she says, her voice small and unsteady. "Can I come in?"

I nod slowly.

"Sure."

I hold the door open as she walks in, dragging her feet as if she'd rather be anywhere else. And truth be told, I feel the same. But this conversation is long overdue and it's about time we finally clear the air rather than continue circling around each other like this.

Beth hugs her shoulders tight as she makes a slow sweep of the room. I wonder if she's thinking about how she condemned me to this apartment after I caught her and Jax together. I'm not going to tell her that it's been a blessing in disguise. Not yet, anyway.

"I ended things with Jax," she confesses.

"Okay . . ." My voice trails off. I'm not sure what she wants me to say to that.

"Look, I know I don't deserve for you to hear me out," she croaks. "I broke your trust and I know I don't deserve a second chance. But you were right. About all of it. About him using me. Manipulating me. And yet you still warned me about him, even if I didn't listen to you."

"Beth, you're my sister," I tell her, crossing the room so the distance between us doesn't feel so unfriendly. "I hated what you did but I still cared. And I didn't want you to end up in the same position I did."

I wish I had tried harder to protect Beth. Looking at her now makes me ache with regret. She looks exactly like how I was two months ago—lost, broken, wrecked with grief from a breakup. I want to hug her and console her and tell her that it may not feel like it now but everything will be okay. That she'll grow from this and one day find someone who'll love and cherish her the way she deserves to.

"Yeah. I should've taken your advice," she admits with a sigh. Her gaze is thoughtful as it returns to me again. "I'm really sorry, Sienna. For everything. I was a stupid, jealous little sister." She presses a finger between her brows to relieve the strain sitting under her skin. "You're just so perfect, you know? You're strong and cool and funny, and when you talk all the guys in the room fall in love with you. I wish I had the confidence that you have."

I want to tell her that that simply isn't true, that I've struggled with boys, too, and I'm just as insecure as the next person, but I don't think that's what she wants to hear. I don't think she'd even believe me. Putting on a brave, tough face was something I've always schooled myself to do because I thought that if I showed that nothing ever got to me, then nothing ever would. And I guess I had others believing it too.

Beth exhales slowly. "I've never had any guy look my way before until Jax. And I don't know . . . I guess it made me feel special when he did. For once, I had someone's focus and attention. And I know it wasn't right, but I was so obsessed with the feeling that I was willing to stick with it anyway." She glances back up at me with sadness. "Even if it meant hurting you."

My body diffuses with tenderness. The weight that had been holding me down has finally lifted and a new feeling takes reign, a feeling of comfort and peace that I had long denied myself all these months.

"Thanks, Beth. I needed to hear that. And I'm sorry too. I shouldn't have treated you the way that I did. You didn't deserve me icing you out. I know I've been a bitch and I'm working on it. I promise," I say, reaching down to cup both her hands and squeezing them. I offer her a small, coaxing smile. "And look, you're an amazing girl, Beth. Any guy will be lucky to you have you. I'm happy to hear you didn't settle for Jax. He didn't deserve to be with you."

She tilts her head. "Really?"

"Yeah," I say, a laugh of disbelief shuddering out. "I can't believe you were jealous of me. I was jealous of *you*."

She looks at me like she isn't sure if I'm joking. "What? No way."

"Yeah. I know I'm the black sheep of the family. Dad clearly loved you more. You were his model child."

"I only tried so hard to be that person because I didn't really know who I was outside of it," Beth tells me with the kind of self-awareness that I've never seen from her before. "Always trying to be perfect. Always trying to live up to everyone's expectations of me. It was *exhausting.* In a way, being with Jax felt like a burden I didn't realize I'd been carrying had been lifted. I know it was incredibly wrong of me to do that, but I was just tired of trying to be what people told me to be and still feeling invisible. He made me feel really special and he embraced who I was."

As twisted as it was, I understand what she means. I felt the same way before I met Jax, and had allowed myself to think that him accepting who I really was equivalent to love.

"He has that effect on girls," I say dryly. "It's annoying."

"I know that it doesn't feel like it, but I think he really did love you," she says, reaching up to squeeze my shoulders. "The way he beat himself up after he put you in the hospital, it was when I knew. I don't think he ever meant for you to get hurt. That was the last thing he wanted." She pauses for a beat, her chest deflating to pull the rest of the words out. Her eyes well up with tears. "When you found out he cheated on you, you thought you were his mistake, right? But that's not true at all. *I'm* his mistake."

"Oh, Beth," I murmur.

The last of my self-restraint falls away and I pull her body into a loving hug. She rests her cheek against my shoulder and clings to me hard, like she'd longed for this embrace for a while now.

"I'm really sorry I let him get between us like this." A sob wobbles her voice. "I'm done with him. I promise. I think I have some things I need to deal with by myself, but I'm swearing off boys like him. And most of all, I just really, really missed you. And I hate that I let us grow apart like this."

"I missed you too," I whisper back.

I do. More than I ever care to admit. But growing apart was what we both really needed. Because at the end of the day, Beth did do me a huge favor. If she'd never gotten with Jax, I would never have realized what a piece of shit he was and would never have found Kayden.

Can I really hate her for something like that?

"And," I make sure to add, "I think I forgive you."

She looks up at me, sniffing. "You do?"

"Yeah," I say, a sigh pulling out of me. "That's what big sisters are for right? And it's been tiring holding a grudge against you. As much as I hate to admit it, I understand why you did what you did. And I'm just glad you finally came to your senses."

Beth pulls away from me enough to say, with a smile, "You can say you told me so. I won't complain."

"I told you so." I shove her playfully, grinning with my teeth. "I freaking told you so."

Her laughter floats up and dissolves into the air, bringing the place a much-needed boost of joy.

"Thanks." Beth sniffs. She's hesitant again, fiddling with her hands before asking, "So would you . . . would you consider moving back?"

Her suggestion catches me off guard. Since I've been living in this apartment it's never crossed my mind that this would be a temporary accommodation. I've grown oddly attached to this place. Protective, even. It's only been my home for two months and I've never felt like I belonged anywhere else.

"I don't know," I say, dropping my hands to my sides and

looking around the place. "I feel like I have some unfinished business here. So I'm gonna stay. At least until I feel like I'm ready."

Beth nods in understanding.

"Will you come over and visit me though?" She says, her eyes filling with hope.

"Of course."

And this time when I look at my little sister, my heart feels feather light, and the anger that had been imprisoning me has now withered away, leaving behind only hope.

One step forward, no steps back.

***

Three days later, when I pay a visit to UFG, I'm shocked to see that it's teeming with people. Apparently, after the disaster that was the finals, public perception toward Breaking Point soured, which meant the management had to lay low for a while. Nobody knows when they'll reopen; some speculate that it might even get shut down permanently to bury the scandal, and the rumors were strong enough that fighters scrambled over to UFG instead.

I doubt Julian is particularly thrilled about a bunch of underground fighters at his gym, but I found out he made them swear off illegal fighting if they wanted to continue training here. Some of them agreed, ultimately deciding that training with an MMA legend would be far more valuable since it would increase their chances of going pro and ensure that they no longer had to rely on Point's fights for cash and glory.

When Julian and I finally have time for a heart to heart, I open up to him about how I'm doing. He's happy to hear I've been trying to patch things up with my family. I think he's tired of being my pseudo-dad for the past few years now, which is completely fair, since I haven't been the easiest to deal with. So I'm more than happy to relieve him of his duties.

"Speaking of duties . . ." he starts off, rising from his chair to unhook a set of keys from the back of the door. He looks at it for a moment, sighs, and chucks it to me. I catch the keys midair, and hiss out a shocked breath when I realize what this means.

"No. Fucking. Way," I say in disbelief as I stare at the keys in my hands.

I feel like Indiana Jones when he found the Holy Grail. With the orchestral music surging in my ears and heavenly light spilling down on me and everything.

"This does not mean that I'm letting you take over operations just yet, okay?" Julian says sharply. "I'm just going on vacation to the West Coast for a couple of weeks to visit some friends and family, and I'd like you to run the gym while I'm gone. You think you can handle that?"

"Is that even a question?" I scoff, closing my hand over the keys. "Fuck yes, I can handle that."

"Don't make me regret this." He glares at me with seriousness. "I'm warning you, if you do anything to fuck this up—"

"You'll hunt me down with a machete? Got it."

I feel compelled to hug him for giving me this opportunity to prove my worth, but then again, Julian isn't the kind who enjoys any kind of physical affection, so I settle for blowing a kiss at him instead.

"Also, before you go," he adds, albeit a little hesitantly. "I know you said you'd never want to compete but if you ever change your mind . . ." He snatches a flyer from his desk and hands it to me. "Tryouts for the next season are in five months. And I think you have a fighting chance, Sienna."

My eyes scroll over its contents. It's all the details I would need if I was interested in fighting for the all-women promotion. I bite my lip in contemplation. A few months ago, if Julian had asked me to fight, I would have turned him down. I loved helping others with their fight, but I think along the way, I started to neglect my own.

Now, for the first time, I have no one else to focus my energy on but myself.

I lift my gaze to meet Julian's. "I'll think about it."

A grin spreads across his face.

"All right, I'm going to squeeze in a workout before I close up," I announce, grabbing the keys and the flyer on one hand and gripping the door to his office with the other.

"Sure," he says. "And Sienna?"

"Yeah?"

"I'm proud of you. You've come a long way."

Well, if I hadn't been feeling teary eyed over him giving me the keys, I'm definitely feeling it now. Tears threaten to flow over the rims of my eyes but I force them back because I don't want him to think I'm an emotional mess.

"Thanks," I blurt out, rushing out of his office.

I'm not usually the kind of person who will get choked

up over something this small. It's probably the therapy that's taking its toll on me.

Crying is a healthy outlet. And a healthy outlet is a healthy mind.

Goddamn you, Dr. Rosenthal.

I do my usual warm-up, starting with a few rounds of light jogging around the space and ending with some lunges. Then I climb into the boxing ring. Covering my hands with my wraps, I begin with mix of jabs, crosses, hooks, and uppercuts together, switching up the pattern every couple of rounds of shadowboxing, while staying light on my feet by pivoting and moving side to side with nonstop motion. It's a killer cardio workout, something that I desperately need since my postbreakup diet hasn't been the healthiest. By the time I'm ten minutes in, my heartbeat is skittering so fast I can hear the blood pounding in my ears like a loud bass drum.

I love the feeling of climbing up the mountain of momentum, wanting to live on top of that summit forever. I used to think this was the only way I could deal with whatever was happening to me. I'd stick to the adrenaline hunt and immerse myself in it until I became numb.

I was born to be a fighter. And when I fight, I live in my emotions.

But maybe my emotions don't have to trap me anymore.

"You should blink less so you can watch your opponent's punch land. Or he might just catch you off guard," I hear a deep voice that momentarily breaks my focus.

I'm surprised that he's come to see me at all. The only time he actively seeks me out is when he feels like his ego is threatened. And I can't think of anything that I've done that would warrant a visit from him today. As far as I'm concerned, we're finished.

"What do you want?" I snap my head toward him in irritation, bracing an arm over my hip.

He's by the foot of the ring, staring up at me like a scared little dog. It's rare to see fear in his eyes. He looks like he's been through hell and back. His dark eyes are tired and a line of stubble shades his jaw, a truly rare sight, since he usually likes to keep himself well-groomed.

"I came here to apologize," he says.

"For . . . ?" I strut in his direction. Closing my hands over the ropes as my head peeks over the edge to look down at him. "You've done a lot of things to me, so forgive me if I can't keep track of them."

His chin tips up and his lips disappear for a moment, curling behind his teeth, braving himself for what he's about to say.

"That night, during the finals . . . when you got hit—" His eyes shut briefly, his entire body shuddering at the memory. When his eyes open again, they are dampened with dread. "I didn't mean for you to get hurt. I *swear*, Sienna, I really didn't see you coming. And when you were lying there, unconscious, it felt like the worst moment of my life. I'm so sorry for putting you in that position and I'm really glad that you made it out okay."

It's hard for me to tell whether Jax is lying or not. I was with him for three years and it was a struggle that left me in limbo for a long time.

But now it's never been so clear. I know his words are sincere.

"I know you didn't mean it," I say. "But thanks for the apology."

"I just wanted you to know that I never wanted to hurt you like that. It killed me this past month knowing that I fucked up with you so many times," he says in a strained voice. A knot forms in my throat at the tormented expression of his features. "I know what I did with your sister was horrible. I had a good relationship with you, and I had to fuck it all up. But I never stopped thinking about you. Never stopped loving you."

Oh jeez, not this again.

"Jax," I start, hopping over the ropes and landing on the ground so I can finally level with him, eye to eye. "This is the last time I'm ever going to say it, so I need you to listen carefully. You don't love me. At least, not in the way I deserve. I deserved a selfless kind of love. Still do."

I think back to what I had with Kayden, and how despite being with him for a brief period of time, it had beaten anything that I had with Jax by a long shot. To be loved by Kayden had been so simple yet fulfilling—from the way he told me how he felt about me to the way he touched me, protected me, uplifted me. I had never known what it felt like to be consumed with real love until I met him.

"You can't have everything you want in life, Jax," I say, a frown curving my mouth. "You've hurt a lot of people and that's not okay. Maybe you need a new start. Away from here, away from me and Beth. Fix what is broken inside of you and go find your happiness somewhere else."

"How will I know what to fix if I don't know which part of me is broken?" Jax croaks.

"I don't know. But I can't help you," I tell him. "Because it's not my responsibility to fix you. I tried fixing you for the past three years and it never worked out well for me." I flick my hand at him. "You got issues, Deadbeat. And I cannot be the person you go to when you get scared to face them yourself."

He nods and looks away, faint lines crossing his tan forehead as he ruminates on my words. Jax has done terrible things to me, and yet in this moment, as I wait for the anger to arrive—

It doesn't come.

All that arrives is pity.

"I'm sorry things didn't work out between us, Sienna," Jax says, hands sliding into the pockets of his pants. "I really am."

"I don't think we were meant to last anyway," I say as I glance at him. "We were just convenient for each other at the time. If anything, you helped me become who I am today. And maybe what happened will shape you into becoming someone else too. Someone better."

"I think you put too much faith in me." He laughs hoarsely at my words.

"I'm not," I say with a hard shake of my head. "I know you're capable of being a good person. I wouldn't have loved you so much if I didn't believe in that. But you can only be that person if you will it to be. And when you do, it won't be because someone fixed you. It's because you wanted to fix yourself to be better for that person."

He nods, straightening his back as relief flows through him. It looks like my words have somehow released him. I truly hope he finds what he's looking for.

"Thank you, Sienna. Truly," Jax says as his gaze sweeps over me. "And really, I'm sorry I ruined what we had."

"That's fine." I shrug. "We're just meant to be with other people."

"You guys look good together. You and Kayden."

"Well, he broke up with me so . . ."

He swears under his breath. "He's such a fucking idiot."

An unexpected laugh floats out of me. Finally, something we can both agree on.

"Yeah," I say sorrowfully. It's hard not to feel choked up over the thought of Kayden. I try to tell myself that I don't miss him, that I don't need him anymore, but my heart always betrays my real feelings.

What I had with Kayden was precious and I will always remember and treasure it forever. I don't feel bitter about the fact that he left. I'm happy because I got to be with such an amazing man who taught me things about myself that I otherwise would never even know.

I don't know what'll happen if he ever comes back. But Brent's right; I can't just sit around and mope until he does.

In the meantime, it's best to just keep moving on and keep living.

THIRTY-SIX

Four Months Later

I watch from afar as Brent and Evans slow dance to their wedding song with their arms tightly wounded around each other.

I let out a tiny laugh as Evans twirls Brent around with one hand and uses the opportunity to crash their lips together. Brent snakes his arms around Evans's neck and kisses him back just as fiercely.

I can't believe my two best friends are *married*.

I'm finally at that age when people are starting to get married. And it's downright weird.

And apparently, Brent and Evans have been married for several weeks. With all the remaining money that Evans had saved up before his parents cut him off, he and Brent had flown to Vegas in July and after a drunken night playing cards and blowing the rest of the money they had, ultimately decided it would be a swell idea to get married then and there.

If I had been there, I would have tried to knock some sense into them and explain what a reckless idea it was to get married before they've even graduated from college. I was utterly convinced that they were going to regret it and all of us were going to have to hear about an ugly separation afterward, but the weeks went by and they seemed happier than ever, stealing every chance they could to flirt and kiss each other. It's nauseating and most of the time I can't stand to be in the same room with them, but I let them have their moment, chalking it up to postwedding obsession.

And now, after a lot of pestering from friends and family—namely me—who were sour they hadn't been there for the elopement, we're here at Red Jacket Beach Resort in Cape Cod as they celebrate their second nuptials. I did get a little teary eyed when they recited their vows. I'd expected Brent to have the long love speech but rather, it was Evans, and he absolutely nailed it.

You are the person who anchors me, brings me back to axis when I'm lost. You are the first person I want to see in the morning and the last person I want to see before I go to sleep, Evans said to Brent at the altar. *I'm so insanely in love with you, and I would rather die than see another person touch you like I do, smile at you like I do, kiss you breathless like I do. I'm happy to be the only person you do all those things with, and I love you so much because of all the craziest ideas I've ever proposed to you, this was the only one you said yes to. And it's the only yes that matters to me.*

Truth be told, I'm happy that they're happy. Even if I

don't necessarily agree with the hasty decision. But I guess different couples move at different paces, and if this is what felt right to Brent and Evans, then I'm willing to support it.

And at least the rest of my friends still have their common sense intact. Though I do hear they're moving on to better things as well. Alex and Daniel are thinking of moving out of the apartment this fall after their lease is up. The start-up company that Daniel and Simon built together is beginning to generate money, and the four of them no longer feel the need to share an apartment. I'm happy for them and hope it comes to fruition because I'm getting tired of hearing Alex complain about the apartment being too crowded.

My eyes linger on Brent and Evans for a little while longer before drifting away to the other couples on the dance floor. Elijah and Patricia are in a tight embrace as they move steadily to the slow rhythm of the song. I haven't had a chance to talk to them all day. They've been so busy accommodating all the wedding guests, and I didn't want to bother them.

Patricia and I have gotten closer since Kayden left town. She's been keeping tabs on him, hoping that he won't get into any trouble while he's away. I'm glad that Kayden decided to keep in contact with his parents after he left. At least they don't have to worry about him.

He still hasn't called me since we broke up. And I get it. He needs to start another life without me in it. So when Patricia offers to give me insight on how he's doing, I tell her I don't want to know. We both need to heal from each other. And the only way I can move on is by knowing very little about him.

For once in my life, I'm happy. Or at least as happy as

I try to be. Sure, there are times when I ache for Kayden's presence. Times when I wish I could feel the brush of his lips on mine again. Times when I long to see his dimpled smile and feel his warm touch. It still hurts to think about him, but I balance the hurt with the clarity of knowing that he's out there, living a better life than when he was here in Boston.

As if on instinct, I glance at the initials on the inside of my arm.

K.W.

Everyone said that I was crazy to get a tattoo of my ex-boyfriend's initials. But I can still remember what Kayden said to me when we were together talking about tattoos:

I don't ever want to forget this. I want to remember you—everything about you. I want to remember what it's like to be with you. It doesn't matter if in five or ten years from now we're just a memory to each other. When I look at your name on my heart, I want to remember that you once had it. And I once had yours.

I'll never want to forget what I had with him. *Never*. I'll always think of him as the man who once owned my heart and inflated it with love and purpose.

"Hey," Evans says as he approaches me from the dance floor, wriggling his eyebrows as he extends a hand to me in invitation. He looks dashing in his navy blue tuxedo, his neat blond hair swept to the side to highlight the brightness in his brown eyes. Despite looking the same, he feels older. More grown up now. "Care to dance?"

"No."

"I'll take that as a *yes*," he declares anyway, pulling on my hand. "Come on. Dance with me. It's my wedding."

I groan, letting him pull me to the dance floor, where he loops a sturdy arm around my waist. I slide my hands over his shoulders, leaning into his sway.

"Technically speaking, it's your second one," I correct him spitefully. "I wasn't invited to the first."

A ridiculous smile crosses his face. "Really? You still mad about that?"

"Maybe."

"What happened to not holding grudges anymore?" Evans teases.

"Yeah, yeah," I mutter as he twirls me around. "You do know that marriage is a lot of hard work right?"

"Yeah, I know, Sienna. I know all of this feels abrupt but it feels right. For us." Evans sighs, reeling me in again. "We'll have a happy and fulfilling marriage, I promise."

"You better," I mutter. "Thanks for leaving my single ass behind, by the way."

"Aww, you'll be fine," he says amusingly. "Besides, you being married would have a terrible 'ring' to it."

I roll my eyes but fail to fight the smile growing on my face at the pun. Brent is such a bad influence.

We end up swaying for the rest of the song in a slow circle, bathing in the silence and just being in each other's presence. I want to tell him the only reason I worry is because I care about him and Brent, and I don't want them to end in a terrible separation that'll scar them. But at the end of the day, I figure it's not my business. I should have faith in them, that they know what they're doing and they'll do whatever it takes to make the marriage work.

Evans's eyes stretch to the two empty seats at the head

table that had been reserved for his parents and I frown, already knowing what he's thinking about.

"Still holding out they're gonna show?" I ask, barely a whisper.

"Maybe." He shrugs, not wanting to let it show that he misses them. "But . . . I think it's okay. I don't need their blessing. I've got you guys."

I squeeze him harder. "I'm proud of you."

"Thanks." I feel him grinning as he rests his chin on top of my head. A sigh pulls out of him as we do another circle. "I think Kayden would be too."

I stiffen at the sound of his name. I can't get used to hearing it without my heart clenching at the flashes of memories that accompany it. It's interesting how differently I've grieved the two relationships I've been in. With Jax, it had been nothing but pure, blinding rage stacked on top of a mountain of ruin and hurt, but with Kayden . . .

I feel only sorrow.

It isn't even the kind of sorrow that makes me feel like if we'd done a few things differently, we would have managed to stay together. I think what makes it worse is that regardless of the what-ifs, the end had still been inevitable.

Someone behind me clears his throat and I turn around to find Brent, hands clasped behind his back, waiting for my dance with Evans to end so he can join his husband again. I let him cut in, joining Cara by the sidelines as we watch the happy couple dancing together, drunk in their own married bliss.

"Look at them go," Cara says, tilting her champagne glass toward Brent and Evans. "Think they'll last?"

"Absolutely," I say confidently, then jerk my head at the couple beside them. "How about them?"

Cara stifles a laugh when she spots her best friend in a heated argument with her boyfriend. To shut her up, Daniel drags Alex to him and smashes their lips together. She's momentarily startled by the gesture but soon enough, sighs and leans into the kiss wholeheartedly, clinging to him like he's her only lifeline.

"Oh, no doubt," Cara says with conviction, cracking a half smile. "Alex and Daniel may drive each other crazy, but it's the type of crazy only they understand."

I laugh quietly to myself. Cara's right; I'll never understand what they have. And I don't have to. Their love is only theirs to share.

"Oh shit," Cara mutters under her breath, cutting me out of my thoughts. "Here comes trouble."

"What?" I follow in the direction she's pointing.

It's then that I notice that the music has died down, and the curious murmurings from guests are the only sounds drifting across the room. The two bouncers who have been guarding the tent have strolled in, cutting Brent and Evans's dance short. Evans has his lips pressed into a grim line and Brent looks shell-shocked when one of the bouncers starts talking. More words are exchanged before the bouncer gestures to someone behind them— a man—as he steps into the tent.

Oh.

My.

God.

It's *him*.

I think my lungs have shrunk a size. Either that or all the oxygen in the room has just been sucked out by a vacuum.

Kayden looks different from the last time I saw him. His dark hair has grown a little longer, the ends curling out from his collar with the rest of it neatly slicked back and tucked behind his ears. The black suit that he's wearing looks tailored just for him, curving over his ripped body and accentuating his lean figure. A dark-red bow tie perches a little crookedly on his collar and he attempts to straighten it out with his hands but to no avail. Deciding to leave it be, his head lifts and his grey eyes are soft, with a warm glow to them as he traces the room in a slow but purposeful sweep.

I can't believe he's here. My ex-boyfriend. The guy I'm pretty sure I'm still madly in love with despite the fact that I keep telling myself I've moved on.

He's here.

The man who broke my heart.

The one who got away.

Every muscle in my body freezes at the overwhelming sight of him. I don't know how to feel. My heart is stammering so wildly against my chest I think it might just fly out of my throat and splatter on the dance floor.

Every single pair of eyes is directed at Kayden. But the attention doesn't affect him one bit. He continues to search the crowd for something, someone, and when his eyes finally find mine, the entire floor feels like it has dropped from under me.

His gaze stretches over me, the weight of it pressing on me like a heavy blanket. His dusty-grey eyes dip from my face, tracing the length of my body to my legs and back up again. My pulse gives an unsteady lurch. I can't seem to tear my eyes away from him either. There are parts of him that look so familiar and other features that don't. I wonder what else has changed that I can't see with my eyes.

Still, when I look at him, everything feels right. Perfect.

Shut up, Sienna. I mentally scold myself. *He left you. He hurt you. How can you possibly have feelings for this man? Haven't you learned your lesson?*

"Lucky," he murmurs.

Guess not.

Because that one word is all it takes to completely undo me.

Kayden strides toward me with bold intent, and suddenly I feel a rising tide of panic growing in my chest knowing that if he doesn't stop right now I might just fall back into his arms willingly and never leave them again.

But I'll never know his intentions because in an instant, Evans intercepts us and slams his fist into Kayden's face, sending him tumbling straight to the ground.

"Evans, what the hell!" Brent screams.

All the guests are scrambling away from the commotion, hoping it won't turn into a full-on brawl. I run over to them and pull Evans away from Kayden.

"Okay, that's enough," I snap at him. "Calm down, Evans."

"Calm down?" He stares at me in disbelief. "Are you serious? This is the guy who left everyone for four months without a word! He abandoned *you*! So I have every right to punch him!"

"It's okay." Kayden gasps as he pulls himself into a sitting position on the floor. "I deserve it."

"Why did you come?" Evans's mouth tightens as he glares down at best friend.

"I came for the wedding." He tries to lift himself up. "Better late than never."

"Unbelievable." Evans huffs, pacing back and forth in a line. "Un-*fucking*-believable."

"Sienna's right. You need to calm down," Brent coaxes his new husband, gripping his shoulders and giving them a shake.

I peer down at Kayden, then extend an arm so that he can take it. When our hands touch, my heartbeat skyrockets at the familiarity of his rough skin brushing against mine. I pull him up from the ground and examine his face. I'm surprised to see a slight gash above his eyebrow. Damn, who knew Evans had a mean right hook?

"The wound needs cleaning," I say to Brent. Kayden continues to stare at me, his dark eyes tracing me so noticeably that I feel acutely aware of every movement that I make. "I'm going to take him out back to fix him up."

"You sure it's a good idea?" Brent sends me a warning look. I know he means to say more. As in, *You sure it's a good idea being alone with him? After the history you and him share?*

"I'll be fine," I assure him.

I don't know if I'm trying to convince Brent or myself.

***

"Tell me if it hurts."

"I think I can handle a bit of disinfectant. I've been through much worse—*Ouch! Motherfucker*—"

"Sorry. But don't say I didn't warn you."

"I'm pretty sure you did that on purpose."

"Well, I guess you'll never know, will you?"

He slumps against a wooden stool as I rub the disinfectant carefully over the wound. It's difficult to concentrate on what I'm doing because his sleeves are rolled up to his elbows, allowing me a prime view of the biceps straining against the fabric. I do eventually manage to pull myself together, cleaning the wound thoroughly and slapping a bandage over it.

We're on the beach, quite a distance away from the tent. I thought it would be better if we were away from the reception for a while since Brent needs to calm Evans down and the rest of the guests are all in disarray from what occurred.

I dispose of the cotton swab along with the packaging in the tin barrel acting as a makeshift trash can and wipe my hands clean on my bridesmaid dress. "There, you're done."

"Thanks." He smiles faintly at me and my heart melts from the simple expression.

Get your shit together, Sienna! You're a hot mess when you're around him.

"Are you gonna head back there?" I ask, grabbing the handle of the first aid kit. It feels heavy as I lift it up. Or maybe it's my strength that's lacking. Everything feels weird. My body no longer recognizes itself when it's around him.

Kayden produces a strained laugh. He fingers the edge

of his tuxedo jacket, folded neatly across his lap.

"I don't think I'm welcome there."

"Well, you can't expect to disappear for four months and think that everyone is just going to welcome you with open arms," I say with a cold shrug. "So, if you want my advice, I think it's better if you stay here for a while. At least until Brent manages to cool Evans down."

Kayden grimaces. Musters a tight nod.

Our eyes lock again and I'm overwhelmed by just how many memories come flooding back to me with just a single look. Those same eyes gazing down at me when we first kissed. The playful gleam in them as he tore off my clothing piece by piece until we were nothing but skin on skin. The playfulness melting into sweet tenderness as our bodies joined together in the way we'd been craving. And then knowing that there was no greater feeling, no greater *love*, than this.

Kayden looks at me, unsmiling. His stare holds me in a tight, unyielding grip. I can't stand the way he's looking at me. The way his eyes pry me open. Like he knows I'm trying so hard to hold myself back from him but it isn't working.

Why isn't it working?

"I'm going to put this back." I force myself to look away as I point to the first aid kit. "And check up on things back at the reception."

A hand shoots up and clamps down on my wrist.

"No, please," he breathes, like it hurts for him to do so. "Please stay."

I hesitate.

Isn't that what I'd longed for him to say? And now that

he's saying it, why don't I feel happy about it at all?

"You're fine. You don't need me," I say, harsher than I mean to be.

Kayden's smile falters. I don't know what else to say so I brave another steady breath and turn on my heel to make my way back to the tent when he calls for me again.

"I came back to see you."

I stop in my tracks. Snap my head back at him.

"What?"

"I came back to see you, Lucky." Kayden is walking toward me now. Every step he takes makes my heart race. "Well, I came back for the wedding. But mostly to see you. I've missed you. So damn much."

And just like that, the anger slips into my skin easily, burning intensely like the disinfectant I'd poured over his wound.

"Don't," I say sharply. "You don't get to do this. You left me. You don't deserve to miss me."

"I know." A lump forms in his throat. He lowers his head, his eyes hooded by his thick eyelashes. "Leaving you was probably the worst thing I've ever done. You needed me and I failed you by leaving. I was a coward. I was afraid because of what I'd done to you. And I left because it was easier to walk away than to fight for you."

A shiver races through me upon hearing his words. I still don't say anything back. I'm glad that he finally came to his senses, but it feels like this is months overdue. And I'm not sure it's enough for me to just let everything bad that happened between us go.

"I'm so sorry for all the pain I caused you, Sienna."

Kayden takes a daring step toward me. Regret flickers in his expression. "When I was gone, I felt really shitty about myself. About what I'd done to you. To us. I've had time to ruminate on it and I realize I wasn't just running from you. I was running from my own fears. My own doubts. And I couldn't face them for the longest time. What we had just made it harder for me to deal with it."

I feel conflicted. He's finally aware of what he's done and is trying to fix those issues. But at the same time, I just can't help but feel frustrated because it took him this long to figure out.

"What do you want me to say, Kayden?" I ask him, exasperated. "What do you expect me to do right now? To take you back? I can't do that. I have a good life here. And you can't just come back out of the blue and screw up all my plans. You don't get to say you miss me and hope that everything will be okay again. Because it won't be. You left people here, Kayden. People who love you. And instead of seeking help from them, you left. You *chose* to run. And you've got to live with that."

I hate what I have to say to him because despite everything I've just uttered—all of the resentment and the anger and the hurt—I still love him. Wholeheartedly. My heart sings for him. Every cell in my body calls out to him. It's pathetic and stupid but it's *true* and I can't keep lying to myself.

"You're right," Kayden says.

"I'm right?" I say, baffled.

"Me leaving Boston hurt a lot of people. I get that. And you're right—I don't expect you to forgive me. Or take me back. I know you, Sienna, and the one thing I admire most about you is that you stand your ground on things that matter. And you should be in control of your own decisions," Kayden says, hands slipping into the pockets of his trousers. He squares his shoulders shyly. "But if you're all right with it, I'd really like a chance to explain myself and where I've been. I want to make it up to you, or at least try to. I'm not giving up without a fight. Not this time."

"Kayden . . ."

"Please," he breathes. "I promise I won't keep you for long."

I bite my lip in contemplation. My eyes bounce back and forth between the reception tent and Kayden. I don't know what to do here. Okay, maybe I do, but it's still not an easy decision to make. Brent and Evans need me by their side. I'm their bridesmaid. The most logical choice would be to get back to the reception and never talk to Kayden again.

But then again, it's *Kayden*. The man I love is standing in front of me after all these months, asking for another chance. The old me would tell him to screw off. But I'm not that person anymore.

And something tells me he isn't the same either.

In the end, my heart wins the tug of war.

In the end, I allow myself to listen to what it truly wants.

"Okay," I say instead. "Just one chance. Lead the way."

THIRTY-SEVEN

We search for a good spot on the beach a couple minutes' walk away from the reception tent. Kayden's hand lingers on my back as we walk, and the heat from his palm sends a sensation of tiny fires across my body. I should have fought back harder when Evans decided I should wear this backless dress for the wedding because it just gives Kayden more surface area to make direct contact with my skin.

Despite that, I don't ask him to take his hand away.

When we've finally found a place—an empty patch of beach amid the tall, billowing grass—I kick off my shoes and plop down onto the white sand, pulling my knees together and hugging them. Kayden follows suit, shrugging out of his blazer and laying it on top of his shoes so it doesn't get sandy. His hair is disheveled from Evans's punch, and his clean, fresh scent tickles my nostrils as he sits down beside me. He makes sure to put a respectable space between us, which I'm grateful for. Otherwise, my self-restraint might find itself in shambles.

We both stare at the vast sea spread out in front of us. Night has completely fallen over the sky, cloaking us in a cold chill as the wind lightly teases my hair. The lull of the water cresting against the shore coaxes the locked box that guards my heart to open, but I clutch the key tightly, afraid of what Kayden might say to me.

The air is dense with an ocean of unspoken words between us, neither of us wanting to be the first to speak. It still feels surreal, with him sitting right beside me.

"I miss this place," Kayden starts off, his voice velvety thick with emotion as he allows the cool breeze to tickle his ends of his hair. "Makes me wish I didn't leave it in the first place."

"Where were you?" I ask.

"I was in Phoenix," he tells me, leaning back on his arms, his elbows digging into the sand. When he catches my confused expression, he adds. "I have an uncle there. Helped out with his car repair business. It was nice. Got some much needed peace and quiet after all the chaos."

I nod wordlessly. At least he had family around him while he was gone. At least he wasn't alone.

"I figured you knew about me being there." He speaks softly, face angling toward me. "Did my mother tell you anything?"

"No. I sort of forbade her."

"Why?"

"You know why," I whisper, picking at a piece of grass on my lap.

Silence follows.

"Maybe, if you'd known, you could have visited me," he says with a strained smile.

Annoyance flares across my skin.

"Kayden, how was I supposed to know if you even wanted to see me? You never even tried to contact me after you left," I mutter, setting the lock of grass down on the sand. "I thought you hated me."

"I could never hate you," he tells me. "And the reason why I didn't call is because . . . well, I knew you would have a better life without me in it."

"You know I didn't need you to make that decision for me." My tone is razor sharp as it slices through his expression to reveal a canvas of regret.

"I know." Misery lodges in his throat, causing his next words to come out strangled but he pushes them through anyway. "I'm sorry, Sienna. I should have given you that choice. I made a lot of mistakes with you, and the worst thing I ever did was steal that decision away." He lets out a lungful of air. "I'm *so* sorry. You didn't deserve that."

"Thank you." I breathe, looking down at my knees. "The apology wasn't necessary but thank you." I pause for a moment, shifting my body uncomfortably. "And well, I think I owe you an apology too. I know the reason you did what you did is because I pushed you into a corner and you felt like throwing the fight was what you needed to do. And I'm sorry for that. I let my need for revenge trump my feelings for you. And I will always regret that. I should have been a better girlfriend."

"Lucky . . ." he starts off, broad shoulders dropping. "I

know we had our issues but I never thought you were a bad girlfriend. You lit up my whole fucking world."

My breath stalls in my throat. I forgot just how much of an effect his beautiful words can have on me.

The air between us doesn't feel so friendly anymore with his compliment. Kayden knows it, too, because he clears his throat and brings the conversation back to its casual roots again.

"So, a little birdie told me you've been staying busy here in Boston," he says, glancing at me.

I give him a look. "Is that little birdie Brent?"

"Yeah."

I'm not surprised. Patricia and Elijah weren't the only ones keeping in contact with Kayden. I know Brent talked to his brother on the regular. And like his mom, he respected my boundaries when it came to Kayden.

I rest my cheek on my knees, facing him fully. "I've been helping Julian at UFG more. And I've also been training."

"With more clients?"

"No," I say. "I'm actually training for myself. I'm entering tryouts for an all-female MMA promotion soon, so I gotta get in top shape."

The first time I announced it to my family and friends, they were stoked to hear that I was finally going to fight for real this time. I'm finally at a point in my life where I'm determined to put myself first and get in that cage to prove to myself that I'm more than just an MMA trainer.

Julian was ecstatic when he heard that I'd entered. *It's about time you got out of your comfort zone*, he'd said. And I agreed, deciding to put my trainer duties on hold, at least for a little while, for a chance to compete. But I assured him that I'm very much interested in coming back to my job once I win a few matches. There's nothing that's going to pull me away from running UFG when he's retired. That's still going to be my future.

But at least the journey there is going to be one hell of a ride.

"You're fighting?" Kayden's expression lights up with a disbelieving smile. "No way."

I nod, smiling back to match his excitement.

"Yeah," I say. "I remember that you said I shouldn't waste my talent, and fight in promotions instead. And the advice stuck with me. I think it's good to have actual combat experience under my belt before I start running the gym full time. And I figure I'll do it now before I get too busy, you know? I'm still going to finish my degree, do my master's in athletic training, but at least I have the real combat experience now too."

"That's awesome. I'm proud of you," Kayden says brightly. His hands look like they want to reach out to me—to hug me—but he stops himself and straightens his back instead, offering me a friendly smile while his hands dig into the coarse sand behind him. Then he says, a little hesitantly, "You're looking for a sparring partner, perhaps?"

"You mean you?" I laugh hoarsely. "I don't know. That'll mean you'll have to be staying in Boston longer than a night."

A knowing grin from Kayden makes my spine go rigid.

"You're moving back?" I say, baffled.

He nods.

I push my knees down and sit cross-legged, scooting

closer to him, eager to know more about his plan.

"Really? How . . . ?" My voice trails off.

"I've got some money saved up," Kayden explains. "So I've decided to go back to college."

"Where?"

"Boston University."

A permanent, giddy smile stretches across my face.

"That's interesting. Because I study there too."

"What do you know?" He says, smiling. "Must be a coincidence."

Shit, he's so cute.

"So what changed your mind?" I prod.

The sea pulls his gaze away momentarily as he heaves a sigh, a hand drifting over his forehead. "Running away was a stupid thing to do. I realize that now. So I wanted to come back and fight the real fight. I've decided I'm going to quit the underground and pursue becoming a social worker. It's what I've always wanted to do, but I always stopped myself short because I didn't think I deserved it. But now . . . I feel like I do. And I want to make Clarissa proud. I want to help foster kids go into better homes, to see that they're cared for and loved. If I can prevent other kids from ending up the same way that Clarissa did, that means I can save lives."

I'm powerless from stopping the huge smile growing on my face. Kayden really has come so far since the last time I saw him. There's an air of confidence around him now in the way that he speaks and holds himself that had always been there when he was in the cage but that has finally followed him out and bleeds into every other aspect of his life.

"I'm so proud of you, Kayden," I whisper, feeling the

urge to reach out and close my hand over his on the sand. His entire body goes rigid at my touch at first, but soon relaxes as he turns my hand to entwine my fingers with his.

"Thanks," Kayden says, staring at our locked hands. His thumb smooths over the back of mine, sending a wave of shivers down my spine. "I guess being away from you did give me a bit of insight into what I really wanted to do for the rest of my life."

"You and me both," I admit. "When you left, it really fucking hurt. But I do think it was necessary. It was a wake-up call for me. The things you said... it made me realize that I was holding onto so much anger. I was just too stubborn to admit it. I've been that way for a long time and I never learned how to let that bitterness go. And if you hadn't thrown that fight with Jax, I would've become someone I didn't want to be."

Kayden's lips curve upward at my honesty. He brings our clasped hands to his mouth and presses a light, comforting kiss on my hand.

"I think I'm in a really good place now." I feel obligated to let him know what's been going on since he's missed out on so much. "Beth and I are slowly mending our relationship. It hasn't been easy, but we're stronger now. And as for Jax... well, I guess we're on good terms. I haven't seen him since he went to LA to visit his dad for the summer. But from what I've heard, he's turned over a new leaf. Just like you."

"Wow." Kayden whistles lowly. "Good for him."

"Yeah. I'm proud of him."

I really am. I never thought I would ever say it, but I genuinely hope Jax finds his happiness. Perhaps one day we can put what happened between us aside and start fresh again.

"I can't believe it." Kayden exhales. "I missed so much of this. This new part of your life."

"It's okay." I comfort him. "I guess since now you're staying, there's plenty of time for me to catch you up. And you can tell me all about your life in Phoenix."

"Well," he says with a humorous edge to his voice. "You didn't miss out on anything interesting. Just a lot of self-loathing and regret about what happened between us." A flicker of sorrow crosses his face, wobbles in his voice. "I know me leaving was abrupt, but I do genuinely think it was good for me, mentally speaking, to not have been here. I think it would have been unhealthy for us if we stayed together, Sienna. And I'm glad we nipped it in the bud before it could fester like that." He lets out a shaky breath and allows his shoulders to sag. "But with that being said, I'm still really sorry. For all the pain I've caused you. I hope you're able to forgive me."

As I stare into the depths of his eyes, I feel released by Kayden and his words. I used to think that giving up was never an option for me because it entailed weakness. I was even willing to compromise everything I ever stood for to make things work. But now I realize that it's better to know your own limits—to know exactly when to tap out. Kayden understood that. And because of him I was able to save myself too. So I can't stay mad at him forever.

It takes a lot of willpower to forgive someone. It takes a lot of strength to let the anger go and live without it.

And I am strong. I wasn't before, but now I am.

I pull myself to Kayden's side and cup his face with both hands.

"I forgive you, Kayden." I murmur. "I do. I think we both made mistakes. But I wouldn't change a single thing about it."

"Yeah." He nods in agreement, covering my hands on his cheek with his own. "Me too."

As much as I hate that Kayden left me, he had to go. He had to figure out what he wanted, whether or not he was going to continue living in the horrors of his past or if he wanted to chase a future with me. And I had to figure out how to fix my own issues by myself. I can't hate him for leaving.

We needed to be apart in order to be together.

"I missed you," I blurt out. "I missed you when you were gone. I tried to be tough and pretend like I didn't need you when really I wished you were here with me."

"Me too." His face tilts to the side to kiss the side of my left palm. "I was worried that if I came back, I would find that your life is so much better without me. You'd be happy and you'd have an amazing boyfriend—"

"I don't," I say quickly. "I don't have a boyfriend. I couldn't be with anyone else after you."

"Thank God. Because if you did, I would have to go tell him to fuck off."

I reel back, looking at him with narrowed eyes. "You wouldn't."

"I won't. Because you don't have a boyfriend," he declares.

I bite my lip, fighting a smile climbing on my face.

"How about you? Do you have a girlfriend?"

The thought of him having a girlfriend makes my stomach churn. If he does, I might have to hunt her down. Maybe befriend her first and borrow her unbelievably stylish stilettos because I'm sure she's a fashionable goddess. And then later, fling them back at her with expert precision in hopes that they'll impale her heart and make her bleed out.

Fortunately, the jealousy that festers within me dissipates when he shakes his head. "No, I don't have a girlfriend."

"That's good." It's difficult to keep the smile off my face. "*Really* good."

"I agree."

We're both smiling at each other right now, too excited to stop.

Who am I kidding? My feelings for Kayden have never changed. If anything, I'm even more consumed by just how much I feel for him. I'll never be able to separate from him again. I don't *want* to.

"What's this?" Kayden catches my wrist, eyes bulging when he notices the tattoo below it.

"Oh God, no." My hand starts to retreat but Kayden isn't going down easy. He clamps his hand down on mine, then flips my hand over, his calloused thumb brushing over the ink.

"Are those my initials?" Kayden looks at me, his eyes twinkling with humor.

I nod, color tinting my cheeks. "It's not a big deal."

He stares at the tattoo again, this time leaning down to press a light kiss on it. I feel that kiss all the way to my toes.

"I really like this," Kayden says, a grin forming on his face. "I want to show you something too."

He sends another infectious grin my way before he slowly unbuttons his linen shirt.

"Um, what are you doing?" I squeak.

Shit, what if he thinks we're about to have sex right now?

On second thought, that's not actually a bad idea.

"Relax," Kayden says soothingly, as if he was reading my thoughts, which makes me flush even harder. He doesn't unbutton the shirt all the way. He tucks the left side of it to expose part of his bare chest. "Right here."

He points to the place above his heart.

"Wow," I murmur, my fingers dancing over the word *Lucky*. "You really did it. You got it tattooed on your chest."

"I told you before." He breathes, warm hands cupping both sides of my face. "I want to remember what we had. You're my Lucky. My lucky charm. When things go bad, I have you to keep me on the right path. You're my Lucky and I'm so fucking in love with you."

Well, there goes my fucking heart.

"Shit," I curse, tears filling my eyes.

Kayden blinks in surprise. "What did I do?"

"*This!*" I gesture to the space between us. I can feel my heart beating so loud inside of me, thumping hard in my head. "I thought I was better off without you. And then you come back and you . . . you ruin all of it. Plans of moving on. All of them, you ruined."

"I'm sorry?" He stares at me in confusion.

"Who am I kidding?" I laugh quietly to myself. "I never got over you. You lingered in my mind every day. I hated you for that."

He swallows nervously. "Well, I hope you don't hate me now."

"No, I don't," I murmur. "I think I love you."

Kayden's entire body freezes, and his eyes grow wide with surprise as he allows the words to sink into him.

"Yeah. I love you," I say with newfound conviction. "I'm glad I get to say it now. I'm sorry I didn't say it before you left. I wanted to be better for you when I said it. I thought I lost the chance."

"But you didn't." A grin appears on his face as he pulls me to him, closer than we've ever been so far today. "Say it again. Please."

"What? I love you?"

He nods and I laugh again.

His gaze drops to my lips, like doesn't want to miss a single thing that comes out of me. So I say it again, making sure to enunciate every syllable.

"I. Love. You."

"*Again.*"

I circle my arms around his neck and smile. "I love you, Kayden. I don't think I ever stopped. I like who I am right now, with you."

"I love you too," he whispers.

My breath hitches. Oh how I've longed to hear him say that to me again. And now that he's finally said them, the words sound even sweeter than I thought they were.

And when I purse my lips, Kayden doesn't hesitate to capture them with his own. There's a collective exhale as our lips meet, as if we've both spent the past few months only dreaming about this moment, never allowing ourselves to entertain the possibility that we'd be reunited like this again. But oh boy, does the kiss live up to expectations, if not completely shatter them. My muscle memory kicks in instantaneously as our lips move over each other eagerly. My tongue sweeps across his bottom lip and I bite it, knowing that it'll summon a loud groan from him, which it does. He tastes the same as he did, soft and sweet and salty.

Kayden threads his fingers through my hair and tugs me closer to him, until we're both exasperated from the little space floating between our bodies and I lift a leg over his so I can straddle his lap and crush my chest against his. I feel the wild thumping of his heart as he presses against me, the excitement giving way to relief when our lips meet again. He deepens the kiss as he grabs the back of my head and pushes our mouths together at a deliciously exquisite angle.

"I've wanted to do that since I first laid eyes on you tonight," Kayden whispers as he pulls away enough to rest our foreheads together.

"We should get going," I say, breathing hard against his lips. "We've been gone for an hour. So much for not keeping me long."

Kayden merely smiles. "You think they think we're hooking up?"

"Probably," I say with a hard laugh. I hop off his lap and get to my feet, patting away all the sand that has stuck to the edges of my dress. I offer a hand to him so I can help him up as well. "Come on. Your family probably wants to talk to you."

He takes my hand and clasps it tightly, like he's desperate to permanently fuse our hands together so we'll never be apart again. "Now, why does that seem like a very horrible reunion?" He groans.

I don't deny that it won't be easy. Instead, I say, with a faint smile, "It's okay. I've got your back."

He grins. "You know I've got yours too."

***

When we return to the reception tent, all eyes are glued on us and our entwined hands. A flush rises to my cheeks knowing that people are going to talk about us, so I excuse myself, striding toward to the bar to grab a drink, while I let Kayden reunite with his family.

Patricia is the first to rope him into a hug, breaking into tears as soon as she does. Kayden clings to his stepmother and soothes her with a smile, telling her that he's all right. Elijah is much sterner with him, briskly pulling his son in for a hug, but once he lets go, starts lecturing him about how worried he's been ever since he disappeared off to Phoenix. I can tell Kayden is getting flustered with the lecture, trying to end it as swiftly as he can by promising never to do it again and announcing that he's staying for good this time. Meanwhile, Brent was the most delighted to hear the news, finally glad to have his brother back after months of not seeing him.

The only one who still appears hesitant is Evans, who looks like he needs a little more convincing. I join the conversation, seeing if Kayden needs help smoothing things over with his friend.

"You okay?" Kayden asks, placing a hand on Evans's shoulder.

"I don't know," Evans says, looking frustrated as he tries to process the news. "I'm still mad at you, you know."

"I know. And you have every reason to."

"Just don't bolt again." Evans punches him lightly on the shoulders, his eyes glistening with rugged emotion. "We're butterfly tattoo bros forever, dude."

Kayden lets out a low chuckle at the new friendship nickname. "I won't. I'm staying for good. And I'm choosing to spend this life however I can with Sienna."

Kayden loops an arm around me and tucks me beside him, pressing a delicate kiss on the top of my head to soothe my worries. I melt into him, allowing my feelings for him take the front again. We mingle with the other guests for twenty minutes more since Kayden has a lot of friends and family he wants to talk to. Everyone is relieved that he has returned, and I'm happy he has a good support system here that he can count on when he moves back.

Later, I feel Kayden's arm snake around me from behind my back. He leans down to kiss my shoulder.

"Hey," he whispers lazily. "You wanna get out of here?"

"You sure the married couple won't mind?"

"Yeah. They've already left."

"What?" I whip my head around, looking for Brent and Evans. And sure enough, they're nowhere to be found. I guess they went back to their place to consummate their marriage.

"All right," I say, nodding. "Let's get out of here."

I let Kayden guide me to the hotel that he's staying at, a couple of blocks down from the beach. We walk together, hand in hand, every step heightening the anticipation for what's to come.

When we're back in his hotel room, he shuts the door behind him, then hoists me up and spins me around, my dress flowing around me like a carousel. I like seeing this new side of him, carefree and light spirited. A gale of laughter flies out of me at his excitement.

When he finally sets me down on my feet, his warm hands glide down my back, resting on my hips. He pinches the fabric of my dress like he wants to rip it off of me this instant. I want him to. But he's a gentleman and likes to take things one step at a time, so his hands drift back up my chest, stopping at my shoulders.

"I really like you in this dress," he says roughly, eyes molten as he toys with the strap of my dress. "But I really want to see how you look without it."

"Then I guess you'll have to help me out of it."

Kayden chuckles, slowly removes the straps, allowing them to fall past my shoulders. Then he turns me, so my side is facing toward him, and pinches the zipper of my dress, tugging it down. I don't know why, but I hold my breath in anticipation. It's been too long since I've done this with him; with anybody, in fact.

When he reaches the end, I let the remaining fabric fall to the floor, and it pools at my feet. His eyes spark with lust as I remove the rest of my undergarments, standing in front of him fully nude with confidence. I'm even more toned now with the rigorous training regimen I've been on for the upcoming tryouts, and Kayden knows it, sucking in a heavy, aroused breath as his eyes roam over my defined, hard muscles.

As he undresses, his eyes never leave mine, as if he doesn't want to miss seeing me get more turned on with every piece of clothing he discards. Desire explodes in my stomach as he kicks his clothes away and straightens back up, fully naked, his hard length, ready and willing for me.

Kayden smiles at me nervously, mirroring my own nerves. We've done this many times before and yet, in many ways, being here with him like this feels like the first time.

He lays me down on his huge, sprawling bed, his body shielding over mine. We don't kiss. Instead we stare at each other with wonder as our hands explore each other's bodies. My hands roam up the muscular planes of his back, desperate to feel every square inch of him. He strokes my hair, then drags his hand down from my face to the curve of my breasts.

Kayden brings one of my breasts to his mouth and the sensation of his tongue against my nipple hits me like a bolt of lightning. I whimper from the wave of pleasure washing over me and I feel him smile against my skin, guiding my hand down to his erection between my legs. We stroke each other like this for a while, teasing and feeling and reacquainting ourselves with each other, knowing full well that the journey is the best part of all.

After a while, I push Kayden over and loop my leg over him so I can straddle him. With another swift kiss, I pull back enough to look into his eyes.

"Condom?" I rasp.

Kayden nods, reaching down to grab his pants from the floor and pulling out the silver packet. Wow, that was convenient. Almost too convenient.

"Please tell me you weren't hoping to sleep with any of the bridesmaids tonight," I say, eyeing the condom with suspicion.

"Technically, you are a bridesmaid," he says, amused.

"So you were hoping to sleep with me?"

"It was presumptuous of me, but . . ." His blush intensifies. "I brought it. Just in case."

"I would be mad at you if not for the fact that this is actually useful right now."

He grins, aiming the condom packet at me. I tear it open with my teeth, and with a knowing smile ravaging my face, I slide down his legs and use my mouth to expertly sheathe the condom over him, rolling over his cock as tortuously slow as I can so I can watch him watch me.

The loud groan that rips from his mouth when I make the maneuver is the hottest, most heavenly thing to ever hit my ears.

When I climb back up, Kayden's eyes are begging me for mercy. I lift my hips, angling myself over his cock and easing down upon it. My inner muscles clutch his thick length, wasting no time adjusting to his size again. Like I said, muscle memory is great. The sigh that leaves both of our lips when I've completely lowered myself is a mixture of heavy bliss and relief.

Kayden's fingers dig into my hips as I ride him. I feel drunk with power when he lets out a series of exquisite sounding moans every time I lift my hips and slam down on him again, heightening the never-ending pleasure we're both feeling. His upper body inclines towards me so our gazes are level with each other.

A smile graces his face despite all the heavy breathing, so earnest and beautiful that my heart clenches from his expression alone, and I lean forward to kiss all the love and affection that I'm feeling into him, so he knows. He knows that I'm all in this time and I never ever want to be parted from him again.

"I love you," I rasp against his lips.

"I love you too, baby," he whispers back.

In an unexpected maneuver, Kayden flips us both around and eases himself into me again, fitting his lips over mine in a tender and loving way. He expresses how he feels for me through his mouth. And as he makes love to me, he tells me a story. *Our* story. He's telling the story of how we met and how we grew to love each other. He tells the story of how our strengths and weaknesses complement each other and how we're invincible because of that. And he tells the story of our broken past, our beautiful present, and our uncertain but hopeful future.

Soon after, neither of us feels like taking it slow any longer. I'm pleading for Kayden to *go faster, go harder*, and he obliges me, fucking me with the incredible precision and strength that he wields. My back arches against the bed with every powerful thrust he makes, unable to keep the growing feeling for much longer. And as our pace intensifies, his hips grinding into mine mercilessly, I'm no longer whispering his name in between breaths but yelling it, unable to contain the intense pleasure cresting over my entire body as he continues to hit that sweet spot inside me.

Kayden moans my name—a desperate plea—which sends me completely over the edge. He follows not long after, slamming into me one final time as he roars with release.

Later, when the euphoric feeling has subsided, Kayden collapses beside me. He tucks us both under the sheets and adjusts me so that I'm lying on his chest. I slide my leg over his body and bury my head into the crook of his neck.

Kayden strokes my hair with his hand, grinning down at me in contentment. He looks wrecked with exhaustion, fighting to stay awake. I don't blame him; we just tried to pack the last four months into all of that, and it was overwhelming indeed.

"I missed this," he murmurs. "I missed you."

"I don't want you to run anymore." I shake my head. "I love you. I don't want you to go anywhere. I want to do it right this time."

"Me, too," he says with a sturdy kind of determination. "I'm here, Lucky. For good. I know we have a lot of stuff to work through but I think we can do it. And I think it'll be much better this time around. We can make this work."

I nod. "We can."

Kayden smiles. "We can."

And then he kisses me.

He holds our future in that kiss. Our future together. I know we will have one. We've come a long way, and because of that, there is a chance for us. Hardships will follow and not all battles can be won. But there is no doubt in my mind that the future is set for me and Kayden.

Because we will fight for it.

Together.

THE END

ACKNOWLEDGMENTS

Perfect Addiction holds a very special place in my heart. When I started this book, I was experiencing feelings of anger and betrayal, much like Sienna, and it was through writing this book that I sought some healing for myself and with the people around me. Even now, nearly seven years later, I find myself relating to her in my darkest moments, admiring her physical and emotional strength to overcome every battle wound and scar. I used to tell my readers I don't have a favorite couple, but now, looking back, I think I've always had a soft spot for Kayden and Sienna. Not only because of their intense chemistry but because of what I feel we can all learn from their shortcomings and sheer commitment to do what it takes to put themselves first—reconcile their own traumas—in order to be with each other.

A special thank you to the entire Wattpad Books team for believing in this story, particularly Deanna McFadden and Rebecca Sands, my editors. Delaney Anderson and Rebecca Mills, my copy editors. Andrew Wilmot, my sensitivity reader. Shout-out to Gyeonguk Na, Agila Thani, FS Cheng, Cheah Wen Khyn, Chew Chee Hui, YouTube, and Google for helping me with MMA research. Also to my boyfriend, Irwin, whom I particularly enjoyed friendly sparring and choreographing fight sequences with. To Nicole, my best friend and favorite beta reader. To Emi, who, before I started the Wattpad version of this book, I had unfortunately cut ties with, but now I'm so happy to be reunited with! And of course, to my parents, who have always supported my dream of becoming a writer since day one. I love you mom and dad.

Also a huge shout-out to Jenna: thank you for bringing so much love to the Perfect series with your TikToks. You are amazing and I love you!

Last but not least, a huge thank you to my Wattpad readers. I, along with the Perfect series, would be *nothing* without your overwhelming love and support. Thank you for being there after all these years—from rallying up to participate in the Wattys 2015 and 2016, to acquisition of movie rights, and finally to publication! Most of you have grown up now, but I'm glad to know that you still think back fondly on the series. I hope these new, published versions of the books elevate the reading experience for you! I have a special *Perfect Addiction* bonus chapter for y'all as a way of saying thank you; be sure to check it out on Wattpad!

A final note to sixteen-year-old me: You did it, girl! I'm so happy for you. You manifested *all of this*! Thank you for being the amazing, hardworking person you are. Everything that I have right now is because of you, you motherfucking GOAT.

See you guys in *Perfect Ruin* and subsequently, *Perfect Redemption*. The journey is far from over.

ABOUT THE AUTHOR

Claudia Tan is an adult romance writer. She graduated from Lancaster University with a BA in English literature and history. Her massively popular Perfect series is a two-time Watty Award winner and has amassed over 160 million reads on Wattpad. The series has also been published in French by Hachette Romans. When she's not writing about swoon-worthy men and badass female leads who put them in their place, she can typically be found strumming her ukulele, writing sad love songs, or binge-watching *Friends*.

Turn the page for a sneak peak of
Book 3 of the Perfect Series

Coming March 2023,
wherever books are sold.

ONE

It smells like shit in here.

A combination of sweat, alcohol, and smoke billows around in a thick, cloudy haze. Harsh spotlights thunder down on us, startling our sight as we weave through the mass of sweaty, vibrant bodies.

Trying to get my vision back, I blink a couple of times as Dakota tugs me forward. Since the three of us are holding hands, my sister Beth gets pulled along as well. We're desperate to stick together. This isn't exactly our scene and I'm not sure what we'd do if we got separated tonight. It feels dangerous in here. Lethal.

"We're almost there!" Dakota screams. Even though we're only a few feet away from each other, the crowd's ear-splitting screams make it so I can barely hear what she says. But I nod along anyway, because she seems like she knows where she's going and I'd be a fool to veer down my own path.

Cheers and hollers ensue from the crowd and grow louder in anticipation of the looming fight.

For housing an illegal sport, I'm surprised at how huge the warehouse is. After receiving a sketchy text message, it had taken forty minutes to get to the abandoned warehouse located outside the city. And even then, there was still a rather long line to get inside. The sheer commitment it takes just to watch blood spill in the ring is truly astounding.

I'm surprised by the turnout. There's at least a hundred people mingling about in the warehouse tonight. And I'm fairly certain I saw some cops cheering along with the crowd.

Guess I don't have to worry about getting arrested tonight.

A sense of discomfort coils around my spine as we push through the energetic crowd. I never thought I'd be spending my first weekend of college attending an underground fight. Ever since Dakota escaped to college with me and Trevor, she'd been obsessed. When she found out that they were resuming the fights after the summer break, she knew she had to cross this off her college bucket list.

I, on the other hand have never expressed much interest in the underground scene. There's something about watching men beat each other up to near unconsciousness in a sketchy, greasy basement somewhere that makes my stomach churn. So when Dakota asked if we wanted to join her as a spectator, I wasn't exactly jumping with joy.

But trust me, you really *don't want to miss this fight,*

ladies, Dakota said with a waggle of her eyebrows while she signed us up for tonight. Clearly I was the only one in the group who didn't get the memo because the second Dakota said those words, Beth let out the most excited squeal that I've ever heard from her.

When I asked Dakota what she meant, she told me, in an obvious tone, *Jax is on the roster, silly.*

As if that meant anything to me.

After some prodding I did eventually manage to squeeze out some information from her and Beth. Apparently, a few weeks ago word got around campus that a newbie named Jax had delivered the first KO of the year, knocking out Perez Mills. This was a big deal because Mills had been the undefeated champion of the underground, winning the title for four years straight before Jax ending all of that in a one-off fight, sealing Perez's fate with a spinning heel kick in his face.

The shock that reverberated through the crowd had been cataclysmic.

I tried to imagine what a spinning heel kick would look like on the way over here, since I've never witnessed an actual fight in my life, and the only thing I can picture is someone's leg flying around like an out-of-control fidget spinner.

Despite my lack of knowledge about the fighting world, I do know that if Jax can make the undefeated champion tap out like that, he must be a damn good fighter. Revolutionary, even.

"Dee!" I scream. Dakota's pulling at my wrist so hard that it hurts. I cut through a couple making out in front of me and mumble a quick apology for interrupting them.

Just when I think I'll never know what normal air cycling through my lungs feels like again, Dakota jerks me forward, hard, and I stumble into an open area. When I peer over the rails, I expect to see a kickboxing ring but instead it's an octagonal cage, which means that this might not be just regular *Rocky* shit. The crowd has surged in volume now. The fight is about to start.

"You all right?" Dakota asks me, her long dark hair whipping at my face as she turns around to inspect me. "Sorry."

"It's fine," I say, wrapping my arms around myself.

Behind me, Beth makes a disgusted face and pinches her nose with her fingers. "It smells so bad in here."

"You get used to it." Dakota shrugs. "Besides, it's totally worth it. We have such a good view of the cage! And you know what that means: direct view of the hotties."

"Dude, you have a boyfriend," I say with a laugh.

"We're in a healthy open relationship," she explains matter-of-factly. "Trevor will understand if I ogle at hot dudes. Hell, he'd probably be okay if I hooked up with one of them tonight."

I smile back, hoping that she's right about that. An open relationship isn't for me but if it works for them, then who am I to judge?

"I wish we could come here every weekend," Beth gushes, her chubby cheeks rife with pink. "I bet they get hotter and hotter every week, especially when they have to train all the time now to prepare for the titles."

"You're so right. Might just nab me one of them after the fight tonight." Dakota winks at my sister.

Beth laughs, and they lean into each other to discuss which underground fighters they'd like to approach.

I wish I could share their brazen intentions with some of these men. Most of the time, I'm usually up for it too. But instead, the only thing I can seem to focus on right now is the discomfort slithering up my spine as more people shove their way into the warehouse. The girl with a pink shaved head besides me offers me a blunt but I politely decline. Not a good idea for me to get high for the first time here. Danger feels like it's sneaking around in every corner, and I should try to stay alert to keep me, Beth, and Dakota safe.

As more familiar faces poke up from the crowd—a couple of high-school friends I haven't seen since I graduated last summer, a few boys from a freshman party I had the displeasure of attending a couple of days ago—I'm surprised by how much of an open secret the underground is in Boston. But Dakota had explained to me that it's because Breaking Point, the gym that hosts the tournament, has an unspoken agreement with the Boston Police Department, and many officers from the force participate in these fights. Breaking Point allows them to get a good kick out of illegally beating up dudes and in return the BPD turns a blind eye to the gym's affairs.

Corruption at its finest.

I look over my shoulder to see several men busy making bets with the bookie about who's going to win tonight. And from what I overhear from a couple of spectators standing behind me, a lot of them have bet big money on that Jax guy.

"I can't wait to see Jax," I hear Beth gush. She tugs on my arm excitedly, her blue eyes shining bright with glee. "I saw him once in Caffeinated but I was too shy to ask him for a picture."

Beth is obsessed with Jax. I don't know what her deal is but she's been crazy for him ever since she started getting into all of this underground madness with Dakota. She'll jump at any chance to see him.

Personally, I don't get the hype. Is he really that hot? Beth has showed me pictures of him on his social media before. He's all right looking. Certainly not *un*attractive but he's no early '90s Brad Pitt either.

"Hey, if you want, I can bring you backstage later to meet him!" Dakota tells Beth and she squeals even more. The sound feels like spikes driving into my ears.

"You can do that?" My sister asks, her expression glimmering with hope.

"Sure I can. My brother's fighting tonight. I should be able to get back there." Dakota winks at her.

Her older brother, Zach, dubbed himself The Sledgehammer in the cage. There's not a lot of talk about him tonight since it's his first fight, but I hope he does well.

"You betting tonight?" I ask Dakota.

"Hell, yeah, I am," Dakota says, wriggling her eyebrows at me. "I've got five hundred bucks on Jax."

"What?" I don't think I've heard that correctly. "That's a lot of money."

"Money that I'll double if he wins!" She exclaims.

I stifle a laugh. I'm amazed at just how confident Dakota is that she's going to earn bank tonight. I don't know any fighter well enough to bet on them yet; perhaps if I end up coming back, I just might.

"You're betting on Zach, too, right?" I ask Dakota about her brother.

She merely laughs.

"God, no. I ain't investing a single penny in him," she tells me flippantly. "I've seen him fight before. He's gonna get beat up so bad. I already told Mom to be on standby in case he gets hospitalized tonight."

Christ.

Before I can say anything else, the crowd explodes as the announcer steps into the ring. He has long, stringy hair and he's wearing a diamond-encrusted suit, which makes me wonder how much he earns doing this. He's no low-wage earner, that's for sure. Banking all that blood money, I suppose.

"WELCOME TO THE VORTEX, FUCKERS!" The guy screams into the megaphone. "THE ONLY RULE THAT EXISTS HERE IS THAT THERE ARE *NO* RULES! SO LET'S. GET. REAL. TONIIIIIIGGGHTT!"

More cheers and leg stomping flare from the crowd. Beside me, Beth and Dakota join in, screaming their hearts out. I cross my arms and close my eyes, immediately regretting my decision to come here in the first place.

"All right, all right! Now the fight you've all been waiting for tonight! On your right, we've got your favorite prince of ghouls, our season regular, Damien 'The Beast' Wells!"

A few cheers erupt but are drowned out by boos when Damien emerges from the left side in a dark-grey robe. He's a stalky figure with Viking tattoos splattered across his chest and crawling up the shaved sides of his head. His expressions are animated, growling and huffing like he's the Big Bad Wolf of the cage.

The guy with the megaphone whistles lowly. "Man! He's going to have to give everything he's got tonight because he's going to be taking on *a legend*! Yeah, that's right, ladies and gentlemen! Over to your left, we have the guy who took down our reigning king, Perez, a few weeks ago, the *it* guy to watch out for this season, Jax 'Deadbeat' Denerissssss!"

The warehouse explodes. Everyone's yelling and screaming his name. Girls are throwing their panties at the ring. I turn to Beth and shoot her a warning glare, telling her not to be an idiot. Everyone's beating their chests and hollering "DEAD-BEAT! DEAD-BEAT! DEAD-BEAT! DEAD-BEAT!" in unison. Beth and Dakota join in, drumming their chests and yelling along to the cultlike chant.

Finally, a shadow emerges from the left side of the cage. My jaw drops to the ground and nearly shatters when I see him.

A black satin robe drapes over Jax's body, and it fits him so well it looks almost like a second skin. His untamed mess of golden hair rests on his sexy, chiseled face, with some strands falling past his striking brown eyes. I wish he wasn't hiding them because they're the best part of him. As if he hears my frustration, Jax pulls his hair to the back with one slick move before lifting his arms up to acknowledge his fans. The entire warehouse goes absolutely insane. A smug grin stretches along his face.

Damn, the pictures that I've seen of Jax don't do him any justice. His eyes are startling, beaming at me with a dark hue across his irises. A myriad of emotions dance across his viper-like eyes—none hint of nervousness. He strides toward the stage, his robe somewhat like a cape, his body language oozing menacing superiority.

I don't realize I'm holding my breath until Beth links her fingers with mine and gives me an excited squeal. A few girls in the proximity—even the girl who offered me the blunt—look like they want to faint from merely bathing in his presence.

Jax sizes up his opponent, scanning him from head to toe, and when he's done, he scoffs and turns away.

I'm holding my breath again when Jax effortlessly shrugs his robe off. It pools on the floor, revealing more of those hard muscles spanning his huge shoulders and back. Holy shit. He's massively built—a broad, rippled chest, an abdomen packed tight with muscle, and arms so huge that they could destroy concrete. I think. I don't really know how much muscle you need to be packing to destroy concrete but I'm sure it's something close to what Jax has.

But damn, he's gorgeous. Cut like a diamond. All hard edges and glistening skin and raw masculinity.

I'm surprised at the sight of his half nakedness, which erupts a deep arousal in my body.

I have to force myself to look away.

Beth and Dakota are jumping up and down, trying to get him to notice them. They're not the only ones doing it. At this point, most of the girls in the warehouse are screaming and hollering at him, attempting to get his attention.

When his eyes rest upon the VIP area, Dakota and Beth go nuts. His eyes suddenly land on me. I hold his stare because I don't know what else to do. I don't want to look away because, well, I don't want to.

Instead, I keep my head up, shoulders straight, and look challengingly at him.

Pleased with my response, a grin greets his lips at the sight of me.

His smile is perfect. Absolutely perfect. It's so beautiful that it speeds up my already erratic pulse.

I shouldn't be this excited. Hell, I don't even know the guy.

But why does it feel like we're not the least bit done with each other?

"Oh my God!" Beth screams. She's pulling on my arm so much I'm sure it's going to detach itself from my body. "Sienna! Did you see that? He's smiling at *me!*"

I'm not going to admit that he was actually smiling at me, so I stay silent instead. I know it would break her heart if she knew the reality of the situation. Instead, I squeeze her arm and smile back, nodding along in agreement.

When I turn my attention back to the cage, Jax's back is now facing me as he clashes his knuckles together, getting ready for the fight. The muscles in his upper body ripple as he leans forward. Damien eases into his stance as well. But his fists have a slight tremble to them, already predicting his fate.

"I want a clean fight, got it?" The guy with the megaphone says to them. Jax laughs.

"No promises," he snarls.

And as the second the bell rings, he pounces.

***

Jax won the fight, of course. Nobody expected any less of him after the Mills fight. The few skeptics in the crowd who were insistent that what happened with Mills was a one-time fluke was swiftly put to rest when Jax had Wells tap out in under a minute by putting him in some kind of headlock then beating him to submission. I barely had time to blink before the referee said the fight was over and the announcer declared Jax the winner.

The rest of the fights after Jax's paled in comparison. The fighters weren't as conniving or skilled like him. They kicked and threw and punched only because they were struggling to survive. Not because they actually could. Jax's arrogance in that cage is not misplaced; every hit that he lands is calculative, falling into an intricate master plan that reduces his opponent into a panic-stricken, blubbering mess. And I loved it. I love how much power he exerts over every single one of them—power that is rightfully *earned*.

No, I have to stop thinking about him. I don't even know him.

I force all thoughts of him out of my mind and instead return my focus on the fight at hand, but it's like he's already made camp in my head permanently.

"You all right, Sienna?" Dakota notices my distraught expression.

"Yeah." I nod back absentmindedly. "Just a little tired, that's all."

She looks like she wants to say more but the sound of

the horn blaring jerks her attention back to the cage.

Now that the last fight has come to a predictable close, people are beginning to move toward the exits. We're squeezing our way through, trying to get to the other side of the warehouse where all the fighters are. Despite the exhaustion setting on her face, Beth is still determined to say hello to Jax.

"Come on, Sienna!" Beth yells. "If we don't move fast enough, he's going to leave!"

"I'm coming!" I mutter. Dakota sends me an apologetic look. She knows that the only reason I came here in the first place was because Beth begged me to tag along.

After about twenty minutes, we finally make it backstage. It's even more crowded than the outside. Fighters loom over us; most of them are the ones who made it out of that cage victorious. Their opponents, on the other hand, are either too weak to move about or getting their faces fixed by poorly equipped medics.

"I'm going to find Zach!" Dakota yells at me. She points in the other direction and tells Beth, "Jax should be around here."

"Okay." Beth nods. When Dakota disappears, my sister turns to me and exhales softly. "Sienna, I'm nervous."

"You'll be fine. Just don't take too long, all right? And make sure he keeps his hands to himself," I tell her, my hands sliding over her shoulders. I squeeze them for reassurance. "If you need help, call me. I'll be right here by the washrooms."

"All right," Beth says cheerfully. "I'll see you soon."

"Good luck." I nudge her toward the hallway and she

smiles at me another time before getting swallowed by the crowd.

I lean against the wall beside the washroom, trying to look inconspicuous by swiping on my phone. It's dangerously low on battery when I decide to send a quick text to Mom and Dad telling them that Beth and I are sleeping over at Dakota's tonight, conveniently leaving out the part about currently being outside of the city watching an illegal sport.

As long as we're with Dakota, Mom and Dad know they don't need to worry about us. They're more preoccupied with each other—the screaming matches between them have gotten worse and I don't think I can even be in the same room as them for more than ten minutes without them yelling at each other for the most mundane things. I'm just hoping it's a phase they can get over.

Around me, fighters run back and forth, some looking pleased and others looking pissed as fuck. The guy from the first fight, Damien, stands in the corner with his friends, flailing his arms around angrily as he recalls what happened in the cage with Jax.

I wince when I catch a glimpse of his face. It's a rather gruesome sight—two of his teeth are chipped and his nose is bloodied and bent out of shape. It's a miracle how he's still talking right now.

"Fuck, I swear I almost had him," he snaps, his body trembling with forceful anger. He smashes his index finger and thumb together. "*This* close! Did you see the uppercut I gave him? The one to the ribs? Yeah, I could have knocked him dead with that shit. Wouldn't even have to break a damn sweat . . ."

I almost burst out laughing. *What a loser.* This guy is delusional if he thinks that he could have won against Jax. Everyone in that warehouse saw Jax beating him into a bloody pulp, so I'm not sure who he's trying to fool.

I look down at my phone and snort, maybe a little too loudly.

"Hey!" I hear Damian yell from across the hallway. I look up and when my eyes meet his, fear clamps its spiky teeth into me. "Yeah, I'm talking to you, bitch." He snarls at me. All of his friends snap their heads in my direction. "Something funny to you?"

Back down, Sienna. You cannot *get into a fight with this guy. He may have lost big time in that cage but he could still snap your damn neck if he wanted to.*

"Uh, yes?" I say, and immediately want to slap myself for saying something. *What the fuck are you doing, Sienna? Do you want to die tonight?* "You said you almost had Jax. I thought that was funny." I shrug.

Damien's nostrils flare with rage. He's walking toward me now, his bulky form shadowing his friends. My heart is slamming wildly against my chest, telling me to *abort mission, abort mission right now!*

"How the fuck is it funny?" His eyes narrow at me.

He's about two feet away from me right now. His friends have me cornered.

"Uh . . ." My voice trails off. *Keep your fucking mouth shut, Sienna!* "Well, you're a liar. Because I saw what happened in that cage with you and Jax tonight," I say nonchalantly. "And unless anyone mistook the match as a friendly little visit from the tooth fairy, I think it's pretty clear what went down."

That comment captures some people's attention. They mingle in the hallway, looking at us curiously.

I retreat from him as Damien approaches, backing myself against the wall. *Shit.* I think I might get seriously beat up. And it's all because my brain doesn't want to listen to my conscience.

"What the fuck did you just call me?" Damien fumes.

He clenches his fists and flexes his arms to scare me. And it does work. A little. I try to swallow down the fear festering in my chest in hopes that I can appear more unfazed. There's no way I'm giving him the satisfaction of knowing that he's successfully intimidated a woman.

"Come on, Damien. You might be halfway to being blind with that right hook that Jax gave to your eye but I'm sure your ears are fine enough hear what I just said," I say with a bored stare. "Is that like a signature move of yours, by the way? Float like a butterfly, KO like a roach that got spritzed with insecticide?" That earns me a couple of laughs, even some from Damien's friends.

Unfortunately, Damien doesn't think it's very funny.

"I didn't KO," he snaps back at me weakly.

"Well, you might as well have because with the way you're lying your ass off right now, it's coming across as a little desperate and embarrassing," I say nonchalantly. "Might wanna grow a pair of balls to own up to your losses. At least if I couldn't take the heat in that cage, I'd be *honest* about it."

He lets out a low laugh. "You talk a lot of shit for someone so small and insignificant. You think you can take the heat? In front of all these people? I dare you to give it a shot," he challenges, and I gulp nervously.

Just as I think he's about to slam his fist into my face, I hear a deep voice echo in the hallway.

"Didn't your mama ever tell you not to hit pretty girls, Wells?" Jax says, materializing from the shadows. All pairs of eyes pivot towards him, even Damien's. His anger seems to skyrocket under Jax's presence. Jax pushes through the crowd and into our corner, occupying the space between me and Damien, shielding me from him. "Or was she too preoccupied with fucking other dudes to give a shit about you?"

"Back off, Deadbeat." Damien warns Jax coldly. "This is none of your business."

"Ah, that's where you're wrong. *She*"—he gestures to me and my eyes widen—"is my damn business."

"What? Is she your girlfriend or something?" Damien scoffs.

"Yes. Is that a problem?" Jax says sharply. "Babe, come here."

When my silence drags, his jaw clamps up in annoyance.

"I said *come here*." He orders me again and this time I begrudgingly oblige him. Jax slips a casual arm around my waist and pulls me to him protectively. He reeks of sweat and alcohol. I swallow the stench down and breathe in through my mouth. "Don't touch what's mine. Otherwise, I won't hesitate to fuck you up like I did in that cage thirty minutes ago."

Damien looks like he's about to have another go at Jax. I

don't blame him. I would hit Jax, too, if I were him. But then again, I'm pretty sure we'd *both* get decked with the amount of shit we just uttered to Damien.

Damien unclenches his fist and lets it drop to his side. One of his friends pats him on the shoulder and tells him to scram. Damien stares at Jax for a couple more seconds, growling with the commanding presence of a cub.

"This isn't over," he says weakly.

"Yes, it is. Or do you want me to toss you around like a fucking pretzel again? Because I'm all for round two." Jax cracks his knuckles. "I might even let you hit me *once* this time before I beat the shit out of you. How about that?"

Damien spits on Jax's feet. His friends tell him to go but he shrugs them off. "I'll be back for you, Deadbeat," he growls. "Watch out."

"Dude, let's *go*." One of Damien's friends hauls at his arm.

"That's right. Stay down or be put down, little dog," Jax coos sinisterly.

Damien hisses out a breath, fiery veins popping in his neck, but his friend gives him a shove from the back, breaking Damien's eye contact with Jax. Damien shrugs off his friend and stalks away in the opposite direction.

I let go of the breath I've been holding, finally allowing my shoulders to relax.

When the crowd disperses, Jax takes the opportunity to turn to me. He cups my face with his hand.

"Hey." His voice softens. "Are you all right?"

I slap his hand away in annoyance. "Why the hell did you do that?"

He stares at me, blinking, shock entering his expression. "What?"

"You know what!" I hiss. "*That*! You calling me out! I totally had the situation under control."

"No, you didn't!" He hisses back. "If I hadn't saved you he would have knocked you unconscious. And God knows what he was planning on doing to you after that."

"Did you really have say I was yours?" I snap. "Like I was your damn property?"

"It was the only way I could get you out of that situation, fuck!" Now he's pissed off at me. Damn, I'm on a roll tonight, pissing off fighters I don't even know. He gives me an irritated look. "Seriously? You couldn't just say thank you? I just saved your life and you can't even put your ego aside to say two words."

"Thank yous are not programmed into my system, sorry." I shrug.

"Wow." He exhales. "And I thought I was a jerk."

"I don't really care what you think I am," I say, and start walking away from him.

He stops me by clamping a hand down on my wrist. "Wait, where are you going?"

I'm momentarily startled by the feel of his rough skin against mine.

"I'm going to find better company than you," I blurt, though a little shakily.

He blinks at me dumbly.

"My sister," I say when I find the strength in my tone again. "I need to find my sister. Good-bye."

I start to walk away from Jax again when I hear him mutter a curse and run after me. He places a heavy hand on my shoulder to stop me in my tracks again.

"Wait," he tells me. "I can't let you go. Not while Damien and his gang are still out there."

I make an aggravated noise. "I don't need your help."

"Yeah you do, actually," he tells me urgently. His eyes dart around the hallway and he lets out a sharp breath. "Look, it's rough out there. There are gonna be guys lingering outside, drunk and high on adrenaline, looking for trouble. And trust me, Damien is the least of your problems. My guess is that you don't come here a lot, otherwise you wouldn't be stupid enough to rile up any of the fighters here. I can help you find your sister."

"Why do you want to help me?" I ask.

"Because I'm a decent human being?" He shrugs. "And you're hot, so that's an added bonus."

"You're disgusting."

"I take that as a compliment."

"Only a fucked-up person would take that as a compliment."

"I am a fucked-up person." He offers me a twisted smile. "They call me Deadbeat for a reason, you know. I have no soul."

I roll my eyes at the absurdity of his words. "Whatever, *Satan*."

"So are you going to just let me stand here like an idiot or you gonna let me help you?" No matter the annoyance, there is a thread of fondness in Jax's voice that makes me hesitate for a moment.

I eye him warily, unable to shake the apprehension churning in my stomach. The feeling of danger slips into my skin again—a feeling I became well acquainted with as soon as I stepped foot into this warehouse—and something tells me I might have just found the source.

All my instincts are screaming at me to leave. I'm sure I can figure out a way to get out of here myself. But then again, if I bump into Damien another time, I might not be so lucky to leave the confrontation unscathed. And I doubt Beth and Dakota will appreciate it if the next time they see me is in the ER on life support.

I suck an unsteady breath into my mouth. Perhaps it would be a better idea to stick with Jax. I mean, if his intentions with me aren't good, he wouldn't have saved me from the clutches of Damien. Which means he can't be all bad, right?

"Fine," I say after a while. "But no funny business, all right?"

A funny grin climbs onto Jax's smug face. "You got it."

"What are you waiting for, then? Lead the way."

Jax nods, extending his arm in an inviting gesture. "Of course. After you, princess."